THE
KING'S
WEAPON

ALSO BY NEENA LASKOWSKI

OF FIRE AND LIES

The King's Weapon, book 1

The Heir's Bargain: Fynn's Story, book 1.5

The Crown's Shadow, book 2

The Throne's Undoing, book 3

THE
KING'S
WEAPON

NEENA LASKOWSKI

OF FIRE AND LIES
BOOK ONE

To those who ever thought they were less,
you are more than enough.

THE SEVEN KINGDOMS OF **VANERIA**

THE
IMIST

THE
WHISPERING
SPRINGS

PONTIA

THE RED SEA

BORGANIA

TWIN

THE THREE
LADIES

TETRIA

F

THE
QUEEN'S
CROWN

PRONUNCIATION GUIDE

Please note: these are fictional characters and places. The following pronunciations are simply the way the author pronounces them. However, if you, the reader, have a different way of pronouncing the names, please do so.

People & Gods:
Barinthian - *bar-in-THI-an*
Domitius - *do-mi-TEE-us*
Esmeray - *es-mer-ay*
Fynn - *fin*
Graeson - *grey-sin*
Kalisandre - *kal-ih-SAN-dra*
Lysanthia - *lis-an-THI-uh*
Misanthia - *mis-an-THI-uh*
Myra - *my-ra*
Pontanius - *pon-TAN-EE-us*
Rian - *rye-an*
Ryla - *rye-la*
Sabina - *sa-BEE-na*

Sebastian - *sa-bash-tin*
Tanzia - *tan-ZEE-uh*
Terin - *tare-rin*
Valrys - *val-ris*

Kingdoms:
Ardentol - *ARE-den-tall*
Borgania - *bor-GAN-EE-uh*
Frenzia - *Frenz-EE-uh*
Kadia - *Cade-EE-uh*
Pontia - *Pont-EE-uh*
Ragolo - *Ra-GOL-o*
Tetria - *te-TRI-uh*

CHAPTER 1

No one else mattered. No one but her mark for the night, who to Kallie's disappointment, had chosen an old tavern that reeked of stale bread, mold, and sweat. Every step Kallie took squished, making her question why she had worn her favorite pair of black leather boots tonight. Even though she frequented the taverns in the lower city during her spare time—which, granted, was too rare for her liking—this one was her least favorite by far. It was cramped, unkempt, and the drinks were subpar. She had no idea how the establishment was in business still, but it probably had to do with its cheap prices. Although, the prices did nothing to improve the quality of the alcohol or the service.

The tavern did, however, have one perk Kallie could appreciate: no prying eyes. Its occupants were always too drunk and too absorbed in their own fantasies to notice anything or anyone out of the ordinary. She suspected that was why her mark had chosen this place to meet his acquaintance.

Kallie leaned against the brick wall and looked beyond the edge of her black wool hood as she scanned the room for the fourth time.

The tavern was more packed than usual tonight. No doubt a result of the king's upcoming ceremony that had all seven kingdoms of Vaneria restless. Men and women crowded the small tables with pints of lukewarm ale in their hands and bland chili on their tables. As midnight neared, Kallie's favorite time was approaching. The time of the night when inhibitions and morals faded as more drinks were ordered and downed by the glass. Sweat glistened behind the ears of men who drank one too many pints, bodies relaxed and swayed as the fiddler plucked a new tune, and lips became looser. An insatiable hunger for a never-ending night hung in the air as anticipation bounced off the sticky walls. In the far corner of the establishment, patrons placed bets on who the princess would choose to marry in the coming days.

And Kallie watched it all with a smirk on her face. None of them knew she had all of the answers on the tip of her tongue. Perhaps, another night she would have joined in on the fun. But as much as Kallie yearned to lose herself in the crowd, the pressures of her father weighed heavily on her. And Kallie's desire to prove she was capable to her father was far greater than her desire to let loose. She had a job to do, and Kallie could not fail.

She wouldn't.

She would have plenty of time to do whatever she wanted once the plan came to fruition. So Kallie waited.

And waited.

Her lukewarm beer, which was only half-consumed, sat forgotten on the high-top table beside her as she observed her mark. In his mid-twenties, he was a little older than Kallie. He wore a plain, black fitted jacket atop a white button-up, both of which were too clean and too well-tailored for this tavern. He had cleanly cut ginger hair and a freshly shaven beard. His attempt at aloofness was dismal, for his scabbard, which hung forgotten at his side as he sat on the barstool, had Frenzia's crest sewn onto it. If someone wasn't paying close attention, their eyes would easily glance over the minute details. However, Kallie wasn't like most of the people here. She was well-trained, well-attuned to the small details. She knew immediately who the man was: Prince Sebastian, the brother of the recently anointed King Rian and the newly promoted captain of Frenzia's largest fleet.

As his acquaintance got up to leave, Sebastian called the innkeeper over and ordered a second drink.

Pushing herself off the wall, she abandoned her pint, pulled her cloak down, and sauntered over to the bar.

"I'll have what he's having," Kallie said to the innkeeper, who then nodded and turned away. As Kallie leaned over the edge of the bar, she felt a sticky residue beneath her palm. Her insides squirmed, but her face remained unfazed.

Sebastian cocked his head in challenge. "Are you sure about that?"

"If it's good enough for the prince of Frenzia, it's good enough for me," Kallie said.

Flinching, Sebastian drew back on his stool as he looked at the nearby patrons sitting on the other end of the bar. "How did you—"

"You don't often see the royal Frenzian crest in a run-down tavern." She chewed on her lip and shrugged one shoulder. "The red hair is also kind of a giveaway."

He looked behind her at the crowd. And Kallie was positive this was the first time Sebastian noticed that he was the only person in the building with bright red hair, a rare and well-known trait of the Frenzian royal family.

He swiveled back on his stool, and from underneath her hood, Kallie noted how his gaze slid down her, his brows raising in amusement. "I suppose I should have worn a cloak." He nodded to the chair. "If my cover is already blown, you might as well sit while we drink. It's not like I can force you to forget who I am."

Kallie smirked and sat on the chair. Crossing her legs, the edge of her cloak floated to the side, revealing tight black leather trousers that hugged her thighs. She did not come here for money but rather for something more worthy of her time.

The innkeeper set down their drinks and walked over to two men on the other end of the bar.

Sebastian raised his glass, the golden liquid sloshing within it, and made a toast, "To disguises."

"And to discovering the secrets beneath them." Kallie clinked her glass against his. When she took a swig of the liquid, the whiskey burned her throat as she swallowed.

Kallie released a deep, quiet sigh. "Good choice, Prince. The ale here tastes like piss." She cast her eyes at the innkeeper, who scoffed. Then, as if to prove her point, one of the men on the opposite end of the bar nearly gagged after taking a large gulp of the ale.

When Sebastian set his glass of whiskey down, she slid her hand on top of his and leaned in. His breath hitched as her lips grazed the tip of his ear. Then with a deep inhale, Kallie pulled from the pit of her stomach and felt the welcoming presence of her gift ready to be unleashed.

And Kallie happily obliged it.

With a sly grin, she whispered King Domitius' words she had spent all morning rehearsing into her mark's ear. As the words left her lips, the bottom of her stomach felt lighter, freer even; however, the hunger still lingered. She craved the taste it left on her tongue, like sweet honey melted over freshly baked rolls covered in butter. But she knew she could not succumb to the pull. She had learned early in her training that if she overused her ability, her body would suffer the consequences. Even this tiny use of her gift would leave her with a nearly paralyzing headache come morning.

Kallie peered into Sebastian's eyes. Once a clear, crisp green, his eyes were now glossed with a faint haze. With that confirmed, she knew her job was done.

Tomorrow, she would find out how effective it was when the palace was crowded with travelers begging for the king's favor.

She downed the rest of the whiskey in her glass, tugged her cloak down once more, and maneuvered through the budding crowd as she abandoned the prince. She pushed open the old oak door and nearly ran straight into a tall, lean woman with a determined face. Kallie let the woman squeeze past her, their shoulders brushing against one another. Once outside, the fresh air brushed against Kallie's face where a coy smile crept across.

Even though she was going to hate the headache she would have to deal with tomorrow morning, she would endure it. Soon, all of the headaches, training, and waiting would be worth it. For every time Kallie used her gift, the princess of Ardentol was reminded that *she* was favored by Sabina, the goddess of passion and manipulation.

CHAPTER 2

KALLIE STARED AT HERSELF IN THE MIRROR WHILE TWO HANDMAIDS fussed with her hair as they ensured each strand stayed in its proper place.

When they were finished, two small braids pulled her dark chocolate hair back into a tight bun at the nape of her neck. A crown with three spikes embedded with glistening diamonds and pearls sat atop her head. The dress she wore hugged the contours of her body while maintaining a sense of modesty. The bodice of her gown was made of a nearly invisible fabric that contained thousands of white gemstones which then trailed down her sleeves, forming a beautiful floral design. The skirt, which was covered with yet more diamonds and delicate embroidery, puffed out at her waist and cascaded to the floor, covering her crystal-encrusted heels.

The dress, the tiara, the shoes—each item was strategically designed to make Kallie appear as the king's most prized possession. The brightest diamond in his safe.

She would not go unnoticed at today's festivities, which was entirely the point, she supposed. Today Kallie would decide whom of the many suitors the king had invited from all over Vaneria she would marry. Her suitors would present themselves and their offerings to her during the ceremony, then they would continue to try to romance her during the ball that followed.

In the eyes of the people, the marriage would seem like a standard alliance; however, Kallie knew it ran much deeper than that for the king. This was the first step in King Domitius' plan to gain control over the seven kingdoms and take revenge against the kingdoms that betrayed Ardentol a century ago.

Kallie rubbed her throbbing temple. The aftermath of her gift and the day's pressure weighed heavily on her head.

"I cannot imagine what it would be like to be in your shoes right now," Myra, Kallie's favorite handmaiden and closet friend, said as she tidied up the vanity.

Kallie sighed. "Feet bound to blister by the end of the night, lungs caged by ribbons, and head heavy. Does that help paint a picture for you?" While Kallie admired all of her dresses, they were always a little too tight and constricting for her liking.

Myra swatted the air as though she was batting Kallie's sass away. "So many suitors to choose from, so many men and women begging for your hand. I don't know how you will choose."

Kallie chuckled. Myra was in love with love, while Kallie, on the other hand, could not care less about finding a suitor or getting married. Kallie had tasted only a small ounce of freedom in her twenty years, so finding a husband had never been a priority. Between the training sessions, the lessons, and the duties of the king's only child, she rarely had the time for something as fickle and destructive as love. Nor did she care to. If it was up to Kallie, she wouldn't be getting married at all.

Until of course, the king told her his plan.

While Kallie was reluctant at first, the king had explained how a marriage between Kallie and another kingdom would benefit Ardentol. The marriage wouldn't have to be about love, it wouldn't even have to last long. It was simply a political maneuver. So, Kallie was quick to come to terms with the arrangement.

She did not want a marriage built on love. She did not need love to be happy or feel fulfilled. She had room for only two things in her heart: her kingdom and her family. The two things she would do anything to protect. She would lie, manipulate, and kill anyone if it was for the betterment of her father and kingdom.

So Kallie knew all too well that love, even forced or fake love, was a powerful tool.

However, if Myra knew the truth behind her marriage, her friend would be appalled.

In the mirror, Kallie met Myra's soft hazel eyes and offered her a small smile. Her friend saw right through it.

Myra's hand fell on her shoulder. "Kallie, what's wrong?"

Kallie looked at her handmaiden who was more like a sister to her. Kallie hated lying to her, but there was no other way around it. "It's nothing for you to fret about."

Myra tilted her head in the mirror and rose a hand to her hip. "Kallie," she said, her tone light yet persistent.

Kallie sighed, squeezing the bridge of her nose. "Days like today— it's hard not to think about her, Mys."

Silence clouded the air between them. When her friend spoke, her voice was quiet. "Oh, Kallie. I have no doubt your mother would be proud of you."

Without Kallie even saying the reason, Myra knew. Because of course she did. Myra always knew. And Kallie tried to force a smile upon her face, but her mouth quivered and the crown dug deeper into her head. She did not know much about her late mother since the king prohibited anyone from discussing her. His love for her mother had made the loss of her paralyzing—the pain so great that he had never spoken her name aloud and had prohibited anyone else from doing so in his presence. And as much as Kallie tried to understand his pain, she also wished he would talk to her. Perhaps if he discussed her mother, it would lessen the heartache.

Kallie could not help but think about the woman who gave birth to her on days when she caught a glimpse of herself in the mirror. When she felt strange in her skin as if a part of her identity was foreign; its origin unknown.

Her ferocity, her stubbornness, those parts of her Kallie knew came from her father. However, when it came to appearances, Kallie and her father were vastly different. Where he had curly blonde hair, Kallie had a heap of brown hair that was easy to tangle, but fairly straight otherwise. The edges of his face were hard, sharp; hers, soft.

So, when she looked in the mirror, Kallie pretended as though she was looking at her mother's reflection. Sometimes she wondered if that was why her father could barely look at her at times.

There was one instance years ago when the king had let slip one detail about her mother. When Kallie was around seven, he had drunk too much whiskey after a meeting with his advisors. In his drunken stupor, he had told Kallie she had her mother's eyes. And like Kallie's, her mother's eyes shifted with the slightest change in her mood. The blue irises appeared darker when she was angry or frustrated, and lighter when she was happy or excited.

It seemed like a simple statement. One that shouldn't have made such an impact on Kallie. But he had never talked about her mother's appearance before, and the tears were quick to fill her eyes. She tried to cover it up, tried to shake it off in the hopes he would continue talking about the woman she knew little about. But when Kallie looked back at her father, he had fallen asleep at his desk, head slumped over a pile of ancient maps time had long since withered.

When Kallie was young, she had dreamed of a love that would be grand enough to break her heart if they were ever parted. A love that would shatter the world and shake the stars. A love that she would burn down the world to protect if it meant saving the person she could not live without. A person who could love the monstrous parts of her.

But then, Kallie grew up, and she saw the truth.

Love weakened.

And love destroyed.

So a marriage that promised her kingdom strength and prosperity? A marriage that would grant her the power to rule over her own kingdom and the power to rule herself? All while avoiding love? She could agree to that. Because a throne was all she wanted.

A throne was control, and control meant freedom.

An agitated voice she knew all too well stirred Kallie from her thoughts.

"Myra, fetch Kallie a cup of chamomile tea."

In the mirror, Kallie locked eyes with the king as Myra scurried past him with her gaze fixed on the ground. No emotion blanketed his face, but the muscles in his jaw flexed and his body stood rigid.

They had broken his number one rule: don't talk about his late wife. Kallie only hoped he would not blame Myra for the mistake later.

As she waited for Myra to leave, she observed her father. Like Kallie's own attire, King Domitius' ensemble was chosen with care. Small silver chains darted across the front of his navy suit jacket, paying homage to the royal colors of Ardentol. He wore matching trousers, freshly pressed. His sword was sheathed in the scabbard that hung from his hip, and his shoes reflected the light perfectly. Everything pristine. Everything in order.

His message to today's visitors was clear: if Kallie was the jewel of Ardentol, he was the chain that held her.

Once Myra turned the corner and left them alone, Kallie finally addressed the king, "Father, you could at least be more . . . warm to the servants."

He huffed in response and assessed her appearance as he

approached. Her father was a stern man. When he ordered the servants to do anything, they scattered across the floor like rats in the street, fleeing to the dark corners of the palace. She witnessed how the people in the kingdom sought out his approval, how *she* sought it out. He was a man both feared and revered by his people, and Kallie hoped to have a presence that exuded respect and command when she ruled.

"Still having headaches from the gift, I see," King Domitius mused. The disappointment painted on his face made Kallie want to shrink back into the shadows. All of the remedies she had tried to prevent the onslaught of her headaches had failed her. She had tried teas, baths, even piercing the cartilage in the inside of her ear. But nothing worked.

"Unfortunately," Kallie mumbled.

"Hopefully that will not be a problem much longer. But, I suppose you accomplished your task last night then?"

She mentally shook the concern from her mind and smirked. "It went without a hitch."

Her father approached her and placed a heavy hand on her shoulder. "Well, we will see tonight, won't we?"

The corner of her lip twitched as she nodded.

He straightened the jewelry box sitting on the vanity. Disgust wrinkled his face. "In any case, avoid using it too much tonight. As long as things go as planned, you will need it soon enough. You do remember the plan, correct?"

Kallie scoffed. "I could recite it in my sleep."

"Go ahead then."

She rolled her shoulders back and spoke with the confidence he had instilled in her, "Once the suitors arrive, I will view their gifts. Then the suitors will present themselves and—"

"Yes, yes. But what of the oath?"

Kallie's jaw snapped shut at her father's interruption. She sucked on her teeth before continuing and gave a tight smile. "Prince Valrys will be the first to present himself, and he will propose the oath as discussed," Kallie smirked, "after feeling a sudden onslaught of passion for our cause to unite the seven kingdoms."

He flicked off a piece of lint from his jacket invisible to Kallie's eyes. "As long as you have succeeded, that is."

She bit back her frustration. "I have."

His left brow raised. "Do not be overzealous of your ability, Kalisandre." The use of her formal name made Kallie's gaze flick up to meet his. Her father rarely used it when talking to her directly. And when he did, it was always to chide her.

She took a deep breath and nodded, knowing he was right. Time and time again he had proven how her confidence was a vice. When she mastered a new fighting technique during training, he would change tactics, proving she was still not good enough. He dismantled her concentration, shook her confidence, and made her fumble for the rest of the day.

However, he could not take away her confidence in her gift. While her father may have been at her side as she sharpened her ability, she was the only one who knew its limits. The only one who could feel it within the pit of her core. Her father did not know how it felt to bare a gift and he never would. No one in this kingdom was born with a gift.

No one except Kallie.

As a result, the king kept her ability a secret and trained her himself, with the aid of the occasional guard under her influence. His lessons were vast and strenuous. They tested her gift, mind, and body. Included in these lessons were assignments to complete while using her gift.

Every mark he threw at her, every assignment she had, she accomplished without a single problem. As she used her gift to manipulate anyone—from servants to strangers on the street to generals in the king's army—she became more attuned to it.

Although no matter what she did, it still wasn't good enough for him. He believed her gift had more potential. And Kallie did not want to think about what would happen if she did not show him the full extent of her prowess soon.

So, this current assignment would be different. She would be tested on all fronts. All of her lessons had amounted to this single task, and her success would prove to him exactly what she was capable of accomplishing.

Kallie gave a slight nod and pushed forward with her recitation of the plan, "Then, after being swayed by Prince Valrys's bold words, the rest of the suitors will feel an obligation to follow his lead and fall in line."

"And Prince Sebastian?"

"As I said, done."

His hand fell from her shoulder. "While you have done great so far," King Domitius said as he folded his hands behind his back, "your cockiness will be your downfall if you do not get a hold of it. This is why we have worked so hard in your training."

"Yes, Father."

"Stick to the plan."

Kallie nodded.

His gaze flicked back and forth between her eyes. "Do not let your mind wander."

"I won't, Father. I can control myself."

He squeezed her shoulder. "I'll see you in the welcoming hall in half an hour for the ceremony."

His footsteps clapped against the spotless floors before Kallie could respond. In the reflection of the mirror, she watched as he made his way out of her chambers. When he reached the threshold,

Myra stopped in her tracks upon seeing the king. She hugged the tray with the tea into the bend of her body as she folded into a bow.

He stopped beside her and Myra nodded, the movement jilted. Then he left, his guards falling into their positions around him.

Only when the king's steps were nothing but a quiet snap on the marble floor did Myra straighten and enter Kallie's chambers. With shaky hands, Myra set the tray on the table and poured the steaming water on top of the herbs in the cup. After adding two sugar cubes and a splash of cream, Myra handed Kallie the white porcelain cup as her complexion returned to its normal hue.

Taking the cup, Kallie stirred the contents with the spoon. "Thank you, Myra." Kallie held the cup up to her nose and let the floral aroma rise to her face. After sipping the steaming chamomile tea, Kallie went to ask what had transgressed between Myra and the king, but another voice at the door interrupted.

"It is time, my lady."

The captain of her guard, Alyn, stood in the entryway, his weight on the back of his heels. He had been recently promoted to captain a few months ago after the previous captain died of a sudden sickness. At the age of twenty-eight, Alyn was the youngest captain of her guard as of yet. He had proven himself to be the best man for the job. He was loyal, trustworthy, and exceptionally good with a sword. Standing before her now, he wore a cold face of indifference. When their gazes met, there was the slightest shake in his demeanor. He always became flustered when Myra was in his presence.

After taking another sip of tea, Kallie opened her arms, her movements careful as she balanced her cup. "And how do I look, Al?" She spun in a circle with an amused grin.

"Oh, stop teasing him, Kals," Myra said, her voice muffled as she covered her laughter with a hand. It lightened Kallie's heart to see her friend smile. The previous encounter with the king long since forgotten. Meanwhile, Alyn's complexion turned pale pink as he avoided the women's gazes.

"But where's the fun in that?" Kallie countered. "So, Al? What's the verdict?"

He cleared his throat. "You look . . . healthy, my lady."

"Healthy?" Kallie's hands flew to her hips.

Alyn nodded. "Yes, my lady."

Myra shook her head and walked toward Alyn. She stopped beside him, then placed a hand on his forearm as she lowered her voice in a fake attempt to whisper, "Don't bother boosting her ego, Captain. It is far too big already."

Kallie rolled her eyes. "And Myra? How does *she* look? Absolutely divine, wouldn't you agree, Alyn?"

Alyn's cheeks turned scarlet, and he cleared his throat again.

Myra whispered to Alyn, barely loud enough for Kallie to hear, "You don't look too bad yourself. Did you get your haircut?"

Alyn ruffled his hair. "Yes, lady Myra."

Myra scoffed though color flooded her cheeks. "I've told you before, Alyn, I am no lady."

He merely shrugged sheepishly, as if titles were of no consequence, so Myra continued, "It looks nice though." Myra then waved at Kallie and headed out of the room, not bothering to wait for them.

As Myra's giggle faded, Alyn's face became a shade brighter, something Kallie had not thought possible. The corner of Kallie's lips tilted upward.

"All right, fine. I don't need your forced compliments anyway," Kallie said, strolling forward, her crystal heels fragile beneath her. "I don't want to hear my father complaining about how I was late to my own engagement." Placing a hand on Alyn's forearm, she let him lead her to the welcoming hall where the seven kingdoms waited for her to reveal her choice. A choice already made for her.

CHAPTER 3

When Alyn and Kallie approached, the guards pushed open the tall oak doors at Kallie's signal. As the doors creaked open, the voices in the welcoming hall quieted to a hush, then to complete silence.

Kallie kept her gaze forward while Alyn guided them down the short marble path toward the dais. On the dais, her father stood with his hands behind his back and with a face of stone. Behind him sat the throne, hand-carved mahogany with silver finishing and the power of the kingdom sewn into the tufting of the white velvet cushion. She had always admired the beauty of his throne and dreamed of one day being able to claim one herself. When Kallie attended these ceremonies in the past, she had pictured herself sitting on the velvet cushion instead of standing off to the side.

Then her heart fluttered.

A throne that mimicked the king's (albeit a smaller one, but a throne nonetheless) now sat next to his on the dais.

When they reached the center of the dais, Kallie removed her hand from Alyn's arm. He bowed, then positioned himself next to the captain of the king's guard, Lundril. Keeping her head high so her crown did not tilt, Kallie curtsied before the king. Her father took her hand when she rose and held it on his arm as they faced the crowd.

A long navy rug leading to the dais divided the crowd in half. Guards were positioned throughout the grand hall. Among the people in the crowd were many whom Kallie recognized, including some of the lords in Ardentol who had made frequent visits to plead their cases during court. Others she knew by the coat of arms embroidered on their jackets or by the paintings she had studied over the years. Then there were those whom she could not place and those who were unfamiliar to her altogether.

Either way, the people of the other kingdoms had followed suit. Colors of all the present territories were represented in the fabrics of the crowd, making it easy for Kallie to identify them. Ardentol's structured navy and white garments made up a large portion of the guests. Diamonds sparkled on many of the Ardentolians' ensembles as an ode to their king who favored the stone. Among the sea of navy, Kallie spotted the Ragolians in icy aqua fabrics, the shade of their treacherous glaciers in the North. Kadia's stark white fabrics dripped with blood-red sapphires reflecting their tundras. Then there were the natural, woodsy tones to symbolize the divided, wood-covered lands of Borgania. And finally, sage green for Tetria, a land ruled by a queen who, according to rumors, practiced uncommon and eccentric rituals in the swamps to the West. The colors of Pontia, however, were nowhere to be found among the guests.

Her father's voice called her attention away from the crowd. "Welcome, all. I hope your journeys were uneventful. Today, we are here to witness my daughter, Kalisandre Helene Domitius, choose her husband at long last." King Domitius paused as the clapping echoed in the hall. Kallie gave a small, closed-lip smile, and the suitors straightened their posture as her gaze swept over them. Some remained stoic with blank faces, while others returned the gesture with their own shakier smiles.

"When she entered my life, she brought a sense of hope to our kingdom. Over the course of these years, she has grown to become a respectable, loyal woman deserving of a worthy suitor. It is our belief that a marriage between Ardentol and one of your territories, be it large or small, is one small step toward rebuilding those relationships we once had in Vaneria. After one hundred years, tensions remain stringent between the seven kingdoms. After one hundred years, our children still feel unsafe traveling throughout Vaneria. And after one hundred years, we have yet to mend what the Great War broke. So let today be the first step of a long road ahead of us toward acquiring the unity, peace, and tranquility that we all so dearly desire."

The crowd clapped, but some clapped with less fervor. Not everyone seemed as excited about the hope for a unified Vaneria as the king. And those reactions did not go unnoticed by Kallie. In due time, they would be dealt with.

While the seven kingdoms remained peaceful since negotiating the treaty to end the war one hundred years ago, it was a strained peace that would eventually falter. Many had already seen the cracks forming, the increased riots in some kingdoms, and in others, the building threat of a coup. Tensions were rising. Yet some kingdoms required more persuading than others, and King Domitius was bound and determined to restore Vaneria to its former glory.

But before he made serious strides in his plan, Ardentol needed a strong forefront. An alliance through marriage was the first building block.

When King Domitius finished his speech, he sat down on his throne and pointed an open hand toward the second throne. Kallie obliged, claiming her seat on the smaller throne beside him. Her palms ran over the smooth carvings of the wooden arms, her skin tingling with excitement. Yet it quickly dwindled when she reminded herself that this throne did not hold any power. This throne was only for show. She straightened and put on a face of indifference. Soon, the king would witness just how successful Kallie had been in her recent assignments. Then with his approval, she would acquire the power she sought.

The herald announced the first suitor: Prince Valrys of Kadia. And so the parade of suitors began.

Age had transformed the prince since the last time she had seen him. His beard was beginning to gray, his eyes wrinkled in the corners. As a prince of one of the wealthier Vanerian kingdoms, Valrys's power dripped off of him. His crown gave the appearance of having been dipped into Kadia's pots of gold. Long, thin spikes protruded from the crown. But Prince Valrys wasn't here for her hand. His purpose today was different from that of the other suitors —though equally, if not more important.

Valrys knelt before the dais. "King Domitius, Lady Kalisandre. I am here on behalf of Kadia. As I am sure you are aware, I am betrothed to Lady Tanzia of Kadia."

Kallie hid the smirk knocking at her lips as she waited for the prince to continue. Waited to hear the words she had planted in his mind when she had visited him a few days ago at the inn where he was staying. Her first target of the week.

"Yes. We are aware, Prince Valrys, but please do continue," King Domitius said from his throne as he tapped his fingers on the edge of the throne's arm.

Prince Valrys put his fist to his chest and fixed his gaze on the ground. "I bring no bribes, no personal suitors, only my word. Kadia has stood with Ardentol since before the Great War, and we will continue to stand by Ardentol in your pursuit of a united Vaneria. As such, Kadia vows to honor the suitor chosen here. And if anyone attempts to go against Lady Kalisandre or her chosen suitor, Kadia shall defend the couple to whatever end. And we encourage those here today who believe in the need for true peace to make the pledge themselves."

The silence broke as murmurs flew through the crowd, and Kallie forced a shocked expression onto her face. Even though Kallie had used her gift on the prince three days ago when he came to Ardentol, the effect had lasted. Now all they had to do was watch and see who followed in his footsteps.

And who did not.

"That is very noble of you, Prince Valrys. Your words will not be forgotten," said King Domitius. Besides the king, Kallie gave a slight tilt of her head.

The crowd shifted as Prince Valrys returned to his spot, then the second suitor with ginger hair strode forward.

Prince Sebastian sank to one knee before the dais. "King Domitius and Princess Kalisandre, I, Prince Sebastian, am here on behalf of my brother, Rian, the King of Frenzia."

King Domitius shifted in his throne. "And why, may I ask, is King Rian, not here himself?"

Sebastian glanced at King Domitius, then averted his eyes just as quickly. "As I am sure your highness is aware, our father, King Lothian, recently passed. Since our kingdom is still in mourning, my brother thought it best if he stayed in Frenzia to support the kingdom in its time of need. However, he did not want to miss the opportunity to offer his hand to Princess Kalisandre, whose beauty is well-known all over Vaneria."

Kallie offered him a small, empathetic smile, then spoke for the first time, "My heart goes out to your family and kingdom. May the gods be fortunate and protect the late king as he makes his journey to the Beneath." Her words would not lessen the grief that plagued Sebastian's or his people's minds. Grief never went away. Kallie knew that all too well. But she said them nevertheless.

"Thank you, Princess." Sebastian nodded. "As such, I volunteered to represent him today and relay his offering to you."

King Domitius said nothing. Sebastian's gaze bounced between the two royals. A moment later, Kallie nodded in encouragement.

The prince cleared his throat. "On behalf of King Rian, I bring no physical offerings, for my brother knows material items only deteriorate with time and he desires a strong marriage, unbreakable by the passing of decades." Sebastian paused, a small chuckle escaping his lips. "His words, your graces, not mine. Instead, King Rian offers this: a strong alliance between our two kingdoms with you on the throne next to him."

The air grew still as the crowd waited to see how Sebastian would handle Prince Valrys's oath. A thin layer of sweat formed on Kallie's palms as she gripped the arms of the chair. The silence that ensued made her question her gift for the first time.

It worked. It had to have worked, she thought.

She had never failed before, and she wouldn't fail today.

Sebastian raised his gaze, and as his eyes met hers, Kallie noticed the murkiness within them. The corner of her lip twitched.

"King Rian and I also promise to uphold the oath that Prince Valrys set forth here today: Frenzia will support your decision, Princess Kalisandre, and defend it against anyone who attempts to oppose it."

Her grip on the new throne lessened at the same time as the people in the crowd shifted uncomfortably.

"Thank you, Prince Sebastian. Your offer does not go unnoticed," said King Domitius.

Prince Sebastian nodded his head once more and returned to the crowd, shoulders back, hand on his hilt.

Tracking him back into the crowd, Kallie noted those who shifted from one foot to the other and those who stood straight, unmoving and unwavering. The precedent had now been set. Everyone now knew those who did not pledge the oath would be making a statement.

But was it a statement any dared to make?

The next few suitors approached Kallie. Lords and ladies from the kingdoms of Ragolo, Kadia, and Borgania placed their offerings before the dais. Among the offerings were ancient family heirlooms and blueprints of land—things Kallie did not need. The suitors from Ragolo and Kadia promised to honor and defend Kallie's choice without hesitation. Just as King Domitius had predicted. Their support and loyalty were not surprising. Ragolo and Kadia had both fought on the same side as Ardentol during the Great War. Although Ragolo's role was minuscule due to its small army, the territory had proven useful. It stood in the coldest portion of Vaneria where thick sheets of ice covered the terrain and made it hard for enemy soldiers to traverse.

Those from Tetria and Borgania, on the other hand, stumbled over the words. One suitor, a young Borganian man, looked back at the crowd as if he was searching for the confidence he needed. This was also not surprising since Borgania had been a divided province during the Great War. Today, it seemed to remain divided. Their hesitation and choice of suitors, smaller lords and ladies with little to offer Ardentol, were a clear indication of their struggle.

However, no matter who stood before her, Kallie did her due diligence. She smiled when appropriate while she feigned a passive indifference simultaneously.

She was not used to holding her tongue or remaining in one spot for too long. She would prefer to be doing something productive, such as training below the castle. Anything besides sitting here next to the king with her hands folded in her lap, like an obedient, silent princess. Kallie reminded herself that her restraint today would pave the way for a greater future.

She understood her small throne was temporary and purely for this event, but she also knew her future marriage could be different if she commanded it.

That was the king's promise to her. While he ultimately would have control over the land through this alliance, Kallie would sit in the seat of power of her future home. And then, maybe her people would look at her with the same respect with which they looked at her father.

Kallie glanced out the ceiling-high window ahead of her that looked over the high cliffs of Ardentol. With the approach of dusk on the horizon, the sky had turned golden. The ceremony was almost over.

Her focus wandered the hall, and she found herself studying the gods looming over everyone in the back of the room. She focused on the statue of the goddess Sabina, the goddess who her father believed bestowed Kallie with her gift of manipulation.

Even though the statue was made of stone, her figure appeared soft. Her hair flowed down her back in cascading waves. A few strands of hair were strewn across her face as if a strong wind had blown by her. As a result, the majority of her features were indistinguishable besides her eyes, which were striking and pierced the soul of any onlooker. Her left hand was folded over her right, and she wore a thin piece of fabric that skimmed over her curves and revealed a bare leg. Power oozed from the stone's cracks.

Centuries ago, the gods had visited the mortal lands of Vaneria. At first, they had hidden their presence from the mortals. However, the passing of time had made it nearly impossible for the gods to hide their unique abilities or their otherworldly physical attributes. The gods were immortal. Their beauty surpassed any mortal, and they could do things no mortal could.

The stories of the gods were often exaggerated and outlandish, but the message remained clear: never trust a god.

Some of the gods, like Barinthian, used brute force to teach mortals lessons. Others liked to turn the mortals against each other, like Ryla.

The goddess Sabina, however, was more subtle in her approach.

In the beginning, Sabina, like the rest of the gods, led a private life in the shadows. No one knew where she had come from, and many were intrigued by the mystery. As the goddess of passion, she could influence emotions. And her favorite emotions to manipulate were the pursuits of the heart. As she became acquainted with the ways of the mortals, she began to shift their minds and infiltrate their thoughts.

By the time the people realized she was not a human, but a goddess, Sabina had already enamored them with her gift. When word spread about her abilities, mortals traveled far and wide to gain a meeting with Sabina. They wanted her to influence others to fall in love with them.

Their requests became a game to the goddess. How far would humans go to achieve their desires? In exchange for Sabina's aide, those who sought out the goddess would provide different services for her. Some would travel to foreign lands to get her different herbs or jewels. Those who were musically talented performed for her throughout the day at her whim. Others participated in physical competitions, which included violent matches, often resulting in someone being carried out on a cot.

Whether the task was simple or onerous, the mortals always accepted them, for humans would do anything when love was at stake.

All requests were the same. The seeker always wanted the love of someone who was not freely giving it to them. After a while, Sabina grew bored of their requests and stopped granting them.

Until one day, a warrior came asking for her help. Rather than asking for someone to fall in love with *him*, he had come to ask Sabina to reignite the passion between his parents. The man intrigued Sabina in a way no other mortal had. After some thought, Sabina granted him his request on one condition: he stayed with her.

At first, the man was rendered speechless, unsure he had heard the goddess right. The warrior was not married but hoped to marry and have children one day. Sabina was infamous for entertaining herself with various companions but never committing to anyone. His hesitation both irked the goddess and enticed her, for no one had ever said no to her before and she wasn't willing to relinquish the feeling. After a few moments—more time than she had granted anyone else—the warrior said yes. His desire to see his parents happy again outweighed his desire for his own happiness.

After a few months, the warrior began to fall for the goddess, and soon enough they were set to wed. Their wedding was to be held at her favorite temple in Vaneria. However, the night before the ceremony, Sabina's fiancé disappeared.

Misanthia, the goddess of war and strife, tried to soothe Sabina. After recounting the night's events and the nights leading up to the wedding, the other gods told her it was foul play for the man's heart was rotten. Sabina was heartbroken. But more than that, the goddess was outraged that she thought she could trust a mortal.

Thus, Sabina began to push the limits of her ability.

Before she had held herself back, but now she relinquished that control. She began manipulating more than an individual's feelings about love and started to shift an array of emotions. She added twists to people's wishes, instilled bouts of jealousy in the seeker's minds, planted seeds of melancholy and anger in their blood. As she released the full extent of her power, havoc ensued.

Over time, she grew to become one of the most powerful deities in Vaneria. People were either in awe of her or feared her.

Once the mortals saw the resulting chaos, they started to pray to Sabina and the other gods for forgiveness. They begged the gods to put an end to it. Out of fear, the people stopped seeking out Sabina's influence as well as the influence of the other gods altogether. Eventually, the gods, including Sabina, slunk back into the shadows of the clouds.

However, there were whispers in the far corners of Vaneria that the goddess had been outcast by the other gods for loving a mortal and that she still loved the warrior even after decades had passed. Some believed she walked among the dead in the Beneath, searching for her lover.

Kallie rolled her shoulders back.

Love is for fools, and I am not a fool.

Kallie had made a vow to herself years ago that she would not be one of the countless souls who fell for love's tricks. She would not lose herself in someone else as so many had done before her.

That was why this arrangement was perfect.

Love was not a part of the equation.

Returning her focus to the crowd, Kallie watched the last suitor leave the dais. King Domitius stood and approached the edge of the raised platform, and Kallie followed.

He addressed the crowd, "My daughter and I would like to thank you again for making the journey to Ardentol. Our objective here is not to take what does not belong to us, but rather to forge a meaningful relationship between our two families and the people of Vaneria. Ultimately, Kalisandre will have the final say in who she chooses to marry, and she will announce her choice at dawn tomorrow. In the meantime, please join us in the ballroom tonight for dinner and dancing."

Kallie bit back a laugh. *Her* choice. At the end of the day, she did not care *who* she married as long as they provided her with power. Even if King Domitius had not told her who to pick, she would be a fool to ignore the opportunity to become queen of Frenzia. Her father was young and healthy. He would be around for many more years to come. If Kallie wanted to become queen sooner, she was going to have to marry or kill someone for it—and committing patricide was out of the question.

King Rian's offer for an alliance between Frenzia and Ardentol was the next step in uniting the seven kingdoms. If someone dared to disagree, she had several ways of dealing with those disagreements. The gift King Rian promised her: a throne with the largest military in Vaneria, a military notorious for being well trained and well equipped, even in these times of supposed peace. And paired with the vows promised today by the suitors who had aligned themselves with Ardentol, she would be unstoppable.

A victorious grin stretched across Kallie's face as the king reached for her arm and led them out the side entrance.

DINNER CONSISTED OF SEVEN DISHES, one dish for each of the seven kingdoms: salmon cakes from Ragolo, baked brie with cranberry chutney from Kadia, smoked asparagus from Tetria, roasted potatoes from Ardentol, venison coated with a red wine sauce from Borgania, poppyseed sweet bread from Pontia, and rich chocolate truffles from Frenzia. However, Kallie only picked at her food. The energy buzzing in her stomach had stifled her hunger, as it did every time she was about to begin a new mission.

Before the feeling could settle and the moment the dishes were cleared, her father asked her to dance with the intent of parading Kallie around the guests. Thankfully, the first song was simple and set at a moderate pace at the request of the king.

As King Domitius guided her along the edge of the dance floor, Kallie locked eyes with Myra who stood near Alyn. Myra's jaw fell open causing Kallie to bunch her brows in question. Kallie casually searched the room for an explanation, seeing nothing amiss. Then in the reflection of the wall-length windows, she understood:

She was *glowing*.

As Kallie twirled around the room, the light from the chandeliers hit the crystals in her tiara, her dress, her heels and ricocheted off of her. The fractured light encased her inside a glittering halo. Splotches of sparkling color scattered across the floor as her father spun her. While the king, clad in dark navy, absorbed the light, Kallie amplified it. She became the diamond her father had spent years forming. The pressure he had put on her only increasing the magnificence. And the eyes of every person in the room were fixated on Kallie as she scattered broken rainbows across the floor.

"Seems our plan is working so far, Father."

"If my plan is to come to fruition, we cannot rely solely on your gift, Kalisandre," he stated.

"Of course, Father."

He peered down his nose at Kallie. "Do not forget: your future actions will send a message and pave the way for everything to come."

Kallie restrained from rolling her eyes. She knew the steps she needed to take. She would not mess this up. Not unless she wanted to disappoint Vaneria. Or worse, her father. "I know, Father."

When the end of the song neared, King Domitius slowed them to a stop near Prince Sebastian. Once the song faded, Kallie picked up her heavy skirt and gave a deep curtsy to her father.

There was a shuffling in the crowd, and Kallie raised her head to greet the suitor she would dance with first.

But the man who stood in front of her was unfamiliar. His brunette hair was tied back in a knot. Loose strands accentuated his chiseled jaw where a shadow of stubble was showing as if he hadn't shaved in a few days. Objectively, the stranger was handsome, but his demeanor, while he stood before her with a half-smirk etched into his face, made him appear arrogant. It was the sort of arrogance Kallie despised. He was not one of her suitors, yet he stood in between her and the Frenzian prince whom the people expected her to dance with next.

The tension in the air was palpable as the stranger waited with an outstretched hand. "May I steal you, my lady?"

Kallie glanced at her father, who stood emotionless next to a frozen Prince Sebastian. Her father's words echoed in her mind. Her choices mattered."I mean no offense . . . "

"Fynneares, but you may call me Fynn," the stranger finished for her with the same cocky expression.

"I mean no offense, *Fynneares*—"

"Fynn," the stranger interrupted, winking.

"*Fynn,*" Kallie said with a strained smile. "However, I really should prioritize those who have come all this way for me."

"And I haven't?" Fynn pressed a hand against his chest feigning injury.

"Considering you did not present yourself to me this afternoon, I can only assume the answer to that is no."

The right corner of Fynn's mouth tilted upward as he offered a hand again, challenging her to accept it in front of everyone. "Then tell me, Princess, how will one dance with a stranger hurt?" The man's accent and overall demeanor were foreign. No one in Ardentol was as brazen as he was.

Kallie never liked backing down from a challenge and a single dance wouldn't do any harm. She placed her palm in his. "One dance."

As a wide smile split his face, his fingers wrapped around her hand. "One dance is all I need."

He guided her away from the crowd and toward the center of the floor. His hand found the middle of her back, and Kallie set hers on his shoulder as he began to take them through the steps. One by one, other couples joined them.

As they moved across the floor, Fynn maintained the distance that separated them to the point where Kallie was unsure if she should be offended or not. But then again, she preferred the distance he gave her. It was more than any of her other unwanted dance partners had provided her in the past.

Fynn followed the rhythm of the music effortlessly. The only element he was lacking as a dance partner was conversation. She waited for him to say something, anything. However, when the first rendition of the chorus came and went, Fynn remained silent. He seemed lost in thought as he looked at her—no, not at her, *through* her.

Preventing her thoughts from spiraling, Kallie focused on the man. She took a deep breath and instinctively felt for her gift at the bottom of her stomach. It called to her, an eagerness tumbling in her core. And it soothed her growing nerves. Kallie knew relying solely on her ability was dangerous. Still, it was a comfort knowing she had access to it in case it was necessary. In case her wit, charm, and skill with a blade ever failed her.

"What brings you to Ardentol, Fynn?" She asked in an attempt to gain some information out of him.

His eyelids fluttered and his brows knitted together as though it was hard for him to focus on her words. Fynn spun her away from him and when he pulled her back, the seriousness had vanished from his countenance.

"You," he said with that arrogant smirk again, as if he had a secret he was hiding that begged to be freed.

Little did he know, she had secrets too. "Me?"

He chuckled. "Wouldn't want to miss my chance to steal the famed daughter of the king of Ardentol before she gets married off to a stranger."

Kallie tilted her head. "You came simply to dance with me?"

He nodded. The fabric of the dancers rustled around them as the musicians picked up the tempo.

"Yet you do not wish for my hand in marriage? Should I be offended, Fynn?"

Another laugh flew from his lips. His laughter was carefree and reckless, a feeling she craved. "Take no offense, Princess."

Kallie's gaze slid over him. "Hard not to be offended."

He shrugged. "If you knew what I knew, you would not be, Princess. Trust me."

She did not.

She narrowed her eyes. "And where did you say you were from again?"

His gaze moved beyond her. "I like to think the people you surround yourself with are your true home." He spun her again.

The muscles in her arms tightened, becoming rigid. She was growing tired of his games. When she was in front of him again, she said, "Not an answer."

A strand of hair fell loose from the ribbon holding back his hair. "Some things are better left a mystery, don't you think?"

By the notes of the song, Kallie knew their dance was almost over. It was her turn to smirk as she tightened her grip on his hand. "I suppose you are right, for I would not want you to know my secrets either."

"The lady has secrets?"

She chuckled. "Every lady has secrets, Fynn, but you will never know mine." Her gaze was unwavering, her voice steady as she pulled on her ability. "When the song ends, you will return me to Prince Sebastian and apologize for stealing me away."

Fynn stared at her, unblinking. A thin haze glazed his brown eyes.

When the song reached its crescendo, Fynn led her to Prince Sebastian. A look of confusion painted the Prince's face. With a single nod, Fynn passed her off to Prince Sebastian and took a deep bow. But when he sank back into the crowd, Fynn's gaze never strayed far from her.

A strange feeling bubbled in her throat, but she didn't have time to flesh it out before she was pulled into another dance. She dragged her attention away from the stranger and onto the prince before her. She cleared her throat and wiped the fog from her mind. "My apologies for making you wait, Prince Sebastian."

"Unnecessary, Princess." Sebastian led her around the dance floor as they performed the standard five-step dance with the rest of the crowd.

The party had only begun.

CHAPTER 4

SUITOR AFTER SUITOR LINED UP TO DANCE WITH KALLIE IN THE HOUR that followed. It was their final chance to persuade her to choose them. She listened to several suitors discuss their various responsibilities, the lands they owned, the people they oversaw. She heard the same conversation, listened to the same surface-level compliments seven times. None of her suitors had asked her about her interests, her desires, her goals.

Because at the end of the day, the only thing that mattered was the crown upon her head. She was a princess, a prize. A way to achieve a higher position in their society. But Kallie was more than that.

When she was queen, she would show the world who Kalisandre Helene Domitius truly was.

Right now, however, she needed to escape.

Before the next suitor could ask her to dance, Kallie slipped away to her table to gain a moment of reprieve. Her headache had returned. No doubt a direct result of her encounter with Fynn.

So much for the chamomile tea, Kallie thought.

She took a gulp of her wine and leaned against the head table. The majority of guests were either dancing, conversing along the outskirts of the scuffed floor, or lingering near the staff to be within arm's reach of the various sweets. Few remained at their tables.

Still, one face remained hidden.

Since their dance, Kallie hadn't seen the man who had left an odd taste in her mouth. She did not trust that Fynn's intentions were pure, but nothing had gone astray yet. And if her long nights at taverns taught her anything it was that there was plenty of night left for things to go amuck.

Between the music and the chatter filling the ballroom, Kallie's headache turned into a migraine. Downing the rest of her wine, she lifted herself from the table and replaced her empty glass with a new one. As she glided toward the doors that led to the gardens and her escape, Kallie politely smiled at the guests she weaved around.

Upon exiting, she headed straight toward a dark corner drowned in shadow and shielded by bushes. Kallie had found herself wandering to this corner of the palace whenever she needed to get away from her guards or just *people*—which was more often than not. After disappearing several times, Alyn was quick to discover her hiding spot. She had assumed Myra had ratted her out. However, Myra had never confirmed or denied it. Either way, Kallie had decided to leave it alone since Alyn's quiet presence never bothered her. Plus, he proved to be of use when he brought a bench over to the enclosure.

Kallie sat on the worn cushion that had molded to her form after many years of use. After sliding off her heels, the tension in her feet dissipated instantly. She peered over the railing. A few of the guests had also ventured outside by this point in the night and to Kallie's surprise, Myra and Alyn were among them.

The captain had never admitted his feelings for Myra, but his pink-cheeked countenance had given him away. Myra, on the other hand, was very vocal when it came to her thoughts on Alyn. Kallie had told her friend time and time again that if Myra wanted to pursue a relationship with him, Myra was going to have to be the one to initiate it. Alyn was too courteous to assume anything (which Kallie found to be annoying, but Myra thought otherwise of it). As the two strolled through the gardens, their bodies leaned toward each other. Myra must have taken Kallie's advice at last.

From her bench, Kallie could hear Myra's soft giggle as Alyn rubbed his hand on the back of his head. Seeing the small moment of happiness shared between two people she cared about brought a soft smile to Kallie's face. But the moment was fleeting once they turned around the corner and disappeared.

Kallie's nerves began to slither to the surface when a burst of laughter sounded from the other side of the garden.

A group of guests had stopped at the semi-circle of benches near the fountain. Although before she could identify the members of the group, a bright glint of light caught her eye.

Her crystal shoes sparkled on the ground, and Kallie cursed herself and the ensemble bound to find a way to betray her at some point. She snatched up her shoes and shoved them underneath the bench. Taking the extra precaution to ensure that her dress would not betray her as well, she sank further into the shadows of her corner. She did not want anyone to know she was there or else they would act differently in her presence.

Properly tucked away into the darkness, Kallie returned her focus to the group by the fountain.

The four guests had spread themselves out among the three benches. Only one Kallie recognized: Fynn.

Kallie's eyes narrowed. Fynn sat alone on the middle bench. His suit jacket hung open, his dark brown curls, now free of the ribbon, flying in the wind. With a glass of wine in his hand, Fynn leaned back as he spread his arms across the back of the iron bench.

On the bench to Fynn's left sat another man who closely resembled Fynn—if Fynn had short hair. Twins, no doubt. And as far as Kallie could tell, identical besides their hair and overall aura. Where Fynn's demeanor demanded the attention of everyone in the room, the twin, whose posture was more rigid, seemed to want to sink into the shadows.

Both of the men's gazes were directed at the third bench where the last two members of their party sat: a woman and another man. The woman wore a pale pink dress, a shade that complemented her russet-brown skin. Her curly hazel hair, streaked with gold from hours under the sun, bounced freely around her face.

The man beside her was hunched over with his head pointed to the ground, his near-black hair falling in front of his face. Like the other men, he wore a simple suit, smoky black, with the top two buttons on his collared shirt unclasped. His elbows rested on his knees as a small glass of clear liquid hung loosely in his right hand. A series of gold rings on his fingers glittered in the moonlight.

Kallie had half the mind to stomp over to Fynn and his party, but the other half of her knew it was futile. As much as she wanted to ask —no, *command* Fynn to tell her what his intentions were, there was no point. At the end of the day, the plan was all that mattered. Tomorrow, Kallie would reveal her choice to marry King Rian. Then the rest of the plan would fall into place. She would meet her new fiancé in Frenzia and would use all of the tools she possessed to find her seat on the Frenzian throne.

A spout of loud, obnoxious laughter poured from Fynn's mouth again. The woman, who had tucked her legs under her, leaned over and poked the sulky man in the shoulder. The man shrugged her hand off of him, unamused. He tilted his head toward the woman. Although Kallie could not see his face, whatever expression lay on it and whatever words he spoke forced the woman to fall back against the bench with a groan.

Then a nearby voice made Kallie jump, nearly spilling her drink. "Princess, your father has asked me to escort you to your chambers."

Kallie looked toward the source. Polin, one of her younger guards, stood scanning the area with his hand on his hilt (as if anyone would be foolish enough to attack her during such a public and well-guarded event). Kallie liked him well enough. He was easy to manipulate.

"Thank you, Polin, but I can make it to my rooms on my own."

Polin cleared his throat. "King Domitius said you would say that. He said that if you did, I was to insist." His voice shook slightly at the indirect demand. "The king also told me to—to warn you that you need to preserve your energy for the long journey ahead of you."

Kallie rolled her eyes. Normally, she would not hesitate to convince Polin otherwise; however, he was right. Unfortunately. She had already overused her gift in the past twenty-four hours (not that Polin knew her father was referring to her ability. He probably thought the king was referring to her journey to her future husband's home). If she wanted to show the king she could rule a kingdom, she needed to show some discipline.

She passed the empty glass to Polin, then gathered her shoes from underneath the bench as she stood. Bare feet on the cold concrete, she placed a hand on Polin's shoulder, who immediately straightened at her touch. The corners of her lip quipped upward. Steadying herself, she slipped on the crystal shoes one last time for the night.

After fixing her skirts, she took Polin's arm. They strolled toward the doors and Kallie glanced over her shoulder at the group of strangers to take one last look.

She inhaled sharply.

Fynn was staring at her.

Did he know she had been watching them this entire time?

He raised his glass to her with a smug smile and a wink. The only answer she needed.

Kallie regained her shaken composure before he could notice it. She raised a single brow, casting a downward glance back in response. Then she spun, her skirts swishing across the cement as she gave her back to the man who left her feeling off-balanced in her own home.

Still, as she dodged the handful of guests in the ballroom, the feeling lingered.

CHAPTER 5

MYRA SHUT THE DOOR BEHIND KALLIE, LEAVING POLIN OUTSIDE HER bedroom chambers to stand guard. Kallie kicked off her heels into the corner of her room. In the shadows of her room, the magnificence of her dress extinguished. The jewels weighed her tired body down as she trudged toward her bathroom with Myra's light footsteps following.

Steaming water filled the tub and the scent of lavender and mint swam in the air. Once Myra unclasped the back of the gown, Kallie removed her arms from the thin sleeves, letting the dress pool at her feet. She stepped over the dress and lifted the plain slip over her head. While Myra dragged the dress into the other room, the jewels scratching across the marble floor, Kallie got into the tub. The hot water singed her bare skin, and Kallie let the heat wrap around her as she sunk deeper into the fiery pit.

When Myra returned, the handmaiden started pulling the pins out of Kallie's hair. "By the gods! I don't know how you wore that dress all night," Myra sighed. "It weighs more than a newborn horse."

Kallie chuckled. With her father's words constantly buzzing in her mind all night, she hadn't noticed. But now that she was rid of it,

Kallie did feel lighter—although she knew the feeling was fleeting. Not wanting to discuss herself, Kallie changed the subject, "How was your stroll with Alyn in the gardens?"

Myra's hands froze in Kallie's hair. After a brief moment, she continued untwisting hair from the intricate bun. "I don't know what you're talking about."

Kallie could hear the blush in Myra's voice. "If you say so, Myra."

Myra tilted Kallie's head back. "Anyway, have you made your choice?"

Kallie closed her eyes as Myra poured water onto her head. The steaming water hit her skull and ran down her back. Kallie wished the water would wash away more than the grime of the day. She wanted to tell Myra the truth about the suitors, but Kallie bit her tongue. For the longest time, the only secret she had kept from Myra was her gift. Now, she was hiding the truth about the suitors and her father's plan from her as well, But it was the only way. Perhaps she could at least be somewhat honest with her friend. "At the end of the day, I'll choose what is best for Ardentol."

"I hope you think about your happiness as well, Kallie." Sadness filled Myra's words. "A kingdom is only as happy as its rulers."

While choosing the king of Frenzia wasn't necessarily her choice, the power the marriage would grant her would provide the happiness Kallie sought. Unlike Myra, love would not make Kallie happy. Love was fickle; love could be manipulated and skewed. Power though, true power over others and herself was something Kallie had always craved. Even though she was a king's daughter and while she loved her father, she needed more. King Domitius was able to do whatever he wanted. He did not need someone else's approval, and Kallie hungered for that sort of freedom.

And deep within, she wanted to show her father she could do more, *be* more than his errand girl.

Every strategy meeting she sat in on, every monthly court session she witnessed, Kallie saw firsthand how the people respected him. How they bowed down to their king.

But it was time they bowed down to a queen.

She would strengthen her gift. She would endure the dangers. She would learn the strengths and weaknesses of her allies and her enemies. And then she would show her father and all of Vaneria she could rule a kingdom. Because that was all Kallie wanted.

To rule. To rule her own kingdom, her own people.

Herself.

Her father had taught her many things, but the most important lesson he had taught her was to take control of her own destiny.

A smile appeared on her face, the first genuine one of the night. "Don't worry, Myra. My happiness always comes first."

Myra squeezed Kallie's shoulders. "Good. That is all I want for you."

Once Myra finished washing her hair, she left Kallie alone.

Kallie stayed submerged in the tub until the scorching water cooled and her skin looked like little prunes. After drying off, she swapped the wet towel for the silk robe that hung on the wooden rod, then wandered into her room. Kallie headed to the windows on the eastern side of her room and threw them open. A breeze swept through and carried in the comforting smell of oak.

Leaving the windows open, she threw on the night dress laid out on her bed. Every choice today and all the days leading up to it had been made for her. From the dress she wore to the words she spoke to the very oils poured into her bath. But tomorrow, she would be one step closer to changing that. Tomorrow, she would be one step closer to becoming her own ruler.

Tucked under the blankets, she faced the window and watched as the moon shifted in the sky, letting her mind wander as she drifted to sleep. She prayed to the gods she would dream of a world she controlled.

THE SMELL of smoke and the explosion of light startled Kallie awake. She crawled out of bed and ran toward the window. Night still shaded the earth, but a bright light streamed into the room from the nearby forest.

The trees were on fire.

The bright flames were too close, too fast. Panic surged through her.

The house would catch on fire at any moment. She had to run, she had to escape. She had to do something.

On shaky legs, she sprinted toward the doors, throwing them open. No guards were in sight. Had they left her to die? She didn't want to think that was the case, but there was no time. Kallie would reprimand whoever was to blame for that misstep later—if they survived.

She ran through the halls, screaming, alerting anyone still asleep. Skidding to a stop at the master bedroom at the end of the hall, she yanked the door handle and immediately wrenched her hand back. Hugging it to her chest, she peeled her hand open. Her skin was scarlet. She shook it while ignoring the searing pain.

Black smoke seeped through the crack beneath the door.

She scanned the hallway, frantically searching for anything that could help force it open. Her parents were still inside.

She pounded on the door with her fists as shouting filled the hallway. Still, she kept slamming her fist against the warm wood.

Then, a noise on the other side of the door caused her hand to freeze above her head before it could clash against the wood again. She might have only imagined the sound, her mind playing tricks on her.

But there it was again. A guttural cough.

"Kallie, honey, get out," said a woman's strained voice.

Tears filled Kallie's eyes as she listened to the throat-scorching cough coming from the other side of the door. She couldn't leave her. Not this time. Not again. She continued to bang her hands against the door. Splotches of red smeared across the door. Smoke continued to fill the hallway. It wrapped around her. Its wisps grabbed onto her, slithering their way up her legs, her waist.

As it grew, the smoke became corporeal and its arms circled her.

But as she tried to pry herself from its grasp, she knew it was not the smoke's doing, but a person's. She clawed at the door, trying to gain a grip on it instead.

"No! Let me go!" she screamed. Kallie wasn't going to leave her there. She couldn't.

"Kallie," the woman's voice was quieter, weaker than before. "It's. . . all right." The coughing resumed. Kallie could hear the smoke filling her lungs, destroying her beautiful voice.

The smoke was getting thicker.

Her screaming turned into coughing as smoke began to fill Kallie's lungs. Her breathing became labored, but Kallie continued to cry out.

The person pulled her closer to their chest. She pumped her legs and arms. She clawed at the air. She pounded at the person's arm wrapped around her, but like a python latching onto its dinner, it was relentless and didn't let her go. The person hissed as she continued to fight and claw at them.

She didn't care if she hurt them.

She didn't care if she died.

She couldn't go through the heartbreak of losing her mother. Not again. Not this time.

Perhaps if she screamed loud enough, it would stop.

Perhaps if she tried harder, it would stop.

Perhaps if she wrenched out her own heart, it would stop.

IT ONLY STOPPED when Kallie woke to a heart ready to burst out of her chest. It might have been easier if she had ripped her heart out in her sleep. Her throat ached, her skin was moist and hot, her sheets were damp. She looked at her right hand, but it was pale pink and there was no visible redness.

She inhaled and counted to ten as she tried to slow her heart rate.

This wasn't the first time her mother's death had haunted her dreams. Kallie had experienced several variations of this nightmare ever since she could remember. Sometimes it took the form of a storm that tore apart their boat and drowned them; sometimes it was a ravaged bull. But no matter the method, the end always remained the same: an overwhelming sense of helplessness.

Kallie exhaled.

Then, her doors flew open and Polin burst through them with his sword drawn, startling her. His eyes scanned the room, alert and ready to fend off an attacker. When he spotted Kallie's disheveled form sitting upright in her bed, the realization hit him.

There was no attacker, only another nightmare that had startled Kallie awake.

He sheathed his sword and made his features appear neutral. "My lady, is everything all right?"

May the gods bless his heart.

Kallie gave him a small, shaky smile. "I'm fine, Polin. It was just a nightmare."

He shifted his weight. It was always awkward when her nightmares got the attention of her guards. But until she found a solution to quiet the night terrors, she only trusted Polin and Alyn to guard her doors at night. Unlike some of her past guards whom she had to release from their duty, they were the only two guards she trusted to keep quiet.

He nodded his head. "I'll be outside if you need anything."

"Thank you."

Polin took his leave. Once she heard the door hinge click into place, Kallie threw the rest of the blankets off of her. She hurried over to the window and let the cool air kiss her skin. Tilting her head up to the stars, she took a deep breath.

She wanted to scream, to cry. Her heart hurt, but she couldn't let thoughts of her mother distract her. As much as she wished her mother could be there, as much as she believed she should be there for tomorrow's events, Kallie knew better.

She could not change the past, but she could change the future.

The seven kingdoms of Vaneria were weakening, strife was building among the people.

She rolled her neck, the top of her spine popping. She forced her lips into a smile and smoothed the wrinkles from her nightgown. Dawn was approaching and with it, her choice would be revealed to all of Vaneria.

She would be done taking orders. She would no longer have to sit idly by as the world turned to shit around her. As kingdoms refused to change, as they continued to let their people suffer in every corner of Vaneria. She would be the piece that united the kingdoms.

She would no longer have to hide her gift out of fear. She would use it to help her people. She would put an end to those who spoke out against them, against her father. Against peace.

Then, with their plan set into motion, Kallie would no longer have to fear the fire consuming her, for she would become the fire.

And she would set the world ablaze and watch it burn before her.

HUNDREDS OF EYES stared at her as she stood on the dais behind her father once again.

Today Kallie wore a simple dress—simple by the king's standard anyway. The off-the-shoulder pale blue dress left her collarbone bare, restricted her movements, and made Kallie yearn for her cloak and leather trousers. The fabric cinched her waist, then flowed to the ground. Similar to the dramatic gown she wore the previous day, Myra had weaved diamonds throughout the fabric, though far fewer than yesterday's extravagant gown. Kallie stood with her arms in front of her, one hand over the other. The picturesque princess each suitor thought she was.

The energy in the room was stifled, sparking with nervous energy. The suitors shifted their weight from one foot to the other. When her eyes landed on Sebastian, his chin tilted upward, confidence dripping off of him.

He knew. They all knew, yet they all waited for the words to leave her mouth. There was no competition here, not when someone offered Kallie an entire kingdom.

But alas, her father wanted it to appear as if the others had a chance.

King Domitius addressed the hall, "After much deliberation, Princess Kalisandre has made her decision." With a hand, her father called Kallie forward.

Kallie took a step toward her father and spoke to the crowd, "I am flattered and humbled to have had so many of you show up to our kingdom and not only ask for my hand, but grant me the comfort of knowing that my choice will be respected. It has shown me how strong we, as separate kingdoms, can be when joined together under one roof, one goal.

"I hope that after today's decision we can continue to build upon the relationships that we have begun to forge. It is also because of this hope that surrounds me today that I have come to my decision," she paused as she scanned the crowd. Dramatics were not formally a part of her lessons with her father, but she had learned them nevertheless. Taking in a quiet breath, a soft, serene smile graced her lips. "Prince Sebastian, please come forward."

Fabric rustled as people shuffled in the crowd to make a path for the prince. Sebastian's gait was sure and did not falter when he approached the dais. He knelt at the edge of the throne and pressed a fist to his heart. "King Domitius. Princess Kalisandre."

Kallie's lips twitched. "Prince Sebastian, yesterday you spoke of King Rian's desire for stability and strength after the unfortunate passing of the late King Lothian. Although I cannot remember when my mother passed, her death still lingers and pulls on my heart, so I can empathize with you and your family. As King Rian and I will learn to lean on each other during these trying times, my wish is that our kingdoms will learn to do the same. I believe that we are reaching a turning point in our history, and forging a bond between our two kingdoms is not only mutually beneficial for Ardentol and Frenzia, but beneficial to Vaneria as a whole. It is my hope that you will relay the news of my acceptance of your brother's proposal to King Rian."

Sebastian bowed his head. "Princess Kalisandre, it would be my honor to share this delightful news with my brother. Your engagement will be the light that guides our hearts back toward the shore during this tumultuous time."

Beside her, King Domitius added, "We look forward to building a relationship between our two kingdoms. Prince Sebastian, we will discuss travel arrangements in my study."

Prince Sebastian nodded and took his leave. The king then directed his attention to the rest of the room to express his gratitude. As his voice bounced off the walls, Kallie began reviewing the next part of their plan and she couldn't stop the smirk that crept onto her face.

THE NEXT FEW days slipped by like a skilled thief in the night. Gone before anyone noticed.

Preparations for the journey were made. Prince Sebastian and his men had already left to notify King Rian about the news before Kallie arrived. Her father and Sebastian had agreed that she would depart a week after Sebastian's party since traveling together would draw too much attention and would only endanger their journey. Kallie and the king had then chosen a select group of soldiers for the journey, including Alyn and Polin. The king also had agreed that Myra would accompany Kallie since Kallie still required her services (and company).

While she waited to leave, the king was insistent on Kallie spending every minute either training, studying, or reviewing their plans. He reminded her that they could not predict what obstacles she might encounter. So, she went to work.

When her body ached for a break, she ignored its pleas. When her stomach grumbled during strategy meetings, she fed off her hunger to accomplish their task. When her eyelids became heavy as she reviewed the countless maps, she threw water onto her face to stay awake. And when her head hit her pillow each night at long last, deep exhaustion blanketed her, keeping the nightmares away.

Today she ran through her training one last time before she embarked on her journey. Over the past decade and a half, she had grown to enjoy her training, often sneaking out in the later hours of the night to train on her own. After donning the mask of a well-mannered royal during the day, Kallie was enthralled by the grittiness of training. The sweat beading at the base of her neck made her feel accomplished. The changes in her body, the muscles in her quads and arms, made her feel powerful and in control. The slick material of her training gear was more pliable than her formal wear and allowed her to move freely. She wasn't restricted by heavy skirts or tight, lung-crushing bodices.

But more than anything, when she trained alone, she enjoyed the quiet—the absence of others watching and judging her. She didn't have her father telling her she wasn't good enough from the way he shook his head.

In the shadows of the night, Kallie could be herself and forget the pressures and self-doubt that plagued her mind. She was able to take a break from the facade she had to wear in front of her father's subjects and visitors. She could turn off the thoughts that ravaged her mind during the day and just exist.

Early on in her training, her father created mazes beneath the palace. He believed they would trick her into thinking it was a game when she was young. Soon enough, the mazes became a habit. The obstacles her father created were exhausting, but they made her think outside of the box and use whatever resources were available to finish the course.

Yet after every success, there was another maze, another trial to beat. Another nod of approval to acquire.

Each maze was harder than the last, and Kallie learned to thrive on the challenge. Shaping her body into something strong and unbreakable was a release she had not known she craved until she had done it. It was the one thing that someone could not claim for themselves for it was hers and hers alone.

And she would use everything she had learned to ensure her journey to the foreign kingdom and her task of capturing the man's heart and mind was nothing short of a success.

Her father would accept nothing else from his greatest weapon.

She would accept nothing else.

So, when Kallie completed her father's latest obstacle course beneath the castle in the training quarters for the second time that night, she ran through it again.

When she slid across the floor to avoid the flying arrows she had triggered, strands of hair fell from her ponytail as the arrows zipped above her head. She rolled onto her stomach, pushed herself off the floor, then sprinted toward the cover that lay a few paces away. Sweat dripped from her brow, but she ignored the urge to wipe it away. She could not afford a distraction. Her concentration needed to stay sharp. This would be her last run through the maze, and it would be flawless despite the ache that was forming in her limbs.

The guard she had manipulated to help her train was waiting for her on the other side of the haystack. She counted to ten, repeating her mantra in her mind.

I am capable. I am powerful. I am control. I am worthy.

And once her breathing was under control, she attacked with the fierceness of a bull.

CHAPTER 6

KALLIE'S BODY SCREAMED AT HER WHEN SHE GOT INTO THE CARRIAGE AT dawn. Her morning stretches had done little to soothe the ache in her muscles. Thankfully, she had a few hours to rest until they stopped.

Myra had fallen asleep on the bench across from her, which was a blessing from the gods. Her jitteriness had made Kallie anxious. Although Kallie could not blame Myra for her excitement. Her handmaiden had lived in Ardentol her entire life. At the age of thirteen, Myra had joined Kallie's service, and the two of them had been inseparable for the past nine years. Where Kallie went, Myra followed. Since Kallie hadn't traveled after an incident when she was eleven, which was before Myra was employed, this was Myra's first time outside the kingdom's borders.

The last time Kallie had been beyond Ardentol's borders was when she was eleven. Kallie had accompanied her father on his visit to Kadia to celebrate the Summer Solstice. Since summer was short in the region, Kadia held an annual festival for a week straight to celebrate summer's arrival. During the week-long event, there were tournaments, grand feasts, and other events that Kallie was not old enough to participate in at the time. After the largest feast, many of the children escaped to a nearby lake. Back home, there were few children around Kallie's age, and she was desperate for friends. However, Kallie had strict orders either to remain by the king's side or be in her sleeping quarters. But Kallie was young, rebellious, and foolish. So without the king's knowledge, Kallie had snuck off to join the others.

At the lake, Kallie had overheard a group of girls around her age bragging about their first kisses. When one of the girls asked Kallie who was her first kiss, Kallie did not want to admit she had not kissed anyone yet. But Kallie's gift had not been strong enough to force them to believe a lie since she was still training her ability. She attempted to lie, but they saw through it instantly.

After a fit of laughter, the girls dared Kallie to kiss someone right there and then.

Not willing to let them think she was afraid, Kallie accepted the challenge. She spotted a boy with silver hair who was tossing rocks along the surface of the lake alone. She had never met him, she didn't even know his name, but he seemed kind enough during the feast.

Kallie walked over to him and asked him to show her how to make the rocks skid across the lake. When he picked up a smooth rock and turned to her, she kissed him. A simple peck. The boy was paralyzed.

And like any girl, Kallie ran.

Straight into her father, who had seen everything. Outraged, he dragged her away as he lectured her about respect and proper etiquette for a royal. But Kallie only heard the girls giggling behind her back.

Afterward, her father prohibited her from traveling with him. However, the travel ban didn't stop Kallie from sneaking out of the castle at night and doing more than planting meek kisses on the mouths of boys.

Nevertheless, this was Myra's first time leaving Ardentol and her excitement was nauseating. When the carriage didn't stop in front of Frenzia's gates after an hour, the excitement diminished. Then when Kallie stopped entertaining her and she had no one else to turn to, Myra dozed off.

After reading a few chapters in a book, Kallie closed it and pulled back the curtain to check on her guards. Peering outside the carriage, she spotted Alyn riding beside the carriage and fiddling with a loose thread on his horse's reins. Every few paces he looked over his shoulders, checking the perimeters. Kallie tapped on the glass.

Eyes wide, Alyn swiveled toward the sound, and Kallie gave him a wide, toothy smile. But the corner of his lip only twitched He then returned his gaze to the path ahead.

Polin then rode closer and upon seeing Kallie in the window, he waved. She smiled back. The two guards began conversing. Unable to hear their conversation through the soundproofed carriage, Kallie sat back in her seat and let the curtain fall. She leaned against the window and shifted in her seat. The leather holster holding her dagger rubbed against her leg and soothed some of her nerves—but not all of them.

Despite the lingering nerves stirring inside of her stomach, she dozed off as the carriage rocked back and forth down the bumpy path that headed toward the Alderian Mountains.

KALLIE'S SKULL smacked against the curtain-covered window and startled her awake. Massaging her throbbing head, Kallie looked over at Myra. The fog of sleep was fresh on her face, her hair disheveled.

"Are we finally there?" Myra asked, hopeful.

Kallie couldn't be sure but she thought she heard footsteps pounding on the ground outside the carriage. She stretched her arms over her head, loosening her sore limbs. "Doubtful. The horses probably need a break."

A loud thud rattled the carriage. Kallie reached for the door, but she yanked her hand back and instead placed her ear against the wall. The soundproofed carriage muffled everything. Something similar to a grunt sounded on the other side, then a sound akin to a scream followed. The back of her neck grew cold as a chill ran through her body. On instinct, she reached underneath her skirts and unlatched the dagger from the holster. She slipped it into the sleeve of her shirt. Whatever was happening outside, Kallie did not want to be in a position where she was fumbling for a weapon.

"Kallie!" Myra hissed. "Why do you have your dagger on you right now?"

Kallie waved her hand in the air as more muffled grunts sounded outside. She grabbed her second, less favored, and smaller dagger from the bag beside her.

"*Two* of them?"

Kallie held a finger to her lips as she listened to the unintelligible shouts outside the carriage, the plush cushioning and thick boards making it nearly impossible to parse them.

Meanwhile, Myra slapped her hand across her face, then lifted it a second later to whisper, "Is all of this necessary?"

"Let's hope not." Kallie held out the smaller dagger. Since Myra was untrained, it might do her more harm than good to wield a weapon she was unfamiliar with. But Kallie would never forgive herself if Myra was stuck in a situation where she had nothing to defend herself with.

Myra shook her head, melting into the cushion as her fisted hands dug into the seat.

Kallie snatched Myra's hand and pried it open. "Take it."

Kallie placed the small dagger in Myra's palm, folding her smooth fingers around it. "Think of it like a large embroidery needle."

Myra scrunched her nose. "No offense, Kals, but that is the stupidest thing you have ever said."

Kallie shrugged, but her handmaiden was right. The Ardentolian guard was made up of men primarily. As a result, Kallie had not been around many women who bore weapons. She made a mental note—when she became queen, she would change that. No one deserved to be defenseless. "Okay, fine. It's very different. But take it. Just in case."

Myra sighed but reached out her hand. "Just in case," Myra repeated.

As Kallie bunched the fabric of her skirt together and tied it into a knot, she started to say, "I'm sure Alyn—" but a whine silenced her. She snapped her gaze up, and Myra's pale complexion told Kallie all she needed to know. She had made a grave mistake mentioning the guard.

"Oh, no! Kallie! What if he's hurt?" Myra's gaze became glossy.

"Don't be silly, Mys. Alyn's one of the best," Kallie reassured Myra.

Still, Kallie's body itched to move even though she trusted Alyn's ability to protect them. She couldn't sit idly, especially at the risk of Myra's tears. She needed to assess the situation. Lifting the corner of the curtain, she peeked out the small window.

Five hooded figures surrounded the right side of the carriage, and no doubt there were more somewhere in the forest. The assailants stood around several bodies prone on the ground. She recognized the coachman, face slack against the dirt, blood spreading around him. A few feet away, a hooded figure slid a sword out of one of her other guards, whom Kallie identified as Orean. Near the first carriage, which contained hers and Myra's belongings, two other guards lay in their blood: Kyen and Fiel.

Four of her men down, only a handful left.

Whoever these strangers were, they had managed to slay her best guards in a matter of a few minutes.

She bit her thumbnail as she continued to scan the scene. A steel sword with a navy leather wrapping and delicate silver embroidery sewn around the grip caught her eye. Myra's handiwork—Kallie was sure of it, for she would recognize it anywhere. And a few feet away, a body lay face-first in the mud. A boot of one of the assailants pressed firmly between the man's shoulder blades. Blonde hair that was normally tidy was now covered in dirt.

Her eyes narrowed. She made to close the flap before anyone spotted her and before Myra thought to look herself. However, when she began to release the shade, the sight to her left pinned her hand in place.

Pushed up against the side of the carriage, Polin stood with his cheek pressed up against the door and his eyes squeezed shut in fear. The attacker towered over Polin as he pressed two scimitars against Polin's neck. The blades dug into his skin, a bead of blood forming.

Anticipating what would come next, Kallie looked away. The splattering against the window made her flinch, but Polin didn't even release a scream as the blades sliced through his neck. She forced herself to watch, digging her nails into her palms as Polin slid down the side of the carriage, hands pressed against his wound in a sad attempt at stopping the bleeding.

She had hand-picked all of her guards. And now they would not be returning to their families or their homes alive because of her choice.

With his scimitars smeared with blood, the figure stood there, and beneath the shadows, Kallie saw the glimmer of a smirk.

She would kill him.

She would kill them all.

Another guard approached the assailant from behind. With an unnatural grace, the figure spun, slicing the approaching guard in the gut with one quick, fluid movement.

The curtain slipped from her damp fingers. She had no time to wash the thoughts away. No time to take into account that she lost two more guards in the time it took her to take a couple of breaths. She scooted over to the opposite corner of the carriage and peered out the other window.

No bodies, no hooded figures.

The attackers must have come from the east and then chose to center their attack on one side of the carriage to draw out the guards instead of surrounding it.

That was their first mistake.

The second was believing she would do nothing. As a princess, most expected her to be tame, weak. But Kallie was neither of those things. She nodded to Myra, who gripped the small dagger with white knuckles. Kallie regretted not preparing Myra, but she had been too preoccupied with her own training. And now, it was too late.

Swallowing the lump in her throat, Kallie cracked the carriage door open. The sound of dying men and metal clashing clogged her ears. Headfirst, she looked both ways and silently hopped out of the carriage, the balls of her feet landing first.

She turned to help Myra. But as she reached her hand out, Myra was being dragged from the other side of the carriage by one of the hooded figures.

"Kallie!" Myra shouted, the notion of being quiet long since forgotten. Tears streaked her friend's face as she was dragged out of the carriage by her ankles.

Rage fueled Kallie as she crawled back into the carriage and scrambled to reach for Myra's hand. Her fingers grazed the tips of Myra's, but Kallie was yanked backward and out of the carriage before she could grab onto Myra. Kallie watched in horror as the small dagger fell from Myra's hand and bounced on the floor as she too was pulled away. Kallie wanted to shout, to reassure her friend that it would be all right. But she was rendered speechless. All Kallie could do was keep her eyes on her friend as though maintaining eye contact with Myra would ensure her handmaiden's safety.

Kallie wiggled against her assailant. Then, pulling her dagger by the hilt, she reared her hand and jammed the blade into the person's thigh.

"You bitch," the attacker spat.

She slid her dagger out of his flesh, twisting it to the right a quarter of an inch as a grin crept onto her face. She hadn't been able to stab a man in a while and she was feeling particularly violent after seeing her people brutalized.

Kallie spun as the man pressed his palm firmly against his thigh where red seeped through his brown trousers. He leaned on his other leg and pulled the sword from its sheath, and Kallie's smile faded in disappointment as she looked at the man's sword.

Kallie had never mastered the use of a longsword. She was decent with the weapon, but she had learned early on that it slowed her down. And her speed was her greatest asset in a fight. Her small stature allowed her to dodge an attacker's maneuvers easily, especially when they were armed with a sword. During her training, many of her opponents believed that she was at a disadvantage when she approached them with a dagger after they had chosen a sword. Against a sword, the common belief was that an opponent with a dagger was easily fought off. The sword had a longer reach and could keep the opponent further away.

However, those men quickly learned the flaw in their logic, because, for Kallie, that was not a problem.

She had been ready for a challenge, but this was going to be easier than she had thought, even with sore muscles.

"Now, you could end this here, Princess, before you make me do something I might regret or—"

"Or you could shut it and fight," Kallie interrupted and the man sneered. "But know I won't go easy on you."

The man chuckled. Then under his breath, he mumbled, "Oh, they're not going to forgive me for this." His foot shifted and Kallie let him strike first.

As his sword thrust forward, she dodged his attack with ease and locked the man's arm against his side. She knocked the sword out of his hand. In a swift motion, Kallie swooped under the attacker's arm and twisted the man's arm backward.

The large stranger was surprisingly quick. The man grabbed Kallie's hand and slammed the heel of his boot down onto Kallie's toes. In the next moment, an elbow smacked into her cheekbone. He twisted around, locking Kallie's head underneath his arm, and forced Kallie to face the other direction.

"I don't want to hurt you, Princess." He said as cold metal pressed against Kallie's throat. Glancing down her nose, she saw a dagger in the man's hand. "But you've left me no choice."

The right corner of her mouth tilted upward. Men prized themselves for their strength, both mentally and physically, but they always forgot about one small thing. Dropping her chin, she jerked her arms upward, spun, and kneed him in the groin.

The attacker crumbled to the ground on impact. "Bitch," he groaned.

She twisted around, then cut off his airway. As his olive complexion turned violet, she whispered, "Next time, learn something new to say when a woman outsmarts you."

His weight shifted as his consciousness began to fall away.

Once he was unconscious, she let him fall to the ground. She scanned the area for her dagger. Kallie spotted it a few feet away from her, but before she could dive for it another cloaked figure appeared and kicked the dagger underneath the carriage. Kallie groaned.

The person before her was leaner than the previous attacker, but their stance was sturdier, more confident.

"Ral always was a little weak. But if he complains to me, at least I know who to blame," the woman said. "Men like to appear tougher than us women, but they can be much softer when it comes to their emotions, don't you think?"

Despite the large hood, Kallie could see the woman slide her tongue across her teeth as she ran the tip of her finger across the blade of her dagger. Tight curls protruded from the edge of her hood.

"You know, I've spent a lot of time thinking . . ." the woman continued while she took a side step to the left.

Kallie tracked her movements, waiting to see how this would play out, but her opponent did not continue. Apparently, the woman wanted an actual response. Annoyed, Kallie said, "So it seems."

The woman sighed. "Let me have this moment. It's been a while since I've talked to a person who might understand."

Another step to the left and they began tracing a circle in the dirt, their dance only beginning.

"The men I've been around have always sought out tools to do their bidding." Another step, this one closer. "Whether that be a weapon, a blade," a pause and a step, "or a woman. But I don't need to point that out to you. Do I, Princess?"

Kallie's fingers twitched at the shift in the woman's tone. Kallie had seen her father's men lean on their weapons to aid them in their fights. Her father had leaned on her from time to time to accomplish some tasks as well. But that, *that* was different. He did not have a gift from the gods. He wasn't using her. He needed her.

They needed each other.

While Kallie aided his pursuits, King Domitius promised her power. And for this woman to question that need, to question Kallie's purpose and worth in a game the woman knew nothing about enraged her.

"Perhaps you should surround yourself with better men then," Kallie countered.

"Perhaps." The hooded woman sucked on her teeth. "But perhaps we should prove to them we do not need any weapon besides ourselves." Smirking, she waved her dagger in the air.

Kallie tilted her head to the side as she weighed her options. Her dagger was under the carriage. The only weapon she possessed was her previous opponent's heavy sword. She could manage it if she had to, but the woman's proposal was too tempting to dismiss. The woman had the aura of someone who knew her own strengths, her weaknesses and knew how to exploit the weaknesses of others.

The sword slid from Kallie's hand.

The moment the sword hit the ground the woman sheathed her dagger and slid across the dirt aiming for Kallie's ankles. Kallie was able to shift her weight in time and somersaulted over the woman's outstretched arm.

Turning around to face the woman, Kallie blew a loose strand out of her face as a maniacal laugh left the woman's lips.

"About damn time," the woman said. Her laughter faded as she stood up and brushed the dirt off her hands. "I've been waiting for a challenge all day."

Then the woman shifted, angling her body. And Kallie made her move, kicking high and aiming for the woman's face. But her opponent blocked the attack and Kallie's leg bounced back to the ground.

Kallie adjusted her weight and swung, but the woman's reflexes were quick and her palm instantly found Kallie's forearm, stopping the momentum and flicking it away. The woman jabbed with her other hand, but Kallie easily ducked under the attack.

In the same motion, Kallie swiveled and rammed her knee into the woman's gut.

Once.

Twice.

With each strike, the woman grunted in pain.

But on the third, the woman pushed Kallie back, her knee hitting nothing but air. Kallie lost her balance. A rush of air hit her face, then the woman's black boot swung at her head.

With the carriage a step behind her, Kallie had nowhere else to go. She crouched low and the boot skated above the top of her head, missing her by an inch. And before Kallie could readjust herself, the woman's knee was coming straight for her face.

The woman's knee smacked into Kallie's outstretched palms and jolted Kallie back a step. But her opponent was off balance too, and Kallie did not waste the opportunity to jam her shin into the woman's side.

Kallie would not lose this fight. She needed to end it. She needed to find Myra.

She pulled her elbow back and struck the woman's jaw. Kallie's punches came in rapid succession. One after another, pushing the woman back with each crash of her fist.

The woman took a large step backward, putting distance between herself and Kallie's fist. "At least Domitius taught you how to fight."

The absence of her father's title did not go unnoticed, and Kallie would not allow him to be disrespected. He had earned that title like she would earn hers one day.

Kallie's breaths came faster. Loose strands of hair stuck to her face, slick with sweat. Kallie noticed a shift in her opponent's stature and adjusted herself for the oncoming punch.

But Kallie was so busy watching the woman's hands that she didn't see the woman's boot this time. The top of the woman's foot jammed into her jaw with a bruising force.

Kallie ignored the pain and swung. But before Kallie could strike, the woman jabbed Kallie with her elbow. Then twisting around, the woman faced her and shoved Kallie backward. Kallie's back smacked against the ground and the air was knocked out of her.

The woman peered down at her and took a slow step forward. "If that leaves a mark, I apologize, but at least it will heal."

Red filled her vision. And in Kallie's peripheral vision, a glint of silver caught her attention. She rolled and scurried underneath the carriage. Fingers on the hilt, she wrapped her hand around her dagger.

In her haste though, Kallie had forgotten what awaited her on the other side of the carriage. A large black boot crashed down onto her knuckles, forcing her to release the weapon.

Two scimitars wiped clean of blood hung at the sides of the towering man. His hood was pulled down over his eyes, but Kallie could still see the cocky smirk on his face. Dark stubble covered his chin. "Did you think you could hide from me, little mouse?" the man said, baring his teeth.

Kallie's heart pounded, but this was not over yet.

As she tried to yank her hand back, someone else grabbed her other arm. Kallie looked behind her and saw yet another hooded figure.

The first man lifted his boot off her hand. His friend made quick work of gathering her hands and tying a rope around Kallie's wrists before she could move. As he tightened the rope, his fingers were coarse on her skin, Kallie's breathing hitched.

His fingers.

He was touching her. Kallie cursed herself for not thinking of it sooner. She pulled at the strands of her gift and laced her words as she spoke, "You will—"

But before Kallie could finish the command, he raised a finger to his lips. And the man with the scimitars spoke over her, his voice deep, wild, "Whatever it is you're about to say, tell us when you wake up."

She turned to the man who nearly crushed her fingers. He reached down, picked up her dagger, and slipped it into the back of his trousers. She tried to ask him what he meant by 'when she wakes up,' but her tongue turned to stone. Then her eyelids grew heavy, her vision blurred.

She prayed to the gods that Myra was okay, that her loss today would not haunt Kallie forever. But she did not have time to think about how much her pride hurt before everything went black.

CHAPTER 7

KALLIE AWOKE WITH HER FACE AGAINST A THIN, COLD BLANKET. HER mind was hazy, her vision was slow to return. But one thing was clear: she had to find Myra and make sure she was okay.

Kallie attempted to push herself up but without success. Her legs were sorer than they had been before. Rough rope dug into her skin. Her heart beat against her ribcage as she tried to think of a plan. She needed to get her shit together before she could try to save Myra. Wherever her friend was.

She took a deep breath, counted to ten to clear her mind. She could do this. Her father had prepared her for this.

After taking another clearing breath, she opened her eyes. Shadows saturated the tent she occupied making it hard to identify the exact details of her surroundings. But she drank in as much as possible in the darkness that encased her. Kallie lay in the midst of blankets strewn across the ground. Somewhere, stone scrapped against metal. Toward the tent's opening, the moon's rays cast a faint ring of light around the silhouette of a broad-shouldered man. He faced the open air with his hood pulled back revealing short, brown hair cut close to his head. The individual was hunched over. A glint of light bounced off a piece of metal in his lap as he sharpened his blade.

If Kallie attracted his attention, she could use him to find Myra. Kallie pulled at her gift laying at the bottom of her stomach. It twirled and flickered. If this was going to work, she needed to remain calm. Keep her temper stifled. Even though all she wanted to do was scream at this man to release her and Myra, the only survivors of their slaughter.

At least, she hoped her friend had survived. Kallie did not dare think about the alternative.

She cleared her throat of the dryness that coated it. "Hey," Kallie whispered.

At the sound of her voice, the man swung his head, but his facial features remained indistinguishable in the darkness.

"These bindings are," she grunted as she tugged at the rope, "a little tight, don't you think? They're making my wrists bleed."

The man grumbled something inaudible, but he stood. Sheathing his freshly sharpened sword, and padded over to her. As he grabbed her wrists to check the binding, Kallie took her chance.

Choosing her words carefully, she let her gift melt with her words. "After you unbind me, you will silently and without alarming the others take me to my handmaiden and let the two of us escape the camp." When she used her gift, she had to ensure that her words could not be misinterpreted and that her intention was clear. If she wanted it to last for a long period, she had to conserve her energy. If it was a simple task, it would require less. Either way, none of her victims knew they had been manipulated afterward.

The man froze. Then, the rope loosened around her wrists and fell off.

Twisting her wrists around, Kallie stood and released a shaky breath. When she looked up at the man, his brown eyes were unmistakable. The man who had stolen a dance—Fynn. But no, this man's hair was shorter. This close, the resemblance was even more uncanny.

Fynn's twin stared down at her, and a fire erupted inside of her. They had infiltrated her home, attacked her carriage, killed her people, and abducted her and Myra. Kallie would make them pay for it all.

However, before she could say anything to the man, Fynn's twin turned toward the tent flap, looked both ways, and ushered her over.

Kallie rolled her neck. Despite the rage that boiled inside of her, she would have to worry about her revenge later, the plan floating in her mind. Right now, Myra was the priority and if the man was leading her, Myra was still alive.

She followed the twin out of the tent and to Kallie's surprise, no one was around. Everyone must have been sleeping in their tents. Kallie wondered how long she had been asleep and how she had fallen asleep in the first place. She tried to recall the moments before everything had gone black, but the events were muddled. The missing information made her stomach churn.

The twin led her to the side of the next tent. He pointed to the ground and put his finger to his lips. Taking the hint to wait, Kallie crouched beside the tent. He peeled back the opening of the tent, then disappeared into the darkness.

Several tents stood around her. The faint smell of a recently extinguished fire coated the air. Then Kallie heard inaudible voices. Her heart rate increased as she sank further behind the tent, melding her body into the shadows as best she could.

She squatted down, quieted her breathing, and wished the twin would hurry up and grab Myra before anyone approached. They didn't have time to waste. Her father and she had drawn up the plan, set it in stone, and marked it into her memory. She needed to begin gathering information and she needed to reach Frenzia.

If she didn't arrive when she was expected to, what would King Rian think?

Her fiancé would think she ran. That she betrayed her word, that she was unfit to rule by his side.

And Kallie was many things—a princess, an enchantress, a weapon, a keeper of secrets—but she was not a traitor.

She would never betray her kingdom or her father. They both had given her everything she held dear: a home, a purpose, and soon, a throne.

She would not give that up.

The wind blew fragments of the pair's conversation toward her and pulled her away from her thoughts.

"Come on, Armen. Are you still mad?" one of the voices asked.

The other person grunted in response. Their footsteps grew louder as they neared the opposite side of the tent. Kallie leaned as far as she dared, straining to hear their conversation. The various jobs her father had tasked her with had taught her that the most important conversations were the ones when people thought no one was listening.

"Did you have to be so rough?" Armen said and his voice made the hair on the back of her neck stand.

That voice. Kallie knew it, but she couldn't place it. It was strained and the name to whom it belonged was unfamiliar.

Kallie took a step forward in the hopes of identifying the figure. However, when her foot landed, her heart sank with it as the snap of a twig sounded beneath it. Her body stilled, her breathing ceased. And the footsteps stopped at the front of the tent she hid beside.

"What was that?" the first voice asked.

Both of the men were silent as they listened. They only needed to take a few steps to their left and her cover would be blown. A bead of sweat slid down the contour of Kallie's face. Only moments away from freedom, yet her foot had betrayed her—no, her curiosity.

Squeezing her eyes shut, she counted each beat of her heart as the silence pressed onward.

"Must have been a critter. There's always some animal lurking in these woods," said the first.

Sweat dripped down Kallie's nose. Her heart beat so loudly she could hear it reverberate in her eardrums, and she hoped it was unheard by the men.

"Maybe . . . " the other voice said, unconvinced. The tension in her muscles strained as she tried to remain still. "But maybe I should—"

But Sabina must have been watching over her, lending Kallie a helping hand. Because as Kallie's legs were about to give out, a small chipmunk scurried past her toward the voices.

"See? Told you. Now, come on. We need to prepare for tomorrow."

The second man huffed in response, but the footsteps continued despite the man's hesitation.

Kallie waited until the footsteps were inaudible, then wiped the sweat from her forehead. Putting her hand to her chest, she attempted to quiet the pounding that threatened to break through her ribs. She regained her composure just as the twin exited the tent, Myra in tow. Her friend's eyes were half-closed as though she had been stirred awake. But as they landed on Kallie, they flew open. And for the second time today, those hazel eyes swelled with tears. Kallie raised a finger to her lips, and Myra gave a shaky nod in response. Quickly, Kallie embraced her friend, pulling her in tight. Myra squeezed her back.

Releasing her, Kallie grabbed Myra's hand and looked at the twin for his final task: their escape.

The twin nodded his head in the direction the two men had come from and started walking. Kallie pulled Myra with her as they walked toward the end of the camp. When they approached the last tent, the twin halted. He looked at Kallie, and for a moment, as Kallie looked into his eyes, she saw a glimmer of unwarranted disappointment flickering there. But then, when Kallie blinked, the expression was gone, as though it had never been there in the first place. He jerked his head toward the woods.

To Myra, Kallie mouthed, "Come on." Then they took off, leaving behind the strange feeling that was beginning to settle within the pit of Kallie's stomach.

THEY RAN. Weaving between the trees, slower than Kallie would have liked, but still, they ran. Their feet pounded against the dirt, bushes scratched their ankles, thin branches scraped their arms, but they did not slow their pace. Eventually, someone would check on the tents the women had occupied and realize that their two captives were missing.

Myra, however, wasn't accustomed to sprinting long distances. So, even though Kallie's training had helped build up her stamina, it did not help Kallie push Myra faster. And Myra's overall lack of athleticism aside, nature was doing everything it could to slow them down. The treetops prevented large amounts of moonlight from seeping through. Thus, they dodged fallen branches by the scattered patches of light.

The one thing they had going for them was Myra's loud, inelegant footsteps. If any creatures lurked in the forest, hopefully, the noise would scare them away.

They needed to get to a clearing so Kallie could see the sky, and then the gods who slept among the stars would help guide them home.

Only a little further. She knew it in her bones that a clearing was near.

Myra's hand slipped from Kallie's grasp and Kallie looked back. Myra was crouched, her hands resting on her knees as she breathed heavily. "I'm sorry . . . I just," she spoke in between her breaths, "need a . . . moment to . . . catch my breath."

Kallie sighed. Stopping reminded her how much her joints ached, and she didn't need the reminder right now. They needed to keep going, lest Kallie lose the adrenaline pumping through her veins. Even if Fynn and his group hadn't noticed they were gone yet, they would be sitting prey for the animals that were not scared off by Myra's clumsy feet.

But Kallie relented. "All right, just a moment though."

Myra nodded.

Kallie took the time to stretch out her hamstrings. Then she bounced on her toes as she watched Myra regain her breath.

Straightening, Myra said, "All right. I'm—"

But Myra never finished. Her unspoken words hung in the air as she stood frozen. Under the faint light of the moon, her face went pale, her eyes widened.

"Myra? Are you well?" Kallie took a step back. "Are you going to be sick?"

"Kallie . . . " Her lips barely moved, her voice almost inaudible. "Don't. Move."

"What? Why?" Kallie's voice was laden with concern.

Then the sound of heavy breathing behind her sent a cold shiver swimming down the length of her spine. Curiosity and fear pulled at her to turn. To see what lurked behind her despite the feeling that tugged on her stomach urging her to stay still.

Her curiosity won.

A pair of large golden eyes stared back at her. Kallie went rigid as she came face to face with a mountain lion perched on top of a dead tree that had broken in half. The mountain lion's back muscles rippled as it crouched, readying to pounce.

Kallie tried to recall anything she knew about mountain lions from her lessons as a child. There was something about their eyes, that if someone were to encounter a mountain lion the person should either look into them or avoid them completely. However, Kallie couldn't remember which one she was supposed to do. She searched her memory, but her mind was empty.

Stare or avert?

If she stared at it, the wild animal might think it was threatened and attack. But if she averted her eyes, it might think it was victorious and her, prey.

By the gods, where's my dagger when I need it?

The mountain lion sank lower.

She had to choose. *Now.*

A giant paw slinked forward, dragging its claws against the peeling bark on the tree, and Kallie took a slow breath. Then she made her choice, praying to the gods that it was the right one.

Swoosh.

A rush of wind skimmed the right side of her face and an arrow struck the mountain lion and pinned Kallie in place. A painful whine left its mouth as it slumped to the ground. Mouth agape, Kallie watched the life drain from the beast.

"Game of cat and mouse, huh?"

Kallie spun around to see gray eyes the color of the moon staring at her. In the faint blotchy light of the moon streaming in through the leaves, she watched as the man grabbed a second arrow from the holster on his back. He nocked the arrow on the string of his bow. A streak of moonlight hit his hands and golden rings glistened on his fingers drawing Kallie's attention. She recognized those rings, the way they clinked together at the slightest movement. Another one of Fynn's crew. The sulky man from the garden stood before her. His bow aimed at her.

He took a step forward as he pulled the string taught and raised the arrow to his cheek. Kallie's heart rate increased. Then the light hit his face and Kallie took a sharp inhale.

On that first night, she hadn't noticed it because his head was down, his hair falling in front of his face. He had hidden it well. Over the man's left eye, a long, pale scar stretched from above his left eyebrow all the way to the bottom of his ear. She wondered what had happened, what had caused the scar. The white jagged mark was stark against his tanned, olive skin.

Without the mark, he might have been handsome. But at the same time, Kallie thought, he *was* handsome. And possibly because of it. It brought attention to his strong, piercing eyes. Rather than hiding the scar though, his dark hair sat an inch above his collar and was shorter near the front, forming a halo of darkness around his face. He was, from an objective standpoint, attractive. But he possessed the sort of beauty that meant danger was near.

And the two blades glistening on either side of his hip reinforced that sentiment. The two scimitars that belonged to the man who had killed Polin, crushed her fingers, and stolen her dagger.

Kallie's gaze bounced from his eyes to the scar to the scimitars.

But she had ignorantly taken her gaze away from the weapon aimed at her. His lips twitched, quirking upward as he let the arrow fly.

And Kallie's heart stopped.

CHAPTER 8

Time slowed as Kallie waited for the blow. But it never came. She was alive.

From behind her, a soft breath released and she pried her eyes open one at a time. She looked at the mountain lion and the head of a second arrow protruded out of its chest. The light within the glowing eyes that screamed murder was now a muted yellow.

"It's cruel to leave an animal in pain, wouldn't you agree?" Kallie turned to the sultry voice. The man lowered his bow, but Kallie did not relax.

"If only you treated humans with the same respect, Gray," a female voice said from the trees.

The man, Gray, scoffed in response. The woman walked out of the trees and her gait was unmistakable, a person born to make others bleed. This was the woman Kallie had fought, and without the hood hiding her features, Kallie knew it was the same woman from the garden as well.

More footsteps crunched behind the woman, and two more figures walked into the moonlight. Kallie instantly recognized the shoulder-length locks and the cocky swagger. Fynn looked over at the unfamiliar figure who accompanied him and tipped his head in Kallie and Myra's direction. "Moris," he said, his tone authoritative and clear.

Without another word, Moris approached Myra who stood frozen in place. Kallie could do little but watch as Moris hoisted Myra over his shoulder as if she weighed no more than a small sack of potatoes.

Kallie wanted to reach out, to strike the man. To do something. But she couldn't for her body betrayed her. She stood as still as the dead carcass behind her. Paralyzed, helpless as she was forced to watch her friend be taken from her. Again.

Once Moris had returned to the shadows of the forest and his footsteps were little more than a ruffle of leaves, Fynn stepped toward Kallie. The left corner of his mouth tipped upward. "No more running, Princess."

And that's when the blood rushed back into her body and the control over her limbs returned. She took a shaky step back putting distance between herself and Fynn.

"Don't make this any harder than it needs to be." Fynn slowed his steps as if he were approaching a wounded animal. "Terin."

"On it, brother," a man's voice from just behind her said.

Startled, Kallie spun around and found the twin approaching her. He had completed her command. She had escaped the campsite. He was free to do as he wished, the goal of the compulsion having been met.

Before Kallie could make a move, the twin's arms wrapped around her and her vision went hazy.

She had never failed twice in a row, but this group was different. They always seemed one step ahead of her. Kallie searched the faces in front of her, trying to find a way out. She reached for her gift as her vision began to go in and out. The strands of her ability lifted and fell sluggishly. Heavy.

Then the crushing of leaves grew louder. A pair of hands entered her vision.

Fynn's voice floated toward her. "It's the only way . . ." His voice was faint and sounded far away.

"No . . . Not again." She didn't know if she said it out loud or if she spoke the words only in her head.

Her panic rose. Then her vision went black against her will for the second time.

WHEN KALLIE REGAINED CONSCIOUSNESS, she first heard the crackling of a fire as the wood popped, the smoke tickling her nose. Then came the hushed voices behind her. She remained still and kept her breathing slow as she listened to their conversation. She didn't know how they kept knocking her out cold, but she would find out. She would find out everything.

"—should have killed him when I had the chance," said a man who Kallie was keen to believe was Fynn despite the absent lightness in his voice.

"Trust me. I know and we will, but—as you have always told me— we have to follow the plan first, Fynn. " This second voice matched that of Gray, the man with the scar on his face. It was unmistakable.

A disgruntled grumble followed.

"Domitius will pay for this. I promise," Gray added. The mention of her father's name had Kallie digging her nails into her palms that were tied behind her back.

She was not their true goal but rather a means to an end. They wanted her father. And every fiber of her being begged her to strike the man who threatened her father's life while simultaneously making her own life seem irrelevant. But she fought the growing urge. She had no weapon, no remaining strength in her gift, and no energy. If Fynn and his comrades were the same people who had attacked Kallie's carriage, the same people who had disarmed her most talented guards, the same people who had ruthlessly slaughtered sweet Polin with no remorse. If they were the same people, she knew she could not engage them. Not when she was tied, unarmed, and weak (although she hated to admit it). She needed her strength to return before she could act.

So, she decided to bide her time and wait to strike until the gods were undeniably on her side. And based on the men's desire to use her as a bargaining chip, her life was safe for the time being. Therefore, Kallie would not run back to her father—no, she would handle this herself. Like she was trained to do. If she could infiltrate their homeland, learn their secrets, and bring them to their knees, she would prove to her father that she was worthy.

Then when she returned, she and the king would attack and set their precious land ablaze. And Kallie and her father would learn who would truly stand by the oath they swore in the welcoming hall.

"You're right. We will stick to the plan. And then in due time, Domitius will pay for what he has done. Are Moris and his squad ready?" Fynn asked.

"They will be," Gray answered.

"Hopefully they do not run into any trouble on their way to the pier in Frenzia. That's the quickest route, so they'll be expecting us to take the princess that way."

"Yes, but we talked about this. Dani believed it was the best strategy."

Fynn sighed in response. "I suppose. The other one will be a good diversion considering they have similar builds."

Gray scoffed. "Similar enough, I suppose." His voice was tinged with hesitation and disgust. "I still think we should have gotten rid of the handmaiden."

Kallie clenched her jaw. They would *not* hurt Myra.

"She's no threat to us, Graeson. She's innocent in all of this. You know that."

Graeson grunted in response as Kallie's muscles relaxed slightly. If Myra were to masquerade as Kallie, she would be safe. It seemed silly though. Myra's hair was blonde, her complexion paler. But Kallie supposed from the back, with the proper attire and a hood, one might mistake Myra for Kallie. They were the same height and had similar builds. It would work for a moment.

Fynn made a noise of agreement. "Unfortunately, it will take us longer to return home."

"Yes, but soon we will all be in Pontia once again and all will be well."

She restrained the smirk attempting to nudge its way onto her face. With the location confirmed, the plan formed in her head.

Recalling the maps she had spent years memorizing, they would most likely travel along the border of Kadia and Borgania. If she was correct, this would mean they would either have to go around the Alderian Mountains or traverse through them. And while she hated that Myra would be taken from her, there was no other way.

Boots clapped against the ground, twigs snapping beneath them. The stirred-up air brushed across her face. Clothes rustled as the men maneuvered around her vicinity.

Fynn whispered, "Has she woken yet, Dani?"

"No," a woman said, her closeness startling Kallie.

One of the men huffed.

"Shouldn't be much longer," said Fynn.

Kallie pretended to stir from sleep. She wrestled with the bindings since her captors would expect her to be surprised by her current predicament. Thankfully, she was a good actress. She grumbled in annoyance when the rope didn't give and found the three individuals staring at her from the other side of the fire. Fynn, Gray, and Dani— the woman whom Kallie had fought—each sat on tree stumps.

Fynn looked down his nose at her as he sat with his legs spread and his head propped on his hand, appearing bored. Flames flickered in his brown eyes and highlighted the shades of gold within his irises.

Kallie coughed. "You all look terrible."

They didn't respond, only stared at her. Unmoving.

The fire crackled and popped. An ember flew out and, for a moment, it danced in the air. As the ember danced its final performance, its bright orange color faded into the air. In its path, a white flake remained, its momentum long gone without the support of the heat beneath it. Her gaze followed its movements as it swayed, side to side. It floated down, then disintegrated onto the dirt by Kallie's outstretched feet.

She looked back at Fynn, raising her eyebrow. "If you're going to tie my hands, you could at least make it interesting."

Fynn rolled his eyes, and Dani snorted beside him as Gray poked the fire with a stick. The air became taught as tensions grew between the four of them.

Fynn was the first to break their silence. "How did you escape?"

Kallie pursed her lips. She would not make this easy for them, for she wanted answers too. She tilted her chin up. "Answer for an answer."

After a moment, Fynn nodded his head and urged her on with a flick of his hand.

Kallie examined the trio before her. Fynn's twin was missing. "What did your brother do to me?"

"You fell asleep," the woman said while she slouched on the stump, her knees spread, her arms hanging over them as she picked the dirt out of her nails.

Kallie chewed on her words. She remembered being surrounded by the group in the middle of the forest after she had almost escaped with Myra. Remembered the twin sneaking up behind her. He was the only one who had been near her when the darkness had consumed her. She recalled Fynn giving him the go-ahead. However, what exactly the man had done to her was unclear. She looked between Dani and Fynn. Something about him drugging her did not sit right with her. They were hiding something.

"How? Because I don't recall being tired."

Dani and Fynn exchanged glances. Dani shrugged.

"Terin put you to sleep," Fynn said.

Kallie's eyes widened. "Does your brother drug people often?"

"Only when necessary." His calm tone did not shake. It was as if it was all right for them to drug innocent people. As if it was a normal occurrence that shouldn't make her insides squirm. It did.

"Your turn," Dani stated. "And we won't ask again. How did you escape?"

A crooked smile rose on Kallie's face. "I didn't."

Fynn tilted his head ever so slightly, his right brow flicking up, scaling his forehead.

Kallie looked around her. "I'm here, aren't I? Not much of an escape, if you ask me." She blew a piece of hair out of her face.

Fynn narrowed his eyes as if he was trying to squeeze the answer out of her.

Kallie ignored him and asked, "Where's Myra?"

"With Terin," Dani answered.

"I want to see her," Kallie demanded.

"Not unless you tell us how you were able to leave the campsite," Fynn said as Dani gave him a strange look.

Let's see how you *deal with traitors, Fynn.*

"Your brother betrayed you," Kallie smirked. "And helped me."

Fynn laughed.

"Terin would never betray us," Dani countered, her words filled with bitterness.

"Are you sure about that? He was fairly easy to convince. Didn't even fight back."

"And how did you manage that?" Fynn asked, his gaze unwavering, a smug expression glazing his countenance.

Kallie couldn't tell him the truth. First, no one was supposed to know she could manipulate people and command them at her will. Second, if she did tell them, she was sure they would make it even harder for her to escape when she needed to. So instead, she pushed her shoulders back, held her chin high, and gave the best answer she could muster. "I suppose he was just enraptured by my charm and beauty."

Dani snorted, and beside her Gray's head fell onto his hands. A soft smirk appeared on Fynn's lips, the look of utter disbelief and amusement plastered on his face.

Kallie was missing something.

"Oh, I suppose that is so hard to believe?" Kallie asked.

"More than you would think," Dani said as she continued to struggle to restrain her laughter.

Heat flushed to Kallie's cheeks. While it may have been a jest, their reaction frustrated her. Even without her gift, she was able to get her way with people by batting her eyes. She didn't think it was hard to believe that Terin would fall for it too. She fidgeted with the bindings around her wrists.

Fynn stood and stretched his arms above his head, the muscles in his arms flexing. He yawned and looked at Gray. "I'm done here. Graeson, keep watch over her." He directed his attention back toward Kallie. "You'll find that Graeson here isn't as easily persuaded as Terin." The manner in which he said the word 'persuaded' sent her mind spiraling, but she did not react to it.

She gave a snide smirk as she said, "Lucky me."

Before turning to leave, Fynn tipped his head to Dani who then stood. He spoke over his shoulder, "We leave at sunrise."

Before Dani took her leave, she squeezed Graeson's shoulder.

With the other two gone, Kallie observed Graeson sitting before her. The air grew colder when a breeze skidded across her skin and the fire did little to coax warmth back into her blood. The flickering fire made the pale scar near his eye starker against his skin. She was blatantly staring at the man, she knew it. But it didn't stop her from doing it. After all, when she saw something interesting to look at, she found it hard to look away. And Graeson was definitely *interesting*, to say the least. Taking her revenge against this man would be fun.

Anger flashed in Graeson's eyes. He took a swig from a nearby flask, and when he set the flask down, his expression was empty, dull.

"Care to share?" Kallie asked.

A crooked smile found its way to Graeson's face. "I'm not very good at sharing."

"I haven't had anything to drink since you decided to attack my carriage. I'm parched." Her tone turned into a whine in the hopes of annoying him to the point where he gave in since she couldn't use her gift on him from this distance.

He grumbled something unintelligible but then picked up a second flask. He walked over to her.

When he reached her, he tipped her chin up. His fingers tensed around her chin as his gaze caught on her cheekbone where the skin was taught and swollen. His expression iced over, his jaw flexed. "Who did this to you?" Graeson demanded, his voice low.

Kallie huffed and shook his hand from her face. "As if it matters."

"Of course it matters," he snarled as he untwisted the cap of the flask. "You are not to be touched. Our people should know that."

"Then perhaps your people shouldn't have attacked me," Kallie retorted.

His hand tightened around the flask, his knuckles blanching. He spoke through clenched teeth, "It will not happen again. I swear it, Princess."

And there it was. He only cared about her safety as it pertained to her title. They could abduct her, bind her, and drag her along with them as long as no one tarnished her appearance. For if they left a scar or a bruise, they would be in deeper shit with her father than they already were. Appearances were everything.

Graeson tipped her chin up once more and poured a stream of cool, crisp water into her mouth. Then when he gave her his back, Kallie spat the water she had saved. The water hit him with a small splash. Graeson froze.

"Refreshing," Kallie said, smirking.

Then he turned around as slow as the river of the dead. He cracked his neck, leaned down. His face now only inches from hers and the anger clear in his glare.

"Next time, Princess," he paused, and with a rough finger, he wiped the water from her chin. Kallie refrained from flinching as she glared up at him. "Swallow."

Straightening, he turned on his heels. Kallie gulped as she watched him return to his side of the fire.

To his back, she snarled, "When my father learns of this, he will kill all of you."

Graeson snorted, the disdain in the small sound thick. "If you get the chance to see Domitius again, please tell him I've been waiting to slit his throat for years."

Years? He couldn't be more than a few years older than Kallie. Maybe twenty-three or twenty-five, yet his words gave the impression he had been harboring this grudge against her father for a long time. Kallie wondered why. King Domitius had never traveled to Pontia as far as she knew. No one from the mainland did. Not anymore, not after the war. So what did Graeson have against him?

Instead of asking though, she snapped back, "He would crack you like a twig."

His tongue swiped over his teeth, making a smacking noise. "I'd like to see him try."

"You're a cocky bastard, aren't you?"

He shrugged and began tracing shapes into the dirt as the red coals in the fire hissed. The color faded in and out as though the dying fire was breathing. Staring at the buzzing embers, Kallie's eyes stung. Her thoughts returned to Fynn and Graeson's conversation.

The men who were in charge of her were bound and determined to kill the one man she loved in this world. The one man who would do anything for her. Heat coated her skin and it wasn't from the fire.

From this moment on, only one thing mattered: neither Fynn nor Graeson would kill her father.

They wouldn't get the chance.

She would kill them first.

CHAPTER 9

KALLIE AND GRAESON SAT IN SILENCE AS THE COALS SHIFTED FROM scarlet to brittle white as they disintegrated to ash. The fire had grown cold and no longer provided heat or light. She adjusted herself against the stump and found Graeson peering at her. She glared at him. But he only shook his head and sunk deeper into his spot.

Despite the time that had passed, sleep never found her. While her current circumstance was not helpful, it was not the reason she could not sleep. Sleep had always evaded her. Either her mind ran in circles, sending her spiraling into an abyss with no end. Or the fear of nightmares kept her on high alert. Kallie was twenty-years-old, yet she feared the terrors awaiting her in the darkness of her mind when her eyes were closed. She envied those who could lay their head anywhere and find instant solace once they shut their eyes.

Therefore, instead of trying to fight a never-ending battle, Kallie stared up at the trees and found a small patch of sky the foliage had left untouched. And she wondered how Myra was fairing wherever she lay her head in this small camp.

Whatever concoction they had given Kallie before must have

knocked her out longer than she had thought. Soon the sky faded from pitch black to a hazy purple as the sun rose beyond the trees.

When a golden hue coated the foliage, scuffling sounded inside the nearby tents. As bodies filed out of the tents, Kallie sat up straighter. People she had not seen the previous day began tearing down tents. Their gazes flicked toward her, and whispers filled the clearing as they worked to disassemble the camp. Then long, unusually unkempt blonde hair pushed through one of the tents and dragged Kallie's attention away from the rest of the group.

"Myra!" Kallie shouted.

Terin shifted his body to block Myra's view and whispered in her ear.

They continued walking. As though she had been slapped in the face, Kallie slouched against the stump while she watched her friend walk in the opposite direction.

A layer of dirt coated the bottom of Myra's light blue traveling dress and her normally spotless black flats. But besides her generally disheveled appearance, Myra was in one piece and Kallie was thankful for that small blessing.

Then when she saw Myra's hands hanging loose at her sides as Terin guided her past the dead fire without stopping, Kallie's wrists burned. Apparently, they had assumed Myra was not the mastermind behind their escape attempt and therefore deemed it unnecessary to bind her hands.

Graeson approached Kallie, stopping less than a yard away. He cast Kallie a downward glance. "Maybe if you cooperated like your handmaiden over there, your hands would be free as well." He looked her up and down. "But you don't like it easy, do you?"

She pursed her lips, then spat at his shoes.

He clenched his jaw, smirking. "Don't test me, Princess."

Kallie sneered. Ruthless killer or not, Kallie was not going to make this easy for him. She wanted him on edge. That was when people made mistakes. "Or what, Gray?"

His fingers wrapped around her arm, then he yanked her up. Unable to use her arms to support her weight, she leaned into Graeson's grip and stood up awkwardly. He surpassed her by more than a foot, her head barely reaching past his chest. Kallie tilted her chin up to compensate for her small stature. Normally, her height did not bother her. She had grown into her figure over the years, had learned to appreciate it and use it to her advantage. Still, men underestimated short women (women in general, if Kallie was being honest). However, next to Graeson and with her clothes in disarray, she felt small, insignificant. Her dress was wrinkled and covered in dirt. Her once-tight bun hung loosely at the base of her neck as sections of hair floated around her face. And her cheek was definitely swollen.

The clean, regal appearance of the Ardentolian nobility long since forgotten—left behind with whatever remained of the discarded carriage and her belongings.

Graeson's eyes darkened, the corner of his mouth twitching as he bent down to whisper in her ear, "You do not want to know what I am capable of doing, little mouse."

She peered at him through her lashes. "Oh, but I think I do."

He tightened his grip around her arm. "You wouldn't stand a chance."

Tilting her head to the side, she asked, "Are you sure about that?"

Graeson chuckled and pointed to himself. "Cocky bastard, remember?"

Kallie blew a piece of hair out of her face. "I suppose it's safer for you if my hands stay tied anyway."

Graeson scoffed and his voice turned deep, haunting, "I highly doubt that."

She glared at him through her eyebrows. He proceeded to reach behind his back to pull a dagger from his trousers. And at that moment, Kallie didn't need a fire to heat her. Her rage from seeing Graeson wave *her* dagger around her face heated her entire being enough to warm an entire house. "That's mine," Kallie said through clenched teeth.

"Is it, now?" He flipped the dagger over in his hands as though he was inspecting it. He shrugged. "Think of it as payment then."

"Payment for what?"

He ran a finger across the blade, the touch gentle as he locked gazes with her. "For saving you, of course." His wide smile, his blatant cockiness, and the way he ran his finger over her blade left Kallie speechless.

Saving her? He attacked her carriage, murdered her guards, abducted her handmaiden.

The man was delusional.

"But don't worry, Princess. It's safe with me." His eyes sparkled silver as light bounced off the steel in his hand. With one hand, he grabbed a hold of both of her wrists while he used the dagger in the other hand to cleanly cut through the rope. The moment Kallie felt the relief from her bindings, she tugged.

However, she was met with immediate resistance. Graeson's grip was firm, unbreakable as he slipped Kallie's dagger into the back of his trousers and grabbed another rope from his front pocket. He placed the rope between his teeth, letting it hang from his mouth. Dark strands of hair fell on his face as he reached around her, engulfing her.

As he adjusted his grip on her hands, he looked at Kallie and her breath caught in her throat. The smell of trees—no, cedar—surrounded her. If he was a different man, perhaps one who did not want to kill her father, she would have found it soothing. Instead, it felt suffocating.

Graeson forced Kallie's hands in front of her. He ignored her pointed glare as he tied her hands once again. Then his eyes lifted to meet hers. "Figured you preferred being tied up."

Kallie snarled. "You should have just kept them tied behind my back."

Graeson winked at her. "Sure, but how would I have shown off my skills with a knife?"

She recoiled. "I think I saw enough of that when you ripped apart my men like a wild animal."

"You saw that did you?" He tilted his head. "As the princess of Ardentol, I would have assumed you were well-acquainted with monsters since your king is one of them."

Kallie stopped snarling and dropped her gaze. She had heard the whispers of the exaggerated stories of her father wreaking havoc when he was young. But they were merely stories that had grown wilder with time. Her father was a masterful swordsman, but he did not go around slaughtering people in his spare time.

He was a man, not a beast.

Graeson pulled the rope tighter, then dragged her toward the rest of the Pontians.

The Pontians were gathered near the last tent standing. There were ten people in total besides Kallie and Myra. Fynn stood in the center of the group, stroking the blackish-blue mane of a horse. Her throat grew dry.

When Kallie and Graeson neared, Kallie stumbled when she saw the man standing beside Dani.

The man stood with his shoulders back, his hands clasped behind him as he rocked back and forth on the heels of his polished riding boots. He wore a simple, loose black shirt that was tucked into black trousers.

Kallie's eyes were playing tricks on her. It couldn't be him. It was not possible.

Graeson tugged her forward as a red-headed woman spoke to the man. When he turned to respond, Kallie had a clear view of the side of his face. She dug her heels into the ground, and a smile found its way to her face.

Alyn.

He had survived. Her lips parted as she went to call out to him, but only air came out.

Kallie's smile faded as she tilted her head at the captain of her guard who was unharmed as he conversed with the enemy. Alyn who stood there in clean clothes. Alyn who stood with a small smile on his face. Relaxed, as if he hadn't been attacked yesterday.

He stood there as if he hadn't failed as her captain.

But Kallie had seen the blood. She had seen the small pools surrounding the fallen guards, the splotches seeping into their clothing. He should have been dead. But . . .

There had been one body absent of blood, absent of any wounds besides the dirt rubbed into his hair. As if . . . As if the attackers had gone out of their way to prevent major harm to him.

Kallie's vision blurred. Her knees grew weak.

She remembered the conversation she had heard before she had attempted to escape with Myra. How one of the voices had felt familiar. Didn't the man verbalize his frustration with Fynn being rough with him? But Fynn didn't call him Alyn . . . what did he call him? And why would Fynn have hurt one of his own men? Unless . . .

She was foolish. So completely and utterly foolish. She should have connected the dots sooner.

Alyn stood before her as if he was a part of this group of attackers because he was. He was one of them.

He was her enemy.

Alyn glanced at Kallie, then turned his attention back to the redheaded woman. He dismissed her, ignored Kallie. Pretended as though he had not spent the past eight years in her guard.

Had it all been an act? Had his kindness been a lie?

Kallie wanted to stab him. She wanted to rip her dagger from Graeson's smug hands and stab Alyn in the back like he had done to her. She wanted to strike him in the chest, tear his heart from his body like he tore Myra's from hers, like he tore Kallie's trust from her. And when she stabbed him, there would be no returning from that wound.

She was done sitting on the wayside.

Kallie rammed her shoulder into Graeson's stomach and slithered from his grip. Alyn's eyes grew wide as she stormed forward and shouted, "You bastard!"

She shoved her bound hands into his chest. Graeson's grip on her arm returned, but he didn't pull her away. And Alyn stared back at her, emotionless, unbothered.

"This is *all* your fault, isn't it? How could you do this? How could you let this happen? We *trusted* you. I trusted you. Myra trusted you." At the sound of Myra's name, his jaw flexed—the only reaction to surface from her words. Kallie hoped his feelings toward her handmaiden had not been fabricated as well.

Alyn's eyes scanned over the small crowd and swallowed.

No one moved. No one made a sound as Kallie stared the traitor down.

But he wasn't a traitor to them. He puffed up his chest. "How could *I* do this? You know nothing, Kalisandre," he spat out her name as if it was venom on his tongue. "I've watched you in that marble palace you call home for years as you ignorantly followed the commands of your so-called king. But you don't even know—"

Graeson stepped in front of her and pushed Alyn back with his palm. "That's enough, Armen."

Alyn breathed heavily as Graeson towered over Kallie's former captain. She had never seen Alyn—no, *Armen* frazzled or angry. He had always been level-headed. Calm, collected.

"I said *enough*," Graeson hissed.

Alyn's gaze flicked from Graeson to Kallie then to the crowd that surrounded them. Everyone had stopped their conversations and were zoned in on the three of them.

Jaw tense, Alyn shoved Graeson's hand off of him and turned around. But before Alyn made it more than a step, he paused and glanced over his shoulder at Graeson. "You can protect her and fight her battles all you want, Graeson, but at the end of the day, she is still just a woman."

Kallie didn't think. She didn't remind herself that she was trying to play nice, didn't hear her old tutor's voice in her head chiding her about proper etiquette. No, she didn't do any of that. Instead, she threw herself at the coward who couldn't even say the words to her and toppled him to the ground. Her fingers dug into his short hair and gripped his head. With her bound hands, she rammed his head into the hard dirt as she straddled his back and locked him in place.

He had insulted her integrity. Insulted her abilities without knowing the full extent of her strength. But that was not what made her steaming with rage. Kallie had dealt with people who belittled her before. It was a common occurrence, an unsurprising cliche that grated her bones every time. And while the commonality of those statements directed at her did not make them any less irritating or appalling, she could prove them wrong. Those words had not caused her to act out in violence, but rather the insult to women as a whole. It was the three words he had said with such indignation: *just a woman.* In the eyes of the people, she was either *just* the king's daughter or *just* a princess. *Just* a prize to be won and given to the highest bidder. *Just* a woman.

It was laughable and illustrated Alyn's ignorance most of all. His tone suggested that to be a woman was an act far less noble than to be a man. To insult the entire gender without consequences, without Kallie fighting back felt to be an even greater slight. And perhaps getting into a physical dispute was not the proper way to take her anger out on him. To make him regret his words. But as people have said to women like her and women around the world: a woman's body is her greatest tool. And Kallie had spent much of her teenage and young adult years fine-tuning that body. So, she would heed those words. And use it.

Kallie extended her arms back, preparing to strike the side of Alyn's head. But her clenched fists struck air when a pair of calloused hands grabbed her arm and pulled her off of Alyn. Alyn's groan brought a smile to Kallie's maleficent countenance.

Heat caressed her skin. She turned and came face to face with Graeson, his face hovering over her shoulder as he pressed her against his chest.

"Do not think for a second that we do not have spies everywhere, Princess," Graeson whispered in her ear, his breath hot on her neck.

Kallie turned away from him, trying to push him off of her, but he held firm. Then quieter he added, "And do not take offense from the fish that lay in the pond at your feet. You, little mouse, should be above that."

The corners of her mouth twitched but were wiped clean when he shoved her forward, forcing her to take a step. As she glanced back, Alyn was pushing himself up from the ground. When the red-headed woman extended a hand, he ignored it. And Kallie was struck by how well he had acted as her guard because this man before her was unrecognizable.

Alyn exchanged glances with Graeson as though Alyn was determined to get the last word. Kallie could hear a faint rumble stir from her new jailer, a feral, animalistic noise that sent her skin crawling.

Alyn's hands shot in the air as he backed away.

Graeson chuckled beside her, then continued forward, leading Kallie toward Terin.

The two towering men sandwiched her in between them, the

closeness making her feel claustrophobic. And though Kallie was surrounded by her enemies, Graeson's grip on her forearm remained. But if she didn't know better, she could have sworn it had loosened.

Ahead of her, Fynn stared at her inquisitively as though he was trying to translate a secret code written on her face. But he seemed to come up empty-head. After shaking his head, he addressed his crew, "Moris and Armen, you know the plan. Fen knows you are coming and should be prepared for you. We should only be a week behind you. If we do not arrive two or three days after that, you know what to do."

Kallie was all too aware of how he skirted around the specifics. But she knew what would be coming. She shifted her weight to the balls of her feet, tipping forward to get a glimpse of Myra. And not far down the line of people, Alyn nodded to Fynn in agreement, and Kallie grinned at the dirt smudged across his previously fresh face.

"Any questions?" Fynn asked his people. When no one responded, he turned his attention to Dani. "Did you bring them?"

Dani stepped forward with a bundle of fabric. "They might be a little big, but they should be fine."

He assessed the pile, then turned his gaze to Kallie and Myra. "Take them to the tent, but be quick about it."

Dani cocked her brow, unmoving. The two Pontians stared at each other as though some invisible battle was playing out between them.

Fynn shifted on his feet. "Please," he mumbled.

Dani smiled. "I'd be delighted to help our guests." She then strolled over to Myra and handed her a stack of clothes. Dani then approached Kallie.

Reluctantly, Kallie brought her hands up and Dani placed the clothes on her arms.

"Let's go." Without another glance, Dani headed toward the last tent standing and Graeson tugged Kallie's arm, jerking her forward.

Kallie edged closer to Myra as they followed Dani. "Are you all right, Myra? Are you hurt?"

Myra shook her head.

"Whatever happens, it will be fine. I promise," Kallie said.

Myra's shoulders shook and Kallie wanted to reach out for her friend, but she couldn't. Before she knew it, Graeson was pushing them inside the tent. Myra scurried under the flap, but Kallie halted when she felt Graeson's fingers still wrapped around her arm. Kallie raised a brow. "Must you follow me everywhere?"

"Modest are we, little mouse?" Graeson asked. And unfortunately for her, it seemed the new nickname was staying.

Kallie tilted her head to the side and gave Graeson a once-over. "Fine, stay. But do not forget, I am engaged."

Graeson scrunched his nose in disgust, and Kallie shrugged as she walked forward.

Once inside, Graeson released her. From the corner of her eye, Kallie saw Graeson turn around to face the tent flap. Her gaze dipped lower and the outline of her dagger beneath his shirt caught her eye. It would be easy to—

"Come on, Princess. We don't have all day." Dani folded her arms across her chest, sneering at Kallie.

Meanwhile, Myra had already stripped down to her slip and was beginning to change into the borrowed clothes.

The rope around Kallie's wrist itched beneath the weight of the strange clothes. "It's going to be difficult with my hands tied."

Dani scoffed, but she reached inside her brown leather jacket and pulled out a small knife. Folding the clothes underneath her arm, her fingers wrapped around Kallie's wrist. "Don't do anything stupid." Then Dani cut the rope in one smooth movement.

Kallie locked eyes with Myra, and Myra shook her head, pleading. As much as it pained her to remain civil in front of her captors, Kallie knew she was outnumbered and vulnerable. There was no point in trying anything. Not now anyway. She looked at Dani and gave the sweetest smile she could bring to her lips.

"Hurry up." Dani shoved the clothes back into Kallie's arm.

Kallie sat the clothes down on the ground and removed her mangled dress. Then she grabbed the new shirt and held it out in front of her, inspecting it.

"Oh, I'm sorry. Shall I go run to the local seamstress instead?" Dani sneered.

Kallie huffed in dismay but began changing into the clothes. Although they were ill-fitting, they were better than her soiled dress. "This wouldn't have been an issue if you had just gathered our things when you so kindly kidnapped us," Kallie mumbled as she buttoned the slim trousers.

"We didn't need the extra baggage," Graeson said from behind her. And then added, "Two women are already more than we bargained for."

Kallie ignored him as she rolled up the hems of each pant leg to prevent herself from tripping over them. She didn't want to give him another reason to get rid of Myra, something he seemed very prone to doing last night. She could make do without her own clothes if it meant Myra was alive.

After tucking the front of the shirt into the waistband, she threw her boots back on. Not the best she had ever looked, but it was better than the mud-covered dress.

"All set, Princess?" Dani tapped her foot.

When Kallie grunted in confirmation, Graeson grabbed her hands before she had the chance to undo her hair. He then made quick work of retying her hands.

"How much rope do you have in those pockets?" Kallie asked.

Graeson's fingers continued to work as he raised a brow. "Why? Care to find out?"

Kallie snorted, then looked over her shoulder at Myra. Her friend gave her a soft, tired smile.

Graeson shoved her forward, and Kallie bit back the snarl in her throat as she stumbled. She quickly regained her footing before they left the tent.

Stepping outside, Kallie found the group sitting atop their horses. Her stomach jolted. She looked away only to find Alyn holding onto the reins of a gray horse as he stood talking to Fynn. But Fynn was only half-focused on the conversation while he tracked Kallie's movements. Alyn turned and locked gazes with Kallie first, then Myra. Alyn's face remained stoic and revealed no emotion. He flicked his eyes back to Fynn and nodded to whatever he had said.

Fury bubbled inside of her again. But before she could act on it, a soft, delicate hand touched her arm. Kallie looked down at Myra gripping her wrist.

"Not worth it," Myra whispered.

Kallie sighed, but nodded and allowed her friend's touch to cool her anger.

Dani then hopped onto a vacant horse with the grace of a dancer. She flicked her curls over her shoulder and leaned over the horse, patting its side. But Kallie stood there, immobile, palms sweating profusely with a growing ache in her neck.

Her former guard approached Myra. Her face turned pale, her gaze locked on the ground. Without hesitating, Kallie eliminated the distance separating her from Myra and turned her body into a shield. Reaching for the strands of her gift in the pit of her stomach, Kallie found it lying there. Heavy and asleep. She stroked it, trying to awaken it, but it didn't move. She had overextended herself the past few days. She was useless.

She had lost her father, her home, and she was about to lose Myra too.

Kallie cursed the gods, cursed Sabina herself. Why bother blessing her with a gift, if it failed her when she needed it the most? If she couldn't even keep her friend from being separated from her, how was she supposed to save and unite a divided people?

Now more than ever she needed to find a way to strengthen her gift.

Kallie squeezed Myra's shaking hands, then touched her forehead to her friend's. When Kallie spoke, she lowered her voice so only Myra could hear, "I'm sorry, Myra. I'm sorry I failed you."

"You haven't failed me. This is not your fault."

"But Mys—"

"Don't." Myra's voice was steady.

"But Alyn—"

Myra squeezed Kallie's hand. "Kals, do not worry about me. I might not be as physically fit as you, but there is more to strength than muscles. I can deal with Alyn. I've dealt with far worse." The corners of her mouth twitched in an attempt to smile, but something dark lurked deep within Myra's gaze. However, there was no time to ask. Alyn had closed the distance.

"They'll pay for this. *All* of them."

"Be careful, Kallie." Myra placed a gentle peck on Kallie's forehead before she pulled away.

Kallie faced the man she once trusted and her hatred of him was plain across her face. She took a step forward. "If you touch her or hurt her any more than you already have, I will kill you when we meet again—and we *will* meet again. It doesn't matter what name you go by. I will find you."

Alyn straightened. "I no longer follow your orders, *Princess*," he hissed her title. "But make no mistake, I am not the monster here and I hope I can witness the moment you learn the truth." With his hand, he ushered a Pontian woman with pin-straight black hair forward.

Myra peered over the woman's shoulders. "I'll see you soon, Kals"

Myra's voice held all of the sadness that Kallie was trying to bury inside of herself.

Kallie swallowed. "Promise."

The woman led Myra by the elbow to a nearby horse. Closing her eyes, Kallie prayed to the gods for her friend's safety.

Her eyes flung open when she felt another tug at her shoulders. She turned to face Graeson who directed her over to his horse that was nibbling grass. These horses were more beautiful than any of the horses Kallie had seen in Ardentol. Their coats glistened in the light and looked as smooth as silk. Several horses had manes and tails that were intricately braided. If the horse's hair wasn't braided, it was clear that someone had taken the time to brush out any knots. And on top of each horse, sat a saddle with elegant embroidery in different colors.

Yet, despite their beauty, Kallie's breathing became labored. She admired the horses for their strength, but her admiration stopped there. Some people were squeamish of rats or snakes, but horses seemed far more dangerous to Kallie. In Ardentol, she rarely needed to ride a horse. Whenever she had ventured into the city for one of her father's tasks, she was escorted by carriage. And while horses pulled the carriage, she didn't have to interact with them.

Having let go of Kallie's shoulders, Graeson approached the large horse with a midnight black coat. He stroked the horse's nose and a glimmer of a smile appeared on his face, his eyes crinkling in the corners.

Kallie twisted the dainty ring around her finger as she reluctantly approached the horse. She stopped a few feet away, leaving more room than necessary between her and the massive animal before her. Her chest heavy.

"This is Calamity," Graeson's voice was surprisingly gentle as he stroked the horse's nose.

She swallowed the lump in her throat. "Fitting."

Graeson shrugged and nodded her over. But when Kallie did not move, he looked back at her, his brows raised in amusement. "Afraid of horses, little mouse?"

Kallie tried to laugh it off, to pretend it was not true, but the laughter was more of a cackle—strangled and hoarse. The corner of Graeson's lip twitched. He reached out his hand. Hesitant, Kallie took a stilted step toward the horse. As Kallie neared, the horse's head swayed. Kallie tried to retreat, but Graeson's grip on her hand tightened.

She snarled at his hand. He was quickly becoming a nuisance.

"She won't hurt you." For the first time, there was no hint of spite or bitterness in Graeson's voice. Instead, he spoke with a tenderness that should not belong on her captor's tongue.

Kallie met his assessing gaze but said nothing.

"Your fear will only make the ride more unpleasant. It will make her nervous."

"She?" Kallie asked.

Graeson nodded. "She's my most trusted horse. Has never let me down."

"Yet," Kallie mumbled.

Calamity struck the ground with her front hoof forcing Kallie back another step. This time Graeson let her retreat. While the corners of Graeson's lips tugged slightly upward, he returned his gaze to Calamity. "She gets a little moody here and there, but she's a gentle giant at her core."

"I don't think she likes me very much."

"She's offended by your lack of faith in her, that's all."

"Oh, is that all?"

With a look from Graeson, Kallie approached begrudgingly, still wary of the beast before her. Sweat glazed the back of her neck. Calamity could easily crush her. Knock her giant snout into Kallie and push her down.

The horse moved its large head, and Kallie fought the urge to retreat again. If she was going to be successful in her plan, she needed to mount the horse. There was no way around it. The journey would be long and she knew asking to walk instead was foolish.

Graeson raised her hand—a hand still wrapped tightly around Graeson's. He placed it on the horse's neck and Kallie froze. The horse's nostrils flared as it smelled her. Then the horse turned its head, dismissively.

"Mount up!"

Kallie jumped at Fynn's command and Graeson's hand fell from hers.

Graeson gave Calamity a final pat on the nose and moved to the horse's side. "Grab the pommel," Graeson commanded, his voice was vacant of emotion, the gentleness from a moment ago discarded.

Kallie wiped her palms on her trousers, then awkwardly grabbed a hold of the pommel with her bound hands.

"Put your foot here." He pointed to the footrest.

Kallie rolled her eyes. Mounting a horse wasn't the problem. But instead of arguing, she followed his directions.

She used her remaining strength and heaved herself up and over Calamity. Not a moment later, the horse shifted under Graeson's weight. Her heart beat against her chest, the sound echoing in her ears.

"Ever heard of personal space?" Kallie asked.

Graeson huffed. "You are my responsibility, and we are not naive enough to let you have your own horse."

"But you *are* naive," Kallie mumbled.

"As are you, Princess."

Kallie may not have traveled a lot during her life, but she was not inexperienced. She knew more about the world than Graeson thought. But she didn't bother responding. He would find out in due time.

NEENA LASKOWSKI

She straightened as he situated himself behind her, leaving space in between them so he wasn't pressing up against her. He reached around her waist to grab the reins, then spread his arms out wide to avoid touching her as though she was infectious.

The action gave her an idea. Perhaps she could use this circumstance to her advantage. Her ability wasn't the only tool she had to manipulate men. If she threw Graeson off enough, she might be able to gain some information.

"Now who's the modest one?" Kallie retorted. Her voice was shakier than she wanted though due to her fear of horses still fresh in her mind.

Graeson clicked his heels against Calamity's side, and Kallie took a sharp intake of breath as the horse moved forward.

"At least I'm not afraid of a horse, little mouse."

Calamity snorted as if in agreement.

Kallie went to glare at Graeson, but instead, her gaze landed on Alyn and his small party heading in the other direction. Myra's head peered over the shoulder of the rider she rode with and locked eyes with Kallie. If Fynn was right, they would only be separated for a few weeks at most. While that was a short amount of time in the grand scheme of things, it would be the longest time Kallie and Myra had spent apart since Myra had become her handmaiden.

By forcing Myra and Kallie apart, her captors were reminding her that they had something over her. A bargaining chip to keep her in line, an unspoken threat: behave or else you will never see your friend again.

As Alyn led his party away, a fleeting feeling passed through Kallie. She should have fought harder—fought in general to keep her friend by her side. A small voice inside of her mind told her to shout, to use her gift again. Told her that she needed her friend at her side. But she squashed the voice and added this moment to the growing list of wrongs her enemy had committed that she kept hidden within the confinement of her mind. There was no point in worrying about what she should have done, for Kallie could only afford to think about what she needed to do.

Taking one last look at her friend, she prayed the gods would protect Myra. And Kallie knew deep within her heart they would be reunited—one way or another.

She turned back around, and as her eyes pressed into Fynn's back, she shoved the feelings further down. Kallie reminded herself of the mission ahead and inhaled.

This group was going to be her biggest mark yet. She was going to tear it apart for what they had done to her, to her family, and to her friends. They would feel the pain they had caused her. Twice-fold.

Kallie leaned back and Graeson straightened, his arms stiffening as she invaded his space. A devilish grin crept onto her face. If Graeson thought her a mouse, then Kallie would play the part and play it well. She would appear sweet, obedient.

But Graeson forgot one thing: Mice were known for finding the tiniest of openings and infesting homes before the owner was even aware of their presence.

Kallie would become an infestation. Bit by bit, she would tear through their walls. She would destroy their homes, their friendships. Their ability to distinguish between truth and make-believe.

And she would make them regret inviting her into their land.

Because at the end of the day, they would only have themselves to blame for the destruction that ensued.

CHAPTER 10

THE ONLY RIPPLES OF CONVERSATION THAT BROKE THE SILENCE AS THE group traveled were Fynn's brief commands.

Myra would have hated it.

If Myra had thought traveling by carriage was tedious, Kallie could only imagine how she was fairing with Alyn—or Armen or whoever he was—and the other half of Fynn's party.

Myra had barely said a word during their short time together, which felt wrong. The only time Myra was silent and not prying in Kallie's business was when her father was around. The king had a knack for making Myra, and many of the servants, on edge. However, this was the first time Kallie had seen true fear flush Myra's countenance. Kallie had never seen Myra so distraught, so broken. But thinking of Myra made Kallie's soul ache, and right now, she could not afford the distraction.

Then her stomach grumbled. When was the last time she had eaten? After being knocked out several times, she had lost track of the time. The last time she ate must have been before they had left the palace. At least a day ago now.

The last time she was this hungry was when her father was giving her a lesson on self-preservation. It had required Kallie to go without food for an extended period. The lesson was brutal and long, but Kallie endured it for she understood the necessity. In the king's youth, he had learned the lesson during a less-than-pleasant journey across Vaneria. And with the possibility of war coming once the king began the next phase of his plan, he wanted Kallie to be prepared for the worst. Though Kallie was sure he did not have the foresight to know she would have to experience the dull pain of hunger so soon.

One of Graeson's hands let go of the reins and disappeared out of sight. A ruffling sound followed as Calamity continued to trot through the Aldarian Mountains. A moment later, Graeson held out a piece of dried meat before her.

Kallie gingerly took it from his hands. Dried meat was not her preferred choice of sustenance. But when her stomach grumbled again, she took a small bite of the tough meat. The piece sat in her mouth and the salt tingled on her tongue. Salt was rare in Ardentol. The kitchen staff used it sparingly to preserve meat during the winter, but the villagers rarely ever got their hands on it, if at all.

Either way, it was good. Really good. Her mouth salivated at each bite. After the strip was gone, she licked the seasonings from her fingertips. When two more pieces appeared in front of her, Kallie snatched them from Graeson's hand and devoured them just as quickly as she did the first.

The group continued to ride beneath the hot sun for several hours. Although few clouds peppered the sky, the breeze in the air kept them cool as spring began to heat up.

When the sound of a stream grew louder sometime later, Fynn raised his fist in the air. Graeson immediately tightened the reins, signaling Calamity to stop. The others followed suit behind them and waited for Fynn's orders.

Fynn swung his foot over his horse and demounted in one fluid motion. He turned to the group. "Quick rest stop for the horses.

There's a small river past these woods. Make sure to fill your canteens."

As Graeson dismounted, he turned toward Kallie. The sun hit his face, casting a bright light across his tanned skin. "Need help down, little mouse?"

She hated the way his tone suggested she could not dismount by herself. She scoffed and gripped the pommel. After shifting her weight awkwardly, she reached for the stirrups. Her foot swung in the air beneath her, searching but coming up empty-handed. She was a few inches shy of reaching the hanging leather strap. Without being able to use both of her hands, it was nearly impossible for her to see beneath her.

She grumbled, then heard a deep chuckle followed by the shuffling of leaves behind her. Graeson gripped her sides, and she wanted to protest but fell short. Unless she wanted to crash onto the ground and risk twisting her ankle, she needed his help.

He tightened his grip around her and tiny goosebumps scattered across her ribcage. As he hoisted her in the air, Kallie forced away the flush of heat that had risen to her cheeks. She blamed it on having little time between her training and the choosing ceremony to seek out the company of men.

He plopped her down on the ground and the heat dissipated as soon as his hands left her.

Then she remembered her plan.

If Graeson thought his touch affected her, he might be more easily manipulated. She turned, gazing at him through her lashes. The ride had made a mess of his hair and his nose was now sun-kissed. She hated to admit it, but the rugged, messy look only made him appear more attractive. And based on her interactions with the man so far, he probably knew it too. She could tell he was the type of man who preferred casual wear to suits. The type who preferred his hair a mess and his collar unbuttoned.

With a contemplative expression on his face, Graeson scanned her from head to toe. And as his eyes slid over her, a foreign feeling flickered beneath her skin.

He cocked a brow. "You might want to wash up while you have the chance."

And then the feeling was gone. Kallie's mouth fell agape. He was not her most charming target, that's for sure. Most men fell on their knees before her, stumbled over their words. But Graeson? No, Graeson was more stubborn than that.

But she would find a way to seduce him. Some men preferred the innocent act, but Kallie had a feeling Graeson preferred someone who bit back.

Luckily, she was a viper.

She sniffed the air. "And you smell worse than a stable. Did you sleep with the horses last night?"

Graeson chuckled and absent-mindedly brushed his wind-swept hair with a hand. "No, just across from you."

Kallie huffed. "Maybe if you allowed your prisoners to sleep somewhere other than against a stump, they would not be so . . . repulsing to you."

She turned on her heel and as she took a step away, she heard him breathe out a response, "You're not a prisoner."

Kallie snorted, lifting her bounded hands over her head as she marched away from him. The burning red marks now ingrained into her skin proved she was nothing but a prisoner.

Graeson spoke to her back, or to himself—she wasn't sure because the words were almost inaudible, "You are much more than that."

She supposed he was a right. She was their hostage. Their key to getting King Domitius's attention.

Either way though, Kallie was done with this conversation. She stormed off in the direction Fynn had disappeared, pretending she hadn't heard Graeson at all.

For the first time in hours, she didn't feel the presence of another person pressed behind her. Although Kallie was not so naive to think her insistent guard wasn't far away.

Trees lined the mountains, but unlike at their campsite, the skies were clear. She had never been to this part of the mountains before. And despite the rope digging into her flesh, Kallie couldn't deny the sense of freedom that brushed across her skin. Underneath the open blue sky with the ground beneath her feet, it was as though a weight had been lifted from her shoulders. There were no towering buildings, no crowded streets, no bustling taverns she had to weave her way through.

She did, however, have her hands tied and her future on the line.

As the wind swept over her, she inhaled the mountain air mixed with the scent of pine. Then she pulled at her gift. The dull buzz that greeted her though told her it was not time yet. She needed more sustenance. If she could solve that issue, she might be able to command one person. But what's to say someone else wouldn't bind her again? She tugged at her bindings in frustration.

As she weaved between the trees and the sound of water grew louder, Kallie spotted a narrow stream beyond the pine trees. Parched, she quickened her pace.

At the edge of the river, she threw herself down onto her knees, which scraped against the grass. Cupping her hands together, she scooped the water and drank. Water dribbled down her face, down her chin and neck, but she didn't care if she looked like a wild animal kneeling before the water. She had half a mind to throw herself into the river and submerge her whole body—clothes and all. To let it wash away the dirt and grime that covered her flesh and mind. Then she'd allow it to carry her away.

But she didn't. Instead, Kallie dipped her hands into the water, splashed water onto her face, and rubbed off a layer of dirt. Whether Graeson was right about her needing a bath or not, the cool water felt refreshing against her dry skin. She reached for her bun that sagged at the nape of her neck and pulled at the ribbon that held her hair in place. She ran her wet fingers through her hair brushing the tangled strands.

As she rolled her neck back and forth, she felt rejuvenated. It was as though she had shed a layer of peeling skin. Her mind was clear. She needed to get the Pontians to talk, to divulge something useful to her so she could make her move. Further down the stream, Fynn, Graeson, and Terin stood with their horses. She wondered who out of the three of them would be the easiest target. It had been easy enough to manipulate Terin, but he had opted to ride at the back of their entourage with Dani's horse in between them. The likelihood of an opportunity arising was slim.

Fynn was clearly the ringleader of the group. While he seemed more open to talking to her, he too had maintained his distance. Kallie annoyingly needed to be in contact with the person she was trying to influence (a fact she had been trying to remedy without success). And despite her desire to cut the snake at its head, there was only one logical answer. One person who was constantly at her side.

Graeson.

But so far in the way of conversation, Graeson had only given her snide comments, insults, and a headache. And when she recalled him using those scimitars on her guards, a shiver ran down her spine. Still, he was the most convenient choice.

He was also the most dangerous.

Those blades were no doubt tucked away somewhere in his bags, which meant they would be in range while they traveled. But as long as she kept her gift strong—once its energy was restored—that wouldn't pose a problem. Ultimately, it was the only option she had, and she was going to take it.

While she untangled the rest of her hair, Kallie continued to observe the men. From what she could tell, they were in a heated argument. The wind, however, was not on her side as it cast their voices in the opposite direction down the river.

Graeson ran his hand through his shining hair in exasperation. While he may have appeared sulky the night of the welcome ceremony and reserved during their ride, Kallie couldn't help but notice how dramatic he could be as well. What caused his agitation? From her side, things were going well for the Pontians. So far anyway.

As she worked her hands through a stubborn knot, Terin left. Fynn gripped Graeson's shoulder, then nodded his head in her direction before he too disappeared back into the woods.

Was *she* the cause? Graeson's bleak expression suggested so.

Perhaps, he was not happy being her guard. Though she didn't understand why. She didn't think she was *that* unpleasant to be around.

But his scowl brought a smirk to her face. Kallie had always enjoyed a challenge.

She leaned over the river and dipped her hair into it as she used her hands to bring the water up to her roots. Once her hair was soaked, she tossed it back. A showering arch of water sprinkled around her. She tilted her face up to the sun and pushed her hair back with a dramatic flourish. The wet hair dripped down her back. Droplets of water slid down her neck beneath her blouse.

The crunching of leaves was the only sign he had approached. She smiled at the sun.

Time to make him unravel.

Kallie stood, reaching her hands up over her head as she arched her back and stretched her limbs. A splash had her arms falling to her sides though. Kallie peeked down at the river.

Graeson was on his knees. As he knelt beside the river, the sun highlighted the muscles revealed by his rolled-up sleeves. He dipped his hands into the stream, mirroring her movements. He rubbed his face with a wet hand, then pushed his fingers through his hair, his rings glinting in the sun. The water from his fingers left streaks in his hair that glistened under the sun.

Kallie swallowed. Hard.

And then remembering who he was, who *she* was, she mentally shook herself from her daze. He was mocking her. Running his hands through his hair in the same way she had to get a rise out of him. Now *she* was the one who was ogling.

But damn, he might have done a better job than she had.

Graeson sighed and pressed his palms against his knee. His damp shirt clung to his arms and his biceps strained against the cotton fabric as he pushed himself up. The look of exhaustion was wiped from his countenance as he looked at Kallie. A bemused grin plastered on his face and a glimmer of challenge shone in his eyes of steel.

Still, Kallie forced her features to appear indifferent. "Can I help you?" she asked.

He looked down his nose at her, the smirk etching deeper into his skin. His jaw flexed as his eyes swept over her legs, her now damp blouse, and her sopping wet hair. "Do you ever think before you act? Only foolish people get on a horse soaking wet. The ride will be miserable."

She tilted her head. "I would think most preferred to ride wet." Her eyes scanned him up and down. "It being less . . . strenuous."

Graeson cleared his throat—not once, but twice. A pinch of red painted his cheeks, and he looked toward the stream as though he had seen something intriguing in the waters all of a sudden. He rubbed the back of his neck, clearing his throat for a third time before he brought his attention back to her. His gaze hovered above her head as he stated, "We're heading out now."

Kallie pursed her lips. She had thought he would pose at least some challenge, but it seemed it was easy to shake his cocky disposition.

How disappointing.

She sighed. She had one chance to get this right. And now was as good of a time as any, she supposed. Wringing out her hair, she awakened her gift, pulling it to the surface. It was weak, but Kallie was sure it had enough strength to get the job done. She placed her fingertips tenderly on Graeson's jaw where it had flexed moments ago. His eyes narrowed in suspicion as she gazed up at him.

"Unbind my hands."

Confusion bubbled to the surface of his countenance as a sliver of haze swam into his eyes. Graeson reached for her hands and grabbed *her* dagger from his waistband. Kallie wanted to snatch it from his hands, but watching him act while under her control made her feel too powerful. Smirking, she let him bring the blade to her hands.

Kallie sighed in relief as he lay the blade against the rope. He dipped his head lower, his breath brushed her collarbone, and a trail of goosebumps formed in its wake.

Anticipation burned in her veins. In a moment, she'd be free.

His lips grazed her ear and the kiss of cold metal on the side of her throat stole her breath away. He clicked his tongue. "You'll have to try harder than that, little mouse."

A shiver ran up her spine as his words lingered on her damp neck, and dread built within her. She sought out her gift again and found it heavy at the bottom of her stomach. But it should have worked. The clothes that were not her own itched, the neckline tightening. At least she had thought she had regained enough strength to give one simple command.

She was sure she had felt it.

Granted, it wasn't as strong as it normally was, but it should have been plenty. The heaviness of it told her otherwise.

Or maybe she was wrong. Maybe, she needed more time to regain her strength. A few strips of dried beef couldn't possibly tie her over. She knew that. She needed more nutrients, more energy.

She huffed. Fine. She would have to try harder. And next time, she would not fail.

Graeson removed the dagger from her neck. Kallie tried to spring for it, but the second she had spent trying to figure out why her gift hadn't worked had cost her the precious time she needed to grab the dagger before he slid it behind his back again. And before she knew it, her hands were sandwiched between his, her cheeks burning in frustration.

He rose a brow. "Distracted, Princess?"

Kallie scoffed. Sure, he was right. She had been distracted, but not for the reasons he probably believed. No doubt Graeson was the kind of man who thought everyone fawned over him. And it was unfortunate her plan would make it seem like she was one of many. But at least she knew the truth.

No man would make her give up her goals.

With a small chuckle, he shoved her toward the woods. The movement caused her to stumble, but his hand returned, stabilizing her.

When Kallie could see Calamity waiting beyond the trees, she dug her heels into the ground as an idea popped into her head. She looked behind her and met Graeson's chest.

Graeson's unamused eyes peered down at her. "Get on the horse," he spat. Away from the river, the previous playfulness was gone and replaced with indignation.

"I need to relieve myself."

Graeson grumbled, but Kallie only blinked up at him. After staring at her as though he was trying to see if she was lying, he rolled his eyes, then tugged her away from the horse.

A few paces away, he shoved her behind a nearby tree.

She strolled over to a spot near a fallen branch hidden from the small group of people on the other side. She lowered her trousers and squatted down. In the open, she felt exposed. She scanned the area, spotting a sharp branch in arm's reach. On the fractured branch, she began sawing at the rope. Small threads sprung from the rope as she sawed.

She had sawed it down over halfway when Graeson's voice rang from the other side of the tree. "Anytime now, Princess."

Kallie groaned. That would have to do for now, she supposed. But now she still faced one problem. "Can you not . . . listen? It's weird."

"Trust me. I'm not," Graeson mumbled.

"That's the problem, isn't it? I don't trust you," Kallie said. Holding back her laughter, she added. "Can you . . . hum or something?"

"What?"

"I don't know just hum. You know . . . to cover the sound?"

Graeson sighed heavily. While Kallie did not think her persistent guard would listen to her, it was worth a shot. But after a moment, he started to hum. It was quiet, but surprisingly in tune. A pleasing sound. Kallie smiled to herself and quickly took care of her business before he became suspicious. Enough of the rope was still intact that it wasn't noticeable but still thin enough that when the time came, she would be able to rip it apart. And if she took any longer, she did not trust that Graeson would not whip around the corner—trousers around her ankles or not.

She pulled her trousers back up, then walked back around the tree to where Graeson waited. Strolling past him, she headed toward Calamity. There was no point in letting her fear get the best of her. She had a job to do.

Taking a deep, shaky breath, she grabbed the pommel attached to the saddle and pulled herself up and over the horse. She looked down and noted Graeson's gaze locked onto her, quizzically.

"Get on the horse," she mocked.

He shook his head, clearing whatever thoughts stopped him in his wake, and quickly mounted. As Graeson settled behind her, Kallie quickly braided her hair into a single plait as she watched Terin approach.

When Terin was an arm's length away, he extended his arm. In his hand, were two items wrapped in cotton.

"For the ride." Terin pushed his hand forward.

When Kallie took the two bundles, Terin nodded at her and sauntered off to his horse.

Graeson reached for one of the two bundles laying in her lap. He stuffed the napkin in his pocket and began eating. Kallie opened the bundle and found a small loaf of bread with meat and cheese in the middle. She sniffed at the loaf and bit off a chunk. Like the dried beef, the bread was sprinkled with salt. She mowed down half of the loaf. When she went for another bite, she felt resistance on her hand.

"Don't eat it all. You'll get sick," Graeson's voice was stern as he forced her hand down.

"Excuse me?" Kallie asked, mouth half-full. Manners be damned.

"You've barely eaten anything and with your irrational fear of horses, you will get sick."

Kallie flipped her braid over her shoulder, the tail hitting Graeson in the chest. "And why do you care?"

Graeson groaned in annoyance. "I do not want vomit on my horse."

Calamity tossed her head as though in agreement.

"And here I thought you cared about my well-being," Kallie grumbled as she bit a small chunk of her sandwich.

"I think you care about yourself enough for both of us." He snatched the loaf from her hand and rolled it back into the napkin.

Kallie's jaw dropped, so she did the only thing she could. She stuck her tongue out at him and turned around like a child.

He drew closer, his head hovering above her shoulder. "Keep

sticking out your tongue and you might wish you hadn't." His tone was both threatening and suggestive.

"Is that a threat, Graeson?"

His tongue slid over his teeth as a strand of hair fell over his scar. "Care to find out, Princess?"

If he wasn't her enemy and her captor, Kallie might push him to see if his word was as solid as hers. But alas, they had their roles to play here, so instead, she turned around. She was not going to play this game of his.

He chuckled behind her and a flask appeared in front of her face. She hesitated but took it. Taking a swig, she swished the water tainted with the bite of liquor he'd had in it before around her mouth and washed the bread down.

After she returned the flask to him, he clasped it to the saddle and signaled the horse into a trot. Kallie took a mental note of the direction in which they headed. They must have been in the north-western point of Ardentol's territory, right at the border of Borgania.

She rolled her neck in an attempt to lessen the tension that was spreading throughout her body. As the parade of hooves clapped against the ground, she wondered how her life had turned into a constant battle against her patience. And she wasn't sure what would crack first. Her patience or her anger.

THAT NIGHT FYNN had chosen to set up camp in a secluded alcove in the mountains since it was tucked away from the paths used by travelers. The small space did not permit them to pitch up their tents. Thankfully, the gods seemed to be watching out for them, for the sky was void of any storm clouds the spring nights often brought into the area. Then, by the time they made camp and ate dinner, dusk had arrived.

The five of them sat around the fire they had cooked their dinner over. Graeson had forced her to sit beside him while the rest of her group had centered themselves on the opposite side. As they sat around the fire now on its last couple of logs, the air grew stiff and the silence, deafening.

Dani tossed a twig into the fire. "Gray, why don't you tell us one of your stories?"

Kallie's interest peaked, but she refused to show it. She needed to get them talking so she could learn something useful. Perhaps a story would do just that.

When Graeson responded, his voice was laden with incredulity, "I'm sorry, what?"

"Come on. Why not?" Dani begged.

"Dani, you are ridiculous. No one wants to hear a story right now."

"I'm sure our guest would love to hear one about Pontanius. Maybe she could learn a thing or two," Fynn said with a crooked smile spread across his face.

Kallie did not know what she could learn from the outcasted god. But maybe the story would allow her to get inside of their heads, so she gave an encouraging nod.

Graeson shifted, pulling his knee closer to his chest, and Kallie could feel his annoyance rise within him. Upon first meeting the man, she believed him to be a closed book. But after being in such close proximity to him the past twenty-four hours, she quickly realized he wore his emotions like clothing: visible to everyone.

"Fine. I will tell one then." Fynn asked. He looked at Kallie. "Do you know the story of Pontanius?"

She shook her head. "We don't celebrate the god, so I know very little besides that he is Pontia's namesake."

"Unfortunate but not surprising." Fynn didn't bother to hide the disgust in his voice. "The people of the mainland tend to look down upon him. And to them, I suppose, they have a good reason to, for he and many of the other gods do not get along. But that is a story for another time. There's another story that I wish to share." Fynn cleared his throat. "Thousands of years ago, when the gods walked on human soil, he fell in love with a mortal—"

Kallie couldn't stop the laughter that slipped from her lips. "Like most of the stories it seems," she mumbled. From the corner of her eye, she saw Graeson staring at her with an amused expression. She shifted.

"While that might be a little true," Fynn said, "don't all great stories involve some sort of great love affair?"

Kallie thought about the goddess Sabina who had been betrayed by her lover, and bile began to build in her stomach. "If you're foolish enough to love," she said.

Pity flickered in Fynn's gaze, but Kallie did not want his pity. She didn't need it. Nor did she need love in her life. The love from her father and friend was more than enough.

"Then call me foolish," Fynn said.

Dani groaned, and for the first time, Kallie agreed with someone in this group.

Hiding her grin, Kallie shifted in her spot, attempting to make the ground less rigid. She let her fingers graze Graeson's. The top of his hand was warm, soft. She let her touch linger there, and his head tilted down to their hands. But to her surprise, he didn't move away. Not until a pop from the fire sparked did Graeson pull his hand free.

He crossed his legs in front of him and cracked his knuckles. And without the warmth of his hand beneath hers, Kallie's palm grew cold. Something within her pulled at her that Kallie didn't recognize. Ignoring it, she shoved it down.

"Fynn, let Graeson tell the story. He knows this one better than you do," Dani said.

Scoffing in disagreement, he leaned back onto his palms. "Fine. Be my guest, Gray."

Graeson sighed but despite his previous refusal, he cleared his throat. The fire sparked again. When he spoke, his voice took on a different tone, one that was ethereal and ancient. "A long time ago, a group of gods entered the mortal world. Pontanius, the youngest of the gods, was among them."

"Obviously," Kallie mumbled, throwing a nearby twig into the fire.

Graeson stared at her, then continued as if she hadn't interrupted. "But he was not like his siblings. While the other gods wanted to use their godhood to trick and deceive mortals for their own benefit, Pontanius wanted to get to know them, understand them. To live among them in harmony. So he decided to abandon the other gods, and he ventured to an island off the Northern coast."

"But why did he view mortals differently than the others?" Kallie asked. She had not heard anyone paint Pontanius in a positive light before, nor had she heard of a god caring about mortals.

"Before some of the gods had decided to visit the mortal realm, Pontanius often spent his days alone. When the idea to visit came about, he sprung for the opportunity to find companionship among the mortals. He had thought he would find what he had been looking for among them." Graeson paused, waiting for Kallie to interrupt again. But when she didn't, he continued, "Pontanius arrived on the island and was in awe of the way the people interacted with one another. He had never seen anything like it, neither in his realm nor on the mainland where the rest of the gods were. The people on the island were kind. They didn't fight over the land, they didn't hoard food from others. They lived as one.

"Upon Pontanius' arrival, he disguised himself. Although humans were built in the shape of the gods, the features of gods were starker, sharper, and would, as a result, appear strange to the mortals. Pontanius did not want to be treated differently. He had already seen how the humans either worshipped or feared the gods on the mainland. He did not want that for himself. Therefore, he transformed his appearance, dulled it.

"He met a small farming family who offered to house him in exchange for manual labor. In the early hours of the day, he helped tend to their crops. During those mornings in the field, he grew close to their daughter, Alisynth. She was beautiful, strong, and intelligent. Alisynth showed him what it meant to truly live. After a while, he grew to care for the daughter. And soon enough he learned that she too shared his feelings. While most would have been ecstatic that their love interest returned their feelings, Pontanius was frightened. Before, hiding his identity felt natural, a necessity even. But if he wanted to pursue a relationship with the mortal, he knew he needed to be honest with her."

Graeson's words floated in and out of her head, pieces of the story never truly reaching her while her mind drifted. It wasn't that Graeson was a poor storyteller. On the contrary, the inflection of his voice was right, but the story wasn't right for Kallie. She wanted to hear a tale about an individual growing into their strength. Holding onto it and never giving it up for someone who would no doubt betray them. She didn't want to hear about a mortal woman falling for a god who lied to her, who was more powerful than she was. She didn't want to hear about how the god inevitably sacrificed some part of himself to be with her. Or how he created a divide between himself and his kind because of her.

And to make matters worse, she found no messages hidden within the parts of the story she heard.

Kallie rested her head against the bag behind her as the heat of the fire made her eyelids heavy.

Tomorrow, she would change tactics. Tomorrow, she would take the reins and lead them where she wanted. She was done waiting. She would stop pretending to be the daft princess in this story.

CHAPTER 11

SCREAMS RIPPED FROM HER LUNGS, TEARING HER THROAT APART.

Her palms were sticky from the warmth of someone's blood. Her breaths were short as the heat of bodies pressed against her. She wanted to throw up. She just might.

"What happened?" A voice asked. It felt far away but close all at once making her head spin.

People moved around her, their movements scattered, but she couldn't see them. Darkness consumed her vision.

"What's going on?" Another person asked, his voice heavy with concern.

Her breaths were coming quicker, sweat beaded on her forehead. Her heart felt like it was going to break through her ribcage. She thought back to her lessons.

She had prepared herself for attacks, for fights. Her coping mechanisms had been ingrained into her brain since she first started having panic attacks when she was younger. She needed to slow down her breathing, gather her senses. Regain control over her body. She began to count with each breath she took.

Inhale, one. Exhale, two. Repeat.

Three.

In and out.

Four.

She unclenched her fingers.

Five.

She relaxed the muscles in her back.

Six.

Her breathing slowed, her breaths lengthened.

Seven.

"I don't know. She just started screaming." A stranger's hand fell on her forehead. She focused on the cool contact and the warmth in her hands dissipated.

Eight.

"She seems to be calming down."

Nine.

"Then what in the hell happened, Terin?"

Ten.

She opened her eyes. Silver spheres hovered above her, shades of black edged her vision. The moon blinked at her and she blinked back. Then the moon disappeared and Graeson stared down at her, his hair floating around his sharp jaw. Then he too disappeared, shoved to the side and replaced by Fynn and Terin's scrunched faces. The twins each took one of her hands in their own. Kallie wanted to pull her hands back, yank them from their grasp. She didn't want them to touch her. She didn't want them to bloody their own hands. But when they squeezed her hand, she knew blood did not cover her hands, but sweat.

She sighed in relief. It was only a nightmare.

"Kalisandre?" Terin asked. And it was the first time she had heard her name spoken. They had avoided saying her name. As though uttering those four syllables would summon the demons from the Beneath to rise from the muck of the rivers and seas. Her name was strange on her enemy's tongue. The last syllable rolled off Terin's tongue and blended in a lyrical sort of way she was not accustomed to.

Kallie squinted at the twins, her focus bouncing between them. Their faces had the ghost of familiarity, but she couldn't understand why.

"Are you hurt?" Fynn asked.

Her mouth was dry from sleep and from her screams. But other than that, she was fine. Because it was only a nightmare. She coughed to clear her throat. "Suffocated."

Fynn's brows knitted together, then settled once again. His concern dwindled as he realized she was not in imminent danger as they all had believed moments ago.

"Huh?" Terin asked, confused. Meanwhile, Fynn had already moved back.

"You're suffocating me," Kallie groaned.

Terin's attention flicked to his brother, then returned to her. Fynn pulled him back by his shoulder. Terin's balance teetered, but Fynn steadied his brother. Then, hooves smacked against the ground.

Kallie pushed herself onto her elbows. Further down the alcove, Dani sprinted toward them on horseback.

Hair blown across her face, cheeks windswept. Out of breath, Dani said, "Fynn, we need to go."

With a quick nod, Fynn began gathering their belongings. Meanwhile, Terin helped Kallie stand on wobbly legs as she, Terin, and Graeson stood watching Fynn stuff a thin blanket into one of their bags.

"Why?" Graeson asked, moving away from Kallie and Terin.

"Tracks. Don't know who it is, but we can't risk it," Dani said, her words clipped.

"Human or animal?" Graeson asked. Several creatures prowled these mountains, creatures of myths and legends, none of which

Kallie had the desire to see while she was restrained and weaponless.

Dani's jaw twitched. "Human."

Kallie sighed in relief, but she was the only one.

Fynn kicked dirt over the fire and their tracks. "You heard her. Mount up."

With an unfamiliar attentiveness, Graeson guided Kallie to Calamity, ushering her quickly yet carefully. As she returned to her spot on Calamity's back, Fynn said from his horse, "We made good distance yesterday, but we will need to ride harder today if we are to make it to the safe-house in the next few days. Necessary stops only."

The others nodded, then they took off. The horses' hooves slapped the ground and Kallie could not help but look over her shoulder. She wondered who would be traveling this far into these mountains. And who Fynn and his men were afraid of if they had been able to kill her guards with such ease before.

THE NEXT THREE days followed the same pattern. Wake-up. Eat. Ride. Eat again. Then try to sleep.

They never pitched their tents, instead choosing to test their luck with the spring weather. And Fynn didn't want the tents to slow them down if they ran into trouble again.

Each night, the Pontians took turns guarding the campsite. And each night, Dani found more tracks, more signs of others traveling nearby, too close for their liking. And every time, they picked up their belongings and continued their trek through the mountains. They made frequent stops to give the horses more breaks since they were unable to stay in one place for too long. They took turns sleeping when they had the chance, but no one found solace for long.

Sleep evaded her captors. And Kallie, out of fear of another nightmare, evaded sleep.

They were all on edge. The silence all-consuming. On the fourth night, they had made it out of the mountains and made camp a few miles away from one of the lakes in Borgania. After dinner, Graeson took care of the horses, brushing their manes and checking their hooves. It was then that Kallie had found out he had been the one who had braided the horses' hair. Graeson had shrugged it off though, saying it kept his hands busy and allowed his mind to settle. He made it seem like a simple act. And perhaps it was, but Kallie saw the attentiveness, the effort in which he took to care for the horses. It made him seem . . . human, normal. As if he was not just a villain in her story.

While Graeson braided a small section of Calamity's hair, Kallie leaned against a nearby tree. She tore her gaze from him. She should not be humanizing any of them. *They* were the enemy.

After a moment of silence, Graeson asked. "Thinking of your fiancé?"

"Hm?" Kallie's brows bunched in confusion.

"The ring on your finger." Graeson looked down at her hands and her gaze followed his. She hadn't realized she was fiddling with the gold ring. It was an old habit she had yet to break.

"Oh, no, this isn't—" She began but stopped as Graeson raised his brow in question. His mountain-gray eyes stared into hers, and she cursed herself. Even though she wasn't in love with King Rian or even particularly interested in the engagement besides for what she stood to gain from it, she at least needed to pretend that she was.

She cleared her throat. "I mean, of course I'm worried that King Rian might grow concerned about my disappearance." She looked down at the slim piece of gold that wrapped around her finger next to her pinky on her right hand. In the center of the metal band, a brilliant amethyst sparkled. The gold band was unlike any of the jewelry she had seen at the markets back home. It had intricate grooves that were unmatched. It wasn't flashy or loud like some of her diadems or necklaces from her father. It was easily the most beautiful piece of jewelry she owned. She never took it off. "But this isn't from him."

Graeson pursed his lips and returned his attention to Calamity's headpiece, undoing the latches.

Although Kallie did not owe Graeson an explanation, she felt the need to continue, to justify her reaction. She didn't need him to think she was lying or that the engagement was a farce. While she intended to lie, the truth barreled out of her mouth before she could stop it. "It was my late mother's."

Graeson looked at her from the corner of his eye, his interest peaking.

She dropped her eyes to the ring as she continued to twist the gold band. "She died when I was a child," Kallie admitted quietly.

Graeson was silent for a moment as he ran his fingers through the horse's mane with a delicate attentiveness. In the quiet that followed, Kallie regretted saying anything. This stranger did not care about her dead mother. After all, he was trying to kill her father.

Then he looked back at her. "Do you remember anything about her?"

His question surprised her, and maybe that was why she answered honestly. "No, not really." A short nervous laugh escaped her lips. "I don't even know what she looked like besides. . ." Kallie stopped. Her enemy did not need to hear this, but for some reason, the words came easily. Too easily. Perhaps, it was the way his tone had shifted or how his gaze had softened. His expression was not one of pity nor the way others had looked at her when the topic would come up. There was an understanding that existed there.

And perhaps it was because, here in a foreign place, away from the prying ears of servants who would tell her father what she said, she felt like she could speak openly about her mother for the first time.

"Besides what?" Graeson asked after Kallie had gone quiet.

Kallie tried to find a spot to focus on. Anywhere but on Graeson, but everywhere else she looked was shadowed in darkness. She clenched her fists as she shifted on her feet. "Oh, uhm . . . our eyes. My father said we have the same eyes." She felt silly when the words left her mouth. She shouldn't have said it. She should have ignored him. What if he was trying to gather any information he could use against her? Or against her father? But then again, this conversation seemed harmless. Her mother had already been taken from her. There was nothing he could gain from the information.

Graeson observed her for a moment silently, then nodded. "Why don't you know anything else?"

Kallie sighed. She hated talking about this, but she felt she needed to defend herself and her family. Graeson already hated the king. No point in giving him more reasons to hate him. "The king still finds it hard to speak about her. When she died, my father was distraught, heartbroken. He destroyed all of her pictures in the palace. They were too painful for him to see. This . . . this ring is the only thing I have that was once hers."

Graeson raised his brows. "I find that hard to believe."

Taken aback, Kallie scoffed. "Well, it is. Everything else is gone."

Graeson's hand fell to his side. "No, not that. I find it hard to believe that the heartbreak was too hard to talk about."

She glared at him, crossing her arms over her chest. "And what is that supposed to mean?"

He exhaled. "Nothing." Then looking away, he continued, "It's just that if I lost someone I cared about, I would want to talk about them. Holding it all in only lets the pain fester and build. Nothing good can come out of that."

"You talk as if you're familiar with the feeling," Kallie said.

Graeson shrugged. "You could say loss is an old friend."

She waited for him to elaborate, but he never did. All too familiar with the pain questions often brought, Kallie didn't press him. Nor did she care to. When she looked into his eyes, she saw something else there. Something she couldn't quite describe. But before she could identify it, it disappeared as though she had imagined it. A figment of her imagination perhaps.

She shook her head, erasing the thoughts of her mother from her mind. The thoughts were making her see things, making her pretend something was there when it wasn't.

They fell back into silence.

Tonight, Graeson was on the first watch. With their conversation done, Kallie made her way over to the makeshift bed he had made for her on the flat ground. Laying underneath the top blanket, she turned to her side.

Darkness blanketed the sky, and she could barely make out the silhouettes of the Pontians, but she knew they were there beside her. Dani had fallen asleep a while ago, Terin and Fynn shortly after. But Kallie lay wide awake.

She didn't know how much time had passed, but eventually, she saw Graeson walk away from the horses to wake up Fynn who lay next to her. The two men slipped into the woods as they spoke in hushed tones, their words too faint to parse.

Sometime later, Graeson returned. He took Fynn's empty spot beside her, practically throwing himself against the ground with an exasperated sigh. In the near distance, she heard Fynn walking in the woods around them, watching, listening for any signs of danger.

No tracks were found that night.

Still, Kallie did not sleep.

CHAPTER 12

Kallie somehow had managed to fall asleep during the ride the next day though. The sound of shouting startled her awake, almost causing her to fall off the horse. But unsurprisingly, Graeson had quick reflexes. His arm tightened around her waist, as she tipped. And for once, she was thankful for his proximity.

She righted herself and shrugged his arm off her. Her hand flew to her thigh on instinct, but her palm fell flat against her pants. She still didn't have her dagger. The paranoia from the past few days had her heart pounding as she searched for the source of the shouting. Were they being attacked?

In the distance, a lanky figure waved at their group, her brows knitted together in confusion. The man was waving them over, bouncing on the balls of his feet. This was not a man planning to attack them. Unless he was a complete imbecile, that is. This must be the safe house Fynn had mentioned. But this was not what she pictured when Fynn had said they would be staying at a safe house. This man was not built for protection. Nor was this farm.

Along the eastern side of the Lucian River, a long stretch of short crops bordered the dirt road that led to the man who stood in front of a small farmhouse. The house was plain, dismissible. And the only house in sight. So perhaps, in terms of safety and privacy, it was a decent choice.

As the group approached, the man directed them to the stable adjacent to the house.

Outside the stable, Fynn hopped down from his horse. A wide grin split his face in two as he walked over to the provincial man. He slapped him on the back, pulling him in for a hug.

While everyone was distracted greeting the man, Kallie examined the stable. Various rusted farming equipment lined the walls, such as hoes, rakes, and shovels. Without her weapon, she would have to make use of what was available.

When Graeson turned around, Kallie feigned a bored expression. "Well?" she asked.

Graeson blinked up at her.

She shook her still-bounded hands at him. "Can I bother you to help a lady out?"

Graeson laughed. "Now you require my help, Princess?"

Kallie groaned. "Fine. I am perfectly capable of dismounting on my own."

"No, no. I wouldn't want you to hurt yourself." He chuckled. "After all, you're always stumbling—over your feet, your words."

Kallie scoffed. "If I do it's only because of this damned rope around my wrist."

He stepped closer and placed his hands on Calamity's back, locking Kallie in place without touching her as if to remind her of her position as their captive. "I recall you saying you preferred it that way."

Kallie's mouth fell open. She quickly snapped it shut as she felt a blush rise to her cheeks. "I—I said no such thing."

He whispered. "See? There you go stumbling over your words

again." He leaned in closer, the smell of cedar cocooning her. "Is it me, little mouse? Do I make you stumble?"

Kallie snarled in disgust. He had been trying to get a rise out of her this entire time, and it had worked. She was flustered, annoyed, and strangely intrigued even though she shouldn't be.

Kallie had always enjoyed playing with someone she couldn't have. And Graeson was the very definition of someone she should stay away from. Someone whom she would enjoy toying with for a time, but a danger once that time was up. His looks alone would have had Myra spinning, but Kallie was not going to be affected by him.

She would use him, manipulate him, then she would destroy him.

"Only because I am constantly shocked by your stupidity." Kallie grabbed the pommel and lifted herself off the horse. She felt his hand go to her back, steadying her as she searched for the footrest. "Perhaps, you could invest in some shorter stirrups," she mumbled, the frustration rising to the surface.

"Planning to stay for a while then, Princess?"

Kallie groaned and regretted saying anything at all.

Once her foot found the small pad of leather, she hopped off the horse, relieved to be on solid ground again.

Graeson placed his hand on her elbow. "And lose my entertainment? I don't think so."

"Are you that easy to entertain?" She jerked her arm away from him, shaking off his hand.

Graeson only shrugged in response.

Kallie cast a glance at the others gathered around the farmer. "Don't you think this farmer will be at all curious as to why you have a person with their wrists tied? Won't it raise suspicions?"

Graeson shrugged again. "Eh, Menz has seen worse."

Kallie opened her mouth, but her words were lost on her tongue. She snapped it shut as Graeson ushered her toward Fynn, Terin, and Dani. Even though the farmer, or Menz as Graeson referred to him, was not much shorter than the other men, there was a stark contrast between Menz and the twins. The men were all clearly strong, but where the twins were bulky, Menz was lanky.

The farmer threw his head back as laughter erupted from his mouth. The sound was vacant of disdain or annoyance and filled with unfiltered amusement, something she was not used to hearing.

"And what, pray tell, is so funny?" Graeson asked, stopping a few paces away from Fynn and the farmer.

Fynn shook his head as he regained his ability to speak. He glanced between Kallie and Graeson. "I'll tell you later, Gray."

"I cannot wait until your mother hears about this," Menz said, still laughing. Then with a gesture to follow, the farmer headed up the path to the small farmhouse.

Menz opened the door and Kallie entered the house behind Fynn with Graeson on her heels. Upon entering, the smell of onions, garlic, and warm broth smacked her in the face. As they passed the quaint kitchen, her stomach grumbled at the sight of the steaming pot on the stove.

"I figured you all might be hungry, so I cooked up a stew for you," Menz said, glancing over his shoulder.

He led the group over to the dining area. The room was just large enough to fit a table for six. Fynn claimed the head of the table in the front of the room. Terin and Dani sat on the western side and Graeson directed Kallie to the chair across from Fynn. Kallie noted how the seat was pushed up against the wall and surrounded by her enemies on both sides, making it nearly impossible for her to try anything.

Sitting down, she took the room in. It was simple, void of decadence besides a few small paintings of the property on the walls. Her eyes lingered on the painting of the house. It was a near-perfect depiction. The colors were bright and lively. Even without people in the painting, the painter managed to convey more emotion within their strokes than any of the royal portraits covering the lavish walls of the palace in Ardentol.

"My late wife painted those," Menz said from the entrance of the room after noticing where Kallie's gaze had gone.

"Lois was a very talented woman," Fynn said.

"She sure was." A proud smile was plastered on Menz's face. Then sighing, he turned around and disappeared into the hallway.

A moment later, the smell of the stew grew stronger, and Menz strode back into the dining room carrying the large steel pot that Kallie had seen on the stove. He tilted his head toward the entry. "Fynn, do an old friend a favor and grab the bowls from the kitchen."

"Of course." Fynn pressed his palms into the table and stood up.

Menz sat the pot in the center of the table. Not a minute later Fynn waltzed back in carrying six bowls and began handing them out one by one. When he reached Kallie, he patted her on the head as though she was a dog rather than their captive. She immediately swiveled her head around and glared up at him with heat in her eyes.

An amused smile was splayed across Fynn's face as he held up his hand as if feigning innocence. Then he continued placing the remaining bowls in front of Graeson and the empty seat for Menz.

"Oh, leave the poor girl alone, Fynnereas," the farmer's light voice sounded from beside her as he reached over her. Menz dropped two spoonfuls of stew into her bowl.

"It's fine, Menz." Kallie rolled her shoulders back. "I'm sure Fynn doesn't get a lot of female attention."

Menz nearly dropped the stew-filled spoon on Graeson's lap. On the other side of the table, Terin coughed.

"Oh, this is going to be fun," Dani said, pulling a faint chuckle from Graeson.

Kallie's head swiveled on her shoulders as she sneered at Dani, "And what is *that* supposed to mean?"

With a half-hearted shrug, Dani said, "Don't worry about it, Princess."

Kallie narrowed her eyes at the smug woman. But the smell of the stew wafting toward her made her stomach grumble. She snatched the spoon with her hand and awkwardly took a bite.

"Oh, come on," Menz groaned. "Why is she still tied up? Where is she going to go?"

Kallie knew they didn't trust her. Why would they? She was their hostage. She was lucky the rope around her wrists was her only restraint. She supposed they needed to keep her in somewhat decent shape though. Lest King Domitius find out and kill them all—though he would do that no matter what.

During the ride to the farmhouse, she hadn't had many opportunities to escape. If she ran, they would catch her. And if they didn't, someone else—or something—would have. Menz was right, she couldn't do much harm at the table. Not when it was five against one. They could at least allow her wrists to heal from the rope burn that was beginning to irritate her skin. And she wouldn't mind being able to eat her stew like a normal, civilized human being either.

Kallie said with her eyes locked on Graeson, "I'm sure *Gray* over here could just feed me instead." Kallie smirked. "After all, he does have a problem keeping his hands off of me."

Graeson choked on a chunk of potato and pounded his fist against his chest as he regained his breath.

Terin added with a shrug, "She hasn't tried to leave since that first night."

"And if she does, it won't be hard to find her." Dani looked her up and down, grinning. "She doesn't run that fast."

Kallie glared at Dani. One of the reasons she did not escape that first night was that she had Myra with her. They underestimated her, but Kallie would use that to her advantage. They knew nothing.

Fynn looked at her, assessing her. Then he nodded to Graeson.

"Fine, but do not blame me if she tries something stupid again," Graeson said.

Kallie thrust her bounded hands in front of her, eager to be rid of the wretched rope. Graeson stood from his chair and grabbed her hands.

Bending low, his lips close to her ear, he whispered, "They might trust you, but make no mistake, I do not."

Smirking, she looked him up and down, their faces only inches apart. "Good."

Grabbing her hands, he cut the rope. He raised it, eyeing the frayed edges where she had sawed the rope days ago. He glared at her, shaking his head. "Wherever you go, Princess, I will follow. Do not forget it or else you will regret it."

"Is that a promise?" Kallie asked, looking at him through her eyelashes.

He glared at her and bit out, "You can bet on it, little mouse."

Kallie shrugged, returning her attention to the stew, which was no longer scorching hot. She began scarfing it down, and with each bite, she could feel her energy returning to her. Tonight, she would be ready.

When she, at last, returned her gaze to the table, she shoved a large spoonful into her mouth. As she swallowed, she found Graeson staring at her, his jaw agape.

Kallie swallowed, then asked, "What?"

When he didn't respond, she wiped her chin with the back of her hand, thinking broth had dribbled down her face. But when her hand came back clean, she narrowed her eyes at Graeson who was still staring at her. "What?" She snapped again.

"Hmm?" Graeson mumbled, blinking.

"You're staring."

Graeson averted his eyes, focusing back on the bowl in front of him. After swallowing down a spoonful of stew, he said, "Nothing."

From across the table, Menz grabbed the large knife sitting in the middle of the table and cut off a slice of bread. "Kalisandre, if you would like more there is plenty."

"Thank you," Kallie mumbled.

Menz tipped his head and smiled softly, setting the knife back down.

Smirking to the side, her eyes fell on the knife. As she stood up, the chair screeched across the hardwood floors and Kallie could have sworn half of the table, besides Menz and Fynn, stopped breathing. She reached over the table and grabbed the knife as Graeson reached to his back.

No one spoke. No one moved.

She dropped her gaze to the blade, running a single finger across the side of the metal. Her gaze flicked to Fynn, who leaned back in his chair, his arm hanging over the back of his chair. His face was nearly expressionless, a hint of amusement sparkled in his eyes. To her right, Kallie heard the sound of the floorboards bending beneath Graeson's weight.

She waved the knife around. As she looked at each of them, some of their faces lost their pigment.

It would be easy to kill one of them. But that was not her objective right now. She had other plans for them. A sly smile rose to her face. "Anyone want a piece?"

The others at the table remained glued to their seat, hands falling beneath the table. No doubt they were reaching for their weapons hidden on their persons. Besides Fynn though, who remained relaxed, calm.

Curious, she thought.

When no one answered, she shrugged a single shoulder. "More for me then." She sliced off a thick piece of the warm bread, the jagged blade scraping against the cutting board. She tossed the knife back onto the table, making it rattle against the table. She ripped off a large chunk and shoved the sourdough in her mouth. With an exaggerated moan, she closed her eyes, as she chewed the freshly baked bread and sunk back into her chair.

As she reveled in her ability to shake them, the tension in the room remained taut. Graeson, who was now back in his seat, stayed alert while he watched her.

As Kallie chewed on the bread, it occurred to her that Graeson never seemed at ease. The only time he seemed relatively relaxed was when he was with his horse. And even then, there was tension in his body.

"Why so tense, *Gray?*" Kallie elongated the nickname she had heard the others use. When Graeson remained silent, unmoving, she giggled.

Dani said, "Oh ignore him. Graeson has always been a little uptight ever since—"

"Dani," Graeson's cold voice cut through the room like a blade.

Kallie glanced between the Pontians. "Ever since what?" Kallie inquired, curious as to why Graeson seemed so bothered. A noise similar to that of a growl erupted from Graeson as he stared at Dani. And he seemed to transform into something akin to a beast, his irises darkening, the muscles in his jaw ticking.

Maybe that was why he treated animals with more respect than humans. He was one.

"Gray, go tend to the horses," Fynn commanded from across the table. But despite Fynn's tone, Graeson stayed fixed to his seat, the muscles in his back flexing.

"*Now*, Graeson," Fynn barked, his knuckles turning white as he clenched his fist.

Graeson slammed his spoon on the table, the sudden movement making Kallie flinch. He pressed his palms into the table, putting half of his weight on them as if the act of removing himself from the table went against some natural instinct. When he finally stood, his silver eyes met Kallie's.

He said nothing as he looked at her. But the way he lingered made it seem like he wanted to say something. Did he blame her for his outburst? It wasn't her fault he couldn't control his anger.

Then before Kallie could wipe off the confusion cast across her face, Graeson stormed out of the room. Seconds later the front door slammed, shaking the paintings on the wall.

"Maybe he should stay out in the stable tonight," Dani murmured. "Let the air cool him off."

"Dani, for once," Fynn said, his voice muffled as he rubbed his hands across his face, "shut the hell up."

Dani shrugged, then continued wiping the edges of her empty bowl with a chunk of bread, soaking up the remaining drops of broth.

Kallie looked between the four people who remained at the table trying to understand what had happened. Terin's gaze was locked on his bowl as if the potatoes and carrots inside it were the most interesting sight he had seen while Fynn sat rubbing his temple. When her eyes landed on Menz, he only gave the slightest shake of his head at her. Perhaps it was best if she didn't know what had transgressed just now.

Menz tilted back in his chair and drummed his fingers against the edge of the table. "Your rooms are prepared for you when you're ready."

"Dani, Kalisandre will stay with you," Fynn said.

Kallie could only assume by the omission of Graeson's name that her insistent guide might, for once, not be attached to her arm tonight. And she knew that this would be her best chance to make her move.

Dani smirked at her as she sucked the tips of her fingers clean.

"Don't bother trying anything, Princess. These are old floors," Fynn added.

Kallie lifted her glass and gave him a sweet smile. "I wouldn't dare."

Raising a brow, Fynn took a sip of his flask and Kallie held in her grin. *Trying* meant failing. And she would not fail.

WALLPAPER SPECKLED with white and pink peonies lined the walls. There were two twin beds, one on either side of the room. In the corner of the room, a small wood burner sat with cold ashes, untouched since its last use. Someone had cracked open the single window between the beds letting the humid air filter in. Since they had arrived, the humidity outside had thickened. All signs pointed to a storm brewing, but perhaps a storm was what Kallie needed.

Kallie strolled over to the window and peered out. The stables sat beneath the window, and from the light of a small oil lamp, she saw the top of Graeson's dark wavy hair. His shoulders were tense as he brushed his horse's coat. She had gained little information over the five days she had been with them. But maybe she could get Dani to divulge something helpful. At dinner, she seemed on the verge of saying something until Fynn and Graeson had stopped her.

"So. . .what's Graeson's deal?" Kallie asked nonchalantly.

Dan sat on the edge of one of the beds as she untied her boots. "It doesn't concern you. Now does it, Princess?"

Kallie shrugged her shoulders, not willing to answer. If the information helped her get rid of these rebels who planned to attack her father, it was part of her duty to gather it.

Dani peered at Kallie. "Or do you mean to tell me you've grown fond of your captor? Kind of strange, don't you think?"

Kallie scoffed. "Do not think my curiosity is a sign of complacency. While my hands are not tied at the moment, the noose around my neck still digs into my skin."

"Poetic," Dani said as she kicked off one of her boots. "But whatever you say, Princess."

Kallie crossed her arms over her chest. "I merely would like to know how long I have to deal with his less-than-pleasant attitude."

Dani laughed. "Oh, that will not be going away anytime soon. Graeson has been like that since we were children."

From the window, Kallie observed the tension in Graeson's body beginning to lessen with each brush stroke of Calamity's hoof. While the man hadn't been *that* terrible to her—especially considering how merciless he could be with a weapon—Kallie wondered what made him seem unpleasant to his friends as well. What made him kill her guards with such ferocity? She hadn't seen those scimitars since that first night, but she hadn't forgotten the way he sliced through Polin, the image haunting her sleep. She could only hope she wouldn't be on the receiving end any time soon. However, the odds were not in her favor. Especially once she made her move tonight.

Dani riffled through her bag. After a moment, she pulled out a rope and walked over to Kallie. With a straight face, Kallie held out her hands. Once Dani grabbed her wrists, Kallie looked into the woman's unfeeling eyes and filled her voice with her gift. "You will go to sleep and stay asleep until morning."

When Dani's eyes hazed over, the woman slumped onto the ground with a loud thud. Kallie had not intended for the woman to fall asleep on the floor and she almost felt bad for the ache Dani would experience in the morning. However, Dani's pain was not Kallie's concern. And when Dani began snoring and no one came barging through the door, Kallie smirked and allowed herself to bask in the successful use of her gift. She felt re-energized and craved the power from the gods as it moved inside of her. She took a breath, letting the feeling simmer down.

The easy part was done. She now had to get out of here.

While she still had plenty to discover, she needed to move. She would get her answers soon enough.

She rummaged through Dani's bag but found it void of anything useful. She then proceeded to check Dani's body and, once again, came up empty-handed. Kallie scavenged the room, careful not to make too much noise to avoid raising anyone's suspicion. She searched under the beds, the small fireplace, the chests at the end of the bed. But there was no weapon in sight. Although the Pontians trusted her not to kill them at the table, they did not trust her to not kill them in their sleep.

Then she saw it.

A letter opener. It wasn't ideal, but it was sharp enough that she could make it work for what she needed. After all, Kallie only needed a distraction.

CHAPTER 13

ONCE DARKNESS HAD FALLEN OVER THE FARM AND THE CREAKING floors had led to the sound of doors closing, Kallie knew it was time. Over the course of her teenage years, Kallie had mastered the art of sneaking out of rooms in the palace to avoid the prying eyes of guards and servants. Therefore, sneaking out of a small farmhouse would be easy—even with the loud floorboards and her enemies near.

When Kallie peeked out the window, the lantern was blown out and the inside of the stable was cast in darkness. She slipped off her shoes to avoid any unnecessary sounds and held them in one hand. With the other hand, she grabbed her stolen letter opener, stuffed it into the band of her pants, and tightened the ribbon holding up her hair. She cracked open the door an inch and peered out. Shadows scattered the hall barely lit by a thread of moonlight that slipped through the curtains of the single window in the hall. All doors were shut, and a soft snore sounded from behind the closed doors.

Kallie sucked in a breath. It was now or never.

She stepped into the hallway, closing the door behind her. Staying on her toes and sliding down the side of the wall, she crept toward the stairs.

Stage one was complete: get past the bedrooms.

When she had followed Dani and the twins upstairs, Kallie had noted that the worst of the creaks had come from the stairs. And one step in particular, about halfway down, seemed to be the loudest. She exhaled and continued her trek, one foot at a time. Using the wall for balance, Kallie avoided overloading one foot so she didn't add extra pressure onto the worn floors.

Half way down the stairs now. The loudest step was just below her. If she could get past this one, Kallie would be able to breathe again.

She put her foot out, slid her hand down the wooden railing, skipping the step. As her toes made contact with the next step and she shifted her weight, Kallie knew she had made a vital mistake. A miscalculation.

The boards beneath her bent underneath her weight. Kallie felt the faintest vibration of the wood as it creaked. *This* was the one she was supposed to avoid. And she had just put the majority of her weight on it.

Her breath caught in the middle of her throat as she stared down into the darkness of the first floor. Somewhere above her, a bed creaked. A bead of sweat dripped down her neck and slid down her back as she anticipated her discovery.

If it's just one, I can control him. I'm fine.

Silence echoed in the dark hallway. No floors creaked, no doors squeaked open. No one came to investigate.

The gods must have been watching over her. She was in the clear.

Counting to ten, she exhaled and continued down the stairs.

WITH THE FRONT door shut behind her, stage two was complete.

Kallie stood on the front patio of the small house. Although she was certain the Pontians would come after her, she did not know how long it would take or how far she would be able to go. Either way, it was worth trying. She had stopped in the kitchen and had pocketed some leftover bread for the ride toward Kadia.

Outside, the moon was half ablaze and half shaded in darkness. Thick ominous clouds peppered the sky. And in the distance, lightning struck followed by a thunderous boom that shook the ground she stood on. The storm was coming, and she was about to ride straight into it.

Kallie prayed to Sabina for success. And with a renewed sense of determination, she slinked around the house to the stable. Unfortunately, she would need a horse for this next stage. Thankfully though, the ride here made her a little bit more comfortable with them—well with Calamity, at least. Graeson's horse was sassy and more human than most of the horses she had encountered back in Ardentol. Kallie grinned, her eyes alight with mischief. Plus, it was a small perk that stealing Calamity would irritate Graeson beyond belief.

Still, with each step, her smug smile lessened, her palms grew clammier. There was no backing out now though. As her father had reminded her multiple times, to achieve great success, one must risk the jump. And better to die trying than to never risk it at all.

Thunder clapped, and Kallie ducked into the stable the moment rain poured from the sky. Through the rush of water, she looked back toward the farmhouse and groaned. She had no cloak. No way to stay dry. She would be soaked once she stepped foot out of the stable. But she could not wait.

Returning her attention to the dark stable, she heard the horses rustling underneath the roof as the rain beat against it. Hay crunched under her feet. With a shaky hand, Kallie grabbed a handful and walked over to where she had seen Graeson brush Calamity.

Despite Calamity's fur melding into the darkness, the glint of

Calamity's large eyes found Kallie. And when lighting struck again, Kallie's heart rattled inside her as the light cast the beast into a sight meant for nightmares. Shadows danced across the stable, almost human, and paralyzed her.

Once the light disappeared, Kallie slowly regained control over her body. She tiptoed closer. Recalling Graeson's words about the horse's perceptiveness, she slowed her breathing in an attempt to slow her thumping heart. When she was an arm's reach away, she extended her hand out, offering the hay to the horse. Calamity swung her nose, sniffing Kallie's hand. Kallie restrained herself enough to not retreat and instead opened up her hand to the horse.

Hot breath filled the air as Calamity opened her mouth. Large teeth neared her hand, slobber dribbled down onto her palm. Kallie wanted to recoil from fear and disgust. But instead of chopping down on her hand, the horse pulled back its lips, its thick breath soaking Kallie's face, and gingerly took the hay out of Kallie's hand. The horse's teeth didn't even scrap against her skin.

Then a clap of thunder echoed and Kallie jumped back a step, nearly slipping on the loose hay on the ground. Her chest tightened, but the horse remained steady. Though the same could not be said for the other horses.

Heart pounding, Kallie brushed the dirt-coated hay stuck to her sweat-slicked hand and patted the horse warily. "All right, girl. We're going to go for a little ride," her voice shook.

Calamity huffed but didn't move away. Taking that as a sign, Kallie moved over to the side of the horse. Then her heart dropped to her stomach.

There was no saddle, no stirrups. No easy way to pull herself up onto the beast.

"Shit," she hissed to no one but the shadows. The saddle was nowhere in sight (not that she even knew how to put it on the horse without startling it). She searched for some sort of stool or anything to aid her. The other horses shifted nervously in their stalls as the rain continued. It was so loud Kallie could barely hear herself breathe, let alone think. Lightning flashed, and the boom of thunder made the metal tools rattle on the wall. Each rustle of hay beneath the horses' hooves sent an eerie chill skating down her spine.

She needed to hurry. She was running out of time.

Across the stable, a barrel sat near rusted rakes and hoes hanging on the wall. She ran toward it, then kicked it with her toe.

Empty.

"Thank the gods," she whispered.

"Or Menz's impressive ability to put away a barrel of liquor by himself."

Kallie froze, hands extended in front of her. She knew that cold voice. The voice that sent shivers up her arms, that made her feel a way she shouldn't. And briefly, Kallie wondered how she had missed his approach, but the storm had been too loud, too consuming. She retracted her hands slowly and moved the letter opener to her back pocket as she turned around.

Smiling, she forced her body to appear calm despite the thudding inside of her chest. "Gray, I was just seeing if Calamity needed some company."

A lit torch that hadn't been there before sat near the entrance and cast a dim light on Graeson. The light bounced off of him as if scared to linger on him for too long.

"Oh, is that so, Princess?" His brow arched as he leaned against the opening of the stable with his arms crossed over his chest, drenched and amused. He shook the wet hair clinging to his face and water splattered against the farming equipment on the wall. He unclasped his heavy, wet cloak and hung it on a rusted nail protruding from the wall. Without his cloak, there was no hiding the sparkling steel attached to his hips. Kallie swallowed. "The girl who fears horses is checking on *my* horse? And in this weather? Should I be flattered or concerned, little mouse?"

Kallie wrapped her hand around the cold metal at her back while trying to avoid looking at the two sharp, curved blades that hung at Graeson's side. "And what are you doing out here?"

Graeson's gaze slid down her body. Amusement sprinkled his face. She was wearing the same clothes from before, wore no cloak, had no weapon, and had a loaf of bread sticking out of her pocket. The right corner of his mouth tugged up. "Same as you, I suppose."

"Hmm." Kallie nodded.

"Mhm." His hand twitched, but he did not move otherwise. And the corner of his lip still pointed up as though it was a permanent fixture upon his face.

Neither of them moved. Time slowed as Graeson and Kallie stared each other down. It was only a matter of time before one of them moved. But the question was who would be first?

Although rage bubbled inside of her, Kallie would force herself to be patient for a little longer.

When Graeson's lips split apart a moment later, she smiled internally. But his words, which were nearly inaudible as the storm raged on, were unexpected. "You know, I really had hoped I would have been wrong," Graeson said as he took a step sideways.

Kallie tilted her head. "Wrong about what?"

He continued to move toward her. His hand slid across a wooden pole that held up the small attic space above them which was lined with barrels and miscellaneous objects. Still, his silver eyes never left her. "You."

Kallie began to walk in the other direction as she kept her back clear from his view. "Me?"

"Yes, *you*. Fynn had thought—he had believed that you would be. . ." He waved his hand around as though he was trying to catch whatever word he was thinking of. "Obedient. But me? Oh, no. You're not that type of person." He twisted one of the rings on his fingers.

"And what type of person is that exactly?" Kallie could not hold back the bite in her words. This man did not know her. Yet he acted like he did.

A crooked smirk appeared on his face. "The type of person to be commanded."

Heat rose to the tips of her ears, but her mouth remained shut. Her fingers flexed around the smooth metal as her rage threatened to boil over.

When Kallie did not respond, Graeson continued. "I've always believed you were so much more, but perhaps I was wrong."

Kallie's brows knitted together in confusion. Why did he care? And why did *she*? The only thing she knew for sure was that he was tiptoeing around the subject as he bought himself time. But if he wanted to play this game, she'd play. At least for a little longer.

"More how?" she asked.

As he thought, he sucked his teeth. "More independent, strong-willed. More of a fighter." He shrugged. "But it seems you are just the king's doll. You do what he says when he tells you to do it." He ran a hand through his hair. "Do you have your own desires, little mouse?"

His words sparked a nerve. She was more than the *king's doll*. And every day she was working to prove it. She had her own goal: power. Her own throne waiting for her to claim it. And she would achieve it. She would achieve everything she had sought to accomplish since she left Ardentol.

"You know nothing, Graeson."

He chuckled. He was *always* chuckling. "I know more than you think, little mouse."

She tipped her chin up. She was done playing his game, and in one fluid movement, she threw the letter opener at his chest.

Graeson caught it in one hand as he dropped his gaze to the dull piece of metal and flipped it over in his hands. "Really? A letter opener? I expected more from the—"

Kallie swung the rusted rake at his head, barely missing him as Graeson ducked, his quick reflexes surprised her even though they shouldn't have. However, Kallie couldn't spend much time admiring his skill. The momentum she had put into her swing caused her to lose her balance, and Graeson didn't hesitate. He threw out a hand.

Kallie tried to dodge his attack, but she tripped over her feet and the rake jammed into her gut forcing out a grunt. She clenched her fists from the surging pain, but there was no time to rest. She rolled onto her stomach and pressed her palms into the dirt, hoisting herself up and off the ground. She reached for the shovel beside her and spun toward Graeson.

He straightened. When he looked at her, his features shifted. It was slight, barely noticeable, but the way he watched her became more animalistic, predatory. "I got to hand it to you, little mouse, you don't give up. Do you?"

A piece of metal caught the faint light of the torch and her eyes flicked to it. Graeson had tossed the letter opener to the side and now held her dagger.

"I want my dagger back," Kallie bit out.

"Oh, this little thing?" He raised it and slid a finger over it, his rings clinking together. "I think I'll keep it. I've grown quite fond of it."

Kallie scowled.

"Come on, why bother?" Graeson stretched his arms over his head. "You're going to lose this fight."

Kallie despised overconfident men. "Oh, am I?" She sneered.

His laughter was deep, emotionless. Haunting as it ran through his body, as though the idea of her beating him was so ludicrous. It sent her into a fury, and she threw the rake. It missed Graeson, and he barked out another laugh. He opened his mouth to speak, but the words never came.

While Kallie may have missed him, he was not her target. She grinned cheekily as the empty barrels that had sat on the long wooden beam overhead came crashing down atop Graeson. He crouched as his arms flew to his head, shielding his body.

Kallie's gaze flashed to the dagger forgotten on the ground, and she tumbled forward, swiping it up. With her dagger back in her hands where it belonged, she prepared herself as Graeson threw the damaged barrels off of him. And before he could get up, Kallie was behind him with the blade pressing into his skin and a smirk plastered across her face. "I suppose I should thank Menz after all."

Then the air shifted and heat pressed against her back. Her smirk fell from her face as Kallie felt cold metal press against her throat.

"Don't make me do something I will regret later," Fynn said from behind her. The sound of the crashing barrels had masked his approach.

But she hadn't lost this fight yet.

Ignoring the sincerity in his voice, Kallie huffed. "You won't kill me." They needed her alive. She was useless to them dead.

"But I can knock you out," Fynn countered.

Despite the threat, Kallie's breathing was even. He would not be able to knock her out while he pressed the blade against her throat. She took a deep breath in, then Fynn removed the cold metal from her throat. Without thinking, Kallie swapped her arms and jammed the dagger into Fynn's side.

He hissed.

Kallie knew it wasn't a death blow, but it provided her enough space between him to—

The world flipped upside down and spun around her.

Her grip around Graeson had loosened without her realizing it, and Graeson had taken the opportunity to flip her over him. She landed on the ground with a loud thud and grimaced.

His instincts were inhumanly quick. In the past, her opponents had rarely ever caught her with her guard down or been given the chance to put her on her ass. She was angry, but not at Graeson. She was mad at herself for giving him the opportunity to take her down.

Footsteps pounded on the ground, stirring her from her thoughts. "You fool!" Graeson spat. "You should have seen that coming, Fynn."

The beams above her swirled, water seeped through the cracks of the roof. A droplet smacked her forehead. She inhaled sharply. She tried to collect her bearings as she waited for her head to stop spinning.

Somewhere nearby Graeson asked, "You all right?"

She couldn't regain her breath to answer though.

Then Fynn responded saying he'd live, and Kallie realized Graeson hadn't been talking to her. After all, why would he be asking about her well-being? He didn't care. She was their captive. The two people who cared about her were miles away.

Fabric ripped and hay crunched. At the same time, the black splotches in her vision faded. She leaned up onto her elbows, the small movement making her head throb while her vision spun in vibrant shades of purple and blue.

When it returned, she stared at a shirtless Graeson. The white fabric was torn and discarded on the floor beside him. Graeson was hunched over Fynn, who now lay on a pile of hay with a piece of the ripped cotton tied tightly around Fynn's torso. A splotch of red seeped through the wrapping where Kallie had stabbed him.

For a moment, Kallie did not know where to look. The bleeding man or the chiseled chest sculpted by the gods beside him.

"We need to tell her," Graeson said. Those five words should not have mattered, but the weight of Graeson's voice, the intensity of his stare as he applied pressure to Fynn's wound, meant something more.

Whatever they needed to tell her, Graeson thought it could prevent things from proceeding in the direction they had been.

"No. We need to wait," Fynn bit out as sweat glistened on his forehead. "We've come this far already. We have to wait."

"Fynn, it's time. She could have killed you. If we continue down this path, one of you will get hurt far worse than a minor stab wound, and I don't know if I can. . ." He left whatever he was going to say hanging in the air around them.

As much as Kallie wanted to find out why a strange flicker of emotion flashed in his eyes when he looked at her, she couldn't. Another, more pressing question lingered between them.

"Tell me what?" Kallie asked as she regained her breath.

"Graeson." Despite the pain from the wound, Fynn's voice was stern, solid. And it reminded her of the way her father's voice would shift when he reminded people of his position.

Graeson looked between Fynn and Kallie, debating who to listen to. And when Kallie locked eyes with Fynn, anger rose inside of her.

If only she could reach him. Grab his hand, his ankle even, something to bridge the gap between them and would allow for her gift to flow through her and into him. She imagined the air between them, the breath that flowed out of her and into his, a rope between them. A connection invisible to the eye but unbendable. Her rage entwined within the space between her words.

She was tired of people keeping the truth from her. Tired of people thinking she was a simple princess with no true power, a woman men dismissed. Ignored. She was in the room. Her whole life she had been *in* the room but never at the table. Even when she played a role in the plans that would ensue, she never had been granted a voice. She had always been talked to and talked over. Forgotten and dismissed. But she would no longer allow that to happen.

Not among these men, not among her people. Not among *anyone*.

She would show everyone she deserved her seat at the table. She was done being the pawn of men. It was time she stepped into her role as a future ruler.

"Tell me the truth." Her voice was commanding and her gift stirred.

For a moment, Fynn stared at her as though he was fighting something inside of him. Then he said three words Kallie had never expected to leave his lips.

"I'm your brother."

CHAPTER 14

Brother?

If Kallie's breath hadn't already been knocked out of her and if her head wasn't already spinning, she was sure it would be now. And Fynn's eyes were now murky, the effects of her gift stirring within them.

Strange, she thought.

She hadn't even been in contact with him. However, before Kallie could analyze why her gift had worked from a distance, she dismissed it as the foreign word—a word she had never thought would apply to herself—took over her entire being.

Brother.

The word sat on her tongue, unspoken. It felt wrong, too strange to belong there. Perhaps, he had meant brother as in a close friend. But no, that wasn't right either. These men weren't even her acquaintances. She was their captive, their bargaining chip, and they were her latest mark.

She had no brothers, no siblings.

When she opened her mouth to speak, air filled her lungs. Yet Kallie felt as if the oxygen refused to provide her organs the necessary levels they needed to absorb the information provided to her. Shades of violet slipped into her vision again.

This had to be a dream, one of her nightmares. There was no other explanation, for if it wasn't a dream, Kallie was afraid to think how it would change her mission.

She studied the two men before her: Fynn slumped onto the floor while Graeson hovered over him as they worked to stop the bleeding. Hanging at her side, her fingers clutched the dagger, blood smeared on the cold metal. Her enemy's blood.

There was one other possibility.

Her fingers tightened around the handle. Kallie pushed herself off the ground and raised the dagger, pointing the tip of the blade at the men. "Do you think me a fool?"

Graeson studied her, his gaze intense and piercing. Then it shifted.

"Kallie," Graeson said.

He had never used her preferred name and it was a tactic to be sure, an attempt to claim friendship or alliance. Kallie, however, saw it for what it truly was: a threat.

His scimitars hung at his side. If he hadn't planned on using them against her tonight, if they were truly allies, then he wouldn't have brought them.

She knew a trick when she saw one. She was, at the end of the day, a master of manipulation. And this charade was no doubt a trick.

She took a step forward.

"We are not playing a game. This isn't—" Fynn groaned as he tried to stand, but Graeson prevented him from moving any further as he pressed down on his shoulder. Fynn took a slow, shaky breath and continued, "This is no trick. We do not think you are daft. Even when you were a child, you were always quick to see the truth."

Fynn spoke as though he knew her.

He didn't.

She adjusted the dagger in her hand, steadied her body.

Fynn swatted Graeson's hand away and pressed his own palm to his wound. "Kallie, there's a lot we need to discuss, about our family, about what happened to you, but perhaps now is not the time."

Kallie halted as small fractures began to form in her mind. They split across everything she knew to be true, everything she had been told. It was as if a pebble had been thrown against a piece of glass, a small web skirting out from the central point of impact.

"Kalisandre?"

She blinked. The splintering ceased.

"Our mother has tasked us with the job of rescuing you," Fynn said as though that would explain everything. It didn't.

She looked back and forth between Fynn and Graeson, and Graeson's demeanor immediately shifted into that of surprise, bordering on disgust.

He raised his hands and leaned back as though the movement would prevent her from stabbing him too. "Not me. We're not related."

Fynn let out a small, strained laugh. "Now *that* would be something, wouldn't it?"

Graeson pressed his palm into Fynn's wound, and Fynn let out a hiss in response.

She ignored them and instinctively reached for the ring on her finger. "My mother is dead."

"*Our* mother is very much alive," Fynn said.

Her fingers stopped rotating the metal. If that was true, then why had she not known? Did her father know? If he did, why hadn't he told her? Why had he let Kallie believe her mother was dead?

"But my father—"

"That vile man is not your father, Kallie," Fynn interrupted with venom on his tongue. "Domitius is the very reason *our* father is dead.

And he is probably rolling in his grave hearing you call his murderer that. He killed our father and then stole you from us."

The cracks in her mind started again and her breaths became shorter, labored. If King Domitius was not her father then who was? And What did that make her? "You're lying."

"I'm not." Fynn sighed. "If you could just wait until we get to Pontia, she'll show you."

"She who?" Kallie asked. Nothing they were saying made sense.

Fynn sighed in annoyance as if it was her fault she had been supposedly lied to her entire life.

"Queen Esmeray," Graeson answered.

"Queen Esmeray? What does she have to do with this?" Kallie asked. According to her father, the queen of Pontia was a haughty ruler with no real skill. A mere figurehead.

Graeson sighed. "She's your mother."

Kallie took a step back. Her mother? But that couldn't be right. Then Kallie remembered how she had opened up to Graeson earlier. Her confusion quickly turned into outrage. "You knew this entire time? Yet you let me talk about my dead mother and went along with it?" She didn't know why the lie hurt, but it felt like she was the one who had been stabbed, not Fynn. She should never have let herself be vulnerable. Vulnerability meant weakness.

Graeson rubbed his face. "I couldn't tell you. We had agreed to wait until we were home."

"And how is that working out for you?" Kallie snapped back.

Graeson shrugged. "Could be better, could be worse."

"Worse? How could it possibly be worse?" Kallie spat.

"Fynn could be dead," Graeson stated.

Beside him, Fynn chuckled, but it was tinged with pain. "Give me some credit, Gray. I am much harder to kill."

Kallie wanted to shout, to scream. To stab both of them—again. She didn't know what to believe. She had never known what it was like to have a mother and had always craved one. However, if Fynn was right, how did she end up in Ardentol with King Domitius? And why hadn't she, or anyone else for that matter, come for Kallie before now? She was twenty years old. If she had no recollection of any of this, then it had been over a decade and a half since they had been separated.

None of this made sense. It was too coincidental.

"How?" She asked through clenched teeth.

"It's all quite—" Fynn groaned and pressed his palm into his wound, "complicated, Kals."

She flinched at the name that only Myra used. And when she spoke, she nearly screamed. "Why would I believe you? You offer me nothing! Nothing more than vague claims you can't back up."

Kallie turned and started to walk away, running her hands through her hair. Her father had once warned her that people would say anything to trick her. To grab her attention, to pull her to their side. She repeated her father's words over and over again in her head, the warnings he had given her before she had left.

Mortals and gods alike were prone to telling others anything short of the truth if it meant they would get what they wanted. And while she had come to master the art of manipulation, she wasn't immune to it.

"Your gift."

Her steps faltered at those two small words, but she continued forward nevertheless.

"You can do things that no one you know can, Kallie," Fynn added.

She paused, clenching her dagger in her hand. "I don't know what you're talking about," she forced her voice to sound unfazed, but inside she was shaking.

"I know, Kals," Fynn said as if he was responding to her thoughts and goosebumps scattered across her skin.

She glanced over her shoulder, found Fynn now propped up

against the wall as he held his side with a new strip of fabric wrapped around his torso. The spread of blood had slowed and the color began to return to his face.

"What do you mean, 'you know?' Know *what* exactly?" Her words were barely above a whisper. There was no point in hiding her fear. It was written all over her face as her deepest secret was being pulled to the surface. Although she tried, she couldn't keep her hold on it as it began to slip from her grasp.

"Despite what you may think, you are not the only one who has been blessed by the gods, sister."

She narrowed her gaze on the man who now claimed to be her brother.

"It's in our blood." Fynn inhaled sharply. "Domitius may have told you that you were the chosen one, someone special, but you're not."

She stared him down. Whatever he said, whatever his reasoning was, it was a lie. She was special, she was unique. Her father had told her time and time again. No one could do what she could. No one had her gift. But still, doubt crept in. "What do you mean?"

"Our family, among many of the families in Pontia, have special abilities the gods granted to us. While yours is unique, it is not the only gift that exists."

Kallie let out a nervous laugh. "Oh? And what can you do besides be an arrogant ass who steals women? That doesn't seem that special of a trait if you ask me."

Graeson, who she had nearly forgotten about, cleared his throat to cover the amusement written plainly across his face.

Fynn ignored his friend though. "I can hear your thoughts."

Curiosity pulled the words from her mouth before she could think better of it. "Hear my thoughts?"

"Yes, that's why Graeson was waiting out here for you. I knew you were planning to escape."

"And you took your dandy time, too," Graeson grumbled, but Kallie refused to glance at him.

A dry laugh passed her lips. "Anyone could figure that out. It doesn't take you hearing my thoughts to know I want to leave."

"Fine. Then think of something right now. Let me prove that I am not lying."

Kallie rolled her eyes. This little game of his was foolish, but she exhaled a heavy sigh and focused on her thoughts nevertheless.

She turned the dagger and examined her favorite weapon finally back in her hands. She hungered for some sense of familiarity and normalcy, something that had felt so far away these past few days. Even though Myra did not always approve of Kallie carrying a dagger, Myra had designed the dagger with the help of Ardentol's top blacksmith for Kallie's eighteenth birthday. If she was going to carry a weapon, Myra had told her, it better at least be one fit for the future queen. The hilt had a simple black leather strap that was wrapped tightly around the handle, perfectly fitted for Kallie's hand. The cross guards had a delicate gold botanical design which continued as it traveled along the center of the blade. Black writing was perfectly etched down the center in Myra's elegant handwriting in an ancient script Kallie did not know. But Kallie knew what the phrase on her dagger meant: *You are the holder of your own fate.*

She craved Myra's light laughter, her unwavering optimism that constantly boarded on the side of annoyance. And the thoughts made her sad, concerned for her friend's well-being.

"Myra's in good hands, Kals," Fynn said, his soft voice pulling her back from the memory, and her thoughts about Myra halted.

Her legs grew weak as she tried to remain standing. If he was telling her the truth about his gift, a piece of information that could be dangerous in the wrong hands, he might not be lying about being her brother as well. Her world was crashing down around her and she didn't know how to stop it. Her control was slipping.

"I—I don't understand," she stammered, unable to hide the shakiness in her voice.

"As I said, it's complicated." He shrugged a shoulder.

"Then, by the gods, make it uncomplicated!" Kallie's voice reverberated inside the stable. Her knuckles grew white around the dagger still clutched within her palm. If he wanted her to trust him, then he would need to provide her with more information than a simple obtuse statement.

"It would be better coming from our mother," Fynn said. "She has a way of explaining things that I do not possess."

She met his gaze. The outrage sitting at the bottom of her stomach from all of the lies that had just been laid out on the table steadied her. It gave her the strength she needed. "I don't care if you can read minds. I don't care if you claim to be my brother or that my mother—who I don't even remember, mind you—is alive. You've let loose this massive beast and expect what? Me to believe you?"

Her words came out like fire taken straight from the Beneath, but she couldn't stop them. They fell from her mouth without a second thought. She was enraged and no one would stifle the fire within her, not now, not ever. Even if some of her words were tainted with delusion. "I don't even know you! You killed my guards. You've separated me from my closest friend. I am not some fickle girl you can manipulate at your will—"

"No. You're right, Princess, because you're the one who does the manipulating," Graeson said, interrupting her.

He had taken a large step toward her. His proximity to her was nearly suffocating, but Kallie refrained from retreating, tipping her chin up. She was fuming. She was angry and broken. If what Fynn was telling her was true, then it meant that so many other things were . . . were what? A lie? A play on her emotions?

The fractures in her mind deepened. Kallie was spiraling. She needed to stop the tornado she was becoming before she was sucked into the center of its vortex.

She exhaled heavily and took a step toward Graeson, eliminating the small space between them. The toes of her shoes brushed against his, his breath kissed her forehead, and her grip around her dagger remained firm. "That might be the first true statement that has left your lips, Graeson."

She touched her gift, knowing very well she had already used it twice today. She could only push it so far. Still, it greeted her, sluggish but present. With her free hand, she grabbed a hold of his chin, the stubble scratching against her fingers. She wasn't taking any more chances, she wasn't waiting any longer.

A crooked smirk pushed at the corner of his lips and she had the sudden urge to slap it from his face. "If you wanted to kiss me, you could have just asked. No need for the charade, little mouse."

No. Slapping him would not be enough. His words made her want to stab him. And it would be easy to do so. Her dagger in her hand was warm against her palm, ready to strike. But it would be too easy.

And right now, she needed answers. For once in her life, neither stabbing nor kissing a person would grant her access to them.

"Tell me why you kidnapped me." Her voice was commanding and clear as she pulled her gift up to the surface.

Kallie searched Graeson's eyes for the sign that her manipulation was working on him. Her heart pounded. She had used her gift twice tonight, but it should still work. She had just enough left; she had felt it. But instead of the fog she was accustomed to seeing, his eyes became brighter, clearer.

She didn't understand. It hadn't worked at the stream or when they were traveling. But during each of those times, she had been low on food, water, or sleep. There was a clear reason. And perhaps she was truly empty right now. Perhaps she had used up all of her gift earlier in the night, even though she had thought she was getting stronger.

The dagger's hilt bit into her skin. Graeson smirked, his jaw flexing underneath her palm.

"It doesn't work on him, Kals," Fynn said quietly.

A fleeting thought passed through her that Fynn was reading her mind at that moment, but she didn't care about that instant of violation. All she cared about was *why* she had failed. Again.

"What do you mean?" she bit out through her teeth, her grip still firm on Graeson's jaw.

Graeson wrapped his fingers around her wrist, his rings cold against her bare skin. "We have a lot to talk about, little mouse," Graeson said. His eyes flicked over her shoulder but they quickly returned to her as if it was nothing more than a twitch. His voice was low and rattled her insides when he addressed her again, "But the next time you want to know my true intent, all you have to do is ask. No need to force it out of me."

Anger and confusion flooded her system. Who she was, who she had been her entire life now stood on shaky ground. The new information about her past, her family, her life story caused a disturbance in the natural order of her system as the fractures created deeper cracks in her mind and her identity.

The residue of the last few days felt heavy on her skin. She became acutely aware of the fingers that didn't belong to her wrapped around her hand. It should have felt grounding, something to stabilize her at this moment when even the earth she stood on began to shake, but it seemed to have the opposite effect on her. She felt trapped. She needed to scream, she needed to rage. She needed to break out of the walls that seemed to be closing in around her.

At the top of her vision, the slightest movement caught her attention. A dip of Graeson's chin, then the air shifting behind her.

She swung her head around, following his gaze.

Terin stood behind her, his face scrunched with pity. The air she breathed turned hot, thick. At some point, it had stopped raining and now the stable felt too small, too quiet. Her eardrums echoed with the silence that threatened to consume her.

Terin was too close. She needed to move, to run, to fight. But the legs she had trained and strengthened for over a decade betrayed her as they grew weak beneath her weight.

Terin reached toward her and when he spoke, his voice was melodic, like a lullaby, and dulled her raging thoughts. "Sorry, Kals, but it's for the best."

Before she could process what was happening, her mind lost focus as the fog began to take over.

Then realization struck. But it was too late.

Her limbs felt lighter. The ground stopped shaking and disappeared beneath her feet. A pair of arms wrapped around her from behind, encasing her with their heat and the scent of home. But even as a blanket of serenity enveloped her, a tick in the back of her mind began to sound. It commanded her not to fall into the fog but to remain standing, alert.

The promise of sleep came. A moment of reprieve where she did not have to think about false relationships, broken promises, half-told truths, or convoluted plans. And it was too tempting.

The arms around her tightened, preventing her from smacking into the ground as the ghost of sleep coated her skin.

Graeson's voice floated toward her, "Your mother will explain everything, I promise."

As Graeson lifted her, she finally understood what had been happening to her for the past week. She understood why she had drifted in and out of sleep against her will. Why she had grown tired out of nowhere, time and time again.

No one had drugged her, for Terin had a gift too.

CHAPTER 15

KALLIE WOKE UP WITH HER HEAD POUNDING AND HER BODY BRUISED. A bright light streamed into her room, increasing her headache.

"Rise and shine," Dani shouted.

"Go away," Kallie mumbled. She threw the warm blankets—a comfort she had forgotten about after sleeping on the ground for the past week—over her head, shielding herself from the light and Dani's chipper voice.

"No can do, Princess. Fynn insists on sticking to the schedule."

Her eyes sprung open.

Fynn.

The events of last night came crashing down upon her with those four letters. Fynn who could read minds. Terin who had the ability to put her to sleep against her will. Fynn who she *stabbed*. The twins who were supposedly her brothers.

And her parents—

No. She would not think about them now. She couldn't. It was too much to handle. She first needed to figure out how this changed her plans. If they were her family, could she kill them? Manipulate them? She didn't know.

She had no allegiances to them, yet a part of her wanted to know more. She had always felt like a piece of her was missing, and perhaps this was why. Perhaps, she had somehow known intrinsically that she didn't belong in Ardentol. But at the same time, Ardentol was her *home.*

She needed to think this through, but maybe when her head wasn't throbbing. She wasn't in the right mindset to make any rash decisions.

Right now, one night would not change her whole world.

Right now, all she wanted to do was forget and pretend as if it all had been one terrible nightmare. If it was a nightmare, it would make everything less complicated. Kallie had planned on killing the Pontians, enacting revenge against them for abducting her and threatening her father's rule. But did sharing her blood change that?

It should.

Still, an invisible thread tugged in her mind reminding her the Pontians were strangers. Only her relatives by blood, not by love. Not by time. They were not her family.

The two people who she had deemed family had been ripped from her. And by *them.*

She pressed the heels of her palms against her eye sockets. As she tried to shove the thoughts away, a heavy weight dropped on her chest. A pile of clothes lay atop her, including a cloak, a new pair of trousers, and a blouse.

"Get dressed," Dani demanded.

Kallie groaned but relented. She changed into the clean set of clothes while Dani shoved Kallie's worn clothes into a bag.

"Here." Dani threw a small glass tube which Kallie clumsily caught in her hands.

Kallie turned the vial over in her hands. "What is it?"

"Lavender oil," Dani said. Then upon seeing Kallie's scrunched face, she added, "For the headache? It should help soothe it a little."

Kallie opened the bottle and inhaled the potent scent. Her headache dwindled slightly and Kallie's eyes grew wide in surprise. "How did you—"

"Graeson and Fynn told me what happened last night. I figured you might need it. I used to get them all of the time before I gained full control of my gift."

Kallie gave a singular nod, as though that explained everything, but Dani didn't explain further. But she did learn one thing: the entire group had gifts. They knew how to strengthen them, something Kallie had been struggling to do since she was little. They were the key to unlocking her gift.

"And what's your gift?" Kallie asked, holding out the lavender oil.

Dani shook her head, so Kallie pocketed the vile. "Some call me the huntress."

"So you . . . hunt animals?" Was that why she had been the one to find the tracks in the mountains every time? If that was the extent of Dani's ability, it did not seem too special.

"Among other things." Dani's green eyes darkened, sending a shiver down Kallie's spine. There was definitely more to Dani's gift, but the woman was not going to be forthcoming with the information it seemed.

Kallie turned around to make the bed. As she folded the sheets over, she said, "So you're a huntress, Fynn can read minds, and Terin puts people to sleep." Kallie threw the comforter over the wrinkled sheets. "And what about Graeson?" If she could learn more about his ability, perhaps she could figure out why Graeson was not affected by her gift. She needed to find out if there was a loophole. Friend or foe, it did not matter. She did not feel safe if he could evade her gift.

When Dani didn't respond, Kallie glanced over her shoulder and Dani was picking at her nail-beds.

"Best if you let him tell you," Dani said. She quickly gathered the rest of their belongings.

"Why?" Kallie asked as she plopped down onto the poorly made bed.

"There are many things you need to learn about our people." Dani strolled toward the bedroom door, bag in tow. "First lesson, we do not reveal someone else's gift without their knowledge."

Kallie cocked one of her brows. "You know, I could just force you to tell me, right?"

"But you won't, will you?" Dani's eyes swung toward Kallie and her gaze flicked to the vial of lavender in Kallie's pocket and smirked. "Second lesson, don't make empty threats." Dani winked as she turned the doorknob and disappeared into the hallway. Dani's footsteps echoed in the small house, the floorboards bending under each step.

Kallie knew that Graeson was somehow immune to her gift, but was there something more to it? Or was that it? The way Dani had avoided her question made her believe that there was more to his gift than they were saying. Either way, Kallie did not know how to feel about not being able to use her gift against him. Although, it did explain why Graeson had been unaffected at the river the first time she had tried to manipulate him. And it did settle some of her self-doubt creeping into her mind. Kallie could only hope it wouldn't be a problem down the road.

If a problem did arise, she would have to find other ways of getting what she wanted.

THE GROUP WAS GATHERED outside around their horses. According to Fynn, they would be heading north to the nearest port. In two nights' time, they would be sailing toward Pontia. He told Kallie nothing else. But she needed to know everything. Now.

She couldn't wait any longer, even if it was only a few more days until they would land in Pontia. Kallie had waited her entire life.

For her entire life she had believed—had been *told*—that she was special, that her mother had died when she was a child. But all it took was one night. One night and everything she believed to be true crumbled in her hands. One night to make her whole world flip on its axis.

One night and she no longer knew who to believe.

And she no longer knew who she was or where she belonged.

She marched up to the twins, her impatience and frustration building with every step. But when she was face-to-face with Fynn with her hands on her hips and the words on the tip of her tongue, hooves pounded on the ground. Fynn spoke before she could confront him. "Menz? What is it?"

With a brisk tug, Menz's horse stopped a few paces before Fynn. And Kallie didn't know what had sent a chill running through her body: the slobbering horse with its teeth barred or the panicked expression on Menz's colorless face.

"Soldiers—Soldiers in town." Sharp breaths broke up his words. "Looking—"

"Menz, slow down. We cannot understand you," Dani said, joining them.

They were all huddled around the farmer as they waited for Menz to regain his breath. The man was keeled over, one hand on his hat, the other on his chest. Kallie twisted her ring back and forth. Even though the kingdoms were at peace, she had grown up seeing soldiers patrolling Ardentol, protecting it. So then why did a few soldiers spook Menz so much?

Fynn crossed his arms. "We need to go, now."

Fynn made to move but Graeson threw out his arm, stopping him in his tracks. "Will someone tell the rest of us what is going on?"

Having regained control of his breathing, Menz finally said, "When I was at the market, there were soldiers and whispers spreading among the people."

"Whispers of what?" Graeson asked, his hand falling to his side.

Freed, Fynn weaved past them. His hand brushed his side where Kallie had stabbed him. For a moment, Kallie felt guilty about the wound she had dealt to her supposed brother.

The feeling was fleeting.

Menz's gaze flicked to Kallie, then back to Graeson. "They are on the lookout for Frenzia's stolen bride. They found the carriages. There are search parties forming everywhere. They're rumored to be going house to house to see if someone is hiding her. Fynn is right, you need to leave. *Now*."

In an instant, everyone began shuffling around her, but Kallie stood paralyzed. Her vision blurred. At some point, someone spoke to her, but she did not hear anything besides the ringing in her ears. She shouldn't have been surprised that soldiers were searching for her. She wished she could have believed that her father—no, the *king* —trusted that she could handle this on her own. But even though he had trained her himself, he didn't. He didn't trust her. He didn't believe in her.

Had he ever?

Domitius knew she would fail. He didn't even bother to give her the chance to succeed. After all, if Fynn was right, she wasn't his true daughter anyway, so why would he?

She ran her fingers through her hair, her nails scratched against her skull. Her mind was split in two, and she needed more time to figure out who she believed. Yet, the ticking of the clock was nipping at her heels.

She was out of time.

"Kallie." Graeson's voice dragged her back from her scattered thoughts. He pointed to Calamity, and she shoved the divided thoughts down as she mounted the horse.

"Scoot back," Graeson ordered.

Her eyebrows scrunched together, the deep crevices in her forehead meeting in the center. "Sorry?"

"Move back." His words were clipped. "If something happens, I'll need full control over the reins."

Kallie scoffed. "Oh. So now I'm in the way?"

He rubbed his face with his hand in exhaustion. "Just move, Kallie."

"Fine." Kallie scooted back, and Graeson filled the space she had vacated.

Fynn brought his horse around, stopping in front of Menz who stood next to his horse with the reins held loosely in his hand.

"I'll do what I can to lead them off your trail," Menz said.

"Much appreciated," Fynn said. "Until next time, my friend."

"Give my best wishes to the queen." Menz tipped the brim of his hat.

Fynn nodded at the man and turned his attention to his crew. "Let's move."

WITH EVERY TURN THEY MADE, with every snap from within the dark depths of the forest, tensions grew. The Pontians knew they were not safe until they had put enough distance between themselves and the soldiers. However, they could only push their horses so far before they tired them out. And that was the last thing they wanted to do. As a result, Fynn opted for a steady pace.

They rode with a blanket of silence covering them, which left Kallie with too much time to think about the new information she had been told. She still didn't know how it impacted her plans. If what Fynn claimed was true, her captors were her family, her flesh and blood. And King Domitius was not.

Still, the people she rode with were still strangers to her, and she had considered the king her father for her entire life. Or at least since she could remember and that had to count for something—didn't it? But did this new information change that?

Kallie didn't know.

She needed answers. She needed to stop her mind from running in constant circles. However, she knew they would not tell her how she had ended up in Ardentol until she spoke to the queen. And Kallie's frustration grew with every mile they traveled. But there were other questions she could ask to fill the time, so she broke the thick silence. "Why does my gift not work on you?" Then she added, lowering her voice as she spoke to Graeson's back, "Or do I have to force it out of you?"

"I'd like to see you try," Graeson said. Over the past week, their proximity had made her adept at identifying the changes in his voice. Kallie didn't have to see the smug smirk on his face to know it was there.

She began drawing abstract shapes along his back with a gentle finger as she glared at the backs of Fynn and Dani on their horses ahead of them. During the ride, Dani had kept eyeing Fynn's wound. Every time Dani had reached for it, Fynn had swatted her hand away.

To Graeson, she said, "You could at least do me a favor and answer *one* of my questions since none of you will answer any of the important ones."

"If my gift isn't important, then I don't see why I need to tell you."

Kallie sighed. "Why is it such a big secret?"

"It's not. Your brothers and Dani know about it."

"So why can't I?"

He turned his face to the side. Her eyes fell to his lips as he gave her a sidelong glance. "Can I trust you?"

Kallie smirked. "You tell me."

He shook his head. "And there's my answer."

Kallie groaned in frustration.

"If it makes you feel better, Fynn can't read my mind either."

Kallie let that information linger in her mind and said, "I didn't think you were in the business of making me feel better."

He huffed a laugh. "I'm not a complete menace."

Kallie shrugged. "Could have fooled me."

In the silence that followed, she listened to the forest come alive. Hidden birds sang in the distance. Hooves clapped against the ground and the wind whistled as it rattled the leaves of the nearby trees. The forests of Borgania were bountiful during the spring months, life springing from every root.

She debated allowing the silence win. But before she knew it, the question that had been tugging at her tongue escaped before she could pull it back. "What's my mother like?"

Graeson sighed, not in exasperation but in what sounded like sadness. "My mother died during childbirth. I never met her, so one could say I don't know what a true mother is. But Esmeray took me in. She treated me like I was one of her own. She never tried to replace my mother even though I never met her. She talked about her constantly, told me so many stories about her that I felt like I knew her."

He paused and Kallie could feel the love and pain starting to mix with each word. It was the same way she had spoken about her mother, but now that was tinged with complicated thoughts and hidden agendas.

"A piece of Esmeray left with your disappearance. Years had gone, but she was still a shell of herself. When the four of us proposed our plan to rescue you, she . . . she was hesitant. She never gave up on you, but hope is a dangerous thing to live off of. And the circumstances of our kingdom are hard to explain. While I'm sure it doesn't seem like it now, she never stopped loving you. None of us did."

Kallie didn't know what to say, so she said nothing. Only laid her cheek against Graeson's back, for once finding stability in his proximity. His muscles flexed, and she thought about moving, but she didn't have the strength to do so. With Terin's apparent help, last night had been the first time she had slept through the dark hours of the night in days. Yet, the jumbled thoughts in her mind made it feel like she hadn't slept in weeks.

THE HORSES PICKED up their pace. Branches of trees flew past them. The jerking of the horse and the swirls of green and brown whizzing past them caused Kallie's stomach to flip. Her hands instinctively tightened around Graeson's waist.

Kallie swallowed. "What's happening?"

"The soldiers have found us," Graeson said.

The fire brewing under her skin heated her entire body. They had been riding for several hours. Still, she was not any closer to understanding who she was, what this group of people meant to her, and how they fit within her plan. She needed more time. But based on the speed at which they rode, she was out of it.

She had to make a decision. And fast.

The five of them weaved between the trees. Ahead of Kallie, Fynn and Dani's horses rode in tandem. After Fynn gave Dani a quick nod, he then turned back, tipping his head toward Graeson. A moment later, Fynn and Dani rode to the left as Graeson headed to the right. And when Kallie looked to the left, Terin had followed after his brother. The trio disappeared in between the trees, the sound of their horses' hooves quieting as the two parties separated, leaving Kallie and Graeson alone.

"Where are they going?" Fear filled her words.

"It's best if we split up," Graeson stated, tone matter-of-fact.

"But shouldn't one of them have come with us?"

He looked over his shoulder and Graeson's stare bore into her. "Do you think I am incapable of protecting you?"

He was confident. But Kallie had always been told overconfidence was the fast track to one's demise. Even though she had seen Graeson fight, she did not know how many people he could handle on his own. And due to the current circumstances, if the opportunity presented itself, she did not know who she would fight with—him or the soldiers.

"You have always been the priority." Graeson's gaze was unwavering, piercing. "I *will* bring you home. No matter what."

Her heart skipped. She had never been the priority, but rather the object used to achieve it. Thus, rendered speechless, she could only give a small nod.

Graeson returned his attention to the road. No further discussion, no further elaboration.

Soon, Graeson brought Calamity to a trot before the horse exhausted herself, and they traveled in silence once again. Without the others riding beside them, the woods felt eerie, more ominous. Each snap of a twig, each crunch of a leaf, each bristle of leaves sent Kallie looking over her shoulders.

Graeson, however, remained focused on the path ahead, seemingly unconcerned by those who chased after them. But for Kallie, paranoia rose with every passing minute. Still wrapped around Graeson, her palms grew clammy. After all of their planning, Kallie had never planned for this. For the moment when she was unsure what she wanted to happen, for the moment when soldiers chased her as she rode upon the horse of an enemy, arms wrapped around him.

Everything was happening too fast. There was no time to process anything. And Kallie was supposed to have time.

The rustling of leaves grew louder behind them and the sound of pounding hooves clashed with Calamity's steps. Kallie had to make a choice. Here and now.

"Use me," she spat out.

"What?" Graeson snapped, his head swiveling around to look at her as if seeing her would change what she had said.

"Use me," she ordered. "I can help."

He scoffed and turned around. "No."

"Graeson, listen to me." Kallie unwound her arms and gripped his shoulders. "They're after me, so use me as bait."

"That's ridiculous," he said as he shook his head.

Kallie groaned. "Why?"

"First of all, we are trying to rescue you, not lose you." Graeson turned his head to the side, glaring at her, but just as quickly he returned his attention to the path ahead. "Second, how do I know I can trust you? You just tried to run away last night."

"You shouldn't trust me." A streak of light through the trees shone on the ring on her finger. "But trust that I need answers, and staying with you is how I get them."

His shoulders sagged beneath her fingers, so she pressed on. "Once they're close enough, I'll use my gift and I'll force them away."

"And if it fails?"

"I never fail."

Except when I've fought you, Kallie thought. But squashed it as quickly as it entered her mind. She would not let him see how her confidence had wavered while she had been captured, while they had destroyed everything she knew to be true.

"You sure about that?"And the way he tilted his head toward her, scanning her up and down, sent a chill coursing through her body that was quickly replaced with the heat of her building rage. While she may not have been able to manipulate *him*, she was not done trying. She needed answers; she needed the truth. And she would get it. No matter what it took.

"My gift is not my only source of power, Graeson."

He ran his hand through his hair. "Fine, but the moment it goes south, I will intervene." He straightened. And when he spoke next, his voice was huskier, colder, "Just know, I make no promises to be merciful to those who go against me or to those who try to take you away from me again."

It was a challenge, not only for the soldiers they would meet on the ground but for her as well. However, Kallie had been trained to conquer every obstacle she faced. She would not start backing down now.

CHAPTER 16

KALLIE KNELT IN THE FOREST, HER HAIR DISHEVELED, HER CLOTHES ILL-fitting. The ride through the trees had warped her appearance. She no longer looked like the daughter of the legendary king of Ardentol, the ruler of the lands filled with diamonds.

And Kallie supposed she wasn't.

After Graeson had agreed to her plan, he let her dismount while he hid in the trees, watching. Waiting.

Soon, a single soldier broke through the trees. Upon seeing her, he pulled his horse to a stop mid-sprint, its front hooves rearing and kicking the air. The sight made her heart pump faster. And for once, she was thankful for being skittish of horses. The fear that shook her body was very much real, making her look like a damsel in need of rescuing.

When the soldier dismounted, he unsheathed his sword. She did not recognize the soldier, but she did recognize the crest embroidered on the sheath. The Ardentolian crest contained three mountain peaks split by a river. And even from her place on the ground, she knew the words lining the bottom: *You must climb the mountain to rule the world.*

She had lived by those words her entire life, and even with the confusion that now surrounded her upbringing, she still lived by them. Kallie's goal had not changed. Just the route she would take to achieve it.

When the soldier was no more than an arm's reach away, he stopped. He knelt, his breathing ragged, either from the ride or from the nerves spiking his body. From this distance, she noted the soft, boyish cheeks, the patches of stubble lining his jaw, the naivety shining in his gaze. He was a recent recruit to the Ardentolian military.

"My lady? Is that you?" He whispered as though she would fly off like a bird in the night.

Kallie feigned a sniffle and forced her body to shake while keeping her head down as she nodded.

"Princess?" He leaned forward. "Are you injured?" He extended his free hand. With smooth, shaky fingers he lifted her chin. When his eyes met hers, she laced her words with her gift.

Upon hearing the whispered command, the haze filled his gaze. Kallie smirked behind the shadow of her hair as the soldier's hand dropped. He stood. She hoped Graeson was still watching from the shadows of the trees so he could see that he was wrong. He had no right to doubt her gift. One day, Graeson would learn the consequences of doubting her ability.

As the soldier returned to his horse, a breeze caught her hair, blocking her vision. Goosebumps scaled her arms. Nearby, leaves crunched and a horse's scream followed.

Kallie stood, the blood rushing from her head as she prepared for an ambush. She reached for her dagger only to remember its absence. Her breath escaped her.

The soldier was dead on the ground, his throat slit. Blood dripped from *her* dagger as Graeson stood over the boy's body.

"By the gods! Why did you do that?" Her heart pounded against her chest. She hadn't even heard the man scream.

Graeson dragged his attention from the dead soldier, his face void of emotion. No remorse, no regret. And Kallie did not understand. The man had done nothing. Had she missed something?

"Graeson, answer me," she commanded.

He looked from Kallie to the body and then to the weapon in his hand. He dug a dark cloth from his pocket and wiped the blade clean, and he kept his focus on the blade. "I told you I couldn't trust you. We do not know how long your gift lasts. He was a threat. He—"

"He was a *boy*," Kallie interrupted.

When he looked at her, fury colored his face. "So was I once. And now look at me, Princess."

Their eyes locked onto each other, and neither of them spoke. Their stubbornness would have kept them there longer, but shouts from the forest pulled their attention from each other as Terin broke through the trees on horseback, his face pallid. Deep maroon splotches covered his clothes.

Terin brought his horse to a stop before them. "Graeson, we need you. *Now.*"

SURROUNDED BY A HOARD OF SOLDIERS, Dani and Fynn stood back-to-back. Three soldiers lay on the ground, but eight remained standing. The two Pontians swung their weapons in a harmonious rhythm as though they were performing a dance they had rehearsed for years. But with every twist, Fynn grimaced. The twitch in his face was slight, unnoticeable to a stranger, but Kallie had spent the past week studying the Pontians. And while Dani was fierce, it was clear their movements were slowing. They were losing.

"Stay with her," Graeson told Terin as he jumped off his horse.

When Terin nodded and Graeson handed Kallie the reins, Kallie opened her mouth to protest, but she hesitated. The look on his face made the hairs on her next stand.

"Do not test me right now, Princess." Graeson shoved the reins at her. "Stay with Terin," he commanded, and this time, she took them begrudgingly.

Graeson weaved between the trees as Kallie shifted in her seat, readying herself to dismount. She would not allow him to command her.

"You will only get in his way," Terin said next to her, making Kallie freeze in place.

"I will not." Kallie knew how to fight and she fought well when she was trying. She would not be a hindrance but an asset. Didn't they understand that? On the other hand, Graeson did just admit that he did not trust her. Perhaps her brother did not either.

"Kalisandre," Terin said, and the look on his face forced her back into the saddle.

She leaned to the right to peer through the trees. The soldiers were too busy fighting Dani and Fynn to notice the creature slinking out of the woods, for Graeson was not a man. Neither a stranger nor a friend. At that moment, he was a beast, the monster in the myths she had been told about as a child personified.

His movements were rigid, yet fluid; confident, yet inhuman as he struck one soldier down, the woman falling to her death in silence. Kallie was both terrified and awestruck as she watched Graeson work. Unlike when she had seen him use his skills before, she was not his mark and could afford to watch this time. His weapons became an extension of himself as he swept the scimitars across the ground and sliced through two more soldiers. And Kallie understood why the others had allowed Graeson to guard her alone.

Graeson fought as if the gods had molded him for the sole purpose of slaying his enemies.

His sharp blades slid across the dirt as he stood tall once again. They hung at his sides, his shoulders hunched like a bear approaching its prey. The soldiers before him stood paralyzed as they took in their fallen comrades. And then one soldier, a burly man, wider than Graeson, charged.

Metal met metal as the sword clashed against the scimitars.

While the man distracted Graeson, another soldier took his chance and slid across the ground, aiming for Graeson's ankles. A thin layer of sweat formed on Kallie's palms as she clenched her fingers around the reins and waited for the blow.

It never came though.

Graeson jumped back, simultaneously avoiding contact with the blade while putting the needed distance between himself and the first opponent.

The second attacker pushed himself off the ground. With the back of his hand, he wiped his mouth of blood. Then the two soldiers sprinted forward.

One swung high, the other low. One was quick, the other rough. Yet, Graeson blocked each blow. Metal clashed, the smell of iron tainted the air.

As the three fought, Fynn and Dani continued their dance with the three remaining soldiers. Dani's positioning seemed jilted though. Then Kallie noted how the woman kept putting herself on one side of Fynn, and Kallie realized Dani was providing support to Fynn's injured side.

While Dani struck offensively, Fynn dealt out only defensive maneuvers as if he was preserving his energy. Still, each move was calculated, careful; his ability to analyze his opponent, admirable.

Then Fynn did the unspeakable and closed his eyes.

Kallie wanted to shout, to yell at him. For what fool intentionally made himself vulnerable to an opponent? Her breath hitched as a strike came toward his neck. A death blow, for sure.

Even though he didn't see it coming, Fynn managed to dodge it.

Then Kallie understood. He was listening to his opponent's thoughts, seeing each move before and as he made it. Even with a fresh wound stunting his movements, his ability to fight, he was still capable.

Still, the Pontians struggled. Exhaustion wore on their movements. Dirt and sweat made their hair stick to the sides of their faces.

And near them, Graeson continued to fight against the two soldiers. Kallie had seen what he could do; she had seen the brutal deaths of her soldiers he had caused when the Pontians had attacked her carriage. Had seen the merciless way he had fought. Yet Graeson had not put an end to the lives of these soldiers. He fought as if something was holding him back.

Kallie turned to Terin. "They need help."

Terin did not look at her, his gaze locked on his brother. "We stay put."

His words sent her emotions spiraling. She did not care for this group of people—blood or not. But she did not want them to die either. They still served a purpose. "Terin, Fynn is injured," she spat. "They won't be able to keep this up!"

"Graeson's here. It will be fine."

"One man is not enough!" When Terin did not respond, she rubbed her palms against her face in agitation. "If you won't help them, then I will."

Terin dragged his attention away from the fight. "No, you will not. You will sit here and do *nothing*, Kalisandre. Your interference will only make matters worse."

"You might be my brother, but you do *not* control me. No man does."

With one hand, she grabbed the pommel, lifted a leg over to the other side, and then Terin's fingers locked around her wrist. "Unhand me," Kallie said through clenched teeth.

"Then stay on your horse. Or else I will force you to stay. And I promise the dreams you will have will make your past nightmares seem childish."

Her heart thudded against her chest. Her gaze dropped to his hand. It would be easy for her to manipulate him. To force him to help or to unhand her—to do anything she commanded because unlike for Graeson, Kallie knew her ability would work on Terin.

But alas, her shoulders sagged. "Fine. But if they die, their blood is on your hands." While she did not want to sit here and do nothing, she also knew she could not waste her gift. So instead Kallie did the only thing she could. She spat on his shoe.

He rolled his eyes, but let go of her wrist. "I swear you haven't changed since you were little."

Avoiding his stare, Kallie righted herself on Calamity's back. Then Dani's voice forced their attention back to the fight, "Gray! Don't you think you've played with them enough?"

A maleficent grin slid across Graeson's face as he chuckled. "I suppose." And the intensity of his voice, the power swirling around him sent a chill through Kallie's body.

She had been right. He had been holding back.

Up until now.

As he looked over his opponent, Graeson's tongue ran across his teeth. The hunger for blood was clear upon his face as he transformed further from the man and closer to the beast, as though he had broken free from whatever cage he had been trapped inside.

Graeson kneed the soldier, forcing him to fold in half, then slammed the man into the dirt. Standing directly above his opponent with his scimitars on each side of the man's face, Graeson turned back to the other soldier who stood paralyzed.

Kallie could neither hear nor see what Graeson said to the soldier, but she saw the fear in the man's eyes, saw the darkened spot growing larger on his pant leg.

After a moment, the man sprinted away from Graeson on wobbly legs and toward the trees where Kallie and Terin hid. When the soldier spotted them, he dug his heels into the ground and raised his shaking hands.

Then recognition befell his face. "Princess?"

Kallie's frustration and disappointment were palpable. *These* were the men the king had sent to rescue her? It was pitiful. An insult, really. They were young, recently trained with little to no experience. Their naivety a five o'clock shadow on their face. Kallie wanted to laugh, but she restrained herself.

The man had suffered enough humility for one day.

And Kallie had one command left inside of her. She had made her choice, and hopefully, it was the right one.

Kallie spoke so only Terin could hear, "Trust me."

When Terin did not move, she took his silence as answer enough and nodded to the man.

"Are you . . . are you hurt?" The soldier asked as his gaze bounced between Kallie and Terin.

After Kallie shook her head, the soldier took a step forward but halted when Calamity shifted on her hooves.

"It's okay," Kallie said, urging him forward. When Kallie reached for his hand, he gave it and she whispered, "Forget this fight. Your fellow soldiers died by the jaws of a creature from the legends of old. Go back to King Domitius and tell him to end the search. His daughter is gone."

When the familiar fog clouded the whites of the soldier's eyes, she released his hand. Without hesitating, he took off into the woods. At least he was faster than the last one.

Kallie returned her attention to Graeson. The soldier on the ground stared at the sky, expressionless. Blood surrounded him.

Graeson wiped his blades off on the grass, then sheathed them. He pulled out a small dagger she didn't know he carried and threw it at one of the remaining soldiers. The dagger struck the soldier's chest, and the man slumped to the ground.

And as Dani's other opponent watched the soldier fall, Dani slid her sword between the man's ribs. Blood spewed from his mouth, and he fell beside his comrade. Dani then spun and slit the last soldier's throat.

As the last enemy dropped to the ground, Dani faced Fynn at last. He put his arm around her shoulders and she helped guide him as they walked toward the trees. Fynn's limp was prominent as he leaned against his comrade. Their breaths came fast as sweat dripped from their foreheads and seeped through their clothes. But by the graces of the gods, neither of them was injured—well, injured from this fight anyway. And while Kallie still thought of them as strangers, she was thankful Fynn had survived. If he had died today, she knew it would have been her fault and she did not know how she would feel if that had been the case. She was not ready to take on that burden.

When Terin and Kallie met the others in the bloodied field, Calamity stopped beside Graeson without Kallie's signal. The horse shook her head at its owner, and Graeson patted the horse's neck, practically hugging the horse as he laid his head against it. Calamity neighed and Graeson's shoulders sagged.

After a moment, Graeson lifted his gaze to meet Kallie's and she shifted on the saddle. "I'm surprised you didn't run off," Graeson said.

"I'm surprised you're not dead," Kallie retorted, but it was a lie. She had seen him fight and was both amazed and frightened by the display.

Having seen through the lie, Graeson chuckled. And Kallie turned away but her lips still twitched.

"Our horses?" Dani asked Terin, the exhaustion in her voice clear.

"Tied up in the woods over here. Come on."

While the others headed into the words, Graeson walked toward the fallen soldiers. Bending down next to one, he pulled his dagger from the body. After he wiped it clean, he returned it to the sheath he kept hidden and then walked back to where Kallie and Calamity waited.

When Kallie scooted backward on the saddle, Graeson jumped up onto Calamity, somehow remaining graceful despite the energy he had already exerted.

He reached to his back and pulled out her dagger. Kallie froze. Did he distrust her so much that he felt the need to threaten her to cooperate? Even after what she had learned last night?

"Prove to me you won't stab me in the back, little mouse."

Kallie eyed it, hesitating.

She did not trust him, nor he, her. So why did he offer her a weapon she could use to kill him? It had to be a trap. A test to see if she was stupid enough to challenge him after he killed a handful of men with the hunger of a wild beast.

He quirked a bow. A test then. But Kallie had made her choice a while ago.

She would stay with them. She would learn from them. But she would not trust them.

Not yet. Not when so many of her questions still danced in the air with nervous energy.

Kallie gingerly took the dagger from him. She ran her fingers across the surface of the blade, the old language still clear: *You are the holder of your own fate.*

A reminder.

And a warning.

Her choice would either be the end of her or the beginning of something new. But either way, it was hers to make.

She only hoped she had made the right one.

CHAPTER 17

TWO DAYS HAD PASSED. WITH THE THREAT OF SOLDIERS SEARCHING FOR Kallie, they rode in silence once again. As a result, no one had given her any more information. Although she had not bothered to press the issue, knowing it was pointless to do so anyway.

The paranoia that had accompanied them had only drifted away once they had made it to the dock where a boat waited for them. Upon their approach, the captain, a man who went by Squires and had a stocky build, greeted them. It was clear that the others were well acquainted with the captain when the tension diminished, and smiles lit their faces for the first time since the fight with the Ardentolian soldiers.

She had been told the journey to Pontia by sea would not last long —about two days. And Kallie didn't know if that was a blessing or not. Traveling exhausted her, paranoia wore on her. But the weight of the answers to all of her questions across the Red Sea threatened to drown her. And despite her stomach flipping when she stepped off the unstable wooden boards and onto the boat's deck, Kallie knew she couldn't turn back. She needed to face whatever awaited her in Pontia.

It was her first time on a boat. During one trip to Kadia, she had seen a ship in the process of being built. But this boat was smaller, though still sturdy in appearance. Before now, she had never needed to board one, and her inexperience was as clear as the sky to the captain upon meeting her. However, Captain Squires dismissed her concerns, then quickly told her about the first time he had stepped on a ship when he was a child. Apparently, in a matter of minutes, he was taking the wheel and navigating the dangerous waters. Now, he preferred the company of the water over people. And that much was clear by his rancid stench of fish and rum seeping from his pores. The smell was sickening.

As Kallie stood at the helm next to him while the boat ventured further from the shore, the captain continued his prattling, oblivious to her uneasiness. He went on about the importance of having the right mindset and so forth.

Then Kallie got sick all over his boots. He shut up real quick after that.

Now, as noon approached, Kallie clung to the railing alone, knuckles stark white, afraid to move as the small passenger boat rocked from the waves. Her stomach sank further into itself. On ground, she could run. On ground, she could retreat. But here, despite the vast ocean before her with no end in sight, she could only go as far as the edge of the boat. And each strike of the wave against the ship was a reminder of the cage surrounding her and only fueled her sickness.

She *almost* wished they were back on the horses.

Kallie wasn't used to sea travel—and apparently wasn't made for any sort of long-distance traveling if this journey was any indication. Nerves were not an unfamiliar companion to her. Whenever she had an upcoming assignment, the nerves would buzz in the pit of her stomach. On one occasion she had traveled to a village a day's ride away from the palace. The village was overseen by a lord who had been complaining a little too loudly about his dislike for the crown. To test her ability, King Domitius had sent Kallie to manipulate the man. It was the first time she had traveled such a distance for one of the king's tasks and the pressure had turned her stomach sour.

But the nerves she experienced now were incomparable as they rattled her bones.

Footsteps approached and Kallie's fingers flexed as she tried to get a hold of the returning sickness.

"Thinking of jumping?" All too familiar with his voice, she simply groaned at Graeson. She did not trust herself to open her mouth—for more reasons than one.

He chuckled as he leaned on the railing beside her. "Well, if you were thinking about jumping, don't. The creatures below are far worse than those above."

"Why?" Kallie asked, the word quiet on her lips. She spared him a glance, noted the smirk on his face. He was making fun of her. Annoyed, she stared back at the sea.

Although she dismissed him, Graeson continued, "According to the stories, a Kraken guards these seas."

Kallie rolled her eyes. "A Kraken? Really? "Do you think me a child?"

"No, truly. They say it protects Pontia from our enemies and can tear apart massive ships before the sailors aboard even know what is happening below the ship. And some say it is as long as four battleships lined up, with four rows of teeth. Others say it only appears that way because of its massive tentacles."

Kallie scoffed. "Surely a myth."

"Myths, legends—what makes them any different from the stories in our history books? We believe in those stories, don't we? And aren't myths based on some truth?"

Kallie shrugged, her grip on the railing loosening. "All right. *If* this creature is real, how do Pontians manage to escape it?"

He turned around, his back against the railing. "We follow the traditions."

She looked at him. "Traditions?"

He tipped his chin and she followed his gaze. Squires and his men were throwing buckets of liquid into the water. The right corner of Graeson's mouth turned upward. "Blood of the enemy."

Kallie inhaled sharply, and Graeson chuckled. "Only joking. It's the blood of goats and some of their organs of course."

"That's disgusting," Kallie said, and just thinking about it brought on another wave of nausea.

He wrinkled his nose, the expression softening his features. "When you think about it." He shrugged. "So just . . . don't think about it."

"Great advice. Thanks." Kallie shook off the image, then her eyebrows quirked in confusion as she thought about the logic behind the act. "But how does that help? Wouldn't that attract it?"

"Think of it as an offering or a sacrifice. If you want something from the gods, you provide an offering in exchange. The goat is our offering to the Kraken."

Kallie nodded slowly. She supposed it made sense, although it still seemed odd. Then as she went to pose another question, the boat hit a wave. She lost her footing, stumbling. But Graeson's hand found her waist, stabilizing her.

They stayed like that for a moment. She should move, but for some reason, she couldn't pull herself away. She couldn't even look away from him. Their eyes were locked onto each other as though there was a magnetic charge between them, keeping them from pulling apart.

At some point, this man had ceased to be an enemy. At least not in black-and-white terms. She had grown up hating the Pontians, believing them to be a kingdom full of selfish, reckless, arrogant people. And while Graeson was arrogant, his actions reckless, and his stubbornness selfish, he didn't feel like he was the enemy. But what did that make him then?

All she knew was that his palm was warm against her side, a simple comfort she hadn't experienced in a while.

She was no longer their captive. Now, she was here by her own doing. She could have left many times. But in the woods, watching this group of strangers fight to protect her stirred something inside of her. And staying with them did not have to mean Kallie had to give up the crown King Rian promised her. She could return to him after she spent some time with the Pontians. She could learn how to strengthen her gift. She could uncover the truth about her past, how she ended up in Ardentol.

She would find a way to have it all.

One of the crew members tossed a bucket onto the ground and the sound caused Graeson to pull away. The magnetic pull weakening. He cleared his throat and brushed his fingers through his hair, messing it up, the ends scattering in different directions. Kallie stared at the hand that had provided her a moment of peace, then quickly turned away from him as she focused back on the waves.

If she wanted the Frenzian throne, she would have to keep her distance. Or may the gods prevent any rumors from spreading. It was different before when they were traveling alone and before she knew the truth. Before, getting close to him served a purpose. Now . . . now things were more complicated than she could have imagined.

"Anyway, if you're hungry, there's food down under," Graeson said, his voice carrying an unusually awkward tone.

Kallie shook her head. "Not hungry, thanks." Which was only partly true. But she needed to forget about what almost happened. She didn't need any distractions—as fun as they could be.

From the corner of her eye, she saw him nod. For a moment, he lingered, tapping his fingers against the railing as though he wanted to say more. Then the moment passed and he abandoned her at the edge of the ship.

A breeze swept by and Kallie hugged herself, the chill of the ocean peppering her skin with goosebumps. This next stage of her journey would be long, she could feel it on the mist of the ocean.

KALLIE SWAYED IN A HAMMOCK, a bucket gripped in between her hands, eyes scrunched shut as she tried to refrain from puking her guts out. Once Graeson had left her side, she had grown tired and had needed to lay down, so she had made her way to her room. Yet sleep once again evaded her.

The ship rode over a large wave, gliding in the air. That second of airtime was enough to cause her stomach to flip. She brought the tin bucket she had found in her room up to her face and dry heaved.

After she regained her ability to breathe, she heard someone knocking on her cabin's door. She groaned, unable to make any other intelligible sound, and hoped whoever it was had heard her. Or just left her alone. Preferably the latter.

A second later though Terin peered through the cracked open door. Her enemy-turned-brother stared down at her with a concerned look. He had given her a similar look when Kallie had tried to escape the camp that first night with Myra. Had he felt guilty for pretending to have abducted her? For playing a part in killing her guards? Or was it full of pity? Pity for the girl who knew little about her heritage and nothing about the supposed truth of her upbringing.

And although a day had passed since the news, Kallie still did not know how to act around the twins. If they were truly her brothers, her flesh and blood, then she supposed she should make an effort in forging some bond with them. Even if it was only a small one. She tried to force a small smile onto her face, but the twitch of her lip was forced. She knew it, Terin knew it.

"Need anything?" Terin asked, his brows bunching in the middle.

Kallie shook her head, regretting the quick movement immediately when it increased her nausea. She needed the sickness to wash away with the waves. And quickly.

"First sick from riding horseback, now sick from the sea? I'm starting to think traveling is not your friend." The corners of his lips tipped into a small smile.

Closing her eyes, Kallie raised her brows in agreement.

He stepped into the small room. "I could help you, you know."

She pried one eye open, giving him a side-long glance. After finding out he had been the one to put her to sleep again and again in those first few days, she had felt violated. While seemingly harmless, she couldn't shake the feeling that every time he slithered into her mind and forced her to sleep that he was making her vulnerable—to him, to Fynn, and to anyone else around. She'd take nausea over losing control over her own mind any day. Though it was ironic since Kallie forced a similar loss of control upon her own victims.

Still, she didn't want Terin's help. She didn't need him to fiddle with her mind and her dreams. She didn't need people messing with her mind. Especially someone who was her enemy only days ago.

She needed to have a clear head when she arrived in Pontia. She needed to face her mother with her mind untouched and focused.

Another wave crashed into the ship. Her stomach flipped with it, but Kallie had nothing left in her stomach to give. She had skipped lunch, and she didn't think she'd be able to eat or drink anything until the ship docked in two days.

"Kals, let me help." Terin knelt beside her. "It's the least I can do."

Although his voice and gaze appeared genuine, she hesitated. Myra was the closest person she had to a sibling growing up. And while Kallie was used to people serving her, she wasn't used to people looking at her the way Terin was now.

She hadn't even known the twins for more than a week and a half, yet she felt this strange bond growing between them. It tugged on her heart, and she didn't know what to do about those feelings. But as the hammock rocked again and despite Captain Squires' promise that the swinging bed would help calm the sickness, she knew she had no other choice. She needed rest. She needed to shut out everything else if she wanted to meet her mother with a sound mind. So when Terin tilted his head and asked once again if he could help, Kallie sighed, then nodded in defeat

Then Terin's hand found hers and a sudden heaviness coated her body.

CHAPTER 18

SOMEONE WAS CALLING HER, BECKONING HER FORWARD.

"Kalisandre," the voice was warm and made her name feel like warm honey dripping over freshly baked bread.

Her eyelids fluttered upward. A man stood before her. And although his face was obscured by shadows, his presence was soothing. It felt like a childhood toy stored away in a chest and forgotten shortly after closing the lid.

The man extended his hand, and a gust of wind blew by them. Mist stroked her face, and with it came the smell of sea salt. The sound of rushing water met her ears.

She took a step forward, and her feet were instantly soaked. Water pooled at her feet and a lake spread out before her. The light of the sun bounced off of the surface causing the water to glisten beneath it. Speckles of orange and purple moved beneath the surface. Fish danced around her feet, the sun hit the scales of their bodies making their color incandescent.

She looked up at the man who stood just over an arm's reach away, a crooked smile splayed across his face. His hand was still extended, waiting for her.

Kallie placed her hand in his. His palm was coarse and warm beneath *her touch. His long fingers wrapped around her hand and squeezed, then he pulled her toward him.*

And smiling, she walked forward, the water raising with each step she took.

VOICES, incoherent and scattered, pulled her from the lake.

"We should have told her," someone nearby said.

"Do you really think that would have been believable?" another asked.

Then silence.

Were they talking about her? They had to be. She wanted to ask why they hadn't told her the truth in the beginning. To ask why they had come up with such a ludicrous plan to get her to Pontia.

Still, she didn't ask any of those questions. She couldn't form them on her lips. She couldn't demand the truth from them if she was unwilling to share hers.

"Do you think—" someone began but got caught off as another interrupted. "Hold on, she's waking."

Fingers wrapped around her wrists and the voices faded into the darkness of her mind as the heaviness came again. Unlike in the past, she didn't fight the darkness but fell into it, happy to put off the truth of everything she needed to face.

THE FACELESS MAN looked down at her, and she reached up to touch his cheek. Perhaps, if she touched his skin, his features would come into focus. But when the tips of her fingers were a hair's breadth away, the man wrapped his hand around hers and brought it to her face instead. His hands

were warm as though they had been in the sun for hours, yet she still could not identify him.

She tilted her head as she leaned into his hand now clasping hers. "Who are you?" She whispered, afraid to scare the man away.

He did not respond. Instead, he guided her deeper into the lake. Wet sand mushed between her toes. The bottom half of her dress was soaked and the fabric billowed around her as the water rose to her knees. The only ripples in the water came from their steps on the otherwise paper-smooth surface.

On the other side of the lake, a towering waterfall surrounded the other half of the lake. Water cascaded off the cliffs, foaming at the bottom, though somehow managing to leave the lake's surface undisturbed.

The water was at Kallie's ribcage now. The man led her toward the rushing water and Kallie's heart fluttered. As they walked forward, the path became slick and marble glittered beneath her feet, forming a pathway leading to the heart of the waterfall.

They followed the path, and as they approached the falling water, Kallie flinched in anticipation.

FIRM HANDS WRAPPED around her and Kallie leaned into the warmth. Her head felt detached from her body as it bobbed back and forth. Her skin, clammy. A cold feeling began to rise in her throat and her stomach churned.

"It's happening again," someone said.

"One more time, Terin," someone else groaned in response, their voice strained.

Then a heavy warmth cocooned her body, a blanket, and replaced the nausea that was quickly forming. She wanted to return to that lake, wherever it was. She wanted to feel the heat of the sun. She wanted to feel solid ground beneath her feet. Anything but this rocking motion. Her mind drifted as she thought of the figure, and she felt herself being pulled back toward the lake.

A PAIR of marble eyes stared down at her. A marble statue of a woman towered over Kallie. The statue was beautifully crafted, the lines of her face appearing impossibly soft for being made out of stone. The statue reminded Kallie of the statues in the welcoming hall in the castle. And the one before her contained some resemblance to Sabina, but at the same time, it was vastly different. Besides the long flowing hair and the overall body shape, this statue was much more detailed. Delicate. Her facial features, which were always hidden in the statues she had seen in Ardentol, were unobscured and prominent. A small pointy nose with large lips had been carved into the stone. The goddess's gaze was soft, yet stern. Powerful.

Why was the goddess here, hidden behind the waterfall? And why did the man take her here?

In the pit of her stomach, her gift stirred. It became wild. Bubbling up as though it wanted to explode from her body. A grating against her brain began, bringing Kallie to her knees. She groaned out in pain as the pain continued, spreading. Intensifying. Her mind was being torn in two.

Kallie looked back toward the man out of fear of whatever was happening to her. But when she turned, he was nowhere to be found. Beads of sweat glittered across her arms. Then her vision flashed white.

CHAPTER 19

KALLIE WOKE TO DARKNESS WITH THE URGENT NEED TO RELIEVE herself. Her body ached from sleep as though she hadn't moved since she shut her eyes. She tried to think back to her dream, but she had little recollection of it. And then her bladder pressed against her. She untangled her legs from the blankets and climbed out of the hammock.

"Ow."

She released a yelp at the voice that was not her own. She was not alone. She squinted into the shadows, forcing her vision to adjust to the darkness. Slowly, an outline of a person formed.

She went to grab her dagger stowed beneath her pillow, but when the individual said, "Watch where you step," Kallie froze. She knew that deep voice.

"Graeson," she hissed. "What are you doing in my room?"

The floorboards creaked. "Well, I *was* sleeping until your large, clumsy feet stepped on me."

Kallie frowned. Her feet were not large. If anything, they were very much average, but she didn't have the energy to argue. "Whatever. Move. My clumsy feet and I have to pee."

In the small cabin space, Kallie couldn't avoid her arm brushing against Graeson's as she slid by him. She opened the door and headed toward the small closet Squires had shown her when they had arrived. She squatted over the bucket and did her business quickly.

After washing her hands in the basin, she shook them dry and headed to the deck, but a lit lantern made her stop in her tracks.

In the glow of the light, Graeson stood overlooking the railing at the bow of the boat. He must have followed her out of the room.

At the sound of her steps, Graeson turned. Although Kallie had planned on returning to bed, her feet were already leading her to the open spot beside him.

She looked out toward the sea. The waves were calmer than they had been in the day. On the horizon, a thin line of gold layered the surface of the sea. Dawn was approaching.

"How long was I asleep?" Kallie asked.

Graeson rubbed the back of his neck. "You were in and out of sleep for the past day and a half."

"A day and a half?"

Graeson nodded. Kallie supposed her body needed the rest after everything. And despite her previous hesitancy to allow Terin to use his gift on her, she was thankful he had. She gripped the railing.

"Nervous?" Graeson asked.

Kallie shrugged and kept her gaze on the open sea before her. "The water seems to be calmer now, so I think I'll be fine." She knew he wasn't referring to her seasickness, but she didn't want to talk about everything else that was on her mind. According to what she had overhead, they would arrive at Pontia's shore by nightfall.

Out in the water, pieces of debris floated, so she used it as an opportunity to change the subject. "What do you think happened there?"

He chuckled softly, shaking his head. "I don't think you'll believe me."

Her eyebrow arched in disbelief. "No."

His laughter that followed was carefree, different from the usual mocking tone she had become familiar with. And it made her stomach squirm, yet her nausea had long since sedated.

"Yes," he said.

Kallie searched the water for the mythical beast, but there were no long tentacles. No strange stirrings beneath the surface. But here Graeson was, laughing at her, but when Graeson spoke she heard no lie tinting his words.

This man who could kill a person without question believed in mythical monsters. And somehow she was not surprised. For wasn't he too a monster? Weren't they all living, breathing beings with unimaginable skills and gifts that most humans didn't even know existed? Perhaps, she should not be so quick to dismiss stories she had once thought fictional.

They watched the boat traverse the waters in silence, and for once, it was not unbearable. It was almost . . . comfortable. Kallie did not think about what the future held or what decision she would make when the moment she was forced to do so came. She forgot the roles they played.

At this moment, he was not her captor, nor was she his captive. At least for the time being. For now, she would allow herself to exist at this moment.

WHEN THE SUN rose and Graeson asked her if she was hungry, this time Kallie nodded. Her nausea had subsided, allowing her to eat a small breakfast followed by a decent lunch with relative ease. Besides joining her for breakfast though, Graeson had made himself scarce throughout the day, helping the captain and his crew wherever needed. The captain at first refused his help, but Graeson had insisted. Since then, he had stayed busy, either tying knots, moving cargo, keeping watch over the seas, or doing some other task that kept him away.

And his absence felt strange. But to avoid thinking about how his absence may or may not have affected her, Kallie joined the others at one of the tables on the deck. Terin had brought out two sets of cards and was currently showing Kallie how to play a game called fifteen-hundred. It was a team-based game where the players tried to form matches with their cards. Face cards held more value than numbered cards, jokers and the queen of spades being the highest. Each player had the chance to sabotage the opposing team. The first person to get rid of all of their cards won the round. The remaining cards in the losing team's hands would be subtracted from their total score. The first team to 1500 points won, hence the name.

As Terin finished dealing out seven cards to each player, Kallie asked, "But how is it fair if Fynn can read our mind and know what cards we have in our hands?"

Fynn picked up his deck with his signature cocky smirk. "I suppose you will just have to work on blocking me."

"Blocking you?" Kallie asked, curious.

He huffed. "No gift is invincible, Kals. Take Terin's for instance. He can only force people to sleep for limited amounts of time. If he puts someone to sleep for too long, the threat of a coma is increased if he is not careful and Terin experiences uncomfortable side effects from time to time as well."

Kallie leaned against the table as she brought her cards together, but she held off from looking at them. "And yours?"

"If there is a lot of activity going on or if I have suffered a serious injury—"

Kallie straightened in her chair. "Like when I stabbed you?"

Fynn glared at her and grimaced. "Yes, hence why I could only focus on reading the thoughts of one of our attackers. But anyway, people can learn to block certain thoughts from me. Of course, this is only helpful when people *know* about my gift and have developed a strong enough will to form walls in their minds. It's not foolproof, and if I concentrate hard enough, I usually can break through those walls. But this," he waved to the cards spread across the table. "This is just a game. I don't need to cheat to win." He winked and began rearranging the cards in his hands.

Kallie took a sip of the rum Squires had let them get into before they sat down to play. Then she concentrated as she picked up her cards. She imagined walls forming around the details she did not want Fynn to know. With tall marble walls in place, Kallie smiled. "We will see about that."

SIX ROUNDS in and two glasses of rum deep, still Kallie did not believe for a second that Fynn was not cheating. The twins were winning by a landslide while the women had only won a single round—and Kallie had a strange feeling it was a pity win.

Dani slammed her cards against the table. "All right, Fynn. You're cheating."

"He has to be cheating," Kallie said in agreement as she tossed her cards face down on the table and crossed her arms.

Terin snorted and Fynn's expression was smug, not a single ounce of innocence to be found in the slight curve of his mouth. "Believe what you want ladies. I am many things: a friend, a brother, a future king, a passionate lover—"

Kallie pretended to gag and Dani laughed beside her.

Fynn ignored the interruption, and continued, "But I am not a loser." He set his last card down on top of one of the piles.

Upon seeing it, Terin reached across the table and slapped his twin on the shoulders, nearly knocking over the glasses. Dani and

Kallie scrambled to prevent them from spilling all over the cards as the men laughed, rejoicing in their suspicious victory.

Sitting back down, Dani spat on the floor. "Honest man my ass."

Between laughs, Fynn said, "Come on. All's fair in love and war. It is not my fault Kallie's mind is so wide open."

Dani scoffed. "She doesn't know any better!"

Kallie wanted to defend herself, but she had nothing to say. The walls she had built around her thoughts of the game were not sound.

"You should have picked a better partner then." Fynn winked.

"Oh, and split you two up? You two would cry to your mother if I ever did that." Dani laughed as she gathered the cards. "By the gods, if you two are ever divided, I don't know what you will do."

"Good thing that is not happening any time soon," Fynn said, squeezing Terin's shoulder.

Dani rolled her eyes and chugged what rum remained in her glass. "Clearly."

Kallie could not tell by Dani's tone if the woman was joking or if there was more to it than that, but the captain's booming voice pulled her focus away from them.

"Prepare yourselves!" Squires shouted from the wheel. "The waters around these parts can be tumultuous as we make to land!"

The threat of a rocky ride made Kallie's palms sweat. Having sensed her trepidation, Fynn ushered Kallie forward toward the ladder to the cabin below the ship. Dani and Terin followed.

Kallie scanned the sky. "It doesn't look like there is a storm coming."

"Not now, but these waters have a way of turning the tide before you know it. If you're not prepared, you will not survive it."

Kallie began to descend the ladder after Fynn. "No wonder you all tend to stay on your island. Dangerous, mythical sea creatures, brutal waves."

Fynn stopped halfway down the ladder and looked up at her. "The kraken is no joke." The look on Fynn's face told her that she had made a grave error in her sarcasm.

"Sorry," she mumbled, hoping the apology would suffice.

Fynn sighed and jumped down to the floor.

"According to the legends, the Kraken was placed in the sea to guard our island and as an added defense, Pontanius makes the sea rage to thwart any enemies from landing."

As if to prove Fynn's point, a wave crashed against the boat and Kallie hugged the ladder. When the ship stopped rocking, she hurried down.

"It was one of our many saving graces during the Great War. The waves on the Red Sea were so tumultuous that it was nearly impossible to pass. Large militaries couldn't manage to traverse the Red Sea. Even if a ship or two were lucky enough to pass the waves, the land was surrounded by cliffs. Only those who knew where the entrance was could land. Pontanius is always watching and knows if an enemy or ally sails these waters. He adjusts the strength of the storm accordingly—though, as you can see, the waters are still tricky to navigate even for an ally."

Fynn pointed to a spot against the wall and she sat on the floor while he helped the others tie down any loose objects. She should have felt insulted that he did not want her help, but she knew if the ship rocked again she would be useless.

The others finished tying down tables, chairs, and anything else in danger of rolling around. Then a few of Squires' crew headed back up to the dock, Graeson among them, while the rest stayed below.

Dani sat in the open spot on one side of Kallie and Terin took the spot on the other side. As they all settled, the crew began sharing stories of their travels. But their stories were loose words that held no weight in Kallie's mind, for the treacherous waves only meant one thing: Pontia was near.

Kallie didn't know if she was ready to face everything she had been avoiding: this new family, the lessons to strengthen her gift, and her mother. Her mother who was alive and ruled her own kingdom. Part of her was proud that she was the sole ruler of a kingdom since it was a title Kallie wished to acquire one day. But another part of her was jealous—no, that wasn't quite right. Envious? Outraged? That her mother did not risk that same title to protect Kallie, to save her. Surely, the queen had the resources. So why had it taken her so long to send someone? The questions only furthered Kallie's confusion.

Fynn had said King Domitius had killed her birth father, but Kallie could not bring herself to believe that. If she turned on the man who had cared for her all of these years, was that not a form of betrayal? Both to him and to herself? The king had not been easy on her, and at times he pushed her beyond her limits, but he cared about her. So did it matter if he was not her flesh and blood?

If she turned on him, would everything she had accomplished thus far be for naught?

Was this family, which was made up of people who she did not know, worth it?

While the queen might be her mother by blood, King Domitius was her father in every other way.

When no answer to her question—a question that would change everything—came, she lay her head back against the wall. She then shut out the chatter and carefree laughter of the twins and Dani as the ship beat against the waves of the storm now pouring down on them.

ONCE THEY HAD PASSED the thick of the storm, Kallie's group and the rest of the crew crawled back up to the dock. The sun was shining down without a cloud in sight. If it wasn't for the miscellaneous puddles splattered across the deck, she would have thought she had dreamt the entire storm.

In the distance, land was at last in sight. Once Squires and his small crew docked the boat and gave the go-ahead, Kallie and the others dismounted after saying their goodbyes.

The port was set a ways off from the palace, but Kallie could still make out the faint outline of it on top of the hill. As the five of them walked alongside their horses to give them time to readjust to solid ground, Kallie observed the streets of Pontia. Several small fishing boats and sailors gathered around the docks. The people waved at the familiar faces of their group with welcoming smiles. However, when they spotted Kallie, smiles wavered and whispers began snaking their way through the cobblestone town.

Kallie could only imagine what was going on in their heads. Did they know who she was? Or was her rescue a secret? Was she a stranger in their eyes? A stranger with red marks burned into her wrists that were finally beginning to turn pink after days of not having them bound. A woman whose footsteps were wobbly as she tried to regain her balance after traveling by sea and who wore ill-fitting, dirty clothes that did not belong to her.

Or was she a woman they all had forgotten about and believed to be long gone, now returned to their shores?

As Kallie passed them, she wondered if any of them also had gifts. If what Fynn had said was true, some of them must. Many of them probably. She wondered what they could do. Could some talk to the fish? Control the weather? Morph their bodies into other creatures?

The possibilities seemed endless, but also fantastical.

And perhaps Kallie allowed herself to get lost in the possibilities because she could not let her mind think about what—or rather *who* —she was going to see all too soon.

CHAPTER 20

DESPITE HER ATTEMPTS TO DISTRACT HER MIND, KALLIE WAS UNABLE TO prevent her ultimate arrival at the palace.

Mirrored gardens lined the path to the palace, small mazes composed of various shrubbery and peonies. Along the stone walls of the palace, wisteria and ivy hung around the tops of the large windows. The light purple flowers a beautiful contrast against the cold stone walls.

After dismounting from their horses, the group walked toward the steps and Kallie's gaze followed the steps up to the main doors. In the middle of a small squadron of guards clothed in matching charcoal jackets and crisp white pants, a woman stood with her hands held gracefully in front of her stomach. She wore a simple lilac dress that flowed down her body like a river. Her dress, her stance, her disposition all made her seem like an extension of the palace. Even without the exaggerated (albeit beautiful) dresses Kallie was used to seeing back in Ardentol or a crown atop her head, anyone would know who she was: the queen of Pontia.

Although to Kallie, she was the woman who had abandoned her. Who had left her identity and existence a secret.

Graeson squeezed her shoulder, and Kallie took a step forward, her legs shaking with every step as she ascended the slick stone steps. Graeson's hand fell from her shoulder. And with each step she took, Kallie straightened, her chin tilted higher and her face turned to stone. She ignored the fact that she wore yesterday's clothes that reeked of sea salt and fish, and instead focused on the woman before her. The soft smile plastered on the queen's face, the twitch of her mouth as the distance between them shortened.

Kallie blew out a deep breath. She refused to think about what was going on in the queen's mind as her supposed long-lost daughter approached. The woman who was supposed to be her mother, the woman who was supposed to care for her and protect her, and do anything for her. Who was supposed to love her unconditionally.

Instead, Kallie found a woman she neither knew nor recognized. Because instead of letting her daughter know that she hadn't died, that she was indeed well and alive, the queen had decided to keep it a secret. To remain a mystery for Kallie's entire life. The queen had chosen this life, a life without her daughter—a life with only her sons by her side—instead of saving her daughter.

Graeson had said Kallie's mother still cared for her, but Kallie let those words fly off into the breeze. For if they were true, things would be different. If they were true, she would not be here confused and conflicted. If the queen had cared, Kallie would not have grown up wondering what her mother's voice sounded like. Because for Kallie, not a day had gone by when she had not wondered about the woman who birthed her. Kallie had dreamed of her mother's eyes. She had wondered if her mother looked down at her from her place among the stars, if she was proud of Kallie.

And even though the woman's eyes were the same shade of blue she had imagined, the woman staring back at her was a stranger.

They shared no similarities. Where Kallie had an athletic build, the woman was slim and lean. The woman's blond hair was tucked into a tight bun at the base of her nape. Not a single strand out of place. A stark contrast to Kallie's unbrushed, undone, sea salt-covered hair that flew across her face as the wind came from the East.

The queen's gaze flicked down to Kallie's hand, and Kallie let go of the ring around her finger and rolled her shoulders back. A flicker of sadness flashed across Esmeray's face, which Kallie quickly dismissed.

When she and the rest of the group arrived at the top of the steps, everyone around her bowed. Everyone except Kallie.

This woman wasn't her queen. She was nothing to Kallie.

Kallie's heart rattled against her chest as the queen greeted each of them individually.

The queen took a step toward Fynn and Terin, and any hints of sadness were wiped clear from her countenance as her lips spread into a wide smile. Her boys were home safe.

The twins rose and moved to their mother, smushing her in between them in a giant embrace. Their height, which must have come from their father, made the woman appear even more fragile. Esmeray patted her sons on the back and squirmed her way out of their embrace a moment later. She approached Graeson next, and Kallie noted the genuine smile that appeared on the man's face.

"Gray." She opened her arms to him and without hesitation, Graeson walked into them.

Something inside Kallie tugged at her, but she tossed the feeling aside. Esmeray let go and tousled his grease-coated hair. When she turned to Dani, Graeson immediately began fixing it.

To Dani, she said, "I have no doubt that my fiercest daughter-in-law was able to keep these men in order."

Daughter-in-law? Kallie began turning the events of the past two weeks in her head. She didn't know how she had missed it while they had traveled together. They all wore some kind of jewelry on their hands. But when Kallie thought about the way Dani and Fynn fought together, it was glaringly obvious in retrospect.

Dani smiled. "I tried my best, your grace, but you know how your boys can be."

A soft chuckle left the queen's lips. "That I do."

The women embraced, and when they parted, she finally turned her attention to Kallie. As their gazes met, Kallie couldn't help but take a step backward. As much as Kallie had dreamed about being wrapped in her mother's arms, she couldn't afford to put her guard down. Not yet.

Not until she knew the full truth.

The retraction did not go unnoticed by the queen and her countenance shifted. Esmeray halted her approach and instead gave Kallie a simple nod in greeting. "We are all glad to have you home."

Home. A strange way of apologizing for the years of abandonment, the years of lies and secrets.

"There is much to be discussed," Esmeray said to the group as she observed them, no doubt noting their disheveled appearances. "But I am sure you all would like to clean up and eat something first. The night ahead of us is sure to be a long one." Her eyes caught on Kallie's and then she swiveled toward the door, waving them forward. "Come. I have already asked for your rooms to be prepared."

KALLIE SAT on a freshly made bed with a silk robe wrapped around her body and her hair dripping down her back in a room that wasn't hers in a foreign palace far from where she had grown up. She stared at a closet half-full of clothes that one of the servants had left while she was bathing. The clothes were in shades of green, blue, and neutral. And unlike her closet at home, the tulle and fuller materials that overfilled that closet were absent.

Kallie grabbed a piece of cold meat from the wooden board that sat on the bed and chewed it. She continued to pick at the food while her mind wandered.

Then a knock came at the door.

Kallie, still half-lost in her thoughts, said, "Come in." Barely giving the guest and their approaching footsteps any attention, she grabbed a ripe green grape. The footsteps stopped and a small cough came from the guest. Kallie rolled her eyes but turned toward the guest. As she raised a grape to her mouth, it slipped from her fingers. It bounced onto the floor as she met a pair of hazel eyes, and a wide toothy grin stretched across Kallie's face.

When Kallie stood, more grapes hit the floor but she ignored them. "Myra!" she shouted.

Kallie threw her arms around her friend, inhaling the familiar scent of lavender. Kallie released her friend and rested her hands on Myra's shoulders and examined her.

Myra seemed intact, and her normal, well-kept appearance was back. No sight of dirt lingered, but Kallie's smile faded when she asked, "Are you . . . are you well?"

Myra laughed. "I'm supposed to be asking you that. Secret family, remember?"

Kallie's eyes widened. "How did you—"

"Alyn told me everything on the way."

Kallie shook her head, and despite the happiness she felt seeing her friend, a fire grew behind her eyes at the mention of her old guard. "Where is he? I'll kill him for what he's done."

Myra's gaze dropped and she released a heavy sigh. "It's fine, Kals. *I'm* fine. Now, come on. We can catch up while I do something about this wet mop you call hair."

Myra grabbed Kallie's hand and dragged her over to the stool that sat before the mirror.

"What were you going to do? Just let it hang there like limp noodles?"

Kallie laughed and the tension in her shoulders lessened. She sat in the chair that Myra pulled out for her as her friend riffled through the various accessories that lay across the vanity. Finally settling on a wooden square brush, Myra began brushing through the knots. And Kallie allowed herself to drop her guard for the first time in weeks as she enjoyed a moment of normalcy—however fleeting it might be.

"So tell me everything," Myra said.

Kallie sunk deeper into the seat. "Not much to tell. My mother's alive, my father is not my father, and I have twin brothers."

"*Attractive* twin brothers." Myra beamed at her in the mirror.

"Gross, Myra. We're related. Is that all that matters to you?" Kallie asked.

"I mean, it sure helps make matters a little more . . . interesting?"

Kallie rolled her eyes and Myra giggled, a noise Kallie hadn't even realized how much she had missed.

"The other one isn't too bad either," Myra mused as she detangled a difficult knot.

"The other one?" Although Kallie's tone was neutral, she could not prevent the heat that rose to her cheeks.

Myra glared at her in the mirror, one brow cocked. "Don't play the fool. It does not look good on you."

Kallie's hand went to her scalp as Myra tugged on her hair. "Graeson's an arrogant ass."

"Oh, so he is just your type then."

Mouth agape, Kallie swiveled around in her chair. "Myra, may I remind you I am engaged?"

"To a man you have not yet met." Myra turned Kallie's head forward. "No one said you couldn't. . . I don't know, look?"

Kallie shook her head in disbelief. Her friend was unbelievable. While Kallie had not thought of King Rian much, Kallie had made a promise. A very public promise.

Then Myra whispered, "What King Rian doesn't know, won't hurt him."

"Enough of that." Kallie laughed and tucked her legs under her. She cleared her throat. "Did you run into any trouble on your way?"

Myra pursed her lips and the light tone vanished from the conversation. "No, not really. Some soldiers were looking for you, but when they realized the only commonality we had was our height and accent, they dismissed us rather quickly."

"That's good." Kallie picked at her nails. "We also ran into some soldiers."

"And?"

"All dead but one."

Myra's eyes grew wide, brush mid stroke and Kallie raised her hands. "I didn't kill them." Her friend's gaze softened slightly, and Kallie added, "The others handled it, but it was . . . difficult."

Myra squeezed one of Kallie's shoulders. "Well, I'm glad you are safe, at least."

Safe for now, Kallie thought.

"So are you going to tell me what happened with Alyn?" Kallie asked in an attempt to change the subject.

Myra sighed. "Nothing happened. As I said, it's fine. Our trip was short. We arrived about a week ago, and soon after we arrived, he ran off on some other trip. I've been spending my time getting familiar with the palace, while a couple of the other guards stayed back and kept me company here and there. But I'm happy you are finally here, Kals."

Kallie smiled as she reached back to squeeze her friend's wrist. "Me too."

Then Myra worked Kallie's detangled hair into a loose braid that hung down the center of her back. Small pieces had been pulled out and framed her oval-shaped face that drew attention to her kohl-lined eyes.

Kallie changed into an emerald floor-length dress Myra had chosen. It had a deep plunge in the center of her chest and a slit on each side of her legs, stopping at the middle of her thigh. The fabric felt like rose petals against her skin, which was a stark contrast to the dresses she had donned back home that restricted her movements and weighed her down. And for once, she didn't mind the change.

While the Pontian palace may have been foreign to her, she felt more at home in her skin than she had in weeks. She let that confidence fill her body as she stood at the threshold of her bed chambers beside Myra.

"Do you have a plan for what you are going to do?"

Kallie straightened, a smirk pushing to the surface. "Always."

CHAPTER 21

Without slowing her stride, Kallie strolled into the queen's study.

Terin sat in a leather chair near the doors, a scraggly white dog with black polka dots lay at his feet. Across from him, Dani and Fynn shared the plush white couch. Fynn's arm rested over the back behind Dani. The three of them paused their conversation as their gazes followed Kallie. But Kallie strode past them, heading straight to the center of the room where Esmeray and Graeson stood whispering near a large oak desk. On the desk, a delicate gold crown adorned with amethyst crystals lay atop a velvet cushion.

Graeson faced Kallie as she stopped next to him without more than an exasperated sigh. His puzzled face seemed to question why she had interrupted them in such an uncouth manner, but Kallie ignored him. She was not here for him.

"I believe we are long past due for that chat, don't you think, Esmeray?" Kallie's demanding tone silenced the room, but she didn't care if the woman held a title higher than her own. Her so-called brothers had refused to tell her anything besides the bare minimum and just enough to sedate her desire to run. So here she stood, ignorant and pissed off, her patience running thin.

The queen shared a look with Graeson. "I see what you mean about her inheriting my brazenness."

Graeson snorted as he leaned his hip against the desk.

Fire rose within her, and Kallie gave the queen a tight smile. "Hard to learn anything from someone who has been in hiding for the past twenty years, wouldn't you agree?"

The queen rubbed her hand across her forehead. "I have not been in hiding, but I am also not going to argue with you on the matter. Sit, and I'll show you the truth."

Kallie didn't move. Her feet soldered to the ground. "Show me how?"

The queen's eyes darted around the room, a sense of annoyance displayed across her face. "None of you told her?"

Fynn shrugged, unbothered. "Haven't you always said, 'seeing is believing,' Mother?"

The queen sighed exasperatedly. With her hand rubbing her temple, she returned her attention to Kallie. "Well, I'm sure. . ." she paused and gave a tight, tired smile. Her hand fell from her face. "Hopefully, your brothers at least told you that our family has a particular set of gifts?"

Kallie shook her head.

"Some families have a distinct set of gifts, whether that be in a craft, the ability for espionage, et cetera. Our family's gifts tend to lean on the mental side. It is one of the reasons our family has stayed in power for so long. I have the ability to show people the past—mine or the past of the person I am communicating with."

Kallie's brows rose, her curiosity increasing. Fynn had told her that their mother's gift was interesting, and now she understood why, though she was having a hard time fully grasping the concept.

Esmeray held her hand out and Kallie looked at it questioningly. "Physical contact strengthens the connection."

Although hesitant, Kallie's curiosity was stronger than her desire to put distance between herself and the woman who stood before her, so she relented. Her coarse hand fell atop the queen's smooth palm.

"The first time might be uncomfortable. Are you sure you do not wish to sit down?"

"I'm sure." Kallie didn't want to delay this any further.

The queen nodded and closed her eyes. Kallie stared at her, waiting for something to happen, wondering how her gift would work. When nothing happened, she opened her mouth to ask, but then the floor beneath her disappeared and Kallie's stomach fell.

The world around her collapsed as she fell through time and space. A rush of noises hit her ears, the sound deafening. Too much sound, too many voices and faces blurred past her.

She tried to cover her ears to quiet the noise but her arms felt heavy.

When her vision returned after a moment, Kallie stood in a dark room. The air was thick and the smell of smoke coated her nose. Kallie scanned her surroundings as she adjusted to the dark, but it felt off, murky.

She tried to move her body, but she couldn't. She didn't know where her body was, she felt like she was floating . . . as though she no longer had a body to occupy.

But that couldn't be right. She could see, she could smell, she could feel the heat starting to consume her.

But she couldn't breathe. She couldn't move.

She was losing control.

Her head began to ache. Her blood began to rise within her and the heat from the smoke became unbreathable, pressing against her body.

Then she realized she was inside someone else's body. The body she inhabited jerked upright. Graceful arms with long delicate fingers extended forward. And Kallie knew that the body belonged to *her*.

This was the queen's gift at work. A memory from her past come to life.

Kallie took a deep breath and counted to ten as the vision consumed her.

ESMERAY WOKE UP. Her gaze sprinted across the room and fell onto the man who slept next to her, his dark chestnut hair spilling across his face and onto the pillow. She crawled to her husband and shook him.

Still, he didn't move.

Markos had always been a heavy sleeper though. It had been a running joke that when their children entered their rebellious stages and began sneaking out of the house—like they had done so often when they were young ages ago—it would be her job to catch them. But now—now, it was no longer a laughing matter.

"Markos! Wake up," Esmeray shouted, shaking him again, more violently this time.

Nothing. He didn't stir and the panic began to settle within her as thick black smoke crept across the bedroom floor.

Esmeray jumped out of bed. In one swift movement, she tossed on her robe and followed the smoke as she sought out the source.

There.

Beyond the smoke, a dim glow seeped from the crack beneath the bathroom door. She sprinted toward it as the smoke began to darken and slither its way through the room, spreading. Esmeray peered into the bathroom and gasped.

That was her first mistake.

Coughing, she covered her mouth with her sleeve. Smoke filled her lungs. Flames covered the exterior wall and were spreading throughout the room, heading toward the main room. The small fireplace that she had custom-built in their bathroom when they had their summer home renovated had somehow erupted in the night.

She swiveled, looking for something to put out the fire, but it was too large, too fast. Too uncontrollable.

A pounding at the door had her spinning on her heels and running to the door that led to the hallway. She reached for the handle and immediately let go as the metal scorched her hand. She shook it at her side.

A small voice shouted from the other side, "Mom! Dad! Wake-up!"

Tears threatened to spill from her eyes, but she stifled them back and kneeled in front of the door. She called back to her daughter, "Sweetie, you need to get out."

Esmeray coughed as the smoke grew thicker and the flames began to spill out of the bathroom. She looked back at the bed, but Markos was still fast asleep. She needed to help him, she needed to get out of here. But she needed to make sure her daughter left first. Nothing mattered more than her safety.

More banging sounded at the door. Frantic movements sounded on the other side of the door followed by her daughter shouting, the frenzied sound tearing Esmeray's heart apart.

"No! Let me go!" her daughter shouted.

Then more screams started. Esmeray put her hand against the warm wood and closed her eyes. She pictured her daughter on the other side. "Sweetheart, it's—" her voice came out more hoarse than she intended. She cleared her throat but more smoke entered. Esmeray managed to say, "It's ok."

In between the incessant coughing, footsteps smacked against the hardwood floors. A tear slipped from her eye, rolling down her face as the shouting faded on the other side. She wiped the tear away with a flick of her hand. She needed to hurry.

She ran back to Markos and put her head against his chest. But his chest didn't rise. And she could no longer hold back the tears. They fell from her eyes in a torrent, almost powerful enough to quench a small fire. But this fire was too big. Her tears would do nothing as they landed on her best friend's chest. Her soulmate.

Her daughter's screams echoed in her mind. Esmeray knew what she had to do.

Covering her mouth, she took a quick breath. The tears muddled her vision. She placed a gentle kiss on his forehead, then ran for the window on the opposite wall of the bathroom. She scanned the area for something, anything that she could use to smash it open. Her eyes landed on the paperweight sitting on the desk covered with Markos's notes. She snatched the circular orb and smashed it against the window, using all the force she could muster.

On the first strike, a small knick marked the glass.

On the third, a web of cracks spread across the window.

On the fifth, the glass shattered. Shards sprinkled the floor. She pulled down her sleeve and used it to wipe away the remaining pieces of glass that lingered on the window sill.

Setting a nearby chair beneath the window, Esmeray stepped onto it and pushed herself through the opening. She wiggled her hips through the window, but something tugged and restricted her movement forward.

She was stuck.

While doing her best to avoid looking at the bed, she looked behind her and noted the fire's dangerous approach. Sweat beaded on her forehead. Esmeray pulled at her robe, ripping a large slit in it. Then she was free. She quickly pushed herself the rest of the way through and dropped onto the ground.

She hissed in pain as her ankle folded under her weight, a less-than-graceful landing for a queen. Leaning against the house, she hobbled her way toward the front yard where she hoped to find her children safe. Her movements were slow and each step sent a shooting pain that ran from her leg to her spine.

When she reached the front of the house, three figures were massed *together as they fought over something. But as the fire grew and overcame the house, she knew she was wrong.*

*It was not some*thing*, but some*one*.*

Fury sparked within her, she raced toward the bodies, her twisted ankle screaming at her and slowing her down. Still, she did not stop. She continued forward, fighting through the pain soaring through her body.

The boy lost his grip and the monster on top of the horse sprinted away with a body thrown across his lap. Long chestnut hair blowing in the wind.

Esmeray fell to her knees. Her daughter's name on the tip of her tongue. Kalisandre.

As the image faded, Kallie's vision darkened and the world spun again. She braced herself for the fall she now expected to come.

The smell of smoke dissipated. However, her limbs remained limp as she tried to regain control of her own body, the effects of her mother's gift throwing her off balance. Kallie didn't know how she managed to remain standing on shaking legs.

Then as her senses came to, she felt the warmth of someone's body pressed up against her. An arm wrapped around her waist, the smell of fresh cedar surrounding her. She turned her head and Graeson stared down at her using his body to keep her upright.

She jerked forward in an attempt to free herself from his hold but stumbled. Graeson's hand only tightened around her, stabilizing her and doing the exact opposite of what she wanted. Yet even though she wanted to stand on her own, she knew she needed the support— although she would never admit that to him or to anyone else.

Avoiding his gaze, she directed her attention to Esmeray. And Kallie couldn't help the water building behind her eyes, but she refused to let them surface. She had felt the Queen's heartbreak, had experienced it as though it was her own.

Kallie didn't want to ask the question she already knew the answer to, but she took a deep breath and demanded the truth anyway. "Show me."

Esmeray said nothing as she took Kallie's hand. And the world spun around her once again, blacking out, transporting her to a far-off memory that Kallie had seen time and time again in her nightmares. Her mind had always prevented her from seeing more as though it were subconsciously sheltering her from the heartache. Perhaps she had been afraid to see the truth. But ready or not, Kallie needed to know.

THE SMOKE WAS GETTING THICKER as Kallie cried out for her mother. Smoke filled her lungs, and Kallie's screams became soundless as they tore her throat to ribbons.

The person wrapped around her tightened their hold, and Kallie pumped her legs, clawed at the air, pounded the person's back. But they were relentless and didn't let go, preventing her from saving her parents.

She dragged her hand across their face, and the person hissed as she continued to fight and claw at them. But she didn't care if she hurt them. She didn't care if she died. She could not lose them.

The person ran.

And ran.

Further away from her parents.

Doors slammed. Someone shouted. And the fire roared on.

The air shifted and a breeze swept over her. The person sat her down, grass brushed against her hands and knees. She was afraid to breathe, afraid to suck in more smoke, but when she inhaled, she didn't swallow smoke, although the charred taste still lingered on her tongue.

Kallie tried to get up, but her arms and legs betrayed her, collapsing beneath her. She crawled toward the front door, toward the flickering light. Toward her parents.

Then she heard it: hooves slapping against the pavement.

Kallie's heart rate increased. The pounding grew louder, and through the smoke, she could make out the faint outline of a horse with a figure sitting atop it.

As the horse sprinted forward, the fire swallowed the house and its rider, the bright flames illuminating them, casting the pair in a ghastly light. The rider wore an iron helmet in the shape of a bull. Two spiraling horns protruded out on each side and angled slits were cut into the helmet in place of eyes for the man to see through. A thick black iron hoop lined with glittering diamonds pierced the bull's nose. And with the light of the fire bouncing off of it, the helmet glowed red and yellow. A black cape tied around his neck by a chunky silver chain flew behind him as he continued forward, unfazed by the smoke.

She tried to crawl away from him, tried to dig her nails into the soft ground, but the rider was too fast. And when her grip failed her, she reached for the person who brought her out of the house. But as she looked behind her, the boy was face down in the dirt, his black hair covered in ash.

Kallie threw herself at him, and at that moment, the bull-headed man scooped her up. She tried to fight, but she was too weak, too frail. Too small to shake the towering man from her. Her lungs began to collapse.

A small hand reached for her and wrapped its fingers around her ankle. A different boy with short dark brown hair pulled on her leg. But like her, he was too weak. The bull-headed man's grip around her was unbreakable. Kallie was being torn apart from both sides.

Then the small hand began to loosen around her ankle as a layer of sweat formed between her leg and the boy's hand. A scream escaped her lips as she felt the last of the slim fingers slip.

The bull had won, and the child had lost. She had lost.

The stranger threw her over the horse and clicked his heels against the *horse's sides. Kallie's head bounced as the horse sprinted away from the burning house.*

As she tried to look back, her vision going in and out, she saw two boys kneeling beside the third on the ground. The house crumbling behind them. Their fits pounding against the ground as she spotted another figure appear in the distance, hobbling.

Tears streamed down her face as Kallie watched her family fade into the smoke. The flames consumed the house and her vision went white.

HER KNEES HIT THE GROUND, her dress billowing around her. A bubble caught in the middle of her chest as though someone had reached down her throat, grabbed her heart from within, and ripped it out of her chest.

This woman, a stranger whom she had known for only a few minutes, had caused her entire world to collapse beneath her.

She should have known. She should have connected the dots.

When Kallie had learned her mother was alive, she knew the king was not her father, but she had not known how she had ended up in his arms.

Everything she knew about her past was a lie, a mirage. A well-crafted story.

She had thought the foundation she stood on, the foundation she had built her life upon was sound, indestructible. The walls she once believed to be made of marble were, in fact, sand and they just got hit by a tsunami. It crumbled in her hands and slipped through her fingertips. Leaving nothing but a few grains in her palm.

She *knew* that helmet. Had grown up looking upon it with awe. Had seen it every day next to the king's throne, displayed proudly inside a stand encased with glass.

The man who Kallie had grown up calling *father* had taken her away from the one thing he could not buy. The one thing she could not manipulate or order. And without even blinking an eye.

Kallie had fallen for his lies and stories so easily.

And why wouldn't she? He was her *father*. He had trained her. He had been the one person she could rely on—except he wasn't. Not at all.

Kallie had done everything for him. She had tricked people, stolen from people, had people killed. All for him. All in the name of reuniting the seven kingdoms.

Had he truly wanted to reunite the seven kingdoms though? Was that just some ploy?

Why had he torn her from her family's arms? From her home?

And why *her* of all people?

Had he cared for her at all? Or just for the gift she bore?

And why had Kallie believed him?

Her thoughts shifted toward the man from Esmeray's memory— the one who had slept through the fire. The one who had died that night. And one thing stood out: the unruly, dark chestnut hair, the tanned skin.

King Domitius had blonde hair. Kallie had always thought, had always *assumed* she had inherited her dark hair from her mother. And there were no paintings to prove otherwise. However, after seeing Esmeray in the flesh, Kallie knew that wasn't true.

Her throat burned and bile began to build up. Her hands lay on her thighs, palms facing the skies, pleading for an answer from the gods.

The air shifted around her, and Kallie lifted her gaze. She knew her eyes were red, her face puffy as she stared at a pair of soft, blue eyes. Kallie swallowed the lump in her throat. "Why?"

Esmeray's delicate fingers wrapped around Kallie's calloused palms. "There is much you do not know about our people's past."

"Then tell me," Kallie said.

"Kallie . . ." Graeson's voice was gentle beside her, but she ignored him.

"No. No more lies." She looked between the two figures before her —two figures who she had not even known a few weeks ago but who carried the truth inside of them. And she did the one thing she never did. She begged. "*Please.*"

From behind her, Fynn spoke, "Kals, are you sure you can handle it? You just—"

She swiveled her head toward him and snarled. "Do not tell me what I can or cannot handle, *brother*," she spat the term she had never used before at him and he halted. His mouth dropped and he sank back onto the couch as Dani gripped his knee.

At the same time, Graeson's grip on her shoulder tightened, almost pulling a laugh from her lips. Did he think he could restrain her? Stop her mind from unraveling?

Too late. They were all too late. The damage had been done.

She yanked her shoulder from his grasp, but she reigned in the anger. "Please, Esmeray."

"All right, but I will need to sit for this." Esmeray pushed herself up, glided across the room with a queen's grace, and sat on the couch next to Dani. The dog that had been laying by Terin's feet jumped up onto the couch beside the queen. Instead of shooing it off, Esmeray began scratching behind its ears.

When Kallie felt Graeson's hand tug her upward, she allowed him to pull her up and guide her to the other couch. They sat down on the couch beside one another. And she didn't know why, but his warmth provided her comfort and she let it envelop her. Fynn handed them each a glass half filled with a golden liquid. She took a sip and let it steady her.

Ankles crossed, glass sitting in between her palms, and her back straight, Esmeray began, "The history of Pontia is one that most have been forced to forget."

"Forced?" Kallie asked.

"Unfortunately, yes. The stories in the history books only explain one side of the events that occurred. However, every story has two sides: the side of the conquerors and the side of the conquered. The story that you know, Kallie, paints our land, our ancestors as the villain. That *we* were greedy and unjust in our choices. That *we* wanted to take what was not ours. That *we* started a war that split Vaneria into the seven kingdoms it now is today. But that is not the entire truth. Not even a little.

"A long time ago, when the gods walked on these lands among humans, one god, Pontanius, chose to venture off the mainlands where the rest of the gods lived. He traveled to a small island off the coast, which the people later named after him—"

Recalling what Graeson had told to her, Kallie interrupted, "And he fell in love with a human. Yes, I know the story. What is your point?"

The queen sighed. "That is only part of the story. Before his mortal wife died, they lived a happy life together with their three children. Pontanius loved his children dearly. One day, another god arrived on the island. At first, Pontanius was outraged that one of the gods dared to step foot on his land. However, when he saw the goddess Sabina—one of the only gods he had tolerated before—and saw the fear written in her eyes and what she hid beneath her cloak, he stopped in his tracks. She was pregnant. And she, like Pontanius, had fallen in love with a human. Although, she was not as lucky as Pontanius who got to live out his life with his beloved.

"The gods were extremely jealous beings. When they found out that Sabina was pregnant with a mortal's child, they grew wary of what her child would be able to do with the blood of both a god and a mortal. They feared the possibilities. But they had one problem: they couldn't kill the goddess, for a god cannot kill another god. It would rip the god to shreds, destroying their soul. So they came up with a different plan. They killed her mortal lover in his sleep one night when he was away from the goddess on a hunting trip. When Sabina discovered this, she knew her children would not be safe once they were born, so she ran. And ran.

"Even though Pontanius had chosen to separate himself from the other gods, the goddess had always trusted him before. A rumor was spread around the mainland that Pontanius had married a mortal, so the goddess thought he might be sympathetic to her cause. As she traveled, Sabina hid her identity and was able to persuade a sailor to take her to the island.

"Luckily, Sabina was right, for when Pontanius and his wife saw that she was with child, they took her in and heard her story. To protect his children as well as the goddess' children, the two gods went to work to protect the island. They brought the Kraken to the island's shore, and together, they made the waters impassable by any enemy. As an extra precaution, they carved out the edges of the land. That way, if someone was able to get past the treacherous waters, they wouldn't be able to reach their land because deadly cliffs encircled it. Only one spot remained accessible and it was well hidden and guarded.

"After a few months had passed, the goddess gave birth to a set of triplets. At the same time, Pontanius' oldest child turned four and started developing special abilities. The child was exceptionally strong compared to mortal children his age, and the gods knew it was a result of the child having the blood of a god. After a year passed, Pontanius and Sabina created a reclusive spring to act as a training ground for their children. They embedded their powers into the waters in the hopes of helping their children learn to control their abilities.

"Long after the children married and had descendants of their own, a good portion of Pontia had developed god-like abilities. As generations passed, the gifts became more focused. The descendants knew these were not normal abilities and therefore kept them hidden from those who did not bear the gifts. After a while though, it became the island's secret. Everyone, gifted or not, protected that secret. And since the people from the mainland were still unable to find a way to travel to Pontia, it was fairly easy to keep it hidden from outsiders.

"However, it was only a matter of time until one Pontian grew restless and traveled off the mainland. His name was Tyson. He was young, naive, and reckless. And he fell in love with the daughter of one of the prominent lords on the mainland, Sloane. However, Sloane was engaged to another. When she tried to break off the engagement since she shared Tyson's feelings, her father, Sorel, was outraged. He locked the princess in a tower, thus separating the lovers. Tyson was enraged and lost control. He used his ability to pull ravage storms from the sky in front of Sorel, and the lord grew curious about Tyson's special ability. Sorel believed he could use Tyson to gain more power over the other lords, so he broke off his daughter's engagement.

"The lord kept his intentions a secret from the two lovers though and instead lied, telling them he believed in their love. He let them marry and have children. But once the children were born and the lord discovered that they too had special abilities, he betrayed them. He locked them up intending to breed them to create a small army of gifted humans.

"Sloane, who was kept in captivity separate from her family, grew deathly sick. But before she passed, she was able to share the secret dealings of her father with a trusted friend. Sloane also told her how to get to Pontia, a secret Tyson had once shared with her. With this knowledge, the woman stowed away to Pontia and shared the horrors of the lord's atrocities with the Pontian rulers. The rulers were outraged that their own kind was being bred and tortured, so they started the Great War in the hopes of releasing the enslaved Pontians. Unfortunately, when the armies arrived at the lord's doorsteps, they were too late. The children were no longer alive."

The queen paused, taking a moment to sip on her whiskey. Fynn brought over the bottle and refilled everyone's glasses.

Meanwhile, Kallie tried to wrap her mind around this new information that contradicted everything she had been told. She had a million questions running through her head, such as what happened to Tyson. But one question was louder than the rest.

"If a war was waged because of these travesties, how does no one know about them? How does no one know about the gifts we possess?"

The queen removed the glass from her lips. "Our ancestor, Queen Marina, had the unique gift of being able to wipe one's memory. She was one of the most powerful gift-bearing mortals. Not only was she able to wipe one individual's memory but large groups of people at the same time. Therefore, one of the conditions of ceasing the war and bringing peace to the seven kingdoms was that the knowledge of our kind be wiped from their minds."

Kallie sat on the information for a minute. The information about how the gifts came to be made sense. She had always known the gods played a role, so that was easy enough to file away. But other pieces were still not adding up. She took a deep breath, readying herself to ask the question that had been on her mind since they were in Borgania. "Why did you wait so long to find me?"

The queen's fingers flexed around her glass as she shifted on the couch. "The moment you were taken I wanted to part the seas, to bring down my wrath on Domitius' head—"

"So why didn't you?" Kallie interrupted, no longer able to contain the pain she felt.

The queen clenched her jaw. "I had just lost my husband and my daughter, our summer home had been turned into rubble. I was not in the proper mental state."

"You could have sent troops."

Esmeray sighed. "No, I could not. We had signed a treaty, so we had to maintain the peace. If we attacked another kingdom, we would be going against that treaty. And since Domitius had covered his tracks well, the other kingdoms would have retaliated and our allies would not have been on our side."

"But I'm your daughter!" Kallie's rage forced her onto her feet. "Was I not worth fighting for?"

"We had to bide our time. We had to have a plan."

Despite Kallie's rage boiling over, the queen remained seated, calm. And her behavior only enraged Kallie more.

"And that took what, seventeen years to create?" Kallie retorted. Graeson reached for her hand but she snatched it away from him.

The queen's calm unfazed demeanor disappeared momentarily, her lips pursed. She took a long swig of whiskey. When she set the glass down, her face was once again neutral. "As queen, I had a choice to make, Kalisandre."

The glass threatened to shatter in Kallie's hand as her fingers clenched around it. "And how do you feel about your choice now, *Mother?*"

Esmeray flinched, the movement slight but unmissable. "I cannot change the past, Kalisandre. The decisions I make—that *any* ruler makes—affect the people, the kingdom. Everyone."

It was not the words Kallie wanted to hear. She understood hard decisions, she had made many and she would continue to make them. But for once, she wanted someone to fight for her, to care for her unconditionally. But her mother—her own mother—had just proven that there were, in fact, conditions involved in her care of Kallie.

Esmeray rubbed her temple. "If King Domitius wanted you that badly to come here, we knew he wouldn't harm you. He was not a reckless man, never has been. He had a plan."

Kallie laughed, the sound cold and cruel. "You could not have known that."

"We have spies everywhere. We were watching." Esmeray sighed. "Please, Kalisandre. I know it is impossible to understand, and I do not expect you to forgive me—"

"Good, because I don't." Kallie crossed her arms over her chest. She never would forgive Esmeray.

The queen pressed on, "Please try to understand. You are here now, and that is all that matters."

Kallie looked at her, then at her brothers. Kallie's gaze softened. Esmeray was right. Kallie was here—with them. That was what mattered now. Her anger would not get in the way of her gaining access to her full ability. She could use them the way everyone else had used her.

So, when Graeson reached for her elbow this time, she did not pull away and sat back down into her seat, the fire fizzing out. Silence filled the room as the anger simmered.

And in the silence, Kallie realized one other detail that didn't make sense in Esmeray's story. "If the waters are so treacherous, how did King Domitius even get here?" Kallie asked.

Esmeray cleared her throat. "Although the waters are dangerous for strangers, it is not impossible to traverse. It seems. . ." Esmeray glanced at Graeson and cleared her throat. "It seems the gods' influence over the land is lessening."

Graeson shifted beside Kallie as Kallie asked, "Lessening?"

Esmeray nodded but said no more. Kallie looked at the others in the room, but they all avoided her gaze. It seemed their trust in her was still not sound.

"And if everyone was forced to forget about the Pontians' gifts? How would that explain why he thought to come here in the first place? How would he have known to take me?"

"We do not know how he came about the information or why he

took you. Our informants, like your previous guard Armen, were only able to glean that Domitius believed you were the key to his plan. The exact details of the plan, however, are still unknown."

Kallie dropped her gaze to the ground, the shiny oak floors staring back at her. The queen was holding back. There was something Esmeray was not telling her. Perhaps if Kallie provided them with information, the queen would trust her more. She searched her memory for any reason why the king wanted her.

With her eyes still glued to the ground, brows knitted together, she said, "He used to say I was the one hope for reuniting the kingdom. It was one of the reasons why I'm to marry the king of Frenzia."

Across from her, Fynn moved to the edge of the seat cushion. "Are you sure there's nothing else?"

She could feel his eyes on her. At that moment, she knew he was reading her mind, hearing her thoughts as she rifled through the many conversations she and the king had. Her shoulders grew tense.

Kallie met Fynn's stare. "No, nothing more."

CHAPTER 22

WHEN THE QUEEN RETREATED TO HER ROOMS, SAYING SHE WOULD SEE them at breakfast, the rest of them remained in the study. Fynn, Dani, and Graeson bounced ideas back and forth between each other as they tried to figure out how the king knew about their gifts and why Kallie was important. Someone suggested that he might have a seer in his possession, but that was quickly dismissed since seers were rare, especially good ones.

The one thing they could agree on was that there must have been a traitor among the Pontians. And if there was one, there were bound to be more.

Now, it was past midnight. Dani and Fynn had already gone to bed. Kallie was beginning to think sleep (or staring at the back of her eyelids as she went over every detail of the night until the sun rose) sounded like a good idea.

She pushed herself off the couch, stretched her arms above her head. The room spun. Kallie didn't know if the dizziness was from everything she had learned tonight or if it was from the copious amounts of whiskey she had drunk to take it all in.

When the room stopped spinning, she took a step. And her foot came down, Graeson was there to stabilize her.

She narrowed her eyes at the floor. Definitely, the whiskey's doing. Kallie shrugged his hand off her shoulder and took another step. Then another. She could do this. She was fine. She had drunk more than she had tonight many times before. But then again, she hadn't eaten much the past two days.

As she continued walking, her steps echoed in the study. No, it wasn't an echo, but the footsteps of another. She swung around without thinking, and her balance betrayed her yet again as she rocked into a stone chest. Terin snickered in his chair, hand covering his mouth.

"And what's so—" *hiccup*, "funny?" Kallie asked.

Unrestrained laughter erupted, but in between his fits of laughter, Terin managed to utter, "Nothing."

Kallie glared at him and the room spun around her again, as if Esmeray was transporting her into another memory. But Esmeray was no longer here.

She put her hands out to brace herself and felt the soft texture of cotton beneath her hand. She followed her hands and found them pressed against Graeson's chest. She looked up at him and found him staring down at her.

Hiccup.

One thick brow turned upward, the corner of his lip tilting with it.

Kallie cleared her throat. Having regained her balance, she took a slow step away from him.

Terin's laughter died down, and with a softness in his eyes, he asked, "Do you think you'll need help sleeping tonight?"

He held no judgment within his voice, only a gentleness filled with concern. But with the amount of alcohol she had drunk, Kallie would fall asleep without any problems. "No—" *hiccup*, "I'll be fine," she said.

"All right, then I'm going to head up to bed." He nodded to Graeson. "Can you help my sister get to her room?"

Kallie scoffed, "I do *not*—" *hiccup*, "need help."

Terin looked her up and down, chuckling.

"I think I can manage," Graeson said, bemused.

Terin nodded and pushed himself out of the chair, then strolled out of the study.

Graeson turned to her and she looked away. "All right, little mouse, let's get you to your room." He held out his arm.

Kallie rolled her eyes. But who was she kidding? If she had to walk up those long steps alone, she wasn't sure she would make it. She gripped his arm and bent down.

"What are you—are you about to—" Graeson took a step backward.

Kallie squatted down, her dress flowing out around her, and slipped off her heels with her free hand. Swiping them off the ground, she used Graeson's arm to help pull herself up.

With a feline smile, she then shoved her heels into his gut, forcing out a grunt. "Let's go then, kitty cat."

Laughing, she pulled Graeson forward and out of the study. She turned to the right, but Graeson tugged her arm, pulling her to a stop.

"This isn't the way to your room," he said.

She tugged back. "I know," Kallie growled, then kept walking down the hallway lined with stained glass windows.

"Then where are we—"

"Food," Kallie said before he could finish his question. She had smelled the aroma of baked bread coming from this direction when she had walked to the study. Earlier, they had passed a kitchen when they first entered the palace, so she believed she had a decent idea of where the kitchen was located.

"We can just ask one of the servants to bring you something. We don't need to barge into the kitchens at this hour," Graeson said.

Kallie followed the pieces of broken rainbows on the windows, then turned at the end of the hall. "Hush. I can very well—" *Hiccup.* She grumbled. "By the gods! If these hiccups do not—" *hiccup,* "go away."

Graeson sighed. "Fine. But then straight to your room."

Kallie giggled and saluted him dramatically. "Yes, sir."

HALF OF A BAGUETTE in one hand, grass beneath the other, Kallie sat criss-crossed on the ground.

No one had been in the kitchens when they arrived, but in the center of the counters sat a crisp baguette waiting for someone to eat it. When she spotted it, Kallie's eyes nearly popped out of her head as she snatched it off the counter. She pranced back to Graeson as she held the baguette over her head, waving it around in triumph. Then Kallie proceeded to drag him out the side doors into the small garden outside.

Kallie ripped the baguette piece by piece. Meanwhile, Graeson hovered, having refused to sit down beside her after mumbling some nonsense about it only encouraging her bad behavior.

The fact that Kallie was even able to persuade him to go to the gardens with her was shocking. It wasn't as if he had much of a say in the matter though. She supposed when you're chasing after a drunk woman with food on her mind, it was always best if you just let her lead the way. Or else, prepare to suffer the consequences.

And a hungry drunk girl was much better to deal with than a sad drunk girl roaming the palace.

As she popped the last piece of bread into her mouth, she whined. "Where did it all go?"

Graeson peered down at her, with an annoyed expression. Groaning, he squatted down to get to Kallie's level, his arms hung over his knees. He put out his hand in front of her, bread extended.

Kallie looked at it, dumbfounded.

His eyes trailed over her. "Take it. You need it more than me."

She met his eyes, and he nudged the bread forward. It seemed strange—to take food from her once enemy. And Kallie still did not know what the present circumstances made him, everything was so convoluted. But this? This seemed simple. A basic transaction. Pushing past the snide comment, Kallie grabbed the bread. Tossing a piece into her mouth, a closed-lip smile stretched across her face. After she ate the last piece, she fell back across the ground, staring up at the stars.

"Is that really a good idea?" Graeson asked, his tone skeptical and clearly disapproving.

"Lighten up, *Gray*." She giggled. With the glow of the moon behind him, she couldn't make out the expression on his face. "I'm not getting up anytime soon, at least not until the stars stop chasing each other. Which one do you think will win?" With wide, eager eyes, she pointed to a cluster of stars.

When he didn't respond, she turned her head slightly. She could see the faint outline of his mouth agape and she burst into laughter. Regaining her ability to speak, she said, "I'm drunk, not crazy. Now calm down and take a seat."

He stared at the night sky and sighed. "Fine, but only for a few minutes, then I'm carrying your ass up to your room, whether you like it or not," Graeson grumbled and lay on the ground next to her. He was so close that she could hear the sound of his breathing.

How did she get here? Why had the gods set her down this path? She was voluntarily lying next to the man who had captured her. In a few days, a simple plan that was clear and straight—gather information from the enemy and then avenge her father's name—

turned into something tangled with strings going off in different directions. She knew what King Domitius wanted her to do: kill them. And she thought she knew what Queen Esmeray wanted her to do: return her loyalties to Pontia and betray her homeland.

But what did *she* want to do?

The fractures on the insides of her mind started up again. She couldn't think. Above her a smoky cloud slinked its way across the moon, dimming its glow.

This wasn't the time for her to be making any decisions. Not when stars winked at her, mocking her.

Kallie blinked, clearing the thoughts from her head, and watched the stars continue to chase each other around the sky. Then as they slowed, she started identifying the constellations of the gods. Sabina had always been the easiest for her to find, for she floated near the brightest star in the sky, the North Star. She recalled Fynn pointing out Pontanius' constellation while they were traveling and connected the line between Sabina's left heel to where Pontanius hovered.

Strange that Pontanius was so far removed from the other gods, but after learning more about him from Fynn and Esmeray Kallie was starting to understand why.

He had been outcasted by the other gods. Separated from them, even in the stars. However, Sabina was there, not too far off, keeping their story secret but remaining a nearby companion. She wondered why the original story about Sabina and her lover was different from the one she had heard tonight. And why did they still celebrate the goddess on the mainland?

It seemed at every turn, the history of Vaneria that she knew was determined to keep the Pontians at arm's length. Perhaps that was why Sabina's story had shifted.

Or perhaps neither of these stories was the whole truth.

She looked back and forth between the two constellations. Both gods slept in the sky alone, separated from the ones they loved forever, for mortals were not meant to be among the stars.

She sighed, and put her hands down beside her, feeling the grass between her fingers and letting it ground her. The blades of grass shifted and warm skin grazed hers, sending a chill up her arm. Neither of them moved as their breaths synced.

Then her finger twitched.

"Sorry," Graeson mumbled.

He went to pull back his hand. But before he could and before she could think better of it, she interlaced her fingers in his. Her mother's ring clanked against his, and Graeson's breathing halted. She shifted to face him.

In the moonlight, his dark hair gave off an almost blue sheen. And feeling her gaze on him, Graeson turned his head toward her. Half of his face now shaded in darkness, while the other half still radiated from the moon's rays. Maybe, like Kallie, Graeson had two sides to him as well. Both of them had monsters that resided somewhere deep within them. Maybe he would understand the predicament she was in. After all, the more time she spent with the man, the more it seemed like they were cut from the same cloth. As though their souls were both tainted by the chaos of their upbringings, the pressures of their kingdoms. Still, they had different roles to play. The princess and the warrior.

She continued to observe his features. If he tried to use it against her tomorrow, she would blame it on the alcohol.

A strand of hair fell across his face, and Kallie had the sudden urge to brush it from his face. But instead, she restrained herself and traced it with her eyes instead. Her gaze fell onto his scar glowing beneath the moonlight. Even though she knew she shouldn't stare in such an obvious manner, she couldn't look away. And neither did Graeson turn away.

Kallie had wondered how he had gotten the scar, but now she knew.

"It was him, wasn't it?" Her words were no more than a whisper. As she ran the tip of her finger along one of the scars, his eyes shut. Wrinkles formed on his face as though he was recalling the memory of that night. When he opened them, she let her gaze meet his. The gray sparkled, the color stark against his pitch-black pupils that bore down into her sea of blue.

"Is that why you hate him so much?" The memory she had relived tonight hadn't shown her, but she thought she knew the moment it happened.

"Kal."

Her gaze skittered across his face. He had never called her that before. It was always *princess* or *little mouse*, but never her actual name. And definitely not a version of her name that no one else had ever called her. And despite her wishes, her breath hitched in her throat.

He sighed. "Does it matter?" His voice was gentle, but sadness laced his words.

"Yes—no." Her mind struggled to understand why she wanted to know, why she had even bothered to ask. Did it matter? Knowing wouldn't change anything. His feelings toward King Domitius should not influence her own. Except it would mean that he had been there. That he had saved her from the fire, had tried to save her from the king. And she didn't know what that would even mean, but she wanted to know.

"Yes," she finally said.

"That night we both lost so much." He rested his hand on top of hers, which had, at some point, stopped tracing the scar and now lay still on his face, practically caressing it. "And there are scars that go much deeper than these."

Her eyes caught on his mouth. She immediately looked away

toward the bushes behind him, but the greenery swirled. In her head, she cursed herself for having drank so much, for her head was still clouded. Everywhere she looked spun, besides when she looked directly in front of her. So she relented and returned her gaze to him. "Like what?"

His thumb moved in slow circles on the back of her hand. "A story for another night perhaps." His gaze was full of promises and unsaid truths. And she wondered what he saw in her expression. If he saw the darkness that lay beneath, her desires, her weaknesses.

Her eyes dropped to his mouth. A sad smile graced his lips, and Kallie wondered how they would feel on hers. Would her touch wipe away the expression? Or would it only increase it?

"Kal."

It was a warning, but Kallie had never been good at heeding the warnings of men.

She inched forward, her forehead pressing up against his, his breath mingling with hers. And she paused, waiting for him to back away, waiting for him to pull back. Giving him a chance to tell her no.

Through her lashes, she saw him staring at her lips, felt his breathing picking up, was overcome by the scent of cedar and citrus. The orange aroma begged her to fill the space between them. But Kallie hesitated.

For one moment of her life, she didn't want to think about the consequences that came from her actions. For one moment, she wanted to do something that wasn't dictated by the king or the gods. For one moment, she wanted to have control.

And perhaps, the gods would be by her side, and come morning, she would have no recollection of this misstep.

She closed her eyes and closed the distance between them. Her lips met his, the softness and warmth almost surprising considering everything she had learned about him.

The kiss was slow, featherlight as if they were testing the waters.

As if the slower they went, the longer they had here under the stars where no one but the gods could see. Where they didn't have to think about fires or lies. Or the past that had them so entwined that it was nearly impossible to separate themselves from the actions of others.

Graeson pulled back an inch, and her lips felt cold without the warmth of his on hers. "Little mouse."

"No," she said, "don't."

She knew what he would say if she let him. How this was a mistake, how she was drunk and didn't know what she was thinking. And while both of those things were true, she was coherent enough to know a part of her wanted this, needed this.

She slipped her hand from underneath his and tugged the fabric of his shirt, forcing his lips back onto hers. His hand moved to the base of her neck, his calloused fingers sending a sweet chill across the skin he touched. And then he met her with the same thirst as he pulled her head closer to his. The softness of that first kiss long since forgotten. Now replaced by something more urgent, bruising, filled with something that would continue to go unspoken between them.

Still, she wanted more. More of him, more of a distraction from her raging thoughts. She tossed her leg over his waist, felt his body against her, felt the strength of his chest beneath her hand, a hardness beneath her leg.

His hand left her neck and she wanted to whimper. She needed his touch, needed the pressure against her skin. But then his hand landed above her knee and skimmed her leg where the slit in her dress revealed her bare skin to the cool night air. His touch was warm, gentle as it stopped at the top of the slit. With his thumb, he began drawing shapes across the skin. And not even the night air could cool the heat building at her core.

She gripped the back of his neck pulling him closer to her. Her fingers traveled up through his hair. She tugged his soft locks, pulling a fierce noise from his lips that sent a shiver down her spine as he gripped her thigh in warning.

Kallie grinned against his lips. The bread had fulfilled part of her hunger, but she was still starving. Her hand traveled down his neck. Brushed over his pectorals, his ribcage, his stomach. Lower and lower.

She needed a release. She needed to feel in control over something. For this one moment, she would neither plan nor scheme, she would not make any life-altering decisions. She would just—

Hiccup.

"By the gods," Kallie groaned.

Graeson chuckled and moved back, then pushed himself up to a sitting position. Kallie threw her head back down on the dewy grass, pressing her hands against her temples. Her body still raged with an uncontrollable heat. But the absence of his body pressed against hers left an emptiness in its place and the heat simmered within her.

Graeson cleared his throat. "Come on." He hovered above her with his hand extended toward her, the moon once again morphing his body into a silhouette.

She tried to make out his features, but darkness consumed him.

The moment was gone, reality crashing back in and she hoped that his shadow cast on her hid her reddening cheeks.

She grabbed his hand and he pulled her up. The swift motion had her insides turning and the heat dissipated completely.

As Graeson tried to lead her forward, she tugged her hand back, wrenching it from his grasp. She bent over at the waist. Her skin now clammy. Before she could stop herself, she threw up onto the damp grass, barely missing his shoes, her hair pulled back by hands other than her own.

CHAPTER 23

With someone having drawn back the white curtains, the sun streamed in through the ceiling-high windows covering the walls of Kallie's borrowed room. As she propped herself up and wiped the grogginess from her face, her head throbbed.

How much had she drunk last night?

A fog surrounded her memory of last night. She didn't remember going to bed. The last thing she remembered was going to the kitchen with Graeson and the delicious baguette she had stolen.

With a hand, she shielded herself from the blaring sunlight that seemed insistent on being an annoyance. The emerald dress she had been wearing lay across the back of a simple oak chair near the closet. Dirt covered the bottom of it. She knitted her brows together, but the sound of someone rustling in her closet made her store away the questions it brought.

A moment later, Myra strolled out of the closet with a flowing piece of fabric in hand and a bright smile on her face. "There's some ginger tea on the vanity table. Graeson stopped by and told me that you might need it."

Kallie sighed in relief, but the mention of Graeson had her mind flipping. Whatever happened last night involved him.

"I was also told that the royal family requests your presence for breakfast." Myra sat her clothing on the back of the chair.

"Thank you, Myra," Kallie mumbled.

Myra offered a small smile in return, but her stance remained rigid, her presence heavy with questions and concerns left unspoken.

"This is weird, isn't it?" Kallie asked, spinning her mother's ring around her finger. "I mean. . . My mother's alive, and my father. . .." The words were stuck in her throat, for saying them out loud would make them real.

Myra exhaled and walked over to the bed, sitting down next to her. "I know. Alyn—I mean, Armen told me what he did when you were a child. I didn't want to say anything when we talked yesterday, since it wasn't my story to tell. Though when you think about it, it does make sense. The king was never. . ."

"Warm-hearted?" Kallie suggested. Her father—no, King Domitius, *not* her father—had never been one to coddle Kallie or been a person she could turn to with her worries. Instead, he had expressed his love by throwing her into training. At least, Kallie had once assumed that was the case. But now she wondered if he even cared at all or if he had been using her this entire time.

Myra huffed. "To say the least."

As Kallie tried to hold back the building tears, her voice was barely above a whisper, "I gained one parent, but at what cost?"

Myra said nothing as she wrapped Kallie in her arms. And at that moment, her friend's touch was worth more than any words she could offer. "You'll figure it out, Kals. You always do."

FYNN, Dani, and Terin were the only three who sat at the table when Kallie arrived. The trio was drinking tea and chatting as the two women walked into the room. Kallie sat in the open seat next to Dani, across from Terin. And as Myra nodded to Kallie and turned to take her leave, Fynn said, "Myra, please. Eat with us."

Myra froze at the threshold, glancing between Kallie and Fynn. Back in Ardentol, the servants never ate at the royal table. It was deemed inappropriate by King Domitius, but it seemed like the customs here might be different.

"While you may still be Kallie's handmaiden, you're our guest, Myra." Fynn signaled to the chair beside Kallie. "Please, sit."

Kallie shrugged, then Myra scurried to the seat next to Kallie and sat down. She placed her hands in her lap and began picking at her nails. Under the table, Kallie squeezed Myra's hand.

The smell of smoked maple wafted into the dining room and Kallie's stomach grumbled. Servers piled into the room carrying trays of various foods, ranging from fresh fruits to warm waffles to assorted meats. The sizzling bacon caught Kallie's attention first. Before the server set down the plate, she was already reaching for a crisp piece shining with grease, hoping it would help her hungover stomach. She also grabbed a waffle, added freshly cut strawberries, and a dollop of whipping cream on top. Meanwhile, the others continued to discuss an issue in a nearby village, but Kallie blocked out the noise as she devoured the bacon on her plate.

In the midst of shoving another strip of bacon into her mouth as though it would disappear if she didn't eat it fast enough, a voice dragged her attention away from the feast before her.

"So all of you are just going to sit there while she eats all of the bacon?" Graeson asked, leaning against the threshold, his arms crossed across his chest.

He pushed himself off the threshold and walked behind her. He reached around her, and the scent of cedar mixed with the smoky maple from the bacon stirred something deep within her. He grabbed a piece of bacon off the platter, then continued his trek around to the chair across from Myra and plopped down in it. A smirk formed on his face as he looked over at Kallie. And the way he was holding himself was different from what she was used to seeing, but Kallie couldn't figure out why.

Then, as he chewed off a piece of the bacon, her eyes dropped to his mouth and her hand instinctively went to her lips.

But that . . . that couldn't be right. I'd remember if . . .

Her hand fell from her lips as the memory of last night flooded back to her. Heat rose to her cheeks and Graeson's smirk turned into an amused grin.

She didn't understand. She must have been incredibly drunk to have kissed him.

Granted, he was attractive, but not so attractive that she would let him ruin everything for her. His strong jawline speckled with a hint of stubble was not enough to make her forget why she was here and the decision she needed to make. Nor was the way his stubborn hair kept falling and casting shadows across his face despite the number of times he brushed it back with his fingers. Like his hair, he was stubborn. Too stubborn for her liking, and his handsomeness would not detract from that fact.

And he was dangerous; his aim, deadly. His ability to shut down his emotions and allow whatever slithered beneath his cool exterior to strike his enemies down without any mercy even deadlier.

Her life was already complicated enough, she did not need a fling with this man making it more complicated for her.

As Kallie sat there, still not having responded, fury rose to her cheeks. When she saw the triumphant expression on Graeson's face, she understood what had transgressed last night. He had no feelings for her. He had seen a moment of weakness and took advantage of the opportunity in front of him.

To him, she was a prize. But Kallie could not be won. She was not some trophy to be displayed on the wall next to the severed heads of wild beasts.

She narrowed her eyes, grabbed the gilded knife, and sliced through the waffle on her plate, the blade scratching against the porcelain." Perhaps if you hadn't slept in, you wouldn't have had to worry about me taking something that wasn't mine."

He must have seen the anger behind her gaze. His brows knitted in the center of his forehead, and the smirk was ripped from his face.

"Yeah, Gray. Sleeping in didn't seem to do you any good anyway. You look exhausted," Dani added, speaking past the bite of waffle stuffed in her mouth.

"Hard to adjust back to my own bed, I suppose." Graeson rubbed his face with his palm as though he could wipe away the deep circles of purple and blue under his eyes.

Kallie turned her attention to her brothers, not wanting to give the man who had taken advantage of her drunken state another moment of her time. "Where's Esmeray? I thought she said she would be joining us."

Fynn began to respond but Graeson interrupted him before he could get the words out, "She's probably out on her morning walk through town, but she should be here soon."

"I didn't ask you. Now, did I?" Kallie sneered.

Graeson looked around the table and shrugged. "Seemed like an open question to me."

Kallie focused back on her food, but she had lost her appetite and poked at the food, moving it around her plate. The group at the table continued their conversation, while Kallie and Myra remained quiet for the rest of breakfast. Once Myra had finished eating, she had run off, mumbling something about seeing a tailor about a dress or something.

Not until most of them were done eating already did Esmeray

stroll into the dining room, laughing. A man with silver hair who followed her stopped at the threshold. His uniform had a sparkling silver medallion attached to his lapel signaling that he was the captain of the royal guard.

At the sight of the medallion, Kallie's thoughts momentarily went to Alyn. Myra had said that he was on some other assignment, but Kallie wondered for how long. She didn't want to see him and she hoped she never would. If she accepted this new family or not, she would never be able to forgive his betrayal. Maybe that was why he had run off when he had returned after being gone for a decade. She had been clear about her hatred toward him when they parted ways weeks ago. And she couldn't promise that she wouldn't kill him on sight.

Esmeray's light laughter brought Kallie back from her wandering thoughts.

"You'll have to remind me next time, Airos," Esmeray said, patting the man's arm.

"Of course, Essie," the guard Airos said with a wide smile.

Across the table, Terin whispered to Fynn, "*Essie?*"

Fynn shrugged and the remnants of bewildered amusement lingered in his expression.

After Airos bowed to the queen and left the room, Fynn asked with a sly smile on his face, "Nice walk, mother?"

Esmeray walked toward the head of the table, and as she passed by her sons she ruffled their hair. "Quite. The weather is splendid today."

"Oh, is that what you were talking about with Captain Airos?" Fynn's brow rose in question as he took a sip of his tea.

Esmeray's cheeks flushed, but she flicked her hand as if no one had seen the way they leaned toward each other when they spoke. She sat down and poured herself a cup of tea. "Oh, enough of that. We have more important matters to discuss." Raising the teacup to her lips, Esmeray cast her gaze upon Kallie. "Such as your gift. How has it been coming along?"

Kallie blinked, straightening in her seat. She was not used to talking about her gift with so many eyes on her. But at least Myra, who still did not know about Kallie's ability to manipulate minds, was gone. "Fine."

"And how frequently are you able to use it?"

Kallie shrugged, unwilling to admit her weakness. Based on the queen's tone and how often the others were able to use their gifts, Kallie had the feeling that her inability to use hers at will was uncommon.

Fynn, however, confessed it for her. "Not often, Mother. One use drains her almost completely."

The queen nodded in response, assessing.

Kallie swung her head and glared at Fynn for having read her mind. "I told you *not* to read my mind."

Fynn shrugged with an amused expression. "Can't help it when your thoughts are so loud."

Kallie rolled her eyes, the movement causing the pain in her head to resurface, and she massaged her temple. And it did not go unnoticed.

"Dani told me about your headaches," Esmeray said before she took another sip of tea.

Kallie dropped her hand. "And what of them?"

"It might be time that you visit the Whispering Springs."

Kallie stared blankly and the queen sighed, placing her cup onto the saucer. "As you know, our gifts come from the gods. And they are not endless. Our ability to use our gifts is heavily entwined with our connection to the gods. And as I told you last night, Pontanius and Sabina created the Whispering Springs to help their descendants strengthen their gifts. It is about half of a day's ride away from here.

Children often go there when they struggle to gain complete control over their gifts."

"I am no child," Kallie countered, crossing her arms.

The queen cocked a brow, and Kallie uncrossed her arms at the pointed look. "You have your father's attitude, it seems."

Kallie at first thought she meant King Domitius, but by the look on her face, Esmeray meant her birth father, Markos. Kallie's gaze fell to her plate, the half-eaten waffle staring up at her.

Esmeray continued, "But I digress. Since you have been gone for so long, it is imperative that you visit the springs. Graeson will take you."

Graeson leaned back in his chair, his arms lazily crossed over his chest, his face indifferent as he said, "Fine by me. We'll leave tomorrow morning."

"Fine, but I'm bringing Myra."

"No can do, little mouse. The land is sacred, people who are not of Pontian blood cannot step foot on the Springs or they will suffer a terrible death."

Kallie rolled her eyes. "You're making that up." When his smug expression did not falter, she turned to Esmeray. "Right?"

"Unfortunately he's not," Esmeray said, taking another sip of her tea. "So it's settled. The two of you will leave in two days. Then you'll come back here and we will work on your endurance." The queen set her cup back down and folded her hands in front of her, resting them on the old oak table.

"Fine." Kallie pushed herself from the table and stormed out of the room.

Behind her, a chair scratched against the floor. She refused to turn around as she made her way up the stairs back to her borrowed room.

When she reached her room, she swung the door shut behind her, threw herself across the bed, and screamed into a pillow.

When the rage still hadn't subsided, she tossed the pillow aside. She needed an outlet. She needed to sweat out everything she had learned over the past two weeks. She needed to let her mind go numb and let her body take control.

She walked over to the closet and scanned the clothes, looking for anything that would allow her more movement and wouldn't be an annoyance. As she searched, she thought through her options. The easiest and simplest option would be to go for a run, but she despised running unless there was a purpose to it. Without an objective, it felt aimless and never-ending.

However, it was better than being here and feeling like a caged animal. Anything was better than this. And it was her only option.

Finding a pair of simple black pants, she threw them on. They hugged her thighs and were skin tight, but the material had enough stretch that she could easily move around in them. She paired them with a plain white blouse, tucking the front of the button-up into the band of her pants and allowing it to billow over. Then after rifling through her closet and pushing past the outerwear, she found a pair of black boots. She slipped them on, then wiggled her toes in them, checking the fit. They were similar to the ones she had worn at home, but stiffer, not broken in yet.

As she finished tying the laces, someone knocked on her door and Kallie sighed. When she opened the door, she found Dani waiting on the other side with her curls tied back by a ribbon.

"Oh, good. You changed. No need to wait then. Let's go." Dani turned on her heels and began walking away.

Kallie stared after her, unmoving. "I'm sorry, but where are we going exactly?"

Dani looked over her shoulder. "To blow off some steam." A wicked smile split across her face, a fire shining beneath her dark green eyes daring Kallie to follow. And Kallie could not help but hope a rematch of their earlier fight was in her future.

KALLIE FACED DANI, both of them panting, sweat dripping from their faces. Dani had brought her to the training grounds on the far side of the property. It was surrounded by thick trees which allotted some privacy. The palace was acres away, and the others were far away deep inside the palace walls.

"You weren't kidding about sweating it all out, huh?" Kallie said, trying to regain her breath.

Dani laughed, but it came out wheezy. When she regained her breath, she said, "I never joke about training. It's all or nothing."

"I can see that." Kallie reached down to her toes, stretching out her hamstrings and lower back. "So I know what I needed to work out, but what about you?"

Dani groaned. "Kallie. Come *on.* That was the whole point of this. To avoid talking about our problems." Dani grabbed her flask of water and took a large gulp, one hand braced on her hip.

"I suppose. But at some point you have to talk about it, right?" She wiped off a droplet of sweat from her forehead and headed to the fresh grass that surrounded the outskirts of the training ground.

Dani followed, then they both sat down. They stretched their legs out in front of them and leaned back against their palms, heads tipped up to the sun.

After a moment had passed, Dani said, "All right. I'll tell you if you promise to tell me."

Kallie closed her eyes. She didn't know much about Dani, but her sister-in-law gave off the impression that Kallie could trust her. She nodded in agreement. "You first though."

Dani smirked. "See, I don't know why Fynn thinks he's so special that he can hear people's thoughts."

Kallie chuckled. She turned her head toward the sun, thankful the clouds dulled the sun's heat and kept it from pouring down on her sweat-coated skin.

"Fynn and I got into an argument, which of course, isn't necessarily new for us. We've always been hot and cold. It's one of the reasons I love him. But. . ." Dani hesitated.

"But he's a stubborn ass who should stop reading other people's thoughts without permission?" Kallie suggested.

Dani sighed heavily in response. "We disagree on a lot of things, especially when it comes to politics. And. . ." Dani was sugarcoating her words as if she was hesitant to give too many details.

Kallie couldn't blame her. Kallie was as much of a stranger to Dani as Dani was to her. And Kallie had yet to be upfront about her inner thoughts.

After a moment, Dani continued, "And he always has to make these elaborate plans, which I appreciate, but sometimes you just need to use your instincts. You know? There's a reason why I'm the youngest general in our military. I was born for this. While Esmeray —who I love dearly of course—raised Fynn to be a politician and to be a man of the people, my parents raised me to be the best hunter, the best strategist. Still Fynn second guesses me. And it's . . . exhausting." Dani released her hair from the ribbon and shook it.

"That's one thing I can understand: the constant need to prove yourself to the men around you," Kallie said and glanced over at Dani. "If you don't mind me asking, why did you marry him then?"

A small smile grew on her face as she flipped her hair to the other side of her head. "Because despite all of the arguments and the disputes, I know that at the end of the day, he's the one I want watching my back. He's my best friend, the other half of my soul. And you only find a love that infuriates you to the core but also makes you burn for the other just as passionately once in a lifetime."

Kallie looked at the clouds. The white bundles glided across the sky as if they had all of eternity to float there. But what they didn't know was that somewhere down their path laid their doom. Something out of their control that would destroy them before they even knew what was happening. Love was a fool's pursuit.

"All right. Your turn."

Kallie exhaled. There was too much she could say. Too many reasons why she needed to escape the palace. So she said the one thing that was the least complicated of them all. "Graeson kissed me."

Gasping, Dani jerked upright. "I'm sorry, what?"

Kallie squinted an eye open and saw the woman staring down at her, mouth agape.

"Or maybe I kissed him?" Kallie groaned, smushing her face into her palms. "I don't know."

"And this is a bad thing?"

Kallie groaned. "Obviously!"

Dani shifted beside her, but Kallie didn't dare look at her. "Why? He's attractive, you're attractive. There are worse options for a partner out there."

Kallie rubbed her face. Dani sounded like Myra. It didn't matter if someone was attractive or not. She did not want a partner. Didn't need one. She was engaged. And while Kallie hadn't figured everything out, that engagement was her way to power. Here, Fynn was in line for the throne and she wasn't even a contender. Her goal had not changed. She did not need Graeson messing it up for her.

And then there was that look on his face: the look of victory.

Before Kallie knew what she was saying, the words had already left her mouth. "Because when I saw him this morning, he had the face of someone who had just conquered someone else." She fell back against the ground, raising her hands to her head.

"Maybe there's more to it than that for him?" Dani suggested.

Through the spaces between her fingers, Kallie gave Dani an incredulous look.

"Did you talk to him about it?" Dani asked.

"Of course not! Why would I do that?" When Dani didn't respond, Kallie continued. "There are no feelings between us. He only did it because I was at a low point."

"So if we're following that logic, why did you kiss him if you have no feelings for him?"

"I don't know. I was intoxicated and lonely. And overwhelmed by everything." Frustration spread through her limbs as Kallie spread her arms out. "And sometimes men provide the best distractions."

Dani nodded, staring off into the distance as if she was working through the information. After a moment, she said, "For the record, Graeson has never been the type to take advantage of women."

Kallie scoffed in disbelief. "Sure, but now I have to go to some stupid springs—"

"*Sacred.*" Dani corrected, holding up a finger.

Kallie rolled her eyes. "*Sacred* springs with him. *Alone.*"

"Who knows, maybe you'll learn something," Dani knocked Kallie's knee with her foot. "And maybe you should give him a chance."

"Dani, I'm engaged."

Why did she keep having to remind people that?

"And given away by a man who isn't even your father. When the people learn the truth, it will be easy to end the engagement."

Kallie dug her fingers through the top of her scalp but said nothing.

And her silence was telling. Dani shifted beside her, her body fully turned toward Kallie now. "You are planning on breaking the engagement, right?"

Kallie took a deep breath and shrugged. "I haven't thought that far . . . but if I did break the engagement off, what would everyone think? People from all across Vaneria witnessed my acceptance of King Rian's proposal. If I break that promise. . ."

"Then your word will mean nothing, and a ruler is only as good as their word," Dani finished for her.

Kallie gave a tight smile. "Fynn is the future of Pontia, but what about my future?"

Before Dani turned away, Kallie saw the hurt in her sister-in-law's eyes. And it was the first time she had felt sorry for the Pontians. They had all been set on rescuing her, but years had separated them. Rescuing her was the easy part. Keeping her was the hard part.

They hadn't thought about what would happen *after* they brought her back to a palace she didn't remember. To a history she didn't recall, to a role she was resistant to play.

The Kallie they knew and loved was no longer there. Or she had grown into something more than they had imagined.

CHAPTER 24

As Kallie sat a top of a horse named Shadow, she regretted taking the reins from Graeson. When Graeson had asked her if she was fine with riding on her own horse to relieve Calamity of their combined weight, Kallie didn't want him to think her a coward. She needed to face her fears. Therefore, with her rage from the other day still fresh, she took the reins, swallowing the large lump in her throat.

The path they took to the springs led them through the village and Graeson signaled them to stop beside what looked to be a bakery.

Without glancing at her, he hopped off. Kallie shifted, but his words halted her. "I'll be back in just a moment."

She stared at his back and watched him disappear into the bakery. As the door shut behind him, the smell of cinnamon, butter, and honey saturated the air. Inhaling the smell, Kallie sighed. But then the memory of Graeson sharing bread with her and the two of them kissing flashed in her mind, and she wanted to gag instead.

Beneath her, Shadow shifted and Kallie gripped the reins, her thighs tightening around the horse. Beads of sweat began to form at the base of her neck underneath her braid. For the most part, she had been fine riding beside Graeson, but now she was responsible for two horses. And her breathing began to pick up. She started counting to ten.

At seven, Graeson walked out, and she exhaled heavily.

When his gaze met hers, his head tilted and he brushed his hand through his hair. "You let your fear get the best of you."

After shoving a bundle in the satchel carrying their belongings, he stepped toward her and Kallie fiddled with the reins.

"Are you sure you're going to be fine? We can turn back and get a double saddle," Graeson suggested.

The word *yes* was on the tip of her tongue, but unwilling to admit defeat, she shook her head.

Graeson waited for a moment as though she would change her mind. But when Kallie didn't, he mounted his horse. "Do you think your fear is because of that night?"

He didn't need to specify for her to know what he meant. She shrugged. "It's possible."

Patting Calamity on the side of her neck, Graeson said, "The horse did nothing besides obey its master." Then under his breath, he added, "Not the horse's fault his master is a monster."

"Obviously. But that doesn't make it any easier." Breathing through her trepidation, Kallie signaled Shadow to a trot. And as she followed Graeson, Kallie tried her best to not focus on the queasiness that kept bouncing in her stomach.

An awkward silence stretched between them and with time, the town disappeared behind them. The grand palace a mere speck in the distance. And ahead of them, a windy path through the hills tipped in gold. The sun greeting them.

The trip had just begun, but Kallie could not wait for it to be over.

THEY HAD STOPPED TWICE during their trek to the springs for a break for the horses and themselves.

Then soon after, Graeson had slowed Calamity's pace down to a walk as they approached a thick batch of trees.

"We're almost there," Graeson said, keeping his eyes on the path.

Graeson led them into the forest that even the sun, which now sat in the center of the sky, couldn't break through. And as they passed the first line of trees, a light chill brushed over her skin. Then a faint tune began to echo in the trees, a beautiful harmony forming.

Deep within the branches of the trees, a splotch of bright scarlet flew from one branch to another. Then another blood-red bird perched on the branch alongside the first, amplifying the tune. Another joined in the song, hidden somewhere among the green leaves. Then another. And another. And soon, the birds were harmonizing with one another, their song reverberating across the forest.

Graeson said in a hushed tone, "I've never seen so many." And for once, Graeson appeared surprised.

"What kind of birds are they?" Kallie asked.

"They're called the Red Spirit, said to be the eyes of the gods."

"They're beautiful," Kallie whispered, afraid that if she spoke too loudly she might scare them off. "Why do you think there are so many?"

Graeson continued to stare at the birds, his face a mix of awe, shock, and concern. "Has to be an omen of some sort," he mumbled, more to himself than in answer to Kallie's question.

But by the bewildered look on Graeson's face, Kallie couldn't tell if it was a good omen or a bad one.

They continued their way down the winding path at a slow pace, not saying another word as they listened to the birds sing.

While Graeson remained concerned, Kallie on the other hand began to feel a lightness within the pit of her stomach. She reached down to her gift, which she had not touched for days, and it danced at her touch. Maybe it was the birds' song or maybe it was this place that was supposedly touched by the gods, but Kallie felt lighter, refreshed.

The feeling only grew stronger as they made their way deeper into the forest, the birds' song intermixing with the sound of rushing water.

A breeze swept through the woods carrying mist that was cold against her warm skin. The rushing water grew louder, the song of the birds coming to its crescendo.

"We're here," Graeson said as he dismounted.

Distracted, Kallie ignored his hand as she took in the sight before her. The trees encircled a large spring. The water at the edge so clear that Kallie could see several feet beneath the surface until the depths of the water began to take over. The clarity was replaced by a beautiful bright turquoise, the sun beating down upon it. On the other side of the large pool of water stood a cascading waterfall that seemed to call to her. A song pulled from her heart, urging her to come forward.

Shaking herself from the trance, Kallie whispered, "This place. . . I've seen this place before."

"What do you mean?" Graeson asked.

"On the boat when Terin had put me to sleep, my dreams took me here."

"Hmm," Graeson murmured. "Terin can influence one's dreams. Perhaps he showed you it?"

Maybe it was Terin's doing, but Kallie wasn't sure that was the case. Although she had no proof otherwise.

She looked down at him, his hand still outstretched, waiting for her to grab onto it. And she looked into his gray eyes, the color mimicking the foaming water behind him. Here, he almost reminded her of someone, but Kallie blinked and the feeling quickly dissipated.

He nudged his hand forward and she dropped her gaze, placing her palm in his and dismounting.

Once she landed, he let go of her hand and she headed toward the springs, the strange sense of urgency leading her. Not bothering to glance back at Graeson, she slipped off her shoes and began to undress.

Piling her clothes on top of a small boulder, she stepped toward the water in nothing but her undergarments. At the edge of the lake, wet sand mushed between her toes.

Letting the memory of her dream guide her, she dipped her toes into the crystal-clear water and headed toward the middle of the pool. As she walked deeper into the water, the coolness of the spring rejuvenated her. Her eyesight felt clearer, her mind steadier as the water rose past her thighs. She wasn't sure if it was the result of being in the water in general or if the essence of the gods was causing her body to react in such a way.

Once she was waist-deep, she paused, instinctively knowing what she would find. And there it was, in the middle of the lake. Large slabs of marble sparkled beneath the water. Kallie stepped onto it, the slate slick beneath her bare feet.

As she moved forward, her balance wavered. She began to fall back into the water, but then Graeson was beside her, one hand on her elbow and the other around her waist, steadying her. But then his hand disappeared from her waist just as quickly as it appeared, although he stayed close behind as she led the way to the rushing water.

With the waterfall before them, she could no longer hear Graeson breathing behind her, the water loud in her ears. Kallie took a deep breath. After exhaling, she stepped into the rushing water, drenching herself. As she passed through the water, she brushed her fingertips through her soaking hair, brushing it all to her back and letting it drip down her spine.

Not a moment later, Graeson broke through the wall of water, equally as drenched. His eyes were squeezed shut. And she couldn't help but stare at his bare chest, water dripping down the defined muscles. He shook his black hair, like a dog shaking off rain, leaving the black strands in disarray. As he ran his fingers through his hair and moved it off his forehead, the scar glistened from the water. His hands left his hair as he opened his eyes. They were brighter than she had seen them, nearly glowing as they met hers, and a crooked smirk that sent her mind spiraling appeared across his face.

She reminded herself why they were here and forced herself to look away. But it was much harder to do than it should have been.

This place was making her feel not quite like herself.

Her attention now directed ahead of her, she observed the cave. When she dreamed of this place, she was unsure which goddess had stood before her, the image unclear. But now, standing before the stone statue, she knew without a doubt it was Sabina.

The stories back home, of how Sabina had gone missing after the betrayal of the human, were nothing but a lie. A way to hide the truth of what had happened between Sabina and the other gods who had betrayed her.

Kallie approached the statue but hesitated when she saw a second statue that Graeson now stood in front of. Kallie had never seen a statue of the god before, but she instinctively knew it was Pontanius that looked down upon them with open arms. A wreath rested upon his forehead, wrapping around his shoulder-length curls. Unlike Sabina whose face was burdened by the grief she carried, Pontanius stood with a hunger for revenge.

Before the towering gods, Kallie felt small and childish. She whispered to Graeson, "Now what?"

"Your family's gifts are closely tied to Sabina. Bow before her and give yourself to her," he said.

Her brows knitted in confusion. "Give myself? What do you

mean?" She felt foolish as if he was playing some game with her. Seeing how far he could push her until he burst out laughing. Although at this point, she was out of her element and she would do anything to gain better control over her gift.

"You'll figure it out." He paused, then his brows scrunched together and his voice lowered as he added, "But, Kallie?"

She rotated the ring around her finger. "Yes?"

"Brace yourself. Sometimes the first time can be . . . overwhelming."

She wanted to ask for clarification, but before she could, Graeson knelt in front of Pontanius. Hesitantly, Kallie followed his lead.

Bowing before the goddess, she wondered how Domitius had known she was linked to Sabina. She had always felt a sense of attachment to the goddess. But now was not the time to question these things, so she welcomed the familiar face looking down upon her. In this foreign place, the goddess she had so frequently turned to back in Ardentol was a comfort.

Placing her hands down on the cold stone, palms down, Kallie laid her forehead on them. Her wet hair fell around her, shielding her from the light and the world around her.

She wasn't sure what she was supposed to do next, so she tried reaching down within herself to her gift. And as she called upon it, her gift rose to meet her, flooding her body with a feeling that tasted like golden starlight, warm and welcoming. It heated her entire being and overwhelmed her senses.

She opened her mind. Allowed herself to think about everything she had closed off and put behind a lock and key, afraid of someone being able to see what lay beneath the surface. The pain, the confusion, the love. Everything she thought made her weak. Everything that made her strong: her determination, her desires. She laid it all out. Opened herself up for the first time in a long time.

And Kallie showed the goddess who she was, who she wanted to be.

An invisible string tugged at the source of her gift, a tether to the goddess. Other strands wove around it, thickening the cord. The connection grew between them, solidified. Then understanding flooded through her.

She didn't know why she hadn't made the connection before. Her gift should have been proof that she was not merely blessed by the gods, but rather their blood—Sabina's blood—ran through her veins. And bowing down before the goddess, bearing all she had to offer, and confessing her deepest secrets, Kallie felt that connection. Felt the link between her and Sabina harden and stretch out before her.

The feeling was intoxicating, like the honeyed wine of the gods. The sense of complete power and control left her wanting more. She wanted to continue drinking the sweet liquor, to let it fill her up.

And then the warmth consumed her. The only thing she could see was the golden light of stars. Feather-light fingertips slid across her shoulders. Then a feminine voice that sounded like raindrops whispered her name.

And by the otherworldliness of the voice, Kallie knew that if she looked over her shoulder she would see the goddess standing behind her. But the fear that resided in her, the fear of the goddess disappearing or something far worse happening prevented Kallie from moving at all.

As the goddess's breath brushed her neck, goosebumps trailed in its path despite the immense heat sailing throughout her body.

"Kalisandre," the goddess said her name like it was sugar on her tongue, "if the truth within is not found, then one may not find what one seeks."

Kallie's brows knitted together. "I—I don't understand."

"Find it, Kalisandre. Find it and destroy it before all is lost."

Kallie shouted, frustrated, "Destroy *what?*"

No response.

She shouted again, this time more urgently, heart thudding against her chest.

When the silence continued, Kallie felt the link begin to drift away and turn to ash. She dared to turn around, but all she saw was the falling water. No sign of the goddess.

And Kallie wondered if the goddess had even been there in the first place. The warmth that previously resided in her drained from her body, leaving her shivering against the cold marble floor.

CHAPTER 25

KALLIE GASPED, INHALING A SHARP, PAINFUL BREATH AS A WARM HAND shook her shoulder. She lay curled up on her side, the ground cold and wet beneath her bare skin.

"Are you all right?" Graeson asked, his voice filled with something akin to panic as he knelt before her, his hair falling around his face.

"What happened?" Kallie's voice was hoarse. She searched the cave for signs of the goddess, for a sign that she was not crazy.

"I don't know . . . one moment it was silent, then I heard you shouting. When I looked over, you were spasming on the floor, but then. . ." Graeson hesitated. When Kallie propped herself onto her elbows and looked at him inquisitively, he forced the rest of the sentence out. "It stopped. Your skin was clammy, and I thought. . ." Graeson didn't meet her gaze.

Kallie tried to push herself up, only to find her body weak. Graeson was quick though and instantly helped her into a seated position.

"Does that . . . does that happen to everyone?" Kallie asked, her voice barely above a whisper.

"The spasming? No, not as far as I know," Graeson said gently.

"But do others see—"

He nodded, apparently already knowing what she would say. And that brought a little relief to her chest.

"I tried to warn you that the first time can be jarring." He said, standing. "Did she say anything to you?"

His words allowed her to breathe normally. It wasn't just her imagination. Kallie recited the goddess's words, "If the truth within is not found, then one may not find what one seeks. Find it. Destroy it."

Graeson was silent as he took in Sabina's ominous words.

"Do you know what it could mean?" Kallie asked.

He shook his head. "I'm not sure." But when he looked at her, his gaze pierced her soul as if he too could read minds like Fynn. She forced her body to remain still. She knew it was silly. Graeson did not share Fynn's gift. Still, all her vulnerabilities and secrets were at the forefront of her mind. And she felt herself forming those walls around her thoughts as she had learned to do. Just in case.

THEY SAT beside the springs while eating the sandwiches Graeson had bought at the bakery earlier that morning. Whatever had happened to her in the caves had caused her hunger to surface by the time Graeson had helped her back to their makeshift camp.

Before sitting down Kallie had thrown on her blouse but allowed her legs and feet to remain in the sun.

They hadn't talked since the cave, which seemed to be the pattern for them. But every so often, Graeson would cast a cursory glance her way. After the hundredth time, Kallie had enough. She bit off a chunk of her sandwich and raised a brow. "What?"

"Are we ever going to talk about it?" Graeson asked.

Her eyes flicked to the waterfall across from them.

He plopped the last bite in his mouth. "No, not that."

The bread became tougher in her mouth, and she struggled to swallow it. She narrowed her eyes. "Then what do we possibly have to talk about?"

He tilted his head and leaned back on his hands, his sandwich already gone." Don't play me for a fool. I know you've been avoiding me."

Her cheeks began to heat and she instantly became uncomfortable under his gaze. She forced a yawn and turned away, pretending as if something in the water caught her eye. "I don't know what you're talking about."

While it might have been true that she had been avoiding him since breakfast two days ago, Kallie didn't know why he felt the need to bring it up. Especially now. That kiss was a moment of weakness, a moment that should never have happened. Graeson bringing it up was just another tactic of his to throw her off. But she didn't understand what his end goal was, which irked her even more.

"Graeson," she looked back at him, face emotionless and tone neutral. "I was drunk. I was emotional and overwhelmed."

"So it was what? A way for you to get your mind off of everything else going on?" Graeson asked. His words made it sound like she was the one using him that night.

Perhaps, a part of her had used him. After all, men had always been a good distraction for her.

She shrugged, turning away from whatever emotion floated in the air between them.

Graeson scoffed. "You are so full of shit, you know that, right?"

She swung her gaze back to him and an icy fire rose in her eyes. "I'm sorry, what did you say?"

"Oh, I'm sorry. Did I hurt the princess's feelings?" Graeson sneered.

Kallie ran her tongue across her teeth and sneered. "Watch what you say next, Graeson."

"Or what, little mouse?"

And the smirk appearing on his smug face after he uttered her nickname in mockery sent her into action. Grabbing a hold of the familiar metal buried in the pile of her clothes beside her, she threw her dagger.

Graeson didn't blink, he didn't even move as the dagger narrowly missed his ear, digging deep into the bark of the tree he leaned on.

"I said it once, and I'll say it—" He stopped mid-sentence as bird poo fell on top of his head as one of the Red Spirits previously perched upon the tree branch flew away, scared off by the dagger.

So they're a good omen then.

And Kallie couldn't help the grin that rose onto her face.

"You were saying?" She tilted her head down and batted her eyelashes at him. The amusement still alive, she leaned back onto her palms and lifted her head to the sun.

The glowing light behind her eyelids darkened. When she opened her eyes, Graeson was bent over her, bird shit still in his hair. Before she could scurry away, he lifted her into the air. His arms wrapped around her legs, restraining them. As she wiggled in his arms, Graeson threw her over his back and stomped off into the water. When he didn't put her down, she pounded on his back with her fists.

The water rose to his calves, then his knees, then below his waist. Kallie bent her legs, keeping them out of the water.

Graeson's hands moved to her hips and he lifted her into the air. He held her there like a small child, her feet kicking. And by the look in his eyes, the anger, and the power he had over her, she knew he wasn't going to just put her down.

Not without a price.

"Graeson," she warned, her legs growing still.

A sly smile graced his face. "Only if you tell me the truth."

She looked back and forth between his eyes. Her undergarments had just begun to dry, but they would dry again. "I already did," she bit out.

Then as his grip tightened around her waist, his arms flexing, she took a deep breath, preparing herself for the plunge.

Water rushed around her, and she pushed against the wet sand, breaking the surface and pushing her hair back.

Kallie momentarily marveled at his strength, for Graeson had thrown her deep enough that she had to tread water, her feet unable to touch the sand. The fabric of her shirt was heavy and floated around her.

She lifted her head to try to see further into the water. She spun around and around but saw nothing. Besides the ripples she had created, the water was still. Graeson was nowhere to be found.

Where could he have gone?

Then the small waves pushed her back, and as she twisted around, she saw a black head of hair appear atop the water.

"You jerk!" she spat, glaring at him as he resurfaced. "You ruined my only shirt"

"And you're a liar," he said, teasing.

She snorted. "And you're not?"

He narrowed his eyes at her, questioning. The man was arrogant *and* a hypocrite. There was no worse combination.

"You *kidnapped* me," Kallie said as she continued to keep herself afloat. "Or did you forget?"

Graeson, who could still stand, shrugged, pushing his hair back. "You say *kidnapped*, but I like to think of it as *rescued*."

"Did you ever stop to think that I didn't need saving? That I was perfectly content living my life as it was?"

None of them had thought about that, Dani had made that clear yesterday. And her words seemed to smack him across the face, his amused expression falling flat.

But then he cocked a brow. "Were you really though?"

Kallie grew silent, unable to answer.

She was happy before, wasn't she? Content, at the least. Her happiness would come once she gained control over Frenzia.

He looked her up and down, his gaze judgmental, harsh. "I at least don't try to run from my problems."

"No, you just throw them into springs," she snarled.

Straight-faced, Graeson said, "I never said you were a problem."

Kallie rolled her eyes. "Right, because I am just something for you to conquer." She floated backward, heading to deeper waters. She didn't care if she was proving him right by putting distance between them. She needed the space.

But Graeson, of course, followed her. Ever the persistent chaser. "What are you talking about?"

She paddled toward the shore. With each stroke, her choices became murkier. "Now who is playing who for the fool, *Gray?*"

"Don't say my name like that," he bit back.

She smirked. His anger only fueled her. Closing her eyes as she floated under the sun, Kallie asked, "Like what, *Gray?*"

"Like we're not friends."

Kallie chuckled. "But we're not."

The tension in the air became taught.

"I suppose not anymore," Graeson said.

After a moment passed, Kallie relaxed, believing Graeson had given up on the conversation.

The past was the past, Kallie reminded herself. She was a different person now. And for better or for worse, she couldn't change that.

Then Graeson broke the silence, "It meant something to me, you know." Her eyes flew open and her peddling slowed, unsure of what to do with those words. "Thought you should know that much, at least," he added.

Hesitating, she flipped over and found Graeson just a few feet away. "Don't do that."

"Do what?"

"Pretend like you care."

"I've never pretended." He swam closer to her but paused when he was an arm's reach away. "Never with you."

"You don't even know me," Kallie countered, treading water in place.

"Kal, I've known you my whole life. And I know it might sound weird to you because either the trauma of that night altered your memory or something else did." A water droplet raced down the side of his face near his scar, and Kallie watched it as it slid down his throat and into the water. "But I never stopped thinking about you."

She swallowed.

"My biggest regret in life was losing you that night. You were never—this wasn't how our life was supposed to go," Graeson said.

"And how was it supposed to go?" her whole body shook, her muscles growing tired, yet her voice remained steady.

He shook his head, then the water pushed them closer. They were now only a foot apart and she did not dare to speak.

"There wasn't supposed to be all of this pain between us. All of this," he motioned toward the air between them, "space."

She looked into his eyes and saw the years of sorrow and searching within them. Why had he waited for her?

He was only a couple of years older than her, maybe two or three. They were children when they had known each other. The memories of which were still buried in her mind as if a layer of frosted glass covered them, blocking them from her view. She did not know how she felt toward him when she was a child. But whether she remembered or not, either way, it did not matter.

She had seen the children in the palace chase each other, turn red when a parent asked them about a friend. And while those feelings could be true and real, they were the feelings of a child. When the world was new and fresh, when the woes and heartbreaks of life had not yet been seen.

Years later, those feelings mattered little.

Right?

Despite knowing that, she asked, "If we take this step, what's to say there won't be more pain?"

Graeson scanned her face. When he spoke, his voice was solid, "I would never hurt you, Kallie."

By his voice and the look in his eyes, she knew he was telling the truth. But he wasn't the one she was worried about, the scar a clear reminder on his face. She had caused that. King Domitius was after *her*. And who knows how he would react now.

When she tried to respond, the question on her lips was much harder to ask than she had anticipated. "And what's to say I won't hurt you?"

But before she could swim away, he grabbed her arm and turned her toward him. Graeson stared down at her. His height granted him the ability to stand while Kallie had to pump her arms and legs in the water.

"Don't you dare turn away from me. Not again."

"You know I didn't choose to do that," she spat.

"No, but this time you are."

He stared at her, and she stared back. She knew she should turn around, swim away from him. That responding to him and continuing to play this game would lead to nothing good. But her body wouldn't let her.

She looked into those pools of glistening silver. "So, let me have the choice that I had taken from me then."

Graeson flinched, but he did not speak. He let the silence bubble between them.

He was letting her make her choice.

However, as he presented her with the option, she didn't know what she wanted. When she searched within herself, her mind was split in two. She knew what she *should* do, what she *needed* to do. But still, she didn't know what she *wanted* to do.

And as she remained there, Graeson made one last effort to persuade her. "Fine. But let me ask you this: don't you feel it?"

Kallie tilted her head. "Feel what?"

His eyes lifted to hers. "The pull between us."

Kallie huffed. What he said was nonsense. The only thing pulling them together was the water. While this place was intoxicating and she probably hadn't recovered from whatever happened in the cave, it was nothing more than the springs playing with them. The gods' lives were not simple, nor were theirs. It was a cruel joke.

Kallie looked around her. "I think you're letting this place trick you."

He groaned in frustration, and a small smile tried to form as she watched his frustration bloom, but she shoved it down.

"It's not just the water, and you know it, Kallie."

The feeling of heavy sand beneath her feet caused Kallie to inhale. She let the top of her toes rest on the sand as she used her arms to balance herself.

Graeson minimized the space between them, but Kallie pressed her palms against his chest, keeping him at bay. Yet as her hands touched his skin beneath the water and his muscles flexed at her touch, she questioned why she was trying to keep him away.

It would be much easier to let him in. This game they were playing was dangerous. And while she was in denial about many things, she knew deep down that that is what they had been doing the past few weeks—playing a game of cat and mouse. It was only going to make it harder for her to ensure her victory in the end.

And they were nowhere near the end.

He placed a hand over hers. "Stop pretending it isn't there. You've felt it since we found each other again. Just like I did."

She couldn't deny that she had felt something there. And despite the anger she still felt toward him—for taking advantage of her when she was at her weakest—it was undeniable that she had been the one to kiss him first. That he had been the one to pull away, not her.

Even though she may not have been able to deny it to herself, she didn't have to be honest with him. "I don't—"

"Kalisandre." His voice was deep and husky, his silver eyes darkened, turning to steel. His hands slid to her waist beneath the water. And the sound of her name on lips was her undoing.

She closed her eyes. Her heart squeezed together, and her lungs tightened. She didn't believe that the water wasn't affecting her mind, her body, and whatever connection pulled them together. But she also didn't believe that it was completely made up either. Because when she looked at him—when she *really* looked at him, she couldn't deny the attraction she felt toward him. The way his wet hair fell across his face, the way water dripped down his skin. The way his skin felt against her hands as she slid them toward the back of his neck. She had felt lust before and she told herself it was nothing more than that.

And when she saw the desire in his eyes, she knew it wasn't a desire she had placed there like she had for her other marks. Nor was it desire for her crown—

She inhaled sharply and jerked her head back.

King Rian.

She pushed him back. "I can't."

"I didn't mean to—we can slow it down." He rushed out, his fingers wrapping around her hand as if he could hold her there.

The way he looked at her, like *he* was the issue, pulled a strange feeling from her. And suddenly she wanted to confess everything to him. For no reason other than to erase that look and the guilt she felt.

"It's not that. I—" she snapped her mouth shut.

His gaze jumped between her eyes. "Whatever it is, you can tell me." His thumb ran circles along the back of her hand as if he could pull the words from her mind.

And she wanted to tell him the truth. Truly. But why did everything have to be so complicated?

She looked up at him. "Graeson, I'm engaged."

She was drifting away and he knew it. He pulled her hands to his chest and pulled her against him by her waist. On their own accord, her legs wrapped around him, the water pushing them up.

"You wear no ring, except this one." He rolled his finger over her mother's ring. "You have not met him. And you've made no vows."

"But I did give him my word," Kallie whispered.

"Kalisandre."

Her arms wrapped around his neck, and she squeezed her eyes shut. She wanted her name to belong on his lips, to stay there forever. She willed it to have the power to break every promise she had made, every vow she had taken, every plan she had made.

But it didn't.

She sighed. "I won't go against my word, Graeson."

"You don't have to, we can explain what happened."

Her eyes flew open. "And say what? 'We kidnapped your fiancé, but really King Domitius kidnapped her first? Oh, and guess what? He's not even her real father!'"

Dani had tried to argue the same point, but a letter would do nothing. It wasn't as easy as telling the other kingdoms the truth. She barely believed it when they had told her, so why would anyone else? It was too strange, too complicated. Too messy.

He sighed and dropped his forehead to hers. "We'll figure it out," he said and kissed her forehead.

And it took all of her willpower to not meet his lips, to not claim him for herself. But as much as she wanted to believe him, she needed him to stop. She didn't need the distraction right now. And that's all he was. Whatever he thought he could gain from this, she would only disappoint him. And for more reasons than she could count.

She had to push him away. And there was only one way to do that.

She rested her head on his chest and said the only thing he could not alter or misconstrue. "He's a king, Graeson."

She felt the absence of his breath on her head. He let go of her waist and brought his hand to her chin, tilting her head up. "Is that really all you care about?" His jaw flexed.

She didn't want to look at him. But she couldn't let him hope there was a chance, so she stared at him, her gaze unwavering. "Yes."

He opened his mouth, then closed it. Whatever words he wanted to say were lost in the space she had forced between them. He released her chin and shut his eyes, his face contorting. She stared at him, wondering if she had made the right choice. But she had never had the choice to begin with, had she?

"I don't believe you," he finally said.

Kallie didn't have a chance to respond as a breeze swept through, brushing against her neck and sending shivers down her back. Her teeth rattled.

Graeson looked down at her, his gaze softening. He cleared his throat. "If you stay in this water, you'll catch a cold. And if you're not going to help get the fire started, you can catch yourself something to eat." Then his eyes lit mischievously.

"What are you doing?" Kallie asked, eyes growing wide as she forced her body to remain still.

A crooked smirk formed on his face. "You may not want to be with me yet, but don't think for a second that I'm not going to stop trying to convince you otherwise."

And at that moment, Kallie learned of another side to Graeson: he was unyielding.

He lifted her out of the water before she could swim away. And with the choice of falling into the water and possibly hurting herself, she wrapped her arms loosely around his neck. "I don't think you can persuade me to give up a kingdom by carrying me."

"Already forgotten our kiss then?"

"Mustn't have been that memorable," Kallie suggested, shrugging in his arms.

Once out of the water, he stood her up in the sand, then he leaned down. His lips grazed her ear and his breath tickled her neck. "Liar."

The huskiness of his whisper against her neck sent shivers down her back.

Kallie rolled her eyes though and shoved him. Walking away, she began unbuttoning her soaking shirt.

He was right though. She was a liar. She was lying about many things, and the kiss was only one of them.

"I saw the way you looked at me at breakfast," he said from behind her. A blush rose to her cheeks as her fingers struggled with the last button. And she was thankful that she was facing away from him because just as she had done when she remembered they had kissed, her hand instinctively rose to her lips. The ghost of his lips still lingered on her mouth even days later.

She took a deep breath. It was only a kiss. Nothing more. A kiss would not unravel her.

CHAPTER 26

GRAESON HAD STARTED A FIRE IN A SMALL CLEARING IN THE FOREST A ways off from the springs to not disturb the sacred grounds. In Graeson's borrowed shirt—a fact Kallie tried not to think about every time the wind swept the smell of citrus toward her—Kallie sat cross-legged by the fire. She let the heat of the fire radiate around her. The remains of the fish Graeson had caught for dinner smoked at the bottom of the fire, turning into burnt crisps.

While they ate, Graeson told her stories of his childhood. His years of schooling, the intense training he had undergone, the constant pranks he and her brothers pulled on each other and Dani. During which, their previous argument was left behind in the waters as if it never happened, and instead replaced with happiness and laughter from his childhood memories. But darkness lurked in the shadows of his stories.

Kallie had noticed fairly quickly that not only was Graeson's mother absent in the stories since she had passed, but also his father. Ironically, the only parental figure present was *her* mother. And she empathized with him. The way he avoided the topic, moving around it at every turn was all too familiar, for she had grown up doing the same thing.

However, Kallie got the impression that his father's role was different.

And despite what she had said before, for some reason, she felt compelled to know everything about this man who sat across from her with his face glowing gold from the flames. She wanted to know both the happy moments of his life and the ones that had caused the scars she couldn't see.

So even though she knew it might be painful, she asked the question she had hated hearing growing up, "What about your father?"

Graeson's gaze dropped to the flames, the laughter on his lips fading. His once soft features hardened, his jaw tightening. "Don't have one."

In the following silence, she observed him, wondering about the rage building behind his flesh. She wanted to know what happened, what his father had done to spark that rage. And she wanted to fix it, to take revenge against whoever hurt this man.

Instead, Kallie simply nodded, for she still didn't understand why she cared about a man she barely knew and who barely knew her. A man who looked like a god and whose foundation was built of the ire that could take down mountains and drain the seas. He was chiseled from marble, but with a softness behind his eyes when a rare smile appeared or a deep laugh left his lips.

Then again, she reminded herself, Graeson was also a man who could not give her what she craved from this world the most.

He was only a man.

Not a king, not a god.

He held no power of his own.

And she needed to refocus on that goal. The purpose of this trip wasn't to get to know Graeson better or to confuse her heart. The purpose was to strengthen her gift, to gain full control of it.

Directing her gaze to the waterfall hidden by trees, Kallie changed topics. "All right, so about this whole 'bonding with the gods' thing. What happens now?"

Previously deep in thought, Graeson focused back on Kallie, who under his direct gaze, struggled to maintain eye contact. "Have you tried reaching for your gift yet?"

Kallie shook her head. She had been . . . preoccupied. She reached for her gift. Normally, she had to dig deep within herself to feel its presence, but at the mere thought of seeking it out, her gift greeted her.

Surprise glossed her features. Her gift flowed, molding to her will. It didn't just sit at the bottom of her stomach but flew through her body and melded with her blood, like another layer beneath her skin.

Graeson chuckled. "Based on the look on your face, I would wager it feels a little different now."

Kallie raised her palms, flipping them over as though she could see her gift coursing through her veins. "Now what?" Kallie whispered, afraid she might scare her gift away and have it crawling back to the pit of her stomach.

"Now, we wait until you can test it," Graeson said, poking the dying fire with a stick. He then placed one arm on his knee that was propped up and leaned back onto his palm.

Kallie sighed, annoyed that the queen had forced Graeson of all people to accompany her since she couldn't use her gift on him. And the golden warmth that had soared through her vanished. "So, can I know more about your gift then?"

Graeson laughed as his gaze trailed over her. "If I have to wait to get what I want, you have to wait too."

Kallie didn't bother to hide her frustration. At this point, the secrecy felt silly. But instead of pushing the topic, she stood and as she headed to the tent, she looked over her shoulder. "Fine. I'm going to bed."

Graeson's light laughter followed Kallie into the tent. After closing the tent flap, she took off her shoes, then claimed the left side of the makeshift bed made of two blankets. Since Graeson had insisted on packing light, they would have to share the small space. Kallie lay down, pulling the top blanket over her. She wiggled against the ground, forming a small divot in the shape of her body.

She had dreaded sleeping on the ground again, believing sleep would be hard to come by again and terrified of the nightmares that would follow. But once she found a comfortable spot on the ground, the exhaustion from the day hit her as she nestled into Graeson's shirt. And soon enough, the sweet darkness of sleep took over.

THE SOUND of the tent flapping in the wind stirred Kallie from her sleep. Blinking her eyes open to the darkness of the night, the glow from the fire outside was no longer present and she could barely make out Graeson's silhouette. She didn't know how far off dawn was, but she wanted as much sleep as she could get. However, despite her efforts to fall back asleep, she couldn't help but track Graeson as he moved through the tent.

He shuffled over to the pile of blankets, his footsteps quiet. He moved slowly so as not to wake her. Before he laid down, she felt a light weight fall across her body. His cloak, which smelled of smoked cedar, lay over her as an extra layer of warmth. His hand lingered on her side and she could feel his thumb lightly moving back and forth over the fabric. And that small gesture made her stomach flutter and a faint smile graced her lips in the darkness while a tinge of guilt coated her throat.

"Soon." The word was almost inaudible on Graeson's tongue.

Soon?

She didn't know what he meant, but the promise behind that single word caused her cheeks to blush involuntarily. And Kallie was once again thankful for the darkness hiding it from him.

As she pretended to be asleep, she decided she would not think about it. So as he laid down beside her and rested his arm near her, for that moment she let herself enjoy the warmth it provided.

Whether she liked it or not, this man might just be her undoing.

CHAPTER 27

"AGAIN," ESMERAY ORDERED FROM HER DESK, HEAD PROPPED ON HER hands as she observed Kallie from across the room.

Kallie rubbed her face. They had been practicing for an hour now to see how far Kallie could stretch her gift. While her gift had become stronger since they visited the Whispering Springs two weeks ago, the queen's long practice sessions were exhausting. From dawn to dusk, they practiced leaving Kallie little time to do anything else. She had barely explored the palace even, something she was meaning to do since she had arrived. Beyond the study, the kitchens, the dining room, and her room, she knew little of the palace. She needed to stretch her legs and her mind needed to rest, but the queen was insistent.

Esmeray wanted Kallie to master her gift. And since she believed Kallie was behind on her training due to the time away from the island, Esmeray had forced Kallie to start practicing using her gift once Kallie had returned to the palace. And Kallie couldn't help but recall the training sessions with Domitius. The long hours spent sweating in the dark corners of the palace, his stern words to keep going, and the fire behind those words.

However, after the constant use of her gift, Kallie feared the headache to come. Some days she was lucky and it never did, but other days she suffered greatly.

She took a deep breath and focused her attention on Terin, who had volunteered to be her practice doll. And several commands later, Kallie was starting to see the aftermath of constant manipulation. His gaze dragged, his reaction time slowed, and her concern grew.

Kallie flicked her eyes to Fynn who stood a few feet behind Terin with his back against the wall. His eyes met hers and she pleaded, begging him this once to read her mind.

Please. We both *need a break.*

Having read her mind, he rolled his eyes and sighed, pushing himself off the wall with his foot. "Mother, do you think it would be a good idea to give them a break? Terin looks like he's going to start drooling soon."

Terin's gaze was still hazy, her previous command binding him to his seat. Kallie didn't know if he was acting to sell it or if he was truly about to keel over.

"Fynn, she needs to practice. You know better than anyone how important these lessons are," Esmeray said, unmoving from her position.

Fynn gripped Terin's shoulders, giving him a small shake. "Mother." His voice was stern, kingly even.

Esmeray sighed. She returned her gaze to Kallie and pointed a firm finger. "Fine, but tomorrow we will test your ability to control two minds at once."

Kallie gave a curt nod, stretching her hands above her head as she stood.

Fynn stepped up next to her. "Want to blow off some steam, sister? We have a lot of years of fights to make up for."

Kallie laughed. She didn't know if she would get used to people calling her *sister*, but she didn't hate it. And so when a toothy smile pushed its way to her face, she let it.

As Fynn and Kallie began walking toward the door of the study, Kallie stopped in her tracks. "Wait. I need to release him." She ran to Terin, pressing her hand to his knee and releasing him from her command. During one training session a week ago, she had learned that after she had given a command to someone, she could take it back. All she needed to do was touch them with the intent of releasing them from her manipulation.

Terin rocked to his side but Fynn was there, propping him up.

Terin blinked a few times, clearing the fog from his eyes. "Remind me why I volunteered for this?" His voice was hoarse and shaky.

"Because I'm your favorite sister?" Kallie suggested, batting her lashes.

"You're our *only* sister," Fynn countered, rolling his eyes. He pulled Terin to his feet. "Come on, Terin. Let's get you some fresh air. You can watch me kick our sister's ass on the training grounds."

Kallie shoved Fynn lightly in response.

"Tough words for a guy about to get beat by his sister," Dani said, appearing from the hall.

"Is that a challenge, my lady?" Fynn said.

Terin groaned, rubbing his temple. "Can you two flirt somewhere else?"

Their laughter followed them through the study doors as Kallie took a step back allowing Fynn and Terin through first. Fynn draped his arm over Dani's shoulders, pulling her toward him, his other arm still near Terin in case he needed support.

Kallie, however, watched from behind as the trio in front of her fell into step with one another. A twinge of jealousy formed in her stomach. Kallie tried to stifle it, but she couldn't and her smile began to fall from her face. She yearned for that kind of relationship. While she had a similar friendship with Myra, it was different. There was an imbalanced power dynamic between her and Myra, one which they often forgot about but was still there, still looming over them. But these three? They were true friends on equal grounds. And Kallie was a mere side character in their story.

They turned the corner to the hall leading to the southern exit of the palace. As they passed the kitchens, the doors were opened and the trio paused when voices flew out. Kallie peered inside.

Graeson leaned over the counter, eating pistachios from a small porcelain bowl while Myra stood on the other side near one of the chefs. The three of them laughing together.

At the sound of footsteps, they turned toward the door and their gazes fell on Kallie and the others.

Graeson, looking back over his shoulder, tipped his head up. "Where are you all off to?"

Fynn said, "The training grounds so Kallie can blow off some steam from my mother's torture."

Kallie's eyes darted toward the chef and Myra, her nerves rising since sharing details about her gift was still not a common practice for her. And from what she had gathered over the past couple of weeks, Myra was still ignorant of her gift. Her friend believed that the training sessions Kallie partook in were only about Pontian politics. However, Myra didn't seem to notice as she snuck a pistachio from Graeson's bowl.

"And you think more training is the best way to allow her to cool down?" Graeson asked, cracking open another pistachio.

"Always," Dani said, crossing her arms as she popped her hip out. "Do you have a better idea?"

He popped the peeled pistachio into his mouth, a mischievous smirk on his face. "You know where we haven't been in a while, Fynn?"

Fynn's eyes narrowed slightly. Even though Fynn was unable to read Graeson's mind, it seemed like he was doing just that at that moment as they exchanged glances.

Graeson shrugged. "Best place to blow off steam in my opinion."

Fynn's gaze turned contemplative and Graeson raised one of his brows as if he was daring Fynn to agree to whatever secret conversation they were having. Graeson's gaze flicked toward Kallie then swung back to Fynn.

Fynn sighed. "Fine. I guess we all do deserve some fun."

"Care to share with the group?" Dani asked, elbowing him in the side.

"We're going out," Graeson said, throwing yet another pistachio into his mouth.

"Out?" Kallie asked

"Is the little mouse nervous?" Graeson asked, teasing. He crushed another pistachio's shell in his hand, releasing a small cracking sound.

Kallie scoffed in response, not bothering to argue with him.

"Myra?" Graeson asked, not taking his eyes off Kallie.

Myra straightened. "Yes, sir?"

"Find something for Kallie and yourself to wear."

"Me?"

"Yes, you. And nothing too . . . formal." A glint of mischief danced in Graeson's eyes.

"Yes, sir." Myra hurried around the counters toward the entrance.

"Oh, and Myra?"

Myra skidded to a stop at the doorway and faced Graeson. "Yes, sir?"

"Please, drop the sir."

"But, sir—"

Graeson tilted his head to the side, taking his eyes off of Kallie for the first time to give Myra a look that read *I'm serious.*

"All right. . . Graeson." Then Myra locked arms with Kallie and dragged her away from the group, making their way to Kallie's chambers.

Upon arriving at her chambers, Kallie found a new vase full of lavender sitting on her bedside table. On further inspection, she found no note of who had left the vase. But she eagerly sniffed it, hoping it would have the same effect as the lavender oil Dani had let her borrow, which was now empty.

Meanwhile, Myra paced inside Kallie's closet mumbling about how ludicrous and cryptic Graeson's request was. And after the fifth time hearing Myra ask, "But what does not *too* formal even *mean?*" Kallie had headed to the bathroom to wash up.

As she used a towel to wring out some of the water from her hair, a knock sounded at the door. Kallie peered out of the bathroom. Finding Myra still pacing, Kallie said, "I'll get it." Then mumbled to herself, "Because *I'm* the one dressed for company."

Myra batted her hand, dismissing her.

Kallie tightened the rope around her waist, her hair falling down her back in a knotted mess. As she twisted the knob, the door pushed open from the other side before Kallie had even cracked it open more than a few inches.

Dani stormed into the room, clothes hanging over her arm. Taking in the sight of Kallie, Dani's eyes widened. "Oh, good! You washed up, but I really hope you plan on doing something with that mop on your head."

Kallie's hand flew to her hair, brushing the ends with her fingers. "You really have a knack for barging into rooms, don't you?"

Dani shrugged one shoulder.

"Why are you here?" And realizing how her words had come out, Kallie quickly added, "Not that I don't enjoy your company but. . ."

Dani gave a slight flick of her hand. "I figured Graeson's clothing suggestion would have sent Myra spiraling." Dani observed Myra who stood in the closet with both hands on her head. "And my assumption was, of course, right, so I thought I'd help. Plus, I grew up with all brothers and those three buffoons, so I never really had the chance to get ready with other women."

Kallie closed the door behind Dani and followed her. "Okay. But you have your work cut out for you. Myra's going insane."

Dani chuckled and set the clothes down on Kallie's bed as Kallie headed to the vanity and began running a brush through her hair. She perched herself on the desk, facing Dani and Myra.

"Let's get started then." Dani rubbed her hands together. "Myra, let's start with you."

At the sound of her name, Myra swung around, eyes wide as if she hadn't realized Dani had entered the room.

"I'm sorry, what?" Myra asked, holding her hands in front of her stomach, twiddling her fingers.

Dani shook her head. "Sit."

Myra hesitated, the discomfort from being told to sit written plainly across her face.

Kallie couldn't handle watching her struggle internally, so she quickly asked for Myra's assistance. Myra sighed in relief, scurrying over to Kallie and leaving Dani to deal with her closet. Myra took the brush from Kallie's hand and began detangling her hair.

Dani surveyed the closet, then looked back at the two women. "If I recall, you're about the same size. Correct?"

The women nodded, and then Dani disappeared into the closet. A moment later pieces of clothing came flying out of the closet, landing on the floor in a pile. One after another, fabrics of different colors painted the air.

When the fabrics stopped flying, Dani strolled out. "I think we'll start with this and see where it takes us," she said observing the large heap lying on the ground. "All right, Myra."

"But—" Myra hesitated, the brush halfway through Kallie's hair.

"Kallie can brush her own hair for once. Can't you, *princess?*" Dani mocked.

Kallie rolled her eyes and took the brush back from Myra.

Dani grabbed a white blouse from the pile and held it out to Myra. "Try this first."

Myra nodded and headed into the closet to change. A moment later, she reappeared wearing a long white cotton blouse that floated down to the middle of her thighs, a few inches above her knees with a tie at the top to tighten the fabric. The sleeves were made of a thin, see-through material that puffed up at the shoulders.

Dani nodded in approval. She then grabbed two corsets from the pile: the first was a black corset with elegant embroidery; the second, a simple white corset with defined boning that tightened in the front. Dani held them up to Myra, one at a time, debating. She tossed the black one back on the ground and handed the white one to Myra.

Myra wrapped the corset around herself, then turned to let Dani lace it up.

After, Dani stepped back to observe the ensemble. She rubbed two fingers across her chin. She reached for the ties on the blouse and loosened them, adjusting the sleeves so they fell off Myra's shoulders. "Perfect," Dani said, smiling.

Myra looked down at herself, then waved at her bare legs. "Uhm . . . aren't we forgetting something?"

Dani waved her off. "Pants will ruin the outfit. The shirt is long enough to be a dress anyway. Wear some tall boots if you must."

Myra hesitated as if she had forgotten how to walk. Then she gave a curt nod.

She began to move away, pulling down at the shirt-dress as she went, then stopped mid-stride when Dani shouted, "Oh! One more thing!"

Myra looked at Kallie with fear in her eyes. Kallie swallowed the laugh building at the back of her throat.

Dani pulled the ribbon from Myra's hair and Myra's blonde locks fell from her bun in soft waves that brought attention to Myra's high cheekbones and soft eyes. "Now you're ready."

Unable to hold back her amusement any longer, a small chuckle escaped Kallie's lips that she quickly smothered with a hand when a blush rose to Myra's cheeks. "Myra, you look good, I promise. Stop worrying."

Myra's face reddened even more, the opposite effect Kallie was aiming for.

"And stop pulling at the shirt," Dani snapped.

Myra released her fingers immediately but began picking at her nail beds instead.

Dani's eyes turned to Kallie with a devious smile on her face. Kallie took a deep breath and got up from the stool. As she approached, Dani reached down into the pile of clothes and pulled out a pair of black leather trousers. "Put these on first."

As Kallie grabbed the pants and slipped them on beneath her robe, she could have sworn she heard Myra mumble, "But *she* can wear pants?"

Kallie kept her mouth shut though, preventing the chuckle that wanted out.

Dani then pulled out another corset. This one was made of a satin fabric that had the appearance of being dipped in blood. "Let's try red first," Dani said.

Kallie disrobed and held the red one against her chest, showing Dani and then Myra.

Myra's nose scrunched. "I don't know . . . it's a bit . . . " Myra hesitated.

"Dull?" Dani asked, but Kallie doubted that was what Myra meant. "I agree."

Dani returned to the pile, rifling through the clothes. She pulled out a black corset that was lacy and made to be worn underneath clothing. But based on Dani's expression, Kallie did not think that was her intention. Kallie sighed but grabbed the corset, holding it up to herself.

Dani nodded, and when Kallie looked toward Myra, she shrugged. Dani motioned for Kallie to turn around, then laced Kallie up.

Giving her a once over, Dani narrowed her eyes as she shook her head. "It's the pants."

She threw a pair of simple black cotton trousers at Kallie.

Kallie slid off the leather pants and pulled on the new ones. Once she had them on, she spun in a slow circle. When she faced the two women, Dani and Myra were both smiling.

"Yep, that did it." Dani smiled at her own success and turned to the clothes she brought with her. "Put your hair up though," she said while she changed.

Kallie walked back toward Myra who began brushing her hair, which was nearly dry, into a ponytail.

Dani approached them wearing a pair of black, loose, linen trousers and a white corset. The corset was practically see-through beside the boning that provided its structure and the small bit of fabric over her chest.

Myra, observing all three of their outfits in the mirror, asked, voice quiet and skeptical, "Where exactly are we going?"

Dani smiled. "You'll see. It's a tavern of sorts, one of our favorite spots."

Myra's gaze met Kallie's, and Kallie shrugged, having been given the same information as Myra.

They finished getting ready. Lining their eyes with coal, putting a little rouge on their cheeks and lips. Then once Dani had given her final approval, they threw on their shoes and set out to meet the rest of their group downstairs.

As they walked down the steps to the main doors of the palace, Fynn's laughter echoed off the walls. Turning around the corner of the staircase, Kallie spotted Fynn and Terin facing the staircase with Graeson standing in front of them. At the sound of heels on the stone steps, Fynn's eyes caught on Dani and a wide smile split his face in two.

Kallie's gaze, however, slipped past Fynn and was stuck on the man next to him. With his back facing away from her, Graeson had not seen her yet. But Fynn's reaction dragged his attention away, and Graeson's eyes immediately landed on Kallie. And she stopped breathing for a moment.

Graeson's jaw dropped as he stood as still as a statue, and Kallie gripped the railing as her heart jumped behind her ribcage.

He was head to toe in black. A crisp black button-up with the top two buttons undone and the sleeves rolled up, emphasizing his biceps and the veins on his bare arms. He wore a matching pair of sleek trousers that hugged him in the right spots. And the all-black ensemble made his eyes even brighter, like the moon in a sea of darkness.

Kallie's cheeks burned, and she was thankful she had put on the rouge.

Then she recalled the power she had felt at the ceremony when she had stood before her suitors and brought that energy, that sense of indifference to her gait. She tilted her chin up and let her gaze slide over him.

As her heels clapped against the stone, Graeson's gaze remained fixed on her.

Once they reached the bottom of the stairs, Fynn tugged Dani by the waist, kissing her cheek. He whispered something in her ear causing Dani to smack him softly in the chest, laughter coating her glare.

Graeson took half a step forward, then paused and fidgeted with his gold cufflinks.

Terin cleared his throat. "Everyone ready then?"

"Yes," Myra said, still fidgeting with her shirt. And then quieter, she added, "I need a drink."

"That makes two of us," Terin grumbled, opening the door and heading out with Dani and Fynn close behind.

Graeson ushered Myra and Kallie forward, then stepped in line behind them. Kallie felt him near her ear, and his voice lowered, "Let the games begin, little mouse."

His breath tickled the side of her neck. One side of her mouth tipped upward into a cocky smirk. She turned her head, her lips nearly grazing him with his face as close as it was. Her nose brushed against his cheekbone. "Oh, but, Gray, they have already begun. And you, kitty cat, are behind." She winked.

Then grabbing Myra's hand, she quickened their pace forcing Graeson to watch her walk away (and to give herself the needed distance from him. Because she knew that if she allowed herself to fall into the scent of cedar and citrus, she would be lost forever.)

Still, despite her confident gait, her heart stuttered as she recited his words in her head. She had made her intentions clear. She had been the one to put a stop to this. And this, as Graeson said, was just a game. He was only trying to see how far he could push her, how much her word truly meant to her.

But Kallie was good at games.

And even better at pretending.

CHAPTER 28

KALLIE HADN'T HAD THE CHANCE TO EXPLORE THE CITY BESIDES WHEN they had walked through it upon arriving or traveling to the springs. Anything she needed, Myra had gone to retrieve. But the little she had seen of Pontia was nothing too extraordinary. But then again, she hadn't seen the village at night. With the night taking over the island, Pontia had come alive. A new kind of energy buzzed around her. Torches lit the streets, people chatted with unrestricted enthusiasm, music swept through the spaces between the buildings. It was blissful and free.

The group had taken a nondescript wagon from the palace, and the driver had stopped outside of the tallest shops in the village. While Kallie waited for the others to exit the wagon, she read the signs on the nearby buildings. The phrases *Jewels of the Springs* and *Weapons of the Gods* were elegantly painted onto two wooden signs hanging above the doors of the shops. Her head tilted to the side. Neither place seemed like a place to blow off steam, though she was curious about the weapons and how they would compare to hers. And she regretted not bringing her dagger with her so she could do just that. But alas, it was buried deep within her closet.

Kallie said, not addressing anyone in particular, "Where did you say we were going again?"

As villagers passed by and glanced toward the group, Kallie noticed Myra from the corner of her eye pulling at the sleeves of her dress. Dani's head turned around at Kallie's voice and glared at Myra, sending daggers with her eyes. Myra's hands fell instantly.

Finally, Graeson answered her, "You'll see soon enough."

Fynn passed the two shops, heading down an alley off of the main street that sank into the shadows. At the end of the alley, an old man sat atop an empty barrel, carving slivers of bark off a small chunk of wood outside a door. As they approached, he jerked his head toward the door, barely glancing at them.

"Always a pleasure, Jinks," Fynn said, then headed inside.

As Kallie passed Jinks, she observed the piece of wood in his hands. The man's body cast it in shadows, but from the light that seeped out the opened door, Kallie caught a glimpse of a tiny, wooden dagger in his hands. His eyes snapped up to meet hers, and the wooden dagger snapped in his eyes. His blade knocked it just right.

Jinks looked down, his brows knitting together in the center of his forehead. He glared at Kallie as though it was her fault the wooden object broke in his hands.

Kallie quickly looked away and hustled inside, shrugging off the feeling the man's accusatory gaze left on her skin.

On the outside, the entrance gave off the impression that it was the back door of one of the shops. And in part that was true, for one of the main shops did have access to it. But instead of turning toward the shop door, Fynn led them down a set of cobblestone steps and toward another door.

Kallie asked Graeson again, "Now will you tell us where we are?"

"The Cavern of Catius," he said nonchalantly as if she would know what that meant.

She didn't.

"Who's Catius?" Kallie asked.

Graeson smiled. "One of Pontanius' many children. He was a little more . . . rebellious than his siblings. The place is named after him."

As Fynn stopped before the door, a small rectangular piece of wood slid across. Inside the small window, a pair of green eyes peered through.

Graeson bent down toward Kallie and Myra to not disrupt the conversation between Fynn and the green-eyed figure. "The cavern of Catius is a place where everyone's identity is as deep of a secret as the barrels of alcohol—and the barrels here are endless."

Kallie raised her brows in question, but before she could voice it, the door opened, and the smell of cigar smoke wrapped around them.

As she walked through the threshold, she felt a sensation brush over her skin. She stopped in her tracks. "What was that?" Kallie asked, scanning the room in alarm.

Graeson smiled and whispered so only she could hear. "That, little mouse, was the doorman's gift. He is the one who hides people's identities. The only people who will recognize you are those you walked in with—and the doorman, of course."

Kallie surveyed the doorman who had returned to his seat, a newspaper in hand.

"Seems like a strange use of such a gift," Kallie mumbled to Graeson.

If Domitius got his hands on this type of gift, there was no doubt in Kallie's mind that he would use it to his advantage. But Kallie supposed that was one of the ways he and Esmeray differed.

Graeson shrugged. "We're not at war. And even then, no one is forced to use their gift a certain way."

Kallie hesitated, wanting to ask more questions, but with Graeson urging her forward, she set her questions aside.

The others were gathered around a table with an array of masks scattered on it. Some resembled the gods, while others took the shape of a variety of animals.

Kallie whispered, "If our identities are secret, then why the masks?"

At the same time, Myra picked up a mask in the shape of a bull, turning it around in her hands. Graeson reached past her, claiming a matte black mask with silver embellishments.

And Kallie's attention was glued to the mask in Myra's hand. It had been three weeks since she had seen Domitius. The lightness she had been feeling before dwindled. Her skin itched as guilt perpetrated through her veins. But before she could worry too much about the past, Dani's voice dragged her back to the present.

"For fun, of course! Because if we're being honest, even if our identities were not kept secret, a small mask would do nothing to protect it." She grabbed a mask that resembled the top half of a fox and held it to her face. Fynn made quick work of the tie at the back of her head, securing the mask in place. "So it's ironic, you see?"

Myra put the bull mask down, grabbing another one. This one was a golden faun with intricate beading. She turned around, and Kallie tied the golden ribbons into a bow that flowed down her waves.

Scanning the table, Kallie's gaze locked onto a black mask made of stiff lace that was adorned with red gems throughout in the shape of a wolf. She smirked to herself. If Graeson wanted to play a game, then tonight *she* would be the predator. Kallie reached back to tie her mask underneath her ponytail. As she began to tie it, a pair of coarse hands slid over hers, stealing the ribbons from her fingers. Graeson stepped closer to her, the heat of his body pressed against her. Kallie swallowed and adjusted her mask. Graeson tightened the ribbons and tied them around the ponytail.

He ran his fingers down the length of her hair, freeing it of any tangles that the ride in the open wagon had caused. As he reached the end of her hair, the back of a finger brushed over her bare shoulder. He dropped his hand, then scooted past her, heading into the crowd, leaving her behind with goosebumps covering her skin. But before he disappeared into the crowd, he glanced back over his shoulder. His silver eyes shone through the black mask in the shape of a panther with a look that dared her to follow.

Clearing her throat, Kallie turned to Myra. "How about that drink, Mys?"

"Drinks?" Dani exclaimed, unraveling from Fynn's hold. "Say no more."

And before Kallie knew it, Dani was pulling her and Myra away from the foyer. Leaving her brothers behind and thankfully heading in the opposite direction than in which Graeson had gone.

Graeson may have wanted her to follow him, but she wasn't going to make it that easy for him. Eventually, he would grow tired of waiting and come find her. Her targets always did.

So, she would lay out the trap and let him get snagged in it.

Dani weaved through the crowd, holding onto Kallie's hand as Kallie dragged Myra along behind her. Kallie was too short to see above the people standing around with their drinks. As a result, she had to trust Dani to guide them in the right direction. Meanwhile, music bounced off the walls. It wasn't any kind of music Kallie was used to hearing in the ballrooms or taverns back in Ardentol. The beat was faster, more chaotic. The people around them moved to the music with unbridled energy as the three women did their best to avoid the drinks that sloshed in the dancers' hands. At that moment, Kallie was thankful she was wearing all black for it would hide any liquid spilled onto her. Although, the same couldn't be said for Myra who was still pulling at her dress.

Soon, the crowd thinned, and Dani stopped before a bar where two bartenders worked. She leaned over the counter, waving one over.

The waiter came over, polishing a glass in his hand, his hair long and pushed back behind his shoulders, a series of piercings lined one ear. "What'll it be?"

Dani twirled a curl around her finger. "Three house specials."

The waiter nodded and then moved to the glass bottles lining the counter behind him. He began mixing some concoction, adding different liquids into the glasses.

"What's the 'house special?'" Myra asked, voice timid.

"Only one of the best drinks here," Dani said, that devilish smile reappearing. "But be careful, it's rather potent."

The bartender placed three tall glasses filled with blue liquid in front of them. He then grabbed a bottle from beneath the counter and poured another liquid on top. As the liquor mixed with the drink, the blue color melted into a light lavender. Myra cooed at the transformation beside her.

Dani handed them each a drink and raised her glass. "To freedom," she said.

A wide grin found its way on Myra's lips and the three women clinked their glasses.

Kallie took a deep breath and sipped the lavender liquid. While it didn't provide the same bite as whiskey, the drink was sweet. The taste somehow reminded her of spring mornings and felt like the sun rising.

When Dani noticed that Myra was still drinking, she touched Myra's shoulder. "I said be careful, not chug it all."

Myra giggled and removed the half-empty glass from her lips. "Sorry." She wiped her mouth with the back of her hand. "We should dance. Do you want to dance?" The liquor must have hit her head quickly because she was talking faster than normal and a buzz of energy radiated off of her.

Dani laughed and Kallie could not help but join in. Myra grabbed

Kallie's hand, her other hand still wrapped around her drink, and led them to the crowd.

If Kallie were at one of the taverns in Ardentol, she would not hesitate to dance. But here, she was too wound up. And Dani must have sensed it, for she danced over to Kallie and tipped Kallie's glass up.

Begrudgingly, Kallie took a large sip of the drink as she listened to the music and began to sway to the beat. As the alcohol swam through her, she reminded herself that no one knew who she was here. She did not have to be bound by protocols or standards. With their identities hidden away by the doorman's gift—which Kallie still had trouble wrapping her mind around—she was free. For a little while at least.

Dani grabbed Kallie's free hand and twirled her in a circle. Soon enough the three of them were taking turns twirling around, unrestrained laughter swirling between them. The music guided their movements as their drinks quickly emptied.

When they reached the bottom of their glasses, Myra, who was smiling wider than Kallie had ever seen, scurried off to get them a second.

Then the smell of smoke floated around her accompanied by a trace of cedar and Kallie's insides flipped, knowing exactly who was near before she even saw him. A pair of hands slid to her waist, featherlight and carefully riding the line between friendly and something more.

"So this is where you have been hiding, little mouse," Graeson's voice was warm against her neck. His nose brushed the tip of her ear.

Kallie smirked. As expected, Graeson had fallen right into her trap.

But fear of being seen this close to him in public made her want to pull away despite enjoying his touch. She didn't want to risk the possibility of a rumor spreading throughout the kingdoms, especially if there were traitors among them. Whenever she went out in Ardentol, she was always careful, always cloaked.

Graeson must have felt her start to move away though because he stepped closer, then whispered in her ear so she could hear him above the loud music, "You don't have to hide here, remember? Your identity is completely hidden. There's nothing to worry about."

Kallie knew the doorman's gift protected her identity, but something inside of her still screamed at her to walk away. She knew better than to stay, to continue down this path. They had talked about it at the springs. Fought over it. And there was no need to rekindle that fight.

Someone bumped into her and Graeson's chest pressed against her back. His lips grazed her neck. "For one night, Kallie, stop worrying." Then he added, "But all you have to do is say no and I'll go. No questions asked."

She took a deep breath. He was giving her a choice.

Again.

No one had ever given her the choice.

And he was right. She didn't need to think about the consequences. Not right now.

She nodded because she didn't want him to leave. She closed her eyes as the music took over. Her hips swayed to the beat again, and she leaned into Graeson, resting her head back against his chest. And the two of them began to find their rhythm. His head hung down near hers, his breath fell against her neck. Her hand skated up his chest to the back of his neck.

When the song changed, they followed it, their bodies melting together. Kallie barely heard the people shuffling around them, laughing and drinking, as she became lost in Graeson's arms.

Then after some time, someone cleared their throat nearby and Kallie sighed when Graeson added some distance between them.

Myra's voice followed, "Where'd Dani go?"

Kallie opened her eyes, her brows knitting together at the question.

"She ran off with Fynn somewhere," Graeson responded, barely lifting his head. And his words quenched some of the concern Kallie had begun to feel.

She hadn't heard them leave. She hadn't even seen Fynn approach, too distracted by the music. And the man behind her.

Normally, She was more observant. And she should still be observant, but Graeson's words resurfaced in her mind: *stop worrying.* Kallie's gaze flicked to the three glasses in Myra's hand. She grabbed one to free her friend from balancing two in one hand, even though she probably didn't need one based on how distracted she had become. But there was no harm in letting go, at least for an hour or so.

"Here." Myra handed Graeson the third glass. "Since Dani's not here, you can have hers."

Graeson took the glass, sniffed it, then took a sip. "Do you even know what's in this?"

Myra and Kallie shrugged. "Dani ordered them for us, said it was the house special," Kallie said.

"Of course she did," Graeson mumbled. "And how many have you had?"

"This would be the second," Myra said, sipping and spinning in a circle, one hand in the air while her hips swayed to the beat.

"And the last," he said.

"Says who?" Kallie stepped away from Graeson. While she may not require a second drink, she did not need this man, or any man, telling her what she could or could not have.

"Do I need to remind you of what happened last time you drank?" Graeson asked, his mouth tilted to the side, as if in a dare.

Kallie rolled her eyes.

"And these," he raised his glass, "are much stronger. But fine. Don't stop on my account."

Maintaining eye contact with him, Kallie took a long swig of the drink. She wasn't buzzed yet, but she made a mental note to ask for a glass of water after this drink. Then drink still to her lips, she shrugged her shoulders at Graeson dismissively. She danced over to Myra grabbing her hand and pulling Myra toward her with a smile on her face.

From the corner of her eye, Kallie saw Graeson shake his head, his eyes roaming over her as she danced with Myra.

But not even a moment later did he take a deep breath, empty his glass, and discard it on a nearby high-top table before joining them with a look of determination on his face. Graeson offered his hand to both of them and Myra was the first to place hers in his. And afraid of ruining Myra's joy, Kallie placed her palm in his as well.

Taking both of their hands, Graeson began twirling them in circles. And Myra's laughter was infectious as Graeson spun her. Kallie tilted her head up releasing the worry she had been carrying with her. She smiled, a true, genuine smile as the room spun around her, Graeson's hand in hers and her best friend beside her.

After a few songs, Terin appeared, whispering into Myra's ear, and Myra's face lit up. Kallie narrowed her eyes as she watched them scurry away.

Alone with Graeson, Kallie made to leave the crowd of dancers, but when she looked at Graeson, his gaze dared her to stay. Dared her to see how far she would let this happiness, this carefree moment take her.

She set aside the thoughts of her parents, of her childhood, of the man she was promised to but didn't know. Instead, she laid her eyes on the man who was here now, at this moment.

And she gave in to it.

She stepped closer to him, placing one hand on his chest and the other around the back of his neck. His hand found her waist and pulled her closer while his other hand slid across her collarbone.

Graeson leaned in, his voice low and sultry in her ear, "Have I mentioned how breathtaking you look?"

Goosebumps sprinkled across her skin and she tilted her chin up. "No, I don't believe you have."

"Hmm. . ." The sound vibrated against her skin. His lips brushed behind her ear and she had never realized how sensitive that little spot was before. And she didn't know how much longer she could restrain herself. This entire time she had been trying to maintain her distance from him in an attempt to prevent any feelings from developing and clouding her judgment. But she wanted to claim those lips.

She wanted to claim *him.*

She inhaled. But it was unhelpful as the smell of him, cedar and lemons mixed with cigar smoke, filled her lungs. She shut her eyes, biting the bottom of her lip.

"Kalisandre."

And there it was again. Her name on his lips. She opened her eyes and looked up at him through her lashes. "Yes?"

"Stop that," his voice was a warning, deep and husky.

"Stop what?" She was practically out of breath as she stared at him, her heart hammering against her chest.

"That." The tip of his finger brushed across her lips and the touch sent a shiver to the bottom of her core. He dragged her lip down. "Biting your lip."

She hadn't realized she was even doing it or that he would even notice. But she refused to give him what he wanted. "And why should I stop?"

"Because if you continue to do that, I will stop holding back." The way his eyes darkened and simmered behind his mask, flicking to her red lips had Kallie wishing he would do just that.

"Is that a threat or a promise?" Kallie challenged, something other than the lavender drink filling her body, making her feel warm inside. She wanted to test the limits of this game they were playing. And the liquid coursing through her only gave her the push she needed.

She pursed her lips to the side, the top of her right cheek brushing against her mask.

He released a rough, almost feral sigh. But he didn't pull her in, only continued their dance.

The music shook the floor, shaking her core.

Or was that her heart shaking on its own?

And just when she thought he wasn't going to do anything, his grip on her waist tightened. He tugged her toward him, her chest pressing up against him. His eyes flitted over her as if debating on whether he wanted her to break her word or not. But he did not close the distance between them.

Not at first.

Not until her eyes dropped to his lips, then back to his eyes. And she stared back at him with the same desire, the same hunger in her eyes. And then she bit her lip.

CHAPTER 29

GRAESON CLAIMED HER MOUTH. AND LIKE THE FIRST TIME, HIS LIPS were soft as they ran over hers. When he pulled away, his teeth pulled her bottom lip, doing well on his promise. But unlike the first time they kissed, she would not forget this kiss when she woke up in the morning.

Even still, the kiss was too quick, too fleeting, and left her wanting more. And she questioned whether *he* had fallen into her trap or if *she* had fallen for his. She wrapped her hands around his neck and yanked him toward her, their lips smashing together almost painfully.

In this moment and this moment alone, she didn't care who was the prey and who was the predator. She needed the warmth, the softness of his lips on hers. The desire burning through their touch.

She didn't care if she was breaking her word. Because at that moment, in a crowded room, no one knew who either of them was. Here in this cavern, she wasn't a princess of any kingdom, she wasn't kidnapped, she wasn't promised to another man. Or confused about where her loyalties lay. She was a woman who desired the man in front of her. And at that moment, she would allow herself to claim him as much as he wanted to claim her.

Kallie leaned into him, sliding her hands from his neck into his hair. Her fingers dug into his soft hair that felt like water running through her fingers. She pulled at his lip with her teeth. And the sound that came from Graeson was guttural as one hand slid up her back resting at the nape of her neck. His other hand ventured below her waist.

And for a split second, she wanted to pull away. Not because she was uncomfortable having him kiss her like this in a public place—identities hidden or not—but rather because she wanted him to herself. She didn't want to share this moment with anyone else.

And she wanted to be honest with him.

But Kallie couldn't move, she didn't *want* to move. Because if she moved away from him, if they broke their kiss . . . if they let go of each other, she feared that whatever spell they were under, whatever bond pulled them together and allowed them to put aside their concerns for once would be broken.

And she wasn't ready for this to be over.

It had barely begun.

So Kallie stayed there, on the edge of the drunken crowd, in the little paradise they had created for themselves. Kissing the man whom she was undeniably attracted to, who caused her whole world to flip on its side. The man whom she had chosen to kiss, despite her mind telling her time and time again that she shouldn't.

It was her choice and hers alone.

His hold on her tightened ever-so-slightly, bringing her closer to him. His tongue slipped into her mouth and she savored the taste of him as she brushed his tongue with hers, the whisper of alcohol on his tongue.

His touch was warm and felt like home, a foreign place she never wanted to leave. A place she could always return to and would always be waiting for her with open arms. It made her question why she kept trying to put distance between themselves. Graeson's hold on her promised her that he could give her everything she wanted, title or no title.

And somewhere deep beneath her gift, she believed that could be true. That he could be the one she had been missing. The one she had subconsciously been looking for.

But then somewhere in her body, something tugged at her, pulled her from those thoughts. It made her wonder if it would be enough, and she wanted to squash that feeling.

Still, it was persistent.

It pulled on her. It kept tugging on her until she felt his tongue begin to retreat and the pressure between their lips lessen. Unwillingly, a soft whine escaped her lips and she dragged her teeth lightly against his receding tongue, to which Graeson responded with a deep chuckle that reverberated throughout her entire body. Only furthering her desire to keep him there.

He pecked the corner of her mouth, laying his forehead against hers.

His breathing was heavy, and she slid a hand from his hair, sliding it down to his chest where his heart beat firmly beneath her touch. And she wanted to know how his breathing would be affected if they went further. She had recalled getting a glimpse into the garden, but her hiccups (and subconscious) had prevented it from going any further. Though she somehow knew Graeson was not the type of man to have let it go any further at that moment.

He removed his hand from her ass and placed it over her hand, holding it in place. "I don't think I could ever have enough of you, Kalisandre."

She looked at his lips and noticed that they were tinted red, and she didn't hide her amused smile. The chuckle that left her lips was true and pure. Kallie took her other hand and wiped the edges of her lips, knowing that he had smeared the rouge that she had applied earlier that night. And as her finger traced the edge of her lips, she watched as Graeson licked his own.

She then wiped the red tint from his lips that were still warm from their kiss with her thumb. And as Kallie went to drop her hand, he grabbed it and ran his teeth across her finger. His hand fell from hers, and she dragged her thumb down along the bottom of his lips, revealing his teeth.

She needed more of him, but the look on his face told her she wasn't going to get what she wanted. And she knew wholeheartedly that he was right.

He would always be right about that.

Music blared around them as Kallie said, "Graeson, I need to tell you something."

His brows bunched as he held a hand to his ear. "What?"

She went to repeat what she had said but snapped her mouth shut and shook her head. Another night, perhaps.

He placed a kiss on her forehead and wrapped an arm around her shoulders. He shouted over the music. "Come on, I have something I want to show you."

GRAESON LED her by the hand through a series of hallways and up several flights of stairs. Her heart raced alongside them as Graeson kept quiet while he guided her.

When they came to a dead end, she wrapped a hand around his arm. "Where are we going?"

He dropped her hand and pointed up. "To the roof." Reaching up to a hatch on the ceiling and using his height to his advantage, he pushed it open. Fresh air seeped through. He then grabbed a ladder propped up against a wall and signaled her to climb.

Kallie looked at him and back at the ladder. "Are we allowed up there?"

"Are you telling me you're not up for some rule-breaking?" Graeson challenged, cocking his brow.

Kallie pursed her lips. She grabbed onto the wooden rail and began climbing up the ladder while Graeson kept it steady at the bottom. Once she reached the top, she hoisted herself up.

The air was less stuffy, and the flat roof was more spacious than it was in the tavern with the wild crowd. But more space meant more space for her mind to wander.

She moved out of the way as Graeson joined her, and she watched him pull the ladder up and through the hole and shut the latch. Kallie looked at him in question.

He shrugged, saying, "It's no fun jumping down when someone tries to prank you by taking the ladder away."

"Fynn?" Kallie asked. Even though she had only known him for a short amount of time, Kallie knew it was something her brother would do to mess with Graeson.

"Don't worry, I got him back later." He winked and the memory brought a coy smile onto his face.

Kallie raised a brow.

"Let's just say, Fynn doesn't enjoy swimming anymore." He waved his hand and walked away from the hatch toward the edge of the terrace.

As Kallie followed him in the dark with only the full moon to brighten their path, Kallie looked up at the stars that filled the night sky.

When she reached the edge, leaning against the railing a few feet away from Graeson, she saw why Graeson had wanted to show her this place. The Cavern of Catius was located underneath the highest building in the village, and on the roof, she could see everything. In the far distance, Kallie saw the path they took to the springs, a thick line of trees on the horizon. And behind Graeson, the palace on top of the hill. From here, the palace looked much smaller and its grandeur faded into the depths of the darkness. Below, people walked on the streets, arms wrapped around each other. And a lightness filled the cool air.

Kallie began pointing at different buildings and areas that caught her attention. She pointed to a small fountain not far off from the shops, bringing Graeson's attention to it.

"It's the fountain in honor of Pontanius' mortal wife. He built it in her name shortly after she passed. According to the myth, he met her in that exact spot," he said, leaning against the wall that wrapped around the roof.

"Do you believe all of that?" Kallie asked.

"What?" Graeson asked, looking at her, his brows creasing in the center.

"All of the stories about the gods," Kallie whispered as if the gods could hear her from wherever they lay in the stars.

Graeson's lip twitched. "Why wouldn't I?"

"I don't know. After hearing the two stories about Sabina, it's hard to know what is true and what has been altered. Then I look at this. And I find it hard to believe that all of this," she waved around to the village that thrived in the late hours of the night, "was the result of a god falling in love with a mortal."

Graeson turned his head toward the fountain. "I don't think it's that hard to believe."

"Really? To be outcasted from your kind? Go into hiding? All because of love? Seems like a fantasy world to me," Kallie said, propping her head onto her hand as she leaned over the wall.

"Love makes people do crazy things, I suppose."

"Love makes people foolish," she repeated the words she had told Fynn weeks ago. And perhaps she said them again to remind herself. She didn't love Graeson. That was ludicrous, especially after having known him for only a month. But she did care for him, more than she thought was possible in such little time.

"Those who fear love are the foolish ones, for they forfeit their own happiness out of fear of the unknown." His voice was quiet, yet steady.

"And risk the possibility of heartbreak?"

"Some things are worth the risk, don't you think?"

Kallie felt him turn to her, but she continued to stare out toward the fountain, refusing to meet his gaze.

"I'd rather be unbroken than left shattered into pieces," she said.

"You don't actually mean that, do you?" He pushed himself up off the ledge.

Kallie turned her head and looked at him. "Why wouldn't I? I haven't believed in love for a long time. It has destroyed too many people." Kallie paused, but when Graeson didn't respond, she continued, "I love my—I loved the king, and look where that's gotten me. Confused and broken. I had thought. . . I had thought before that those in your family were the ones you could love unconditionally, but it turns out that's not true either. So why would I give my heart to someone and risk them breaking it, too? Or risk breaking theirs?"

Graeson looked at her, his eyes flicking over her face. He opened his mouth, closed it, then opened it again. "Do you think you would break someone's heart?"

Kallie sighed and looked away to where two women sat at the edge of the fountain. Hands grasped together, foreheads touching. "It's not that I would *intentionally* break someone's heart or that I would even try to have that much power over someone . . . but sometimes you betray someone without meaning to, without even knowing how much you meant to someone before it's too late."

One of the women kissed the other on the cheek, caressing her face. Then, her hand fell and she walked away, leaving the other woman alone in the dark. The woman who sat at the fountain watched the other walk away, but she didn't move, she didn't go after her. Instead, her head dropped into her hands and her shoulders began to shake.

Case in point, Kallie thought.

She raised a shoulder, then dropped it. "I don't know. Maybe it's silly, but I'd rather just . . . not deal with that kind of heartbreak."

From the corner of her eye, Graeson ran his fingers through his hair and he leaned back over the wall. "To hold yourself back though, out of fear, can't you see that it is almost worse? You're intentionally preventing your own happiness."

Kallie rubbed the back of her neck. "I don't know, maybe one day I'll think differently, but right now, that's how I feel."

Graeson grew silent as he stared out toward the village. Nearby, an owl howled in the night. Trees rustled in the wind and a hoard of birds scattered from the treetops. And Kallie wondered how she had ended up here. How her life had gotten so complicated to the point where she no longer knew right from left. And how it would have been different if she had been raised on this island.

Would she and Dani have grown up to be best friends? Would she have grown up training alongside her brothers? Not in secret underneath the palace, but in the open training grounds? Would she have struggled with control over her gift for as long as she had? Would her birth father have trained her? Or her mother? Or a stranger?

Would she have been forced to marry out of duty or for the heart?

Perhaps she would not have feared love for so long. Perhaps she would have embraced it after growing up in a house overflowing with it.

There were too many possibilities for her to work through. And she knew it was all for naught. Nothing would change what her life was now or what she had done. And the part that tugged at her mind the hardest was that she didn't know if she wanted it to. Everything had happened for a reason. And even though she didn't understand all of it right now, one day she would.

One day she would be able to enjoy the happiness that her life offered her.

But today was not that day.

Kallie looked at the village, her gaze turning toward the pier in the distance. Just north of it, she saw a blotch of bright light. A breeze swept over her which sent a cascade of prickles across her skin that she couldn't shake off.

"What's going on over there?" Kallie asked, hoping she was wrong about the feeling in her gut.

Graeson tilted his head in the direction of the flickering light, silent as he assessed it. And Kallie squinted to get a better look. Above the light, near the clouds, a stream of thick black smoke billowed in the air. A thin layer of sweat coated her palms. Smoke only formed like that for one reason.

"Graeson," her voice shook. That wasn't a blotch of light. "Are fires normally that large here?"

"No. No, they are not." He pushed off the wall and headed toward the hatch.

"What occupies that land?" Kallie asked, struggling to meet his stride.

"Mainly unused land, but houses are not far away from it. Grab the ladder," he ordered, his words coming out faster, distracted. "We need to find the twins."

Kallie passed him and grabbed the ladder. She handed it over to Graeson who then dropped it down the hole.

"Go." Graeson ushered her forward. "Quickly."

Wiping her hands on her trousers, she descended. Once she landed, Graeson was no more than a breath away, his shoes slamming against the ground from the drop. He tossed the ladder onto the floor and shut the hatch. He grabbed her hand and started jogging down the hall. Kallie picked up her pace to match his long strides.

"Do you know where they went?" she asked.

Graeson didn't respond and headed down a hallway. He stopped at a closed door. "I have a pretty good idea." He knocked on the door.

After a moment, a muffled voice came from the other side, "Occupied!"

"Is that...?" Kallie asked, recognizing the muffled voice.

Rolling his eyes, Graeson banged on the door again. "Fynn, get your ass out here."

Kallie heard scuffling on the other side and a feminine squeal. "Wait—are they...?"

Graeson grunted, unamused and annoyed.

The door cracked open, and Fynn's head popped out. He slid through the small crack, shutting the door behind him.

"Where's Dani?" Graeson asked, looking behind Fynn as if she was hiding behind Fynn. "We might need her and her units."

Fynn brushed back his tousled hair. "She needs a minute to... be decent." His mouth turned into a knowing smirk.

Kallie shivered, not wanting to think of her brother in that situation, and Fynn shrugged in amusement.

A moment later, Dani appeared from the room, her hair flattened and frizzy and rouge smudged around her mouth. As she locked eyes with Kallie, Dani wiped the edges of her lips with her nail. A wide smile appeared on her sister-in-law's face.

With Dani present, Graeson turned on his heels. "Come on, we don't have time. We need to find Terin."

Dani fell into step beside Graeson, the face of a general quickly forming. "What's the situation, Graeson?"

"There's a fire by the pier. And not some kids fucking around kind of fire. It's spreading. Beyond that, I don't know much, but my gut is telling me that it's intentional."

Fynn looked between Graeson and Kallie as they walked, then he stopped abruptly in his tracks tugging Kallie to the side. Fynn grabbed her shoulders and forced her to face him. Kallie's entire body tensed up under his gaze as his eyes narrowed on her. And when he said her name, the voice of a future king echoed in the halls.

"Kalisandre, what did you do?"

CHAPTER 30

THE OTHERS HALTED, AND KALLIE'S EYES WIDENED IN SURPRISE AS SHE looked between the three of them, their attention focused on her. "I don't know what you are—"

But before she could finish, Fynn had taken another step toward her. Her back smacked the wall.

Fynn tilted his head, his eyes turning into slits. "What have you been hiding from me, sister?"

A chill snaked its way up her spine as he began rifling through her mind. "Why don't you let me in your mind, Kalisandre?"

Kallie spun the ring around her finger as she thought of what to say, of how to explain herself. The walls she had built were breaking inside of her.

Graeson stepped beside Fynn, their conjoined bodies barricading her against the wall. Their body heat reverberated off them and wrapped around her neck. She couldn't breathe.

She didn't know why she had thought she could have it all. She should have known better. She should not have let herself forget who she was, what she did, and why she came here.

Graeson glared at her, pain lacing his words, "What did you do, Kalisandre?"

And this time, when Graeson said her name, a different feeling arose within her, one she didn't care for. One that made her want to shrink back into the shadows and disappear into the darkness.

She met Graeson's gaze and the desire and heat that had filled them earlier that night was replaced by something that shook Kallie's insides.

"Graeson, I can—"

Graeson grabbed her shoulder, his grip tensing. His iron eyes bounced back and forth between Kallie's. When he repeated his question, his voice was not an inch above a whisper, "What did you do?"

Standing before her, he was unrecognizable, transformed into something cold, unfeeling. Feral. His voice was animalistic and predatory; his face, void of any warmth. Gone was the man who had lain next to her in the grass. Gone was the man who had thrown her into the lake, who had danced with her and shown her the stars.

The man before her could strike down his enemy without a moment of hesitation.

But the beast had always been there, hadn't it? Deep beneath the surface, lying in wait.

And seeing this version of Graeson return made her insides flutter. Perhaps she wasn't the only one who was hiding their true self. And as she inhaled, readying herself to explain to Graeson the truth, Fynn stepped between them. He knocked Graeson's hand off of her and stole the words from her mouth. "Graeson, let her explain herself. I'm sure there is a good reason why our land is on fire."

But Graeson didn't move, for the monster had been unleashed. His eyes slid down her as though he was assessing where best to strike.

Fynn reached out to Graeson. "Gray." A warning, an order.

Graeson's gaze dropped to the floor. Then he took a step back as he inhaled.

At some point, Dani had inched closer, moving to Fynn's other side. Kallie looked between them and her throat seized up. Because despite her efforts in maintaining distance between herself and the Pontians for this exact reason, she had failed and had grown to care for them. And if present circumstances showed her anything, she needed to shove those feelings down.

Fast.

Fynn returned his attention to Kallie. And by the pain that glimmered in his eyes, she knew that her brother had read her mind, had discovered the truth. Despite her efforts in guarding her secrets, she had failed. "Why did you tell that soldier where you were in the woods?"

Or at least, part of the truth.

She hadn't completely failed, not yet. She could recover from this.

Her shoulders folded inward and she did not meet their eyes as she spoke. "I—I didn't mean to. The soldier was so . . . young, scared. If I had told him anything useful, I did not mean to." She dragged her gaze up, focusing on her brother, and pleaded. "You have to believe me, Fynn."

He stared at her, unmoving. Then his head dipped down and his next words released the tension from her shoulders. "I believe you."

A sharp inhale to Kallie's right had her turning her attention to Dani. "Really, Fynn?"

Fynn turned to his wife. "We don't have time to argue over this. Our kingdom is burning down!"

"But—"

"Fynn is right." Graeson rubbed his temples.

Dani's mouth fell agape, then she quickly closed it. After staring Fynn down, she shook her head and turned on her heels. "Fine."

Fynn's fingers wrapped around her wrist, spinning her back around. "Where are you going?"

Dani shook off his grip. "As you said, our kingdom is in danger and we are running out of time. I need to gather my units and assess the situation."

Fynn grabbed her arm once again, halting her. "I'm not leaving you."

"Fynn," Dani's voice was tense, but her eyes had softened as she looked upon her partner.

His voice softened as Fynn caressed Dani's cheek. "I'm not leaving you."

"No. You need to stay in the castle. You're the next in line. You can't go into this situation when we don't even know what the situation is. It's reckless," Dani said.

"I said, *no*." His voice turned commanding, transforming into the voice of a king.

They stared at each other, and Kallie wasn't sure who would win this battle.

Graeson turned around, not looking at Kallie, and stepped in between the couple. "There's no point in fighting about this either, as both of you have pointed out now, we don't have the time. If Fynn thinks that he might be in danger, he'll retreat. Right, Fynn?"

Fynn's gaze flicked toward Graeson, who stood waiting, staring at him. He gave a quick nod. "Right."

Dani bounced from one foot to the other, then shut her eyes in defeat. "Fine. Have it your way." She stepped up to Fynn, poking him in the chest. Though her figure was leaner than Fynn's stocky build, Dani exuded just as much strength and power. A born leader. They both had a fire that burned within them, both were knowledgeable and skilled. Both would make great rulers together one day. "But at the first sign of trouble, when I say leave, you leave."

Fynn nodded in agreement and Dani took his hand. "Gray, take Kallie back to the palace and find the others."

Graeson nodded. "I'll be there as soon as I can."

Before they took off, Fynn looked back at Kallie and gave her a tight smile, his eyes flicking over her, sadness filling them. And seeing the disappointment on his face when he looked at her had the guilt swishing in her stomach again.

And for a moment, she wanted to take it all back. But she couldn't. It was already happening and there was no undoing what she did. So, she took a breath and shoved the feeling down as her brother and Dani ran off down the hall hand-in-hand.

Then Graeson seized Kallie by the crook of the elbow and pulled her along with him. They ran toward the music that shook the walls, and Kallie became painfully aware of how Graeson still had not looked at her.

The fantasy world that they had built and had foolishly thought that they could exist inside began to crumble with every step they took.

AFTER CIRCLING the crowd twice with no luck, Graeson took a deep breath, then pushed into the crowd of dancers. Graeson's head swiveled above the crowd as he searched for Myra and Terin. Meanwhile, Kallie remained unable to see anything and was dragged along behind him like a child as she dodged drinks. She made herself as slim as possible as Graeson shoved his way through groups. He pulled her to the left with a new sense of urgency.

As the crowd parted, Kallie finally saw them. Terin was dancing with a girl in a rabbit mask while another masked man spun Myra around, one of her hands waving in the air as she held up an empty glass.

Terin locked eyes with Graeson and his face dropped once he took note of Graeson's sour expression. He whispered into the girl's ear who promptly pouted at him. He bent down and whispered again. Sighing, the girl nodded and left, practically hopping away to the beat.

Graeson stepped up to Myra and the masked man who continued dancing. Myra's eyes opened and she shouted, her hands waving in the air, "Graeson, dance with us!"

With one look from Graeson, the masked man scurried off.

Myra didn't notice her dance partner's absence. "Kallie, you too!" She drew out the last syllable of Kallie's name, smiling widely and running over to pull Kallie into her dancing circle.

"Myra, no. Wait," Kallie said, trying to pull her grip from her friend's hold. But Myra, drunk on the lavender drink and the pure freedom that now ran through her body, was relentless and tugged back.

Myra spun Kallie around. And when Kallie faced her once more, Kallie grabbed Myra's shoulders. "Myra. Listen."

Myra wobbled underneath Kallie's grip, but she stopped dancing, brows knitting together. "Hmm?"

"Myra, we need to go. Something is going on by the pier." Kallie searched her friend's eyes and watched as she slowly absorbed her words.

Myra nodded, the terror and confusion sobering her up enough to understand Kallie's tone. Kallie grabbed her hand, then the four of them hurried out of the building.

They took the wagon back to the palace, Fynn and Dani having taken off on foot toward the fire. As they made the journey back to the palace, they watched from a distance as the fire spread toward the village.

When the driver of the wagon came to a full stop, they jumped out. Terin helped Myra, who was still coming down from her buzz.

When Myra hit the ground, Kallie grabbed her hand and they all sprinted up the marble steps toward the palace doors.

Graeson stopped in front of the two guards who stood posted at the front doors and informed them of what was going on at the pier. After exchanging glances, one of them ran off inside, disappearing down the hall.

In the entryway, Graeson turned to Terin. "Take her to the safe room and grab the queen."

At his words, a fire stirred to life inside of her. She would not be thrown into a room and locked up while others were fighting her fight. She would not be hidden away. She had been hiding her entire life. And she wouldn't do it anymore. Not after finally realizing what freedom meant.

This was her life, her doing.

Her choice.

She took a step toward Graeson. "I'm going with you."

Graeson didn't flinch, but he didn't bother to acknowledge her either. Instead, he looked right past her and spoke to Terin, "If they've come to take your sister, we need to make sure that they are unsuccessful. *Do not* let her out of your sight."

Kallie felt like she had been slapped across the face. And she didn't know what hurt worse. The fact that he didn't bother to look her in her eyes to give her a chance to apologize. Or that he seemed to have forgotten everything that they had said to each other over the past few weeks.

Or perhaps what hurt the most was that he didn't even bother to say her name as if it was now poison on his tongue. And she cursed herself for once thinking that she had feelings for the man who stood before her. The man who didn't even acknowledge her presence, who ignored her very existence.

This was why she had sworn off feelings of love. Before it warped the mind, it made an individual feel as if their self-worth, their existence depended on the person they loved. But love shouldn't make someone feel less than they are. It should empower. It should make the person feel untouchable, unbreakable.

However, standing here in the stone hallway, Kallie felt frail and disposable.

This was not love. This was merely infatuation. Graeson had only been someone for her to hold onto when everything else in her life was falling apart. And now it was time to let him go too and stand on her own two feet.

While she tried to understand what was going on in her head, Terin nodded and Graeson turned on his heels.

Kallie stared at the back of his head, at the dark strands of hair that had just run between her fingers. And despite her anger, she still wondered if he would look back at her as he walked out of those doors, if he would grant her one more chance to see those silver eyes that tore through her soul.

Because once he slipped past those doors, once they went their separate ways here, everything would change and Graeson would never look at her the same.

And she hated herself for feeling that way, for wondering. Because despite her betrayal, she still thought that maybe, just maybe, if he turned around and gave her a chance, whatever happened next would pass. They would be able to return to the cavern, pretend like they weren't the people they were. Pretend that they didn't have any responsibilities or owed anyone anything.

However, when he stopped at the opened door, her heart shook uncontrollably. She was wrong, she did not want to meet his gaze. Did not want to see the hurt, the pain.

And by the blessings of the gods, she did not have to, for his head turned to the side, eyes downcast. His lips parted as if he was going to say something, but instead, he shook his head and walked out.

If he had let her explain that when she saw the guard in Borgania, she was still unsure of who to trust. If he allowed her to explain her motives, her reasonings, perhaps he would understand. But there was no going back now. They both knew that.

Graeson would forever view her actions as a form of betrayal. As if she had a choice in the matter. And no explanation, no excuse would unravel the mess Kallie had created.

The guard closed the old oak door as Graeson raced down the steps. He ran away from her and toward the blazing fire that would surely destroy everything in its path.

CHAPTER 31

Kallie stared at the closed door, paralyzed as the scent of cedar dissipated. And a piece of her heart peeled off and withered away as the man who said he would always save her walked away from her without saying a word.

She didn't know how it got to this point where a man, a single person, could have affected her so much. She didn't know if she wanted to run after him and yell at him or beg him to listen to her and forgive her.

As Kallie tried to sort out the confusion rolling in her head, Terin interrupted.

"Myra, warn the staff. They'll know where to take you to remain safe." The order was awkward on Terin's tongue as he shifted on his feet.

Myra nodded, turning to Kallie. She pulled Kallie into an embrace. A sense of calm slid over Kallie's sweat-coated skin at Myra's touch.

Myra whispered into her ear, "Stay safe. I'll see you soon, Kals."

With a tight smile, Kallie nodded. Myra turned on her heel,

scurrying down the hallway. Her friend's lingering touch brought her back to reality. The past few weeks Kallie had spent here on the island had made her forget who she was. She had never needed a man to save her. And she didn't need one now.

So, Kallie did what she did best. She shoved her feelings down and reached for the thing that would always be with her no matter what happened on the outside.

She rolled her head back, her neck cracking as she brought it around, and fixed her gaze upon Terin. His eyes narrowed as Kallie straightened.

But after the past few weeks, she had learned his reaction time. And having strengthened her connection with Sabina at the Whispering Springs and having practiced using her gift tirelessly, Kallie was faster.

"Take the queen to the safe room and protect them," she commanded.

Terin's eyes became hooded, glazed over. He turned on his heel and headed down the hall without another word. And Kallie watched her brother walk away from her.

Finally alone, the silence of the empty hall wrapping around her, water billowed behind her eyes and tried to push its way out. She took a deep breath in.

And only when she ran up the staircase to her chambers did she let the tears fall, not bothering to wipe them away. She mourned the loss of her friends, knowing she had just ruined everything by leading the enemy to their doorstep.

This was her fault and she deserved to feel the pain of her own actions. She deserved to feel like the fool she was.

She took a deep breath in, then exhaled, releasing all of her emotions. She had one more job to do and she needed her tools to accomplish it first.

THROWING THE DOOR OPEN, Kallie sprinted to her closet, passing the pile of clothes that still lay on her floor from Dani. She scanned the clothes hanging on the wooden rail, eyes skipping over the beautiful silk gowns she would never get the chance to wear. But she couldn't worry about that now. It was somewhere in here, but Dani's escapade through her closet had rearranged the items that had been so meticulously organized.

Her gaze flicked across the items, searching. And she sighed in relief.

There.

Shoved behind the emerald green gown she had worn that very first night now freed of stains hung the black woolen cloak she sought. It wasn't the same one she had in Ardentol, for this cloak was made out of a lighter material. But it would do. When Kallie had first arrived in Pontia, she had asked Myra if she could procure it for her and her friend had done a good enough job. Upon receiving it after she and Graeson had returned from the springs, Kallie had stored her dagger in the pocket hidden on the inside of the cloak.

She snatched the cloak and threw it over her clothes, not bothering to take the time to change. Cloak in place, weapons hidden, she hastened back to the door.

Hand on the wall, she took one last look back at her borrowed room, the clothes, the bed, the vase of lavender that sat on her bedside table. Taking one last moment to remember it all.

She brushed off the remains of the tears and pulled out the ribbon holding her hair. Her hair cascaded down her back. Tucking it inside the cloak, she slid her hood up and tugged it down.

Tonight she would remember who she was and what she fought for: her home, her family, her freedom. Her power.

MANEUVERING through the castle unseen presented no issues. The guards who normally patrolled the hallways had been called from their posts and stationed elsewhere due to the attack. Kallie assumed their new posts were near the most vital points in the castle: the exterior doors and the safe room.

Therefore, getting out of the palace would be another story.

Her gift had gotten stronger from the continuous practice Esmeray had put Kallie through the past couple of weeks. It stirred in her body, a continuous flow underneath her skin, not having weakened in the slightest from its earlier uses. And it set her blood ablaze.

Using her gift stirred up an intoxicating feeling inside of her. With a deep breath, she stifled the feeling that was beginning to slither its way into her mind. She needed a clear head so she could leave the castle and find those who had started the fire.

Only she could stop this. Only she could prevent people from getting hurt.

Because as much as she hated to admit it, she had begun to care for these people—her brothers, Dani, her mother, and even Graeson despite the confusing thoughts about him.

Slinking her way down the hall to avoid any unwanted attention in case the staff still wandered the halls, Kallie made her way to Esmeray's study.

Reaching the door, she cracked it open. Darkness greeted her on the other side. She slithered her way through, shutting the door behind her quietly, the latch clicking into place.

The room was dark, but Kallie had spent plenty of time here so she knew the layout of the room well. She maneuvered around the sitting area where she had sat with everyone as her mother had told her the truth behind the divided kingdoms, where she had spent weeks training nonstop. She headed toward the desk where her mother had brought her down to her knees shaking as she showed her the truth behind that fire that haunted her dreams. Behind the queen's desk, the curtains were drawn closed, shielding the room from the moon's light.

Kallie drew back the golden velvet curtains and light spilled into the room, casting a spotlight on the bookshelves lining the wall. Following it, she spotted a small painting on top of a stack of books. She needed to keep moving, yet she found herself walking toward the painting nevertheless.

Encased in a golden frame, the painting was no bigger than the size of her palm. Five figures had been painted in an ovular shape atop a white background. A simple family portrait. Nothing extraordinary, yet none covered the palace walls in Ardentol.

She instantly recognized Esmeray's feminine face and signature pulled-back hair. But the smile the queen wore was different from the one Kallie was now familiar with. This one was light, hopeful. Beyond doubt, her mother was beautiful. And remained so.

Kallie's gaze then darted to the man who stood beside Esmeray. He towered over the queen. And Kallie knew by the dark chestnut hair that fell gently around his face that this was the face of her birth father. His jawline was firm and chiseled. His nose was Kallie's nose; his almond-shaped eyes, her eyes.

And in his arms, smushed together, were two identical twin boys. Terin hadn't adopted his short hair yet, and Kallie could barely tell him apart from Fynn. But Fynn's goofy smile that lit his face and Terin's soft, gentle gaze distinguished the two well enough for her.

At last, she turned to the final figure in the painting: a small baby bundled up in a blanket, a head full of dark hair popping out, who slept in Esmeray's arms. Kallie's lip twitched and she shook the painting from the frame, folding in the corners of the thick parchment carefully to not crack the paint. Then she slid it down the front of her tight corset. Setting the empty frame back on the stack of books, she returned to the window.

Her fingers ran along the edges of the window. Finding the latch at the bottom of the window, Kallie unlocked it. With a quick push, she thrust it open and flicked the cloak behind her as she stepped out with one foot, then the other. She threw the curtains closed before she shut the window behind her. Then she bounded down the hillside of the property where smoke continued to fill the sky.

As she approached the edge of the property, she squeezed her way through the gate and looked out toward the pier.

The fire had started due north of the pier. But between the time she had spotted it on the rooftop of the Cavern of Catius to now, the flames had crept toward the nearby houses. On the roof, she had barely been able to make out the houses. However, now she could see the clusters of houses that were illuminated by the flames, the fire having already overtaken the closest ones.

Her hands began to shake as the memory of that night seventeen years ago rose to the surface of her mind. She only hoped that no child below would have to experience the same nightmare.

Quickly clearing the thoughts from her head, she scanned the area. She recalled Dani mentioning that her units, along with a good portion of the military, were housed in the quarters south of the pier. At least they were not too far away to help those in need then. However, Kallie was too far to see if help had arrived in time. She didn't know where the villagers would run to seek refuge. And she could only pray to the gods that the people inside had plenty of time to spot the fire and evacuate.

She headed down the steep hill as she planned her next steps. She had one chance, one chance before more people unnecessarily suffered because of her actions. She didn't know where she should go or where the attackers would be stationed. But she had to keep going.

The muscles in her shins strained as she made the decline down the hill. She thought back to her training lessons with the king. To all of the times she had sat in the far corner of the king's meeting room while he and his advisors discussed safety procedures and possible ways to attack if the time arose. If the purpose of the attack was to rescue her, they would have assumed she would not be by the fire. For why would someone who was supposedly kidnapped run off *toward* a fire?

An explosion shook the ground beneath her.

Her head swung back toward the palace as she pivoted, and Kallie lost her footing in the process. The ground beneath her became loose. Then her heel slipped, skidding over the dirt, and her knees hit the ground. Her palms followed, smacking down. She hissed as her skin rubbed against the grass and dirt. Her palms were sure to be red now.

Kallie lay there for a moment, then pushed herself up, using the strength in her legs to her advantage. A sharp pain surged in her ankle, and she hissed out a curse. She closed her eyes, scrunched her face, then took a deep breath.

The fire had been a distraction. After all of the strategy meetings she had sat on, she should have known. However, she must have zoned out during those conversations, distracted by her upcoming assignments. She should have listened to the men around the table more closely, she should not have gotten in her head. And now she was paying the price with a sprained ankle.

She grunted from the pain. And knowing that the incline would be nearly impossible to climb with it, Kallie began to crawl. The grass scratched her right knee, the fall ripping a hole in her trousers. She dug her nails into the dirt as she clawed her way up the hill. Dirt clogged beneath her nails, and the grass burned her knee. She hadn't realized how far she had descended the hill. She yelled at herself internally for being so foolish, for not having thought this through before she had ventured down the hill.

She should have known the attackers would have been heading for the castle.

Smacking her hand against the ground, she wanted to scream.

She should have been smarter, quicker. She should have been *better*.

Never again would she let this happen.

Feeling the hill beginning to flatten, she pushed herself up, placing her weight on her left leg. She clenched her teeth together as she took her first step forward.

I am better than this, Kallie told herself.

She approached the gate and inhaled. Distorting her body so she could slither her way back through the metal bars, she led with her uninjured leg. The iron bars pressed against her, squeezing her, and she used her hands to push herself through.

Once she passed the bars, Kallie took a deep breath, then she recited her mantra in her head as she made each step, her right foot dragging behind her.

I am capable.

One step.

I am powerful.

Another step.

I am control.

And another.

I am worthy.

She would make it back to the palace. She would storm through those tall oak doors. And she would finish this.

Then she would prove to *him* that she was more than what he believed her to be capable of. She would show him that she could stifle the pain surging throughout her body. That she could shut down her emotions in order to achieve what she wanted—what *they* wanted.

She would prove to him that she was worthy of his time. Worthy of his love.

She was not going to let them take everything away from her, everything she had gained.

No one would take that from her. Never again.

CHAPTER 32

HER HAND SCRAPED AGAINST THE COOL STONE WALL OF THE CASTLE, rubbing against the burns on her palm from the grass.

Kallie straightened out her plan as she thought of where the attackers might try to enter the castle. Depending on how many they had with them, they might have tried for one of the side entrances, taking out any guards along the way. Or if there were only a few of them—or if they wanted to be more subtle—the attackers might have tried to go through a window.

But Kallie didn't know. There was no way for her to know. So, she decided to head toward the western entrance which led to the servants' quarters and, conveniently, was the closest entrance to her now.

She neared the corner and slowed her approach, creeping as quietly as she could as she hobbled over to it. She peered around the corner.

Through the crack between the wall and the tall bushes, she didn't see anyone guarding the door. And she thanked the gods as she exhaled. Kallie rounded the corner heading toward the door, but something on the ground caught her eye forcing her to stop in her

NEENA LASKOWSKI

tracks. Her hand swung to her face muffling the gasp that had slipped from her lips.

The ground was covered in soot and the smell of smoke in the air was prominent, thick. And then there was something else in the air. She had never seen nor smelled anything like it. It was . . . horrifying. Gagging, she plugged her nose.

Then, amidst the black dust were three Pontian guards dead on the ground. Two of the bodies were nearly unrecognizable, their bodies charred. As Kallie stepped over the third body, which had been stabbed in the gut, a gurgling sound had her head swiveling.

The guard was still alive.

Her heart tightened as she took in his face. His cheeks were soft, and patches of stubble grew on his chin. He couldn't be more than eighteen. Blue eyes flung open, hazy but alert. He held his side, his breathing quick and short, filled with an unnatural wetness.

His gaze met hers as she knelt beside him. She reached out and placed her hand over his, pushing down against the open wound, trying to prevent more blood from spewing out of his body, but too much had been spilled already. There was no saving this man.

Still, she could offer him some comfort. Swallowing, she dropped her hand from her nose and lay it on his cheek. His face cold beneath her warm skin, and at her touch water filled his eyes. Kallie hadn't spent much time around the dying, but she knew he didn't have much more time left.

"It's okay," she said, forcing her words to sound calm, soothing.

"I—I failed," the man's voice shook.

Her lips formed a soft, sad smile. "You did all you could."

Tears fell from his eyes, sliding down the sides of his face. She wasn't sure if it was the pain of the wound that caused his tears or the pain of knowing that what he did wasn't enough.

Unsure of what to say, Kallie said the only thing she could, "You did well. But it's time for you to rest, now. Rest easy knowing that you were brave, that you were enough, soldier."

The man attempted to form a smile on his lips. He grimaced in pain and scanned the air as he gripped her hand tighter. "Frenzia," he hissed.

Kallie tilted her head. "What about Frenzia?"

"Here," and as the word left his lips his chest fell and did not rise.

Frenzia's men had come for her. Her *fiancé's military* had come for her.

And Kallie's body shook.

She let her tears go and bent down, placing a kiss on the man's forehead. Even in the end, he tried to do more. Tried to be of service. And Kallie's heart ached for the soldiers that died believing that they were never enough. For those who continued to fight to prove themselves to their commanders, their families, their kingdom.

She knew that feeling all too well. Weeks ago many of her men died fighting the hard fight.

Kallie placed her hand over his eyes and gently shut the soldier's blue eyes. She sent a soft prayer to the gods.

It was a well-known fact that the Frenzian military was well-equipped. It was one of the reasons King Domitius had sought the marriage between the two kingdoms, so he would have access to it. However, Kallie had assumed when people commended the military that they had been referring to its size, training program, loyalty, and ability. She had not expected it to be because of the weapons they possessed. She had never seen anything like the aftermath of whatever weapon they had created and used here today.

It was dangerous.

It was frightening.

And it would destroy entire kingdoms if used on a larger scale.

And they had brought those weapons here.

Kallie brushed away the hair that had fallen in her face, then stormed into the castle. The pain that spiked in her right ankle as it hit the sleek floor was a constant reminder of what she was fighting for. Only urging her faster through the halls. Each slap against the wooden floor echoed the king's warnings in her head.

Don't be overzealous. Don't be cocky. Stay focused.

And despite all she had learned, he was right. Her confidence in her safety had led her to this moment. She had let her mind wander, let herself enjoy the world around her. And consequently, she had lost sight of the task at hand and lost sight of who she was. But now, as she dragged her throbbing ankle behind her toward the safe room, she would refocus on her goal.

Her gift coursed through her veins.

She was ready.

She had to be.

KALLIE SKIDDED to a stop as she reached a fork in the hallway. Slowing her breathing, she listened as she decided which direction she should take.

She had never been to the safe room. Up until now, she had been using her instincts to guide her, but a decision had to be made.

She wiped off the moisture that beaded on her forehead with the back of her hand. And then she heard them.

Rough voices sounded from down the hallway on the left. Without hesitating, she let the faded voices guide her. She passed several closed doors. The usual warmth of the halls now cold and silent. The floors that once sparkled, now dull. This section of the castle was rarely used it seemed.

The voices led her down another hall and grew louder as Kallie drew nearer. She slowed her pace, quieted her footsteps. She could now pick up bits of the conversation.

"What if she's not here?" one of the voices asked.

"She will be," the other replied.

"And if there are others?"

"You heard what the king said. Kill them."

Her stomach dropped. Kallie didn't know how many were in the safe room, but she knew at least Esmeray and Terin would be there. Even though her actions had brought these men to these shores, she couldn't let the Frenzians kill them. She just needed to get close enough to them, so that she could change the tide with her gift.

At the end of the hall, there was another turn. Kallie paused before she crept down it. She peeked around the corner. Three men stood before a door on the opposite wall, their backs turned away from her. One of them began touching the border of the door. She scanned the men, spotting the royal Frenzian crest and a man with bright ginger hair. He was unmistakable.

It seemed her target long ago did not learn his lesson that first night.

Prince Sebastian—the captain of Frenzia's navy, her fiancé's brother—stood before the door.

Kallie waited behind the corner, anticipating their next move as Sebastian drew his sword, nodding to the soldier standing next to him. At Sebastian's signal, the soldier approached the door. Holding a handkerchief over his face, he lit a match with his other hand as Sebastian backed up against the opposite wall.

Kallie's eyes narrowed. Then a faint sizzling sound sparked. The match caught a hold of something and a small flame began to travel around the edge of the door. As the burnt line connected, the soldier pushed gently against the door and it fell inside the room. Sharp screams followed the fall inside the room.

Prince Sebastian stepped under the archway and onto the fallen oak door, sword at the ready. "Where is she?"

When only silence answered him, he spat the question again, "Where is she?"

After a moment, someone inside the room cleared their throat. And then Esmeray's voice filled the hallway, strong and steady as she responded to the armed man before her, "I'm sorry, but you are going to have to be more specific than that."

Annoyed, Sebastian scoffed. "Kalisandre."

"I'm sorry, but Kalisandre is not here."

Sebastian groaned in annoyance. But it wasn't a lie.

Not quite.

"If I have to ask again, I will not hesitate to kill everyone in this room. But if you tell me where she is, I will turn around and pretend as if I saw none of you."

Sebastian was lying and Kallie knew Esmeray saw through his lie as well. The queen was too valuable for him to kill, but it did not mean he would not kill everyone else.

Still, the people in the room remained silent. Sebastian's fingers tapped against his scabbard, waiting. Ticking down the clock. Kallie swallowed, twisting her ring.

When Sebastian nodded to the soldier beside him, the man stepped into the room, two short swords drawn at his side.

Kallie took a deep breath. She had one chance to get this right.

She pushed the hood of her clock back from her face and let it fall onto her back.

"Prince Sebastian!" Kallie shouted, making her voice small and weak as she came around the corner, dragging her foot behind her more dramatically than necessary.

The three Frenzian men swung their heads toward her and Sebastian's eyes widened as he found Kallie before him. His eyes scanned over Kallie. Her black pants were slathered with dirt, holes torn at the knees from crawling. Dirt and blood coated her fingernails and hands. The risqué corset pinched her waist, her collarbone bare with dirt smeared on it. She was far away from the elegant princess the king had raised. But she never felt more like herself.

Using the wall to prop herself up, Kallie trudged down the hall, the half-dried-up blood from the soldier outside smeared on the wall. When she was across the door of the safe room, she let herself slip down the wall.

And before she even hit the floor, Sebastian was in front of her, hoisting her up by her armpits. "Princess Kalisandre?" His voice was laden with concern, for to Sebastian, she was still his brother's fiancé. To him, she was a victim and he was there to save her from her kidnappers.

She had never been a victim though.

He lifted her. As he wrapped his arm underneath her, the smell of iron and smoke hit her nose. She noticed the once-white handkerchief stained red peeking out of his pocket, the black soot on his lapel.

"Are you well? Are you hurt?" Sebastian asked.

Kallie forced her voice to shake, which took little effort at this point. "I'm ok. It's nothing. Just my ankle. . .I had to. . . I—" Tears billowed in her eyes as she feigned weakness. And she hated herself for pretending to be weak, but she knew that the man who stood at her side would believe it.

Any man would believe a weak woman.

Besides one. That man, however, wanted nothing to do with her anymore. And she couldn't blame him. Their fairytale moment was over.

"Shh. It's ok. We're here. We'll get you back to our kingdom, wash this filth from you." The double meaning of his words did not go unnoticed as his gaze flicked toward the people in the safe room before returning to Kallie.

Kallie gave him a tight smile, his gaze shifted. Her stomach almost turned as she took in the ecstasy that coated his eyes. It wasn't for her though, but rather a hunger for blood. She forced her face to remain neutral as she looked at him.

"Let me deal with these savages first, then we will leave and take you back to the ship and to my brother."

Was King Rian here?

Kallie recalled them mentioning a king's orders earlier. And her heart beat faster.

Shuffling sounded from the room and she glanced over his shoulder. Terin, Airos, and a few other guards had taken up fighting stances in front of Esmeray. Kallie turned her gaze away from the people now held hostage by Sebastian and his men.

Kallie feigned a smile and focused back on Sebastian as she reached down inside her. "Prince Sebastian?" Her voice was quiet, feminine.

Sebastian looked at her. "What is it?"

Speaking so only he could hear, she commanded, "You and your men will take me to your ship, but you will leave these people unharmed. And if your men kill or harm them, *you* will kill him in return."

His eyes glazed over, and Sebastian looked back to his men who stood just inside of the room. He tilted his head, ordering them to leave the room.

One soldier headed out as the other turned to the people inside the safe room and addressed them, "If you follow us, you die." He turned on his heels and waited behind Sebastian as the other took his place in front of him.

Kallie rolled her eyes at the threat. Then without bothering to ask if she needed his assistance, Sebastian put one arm behind her knees and lifted her into his arms. Kallie wanted to shake him off. She didn't want to appear weak or in need of his help. It was not who she was. But it was exactly what she needed to do.

She *needed* these men to think she was weak, small. And so she let Sebastian lift her off the ground.

"My brother would never forgive me if he knew I let you walk on an injured ankle," Sebastian said, walking forward.

And then the sound of footsteps behind them had her sighing. For once during this journey, she wished things could be easy. But it seemed the gods had other plans.

"Kals," Terin said, voice rough.

She should have known her brother wasn't going to let her go that easy. Kallie looked at him, giving him a tight smile. "Terin, don't. It will only make it worse."

"But Kallie, you can—"

One of the soldiers stopped Terin in his tracks as her brother dared to take a step forward despite the previous threat. And Kallie prayed to the gods for mercy here. He was not the fighter. Fynn was. And Fynn was not here.

Kallie knew what her brother wanted her to do. He wanted her to command them all, Sebastian and the other two Frenzian soldiers. But even if her gift was stronger than it used to be, she hadn't had the chance to practice using it to command multiple people at once. They were supposed to do that in tomorrow's session. And she couldn't risk failing, not again.

And even then, Terin didn't understand what he was truly asking her. It was so . . . complicated.

Still, he wouldn't let her go without an explanation, so with pain in her voice, she looked him in the eye and said, "Terin, I can't."

He took another step forward, the Frenzian soldier raised his sword. "But I can—"

Kallie caught him off. "Terin, stop. Stay with them. Protect them." Heat rose behind her eyes and her voice ached. "*Please.*"

Fog seeped over his eyes and he took a step back, his outstretched hand falling to his side, limp and lifeless. He gave her a single nod before he turned back to the safe room where Esmeray had popped her head out. Esmeray reached out her arm and pulled her son toward her. She looked at Kallie, meeting her blue eyes, the blue eyes they shared. And Kallie couldn't help but think of that horrid moment years ago as it replayed in front of her.

But this time it was different. This time Kallie was choosing to leave. This time Kallie knew what was happening.

The parchment hidden in her corset rubbed against her skin and burned against her chest as her heart began to shed another layer that crumbled to ash. But this was the only way. The only way to save them.

The only way to achieve what she wanted.

CHAPTER 33

while Kallie lay in the prince's arms, not hearing anything they said, their words floating past her. Only the sound of screams filled her ears. They descended the hill and Kallie bounced in Sebastian's arm. Her body became numb with every step as the spring night settled around her.

Sebastian said something to one of his men and one of the soldiers disappeared in the direction of the fire.

Kallie no longer cared though. And her gaze wandered to the sky where the constellations hid behind the smoke. She supposed she preferred it that way, for the gods to be hidden. Perhaps since she could not see them, the gods couldn't see her either.

The moon's light, however, showed through the heavy smoke, lighting the pathway back to wherever Sebastian's boat was docked. And she focused on that.

The moon was full and bright as it orbited the world, circling the world as it ran away from the sun. As it did, it led a lonely life. And it must have been exhausting to continuously run in circles. But at least the moon was able to provide the world with light while the sun was away. And Kallie tried to smile at that. Although lonely, the moon had its purpose. And it was unwavering in its pursuit to provide for the world it revolved around.

And wasn't that better anyway? To have a purpose rather than to wander aimlessly—with or without the company of others?

Kallie sighed and returned her attention to Sebastian. His brows knitted together, worry spreading across his face. His mouth moved but she heard nothing. His mouth moved, yet she couldn't bring her attention to focus on it for his mouth wasn't the one she wished to see. His arms weren't the ones she wanted to be in and she began to question everything she was doing.

Sebastian gave her a light shake as he continued walking. "Princess?"

Kallie forced herself to meet his green piercing gaze and made a noise of acknowledgment.

"Are you sure you are well?"

Kallie could almost see the wall he had built between himself and his emotions. And Kallie wondered if his hesitancy wasn't out of concern for her well-being, but rather out of concern that his brother's fiancé was broken. That she was unfixable, unworthy to be Frenzia's queen.

So Kallie, pushing past the tears that threatened to surface, offered him a soft smile as she shook her head. "No, I'm fine. Just tired and ready to see my king."

He nodded. "We'll be on the ship soon. I'm sending word to my men."

Kallie gave a single tilt of her head and rested her head against his chest. The fabric of his military coat was rough against her skin, her body rigid in his arms.

KALLIE'S FEET hit the deck, the wooden floorboards of the ship creaked beneath her weight, and her body shook from the sea's mist. Her stomach grew queasy as the memory of the last time she was on a boat surfaced. And this time, Kallie would need to find other means of dulling her senses to quell nausea.

In her peripheral vision, she noticed Sebastian whispering to someone. The soldier headed down the ladder, which she assumed led to the sleeping quarters, and the soldier disappeared into the darkness.

Kallie stretched her legs, hissing as she moved her ankle. She hobbled over to the edge of the ship and leaned against the railing as she overlooked Pontia one last time. Frenzia had docked their ships a ways down the pier. It was closer to the village but remained hidden behind a wall of trees. And the fire was still in view.

Soldiers shuffled behind her. Their paces quick as their anxiety-driven energy fueled their race to prepare the ship for their journey back. But her attention wasn't on them.

It was on the sight ahead of her.

The fire had spread deep into the bundles of houses. The first row of homes was destroyed. Holes filled the roofs and the walls, entire infrastructures collapsed in on themselves. In the distance, silhouettes of people were gathered between the pier and the blazing fire. Kallie couldn't see them clearly but she imagined them holding each other, their distraught faces glowing from the flames. She imagined their faces as their homes crumbled before them as ash covered the ground. The black smoke rose all around them while the flames consumed everything they once owned. She imagined children huddled together, tears streaming down their innocent, soft faces as everything they knew and loved burned to the ground.

She had never wanted any of this to happen.

Shadowed figures ran between the fire and the water. A line

formed as people passed buckets filled to the brim with water back and forth, throwing the water onto the fire.

Still, their efforts were abysmal at best. But bucket by bucket, the Pontians took out small sections of the fire in an attempt to decrease the size of the fire and prevent it from spreading even further.

The floorboards creaked behind her, and Kallie turned her head slightly, not able to take her focus away from the fire entirely. As if it would all burn to the ground if she looked away. At some point, Sebastian had disappeared, and now the person who had disappeared down the hatch, a young female soldier, stood next to her.

"My lady, I've been instructed to wrap your ankle," the soldier said, showing Kallie the wrappings she held in her hands.

Kallie nodded. And because of growing nausea, she leaned against the railing and reluctantly put her back to the fire.

The soldier knelt and began wrapping Kallie's ankle. As she finished tying it tightly around her ankle, which was now stiff from the binding, a commotion came from the stern gaining Kallie's attention. A crowd was forming at the back of the ship.

"What's going on?" Kallie asked.

The soldier stood and looked toward the crowd. "I don't know, my lady. But I can take a look for you if you wish."

More sailors ran by them. Kallie pushed herself off the railing. "Help me down there," she said.

"But, my lady, if something is amiss, do you really think it best?" The soldier held her hands in front of her stomach, the act eerily similar to how the servants stood in front of the king. Was this what it would be like to be queen?

Then again, no one question Domitius's commands.

Kallie glared at the woman, her gaze cold, words clipped, gift at her fingertips. "Take me to them."

The woman's eyes glazed over. Her arm rose and Kallie grabbed onto it for support as they hurried to the stern.

Frenzian soldiers had formed a semi-circle around whatever was going on in the epicenter. Their feet stomped the ground, a cacophony. Their weapons gripped firmly in their hands, the taste for blood laced their shouts growing louder with each stomp.

Kallie had seen many brawls in Ardentol's taverns. And by the sound of their hollers and the sickening feeling growing in her gut, Kallie knew she would not enjoy seeing whatever she found in the center.

The woman guiding Kallie pushed aside a pair of soldiers who grumbled angrily in response. But when their eyes fell upon Kallie, they tilted their head down and backed away, eyes darting to the floor. As they parted, an opening was created for Kallie and her escort. And Kallie's breath caught in the center of her lungs.

Sebastian stood at the center of the crowd, facing the ship's railing with his back to his crew. And beyond him, broad shoulders peaked out. Then as Sebastian began to circle, his sword out in front of him, the moon's rays shone on his opponent.

Fynn stood before Sebastian. Her *brother* was surrounded by his enemies. His hair disheveled, ash smeared across his cheek, the same black soot she had seen at the palace covered his clothing.

He should not be here, Kallie thought. He promised Dani he would leave if he was in danger, not run straight toward it and board an enemy ship.

Without Sebastian's body hiding Kallie from view, Fynn's eyes instantly locked on hers and a plethora of emotions coated his face, the most prominent emotion being the blazing determination. And Kallie wanted to burst into tears.

He had come for her.

He had fought for her.

And now he had taken his eyes off the enemy *because* of her.

Having noticed the distraction, Sebastian took advantage of the opportunity granted to him and struck. And if his opponent was anyone else, Sebastian would have hit his mark. If he was anyone else, his opponent would have already been bleeding out. But Fynn was no ordinary man.

With a quick side step, Fynn avoided the attack. Sebastian swung again, but Fynn dodged beneath it. Her brother pivoted on his feet, then jabbed at Sebastian, pushing him backward.

And the crowd shifted back a step as their leader neared.

Sebastian grunted in frustration and swatted Fynn's sword down. And the corner of Fynn's lip twitched as Sebastian aimed for his chest.

And when Fynn blocked the strike yet again, Kallie knew her brother was reading Sebastian's mind, knowing Sebastian's every move right when Sebastian thought of it.

Time and time again, Fynn dodged each attack Sebastian threw at him.

Sweat beaded on Sebastian's forehead, the crowd tensing as they watched one of their leaders miss every strike. As their leader continued to fail.

This time when Fynn fought, he did not have a fresh wound hindering his movements. This time, the true fighter was revealed and it was a wondrous sight to behold. And Kallie hid the smile creeping onto her face from the surrounding Frenzian soldiers.

Sebastian's cheeks reddened, his frustration building as the two men continued to circle each other. His moves became tenser, more reckless as he struck his sword through the air.

Nearing his wit's end, Sebastian grunted, then charged. But Fynn continued his dance around the sword, dodging and blocking every swing, every slice, every jab with that all too familiar smug smile.

The soldiers began to shift on their feet, unsure of whether they should help their leader or stay planted where they stood. But alas no one in the semi-circle seemed brave enough to find out what would happen if they intervened.

Then one man shouted, "Shall we get the grenades, Commander?"

"And risk blowing us all up or blowing a hole through the ship?" Another soldier asked in horror.

Grenades? Kallie had never heard of those before and she had the strange suspicion that whatever they were, they had caused the horrendous sight at the palace. And by the way Fynn's movement stuttered for a moment, he had experienced them too.

"No grenades, you imbeciles!" Sebastian shouted at his soldiers, his voice taking on a higher pitch. "This is my fight. Let us show our guests what it means to be a Frenzian." The corners of his lips quirked up, forming a cold, heartless smile.

Fynn now was a few feet away from her, his back to her. And Kallie's heart thudded against her chest. She didn't know what to do. She didn't know how to help.

She felt for her gift, but the pulse of her gift was not as strong as it once was. She had given too many commands out today between her training and the events of the night. But Fynn wasn't that far away, she could reach out.

Would Sebastian and his soldiers be suspicious of her though? As far as she knew, they did not know about the gifts she and many of the Pontians possessed—although, at this point, anything was possible. Still, she wouldn't risk it. Just in case. But she was running out of options.

Sweat coated her palms as she dug her nails into the flesh, her knuckles turning white.

Then the soldier fidgeted beside her. And Kallie panicked.

She turned to the soldier who had bound her ankle and pulled at her gift as Kallie gripped the soldier's arm.

"End this."

CHAPTER 34

THE COMMAND RAN THROUGH KALLIE AND INTO THE SOLDIER BESIDE her. The soldier took a step forward, and Kallie's hand fell to her side.

Sebastian's attention flicked toward the movement, granting Fynn the opportunity to slide across the floor as the soldier swung at him with a dagger.

Kallie clasped her hands in front of her mouth. *That* was not what she had meant when she had told the soldier to end the fight. She should have known to be more careful with her words. But she had panicked. She had been careless. And she yearned to call out to her brother, to apologize to him, to tell him she didn't mean for this to happen.

For any of it.

However, Kallie remained silent, unwilling to add another distraction to the mix as Fynn fought against two opponents.

Kallie glanced at Sebastian as her brother hopped back onto his feet. Sebastian glared at the soldier who dared to interfere, a nameless soldier whose rank Kallie hadn't even bothered to notice. And by the look on Sebastian's face, she knew he felt insulted as the woman came to his aid.

"Return to your post, soldier," Sebastian ordered, focusing his attention back on Fynn.

"Sorry, commander, but I cannot. I must put an end to this," the soldier's words were void of emotion as Kallie's command flowed through her. The soldier would not stop until her task was finished.

Sebastian scoffed and demanded a sword from a nearby soldier who gave it to him willingly. "So be it, but do not get in my way or else it will be *your* head that I will slice off." Sebastian twirled the two swords in his hands, the iron flickering in the moonlight. At the same time, the soldier slinked off to the other side of Fynn, locking him in between them.

Kallie watched as her brother took a deep breath and a scream almost escaped as Fynn closed his eyes.

And his two opponents did not hesitate. They charged.

Sebastian swung high as the soldier slid low across the ground with the dagger in her hand. But before they made contact, Fynn's eyes flung open. He kicked out his foot, locking the woman's outstretched arm in between his legs and knocking the dagger out of her hand while simultaneously dodging Sebastian's attack.

Sebastian had not lost all of his energy yet though and was quick as he swung with the second sword.

Still, Fynn was quicker. He twisted the woman's arm, the cracking of bone loud and the woman's scream that followed even louder. Fynn didn't bat an eye though. He picked up the dagger laying at the soldier's feet and braced himself against the wall of the ship as the clang of metal mixed with the sobs of the woman. Sebastian pushed against the dagger, but Fynn was unrelenting as he shoved back. Sweat gleamed on Fynn's forehead, his teeth clenching.

And Kallie could have sworn that at that moment her heart stopped as she watched her brother struggle against the prince.

Meanwhile, the soldiers around her became restless. Hungry. One moved forward, weapon drawn. But the soldier was slow, and Fynn easily knew what was going to happen as the soldier approached clumsily with his sword. At the last minute, Fynn let one hand free. He turned the enemy's sword on him. And the man was impaled by his own sword before he even saw it coming. The soldier fell backward and into another soldier, the weight of the first causing the second soldier to topple over.

In one movement, Fynn returned his hand to the dagger and with renewed vigor, pushed back. Sebastian's foot slipped an inch as Fynn used his entire body weight to push against Sebastian. But then another soldier stepped over the two bodies on the floor.

And another.

Until several charged forward and chaos broke out on the ship. As though the Frenzians were starving animals with a grand feast placed before them, they pounced on Fynn.

And even with his ability to read their minds, Fynn was helpless as they came at him with weapons drawn. There were too many minds to read, too many weapons to dodge. Their swords slashed against his clothes, his skin. Blood splattered across the floor.

Enemy or friend, Kallie didn't know. Only stood there in horror, unable to form words. Unable to form a thought as she stood paralyzed. Unable to do anything but watch her brother get swamped by rabid men.

She heard screaming.

So much screaming.

Her knees hit the ground.

This was all her fault. And she couldn't get to him. There were too many bodies, too many weapons. Too many mistakes.

It wasn't supposed to be like this. No one she cared about was supposed to get hurt.

But she wasn't supposed to care for him, was she? For any of them.

Her throat felt like glass and as she raised her hand to it, she understood why. It was she who had been screaming. And she could do nothing to stop the events that unfolded before her. She had let this happen. And she couldn't even crawl to him to apologize. To tell him how sorry she was for everything she had done. For bringing these monsters to shore. For being one of those monsters.

And to tell her brother she loved him. Something she had never said, and now would never get a chance to do so.

They hadn't had enough time. She had just gotten to know that goofy smile he wore on his face. She had just gotten to know the way he looked at his wife, how he and Terin conversed without saying a word aloud. How his laughter filled every room he occupied. How despite everything going against her, he still believed in her, fought for her. His sister who had never been forgotten.

Even when she had forgotten them.

And then, in the back of her mind, she heard a small voice, faint and far away: *I know and it's okay. But find it, Kals. Find it and destroy the link.*

And she didn't know how, but she could have sworn it was Fynn's voice in her head. Fynn's words. She didn't know if speaking within someone's mind was a part of his ability or if the horrors that lay in front of her had caused her to start hearing things, but she didn't think it was her imagination. The voice, though faint, was distinctly Fynn's. The presence knocking on her mind was unmistakably his. And the tears fell hard as the full weight of his words began to settle in her mind.

He knew. He knew *everything.*

CHAPTER 35

THE FRENZIAN SOLDIERS BACKED AWAY FROM FYNN'S BODY, AND KALLIE gagged as she saw what was left of him. They had brutalized him, scarred him. His handsome face was now marked with tiny cuts. Blood seeped from his wet clothing. And his brown eyes were void of any light as they stared out toward her.

The world spun around her as the soldiers returned to readying the ship, their actions more urgent, hurried to avoid any more unwanted guests.

Kallie heard nothing as they moved past her. Felt nothing. Only stared at her hands that lay shaking in her lap. Trying to force them to stop, to lay still, but she couldn't. She couldn't do anything.

She hadn't been able to do anything when it mattered, and now she sat there, shaking.

A pair of boots entered the corner of her blurry vision. Blood coated the leather.

What color were they originally? Brown? Black? She didn't know.

There was just blood. More blood than she could have imagined from a single body. Her stomach turned and vomit spewed across the boots.

The owner of the boots groaned in disgust. "Dispose of it," he said.

A reply came from somewhere nearby, but Kallie couldn't focus on whatever their words were though. She could only stare at her shaking hands.

Then someone dragged her up by the elbow, forcing her onto her feet, and she met Sebastian's green eyes, his face half cast in the shadows. The light that shone on one side of his face made his features appear shaper, harsher than she had noticed before. Speckles of red freckled his face. His eyes scanned her. And she could only imagine what he saw. A woman in ragged clothing, strands of loose hair around her sickly face, her body shaking, her face wet from tears, eyes bloodshot. The beauty that had once existed was left discarded. A shell of a human in its place.

This wasn't supposed to happen. *He wasn't supposed to die,* she thought.

She felt the weight of his arms press down on her shoulders and he tried to get her attention. Sebastian shook her, the movement jumbling her and causing her ankle to throb in pain.

When she tried to look away, his palm met her chin, forcing her bloodshot eyes to meet his. "Filth or not, this is not a sight for a princess."

She looked up at him through her brows, pursing her lips. She gnawed on the inside of her cheek and forced the tears to remain behind her eyes, refusing to let another tear fall before this man.

"This is what happens to those who try to take from Frenzia," Sebastian stated. Though she did not miss the threat behind them. "You are safe now and that is all that matters." His words were meant to comfort her, the kidnapped princess. His future sister-in-law. The future *queen* of his land.

But they didn't.

A fire built within her. Her stomach filled with rage. It threatened to boil over as she stared into those green eyes, a shade of green that mimicked the treetops in the forest that surrounded the springs. A shade of green that once felt like freedom, joy, and love. But now as she looked into that deep green shade, she felt the space around her close in, suffocating her. She couldn't breathe. The oxygen lodged itself in her lungs as she inhaled. Her lungs felt like stones, with the air pressing against them, wanting to come out, banging on the walls.

Then there was a splash of water behind Sebastian.

Kallie jerked her head toward the direction in which the sound came from and her heart sank. Two soldiers stood at the back of the stern, wiping their hands on their trousers as they turned away from the railing. They saluted Sebastian and walked off.

She shoved past Sebastian. He shouted her name, but she didn't turn back, didn't stop. She needed to see it for herself. She needed to know what that splash was. As much as she didn't want her intuition to be true. But her brother's body no longer lay on the floor. All that remained was a puddle of blood smeared onto the old wooden boards.

She pressed herself into the railing, the metal slamming into her gut, but she didn't think about the resulting pain. Everything already hurt anyway. She could only think about what she saw in the water.

Ripples formed on the surface of the sea, spreading as the boat began its slow descent away from the shore. And in the center of the ripples, a hand bobbed on the surface, then a body.

Fynn's body.

They had *thrown* him overboard as if he was an empty barrel of rum that the sailors no longer needed and had thus discarded. As if he was unnecessary cargo rather than a human being.

Her stomach turned.

As the ship began to push away from the shore, his body floated over the waves that crashed into it and headed toward the shore. The water darkened around him.

And a hysterical laugh left her lips.

Kallie wanted to scream. She wanted to shout. She wanted to yell at Sebastian and his men. But her throat was dry. And then someone out on the shore screamed for her.

At the edge of the shore, not even fifty yards away, two figures stood on the beach hidden by the shadows of the trees. She squinted past the layer of dried-up tears coating her eyes. One of the figures collapsed onto their knees, shaking. Screaming. And Kallie knew who it was even with the moon casting a shadow over their features.

Dani, who knelt on the sand as she watched the love of her life, her husband, her partner, her soulmate ride the waves of the Red Sea. His body mutilated, destroyed. The beauty stripped from him. His humanity stolen from him by Frenzia's soldiers.

Kallie wanted to reach out for her, for the woman she had grown to care for over the past few weeks even though she knew she shouldn't have. She wanted to jump over the railing. Drop into the water, let her knees crash beneath her weight as they hit the sand for the woman who was by law, her sister. And in another life, her best friend.

But instead, Kallie remained pressed up against the railing.

The second figure crouched down beside Dani, wrapping her into their arms as if they could shield the pain away from her. The moon's shadow hid the person's face. Since the two figures melted within each other's forms, it was hard to identify the figure's body.

Fynn's body floated closer, and Dani shoved the other figure aside and ran to him. Water sprayed all around as she stomped into the water, her arms in the air to balance herself. The fish beneath the surface scurried away as the woman shook the sea.

When she finally reached him, she raised a hand to her face, and Kallie could have sworn she saw it shake in the darkness. Knee deep in the water, a scream caught in her lungs as Dani looked upon the man she loved. Her knees gave out, the water scattered and sparkled in the moonlight, tears falling from above. Her scream pierced the night as she pulled him closer, his head cradled against her chest.

The second figure then joined Dani. The broad shoulders, the lean build were all too familiar. As he came closer to Dani and toward the ship that began to sail away into the wild sea at a painfully slow pace, Graeson stepped into the light. His sun-kissed skin glowed under the moonlight, his dark hair covered in ash dulled its normal sheen. And those eyes, even with the sea separating them, pierced her soul.

He would never forgive her for bringing the enemy to their shores.

He would never forgive her for the destruction tonight had brought onto innocent lives, the destruction of his homeland.

He would never forgive her for the death of his best friend, Dani's husband, the next in line for the throne. Her brother.

And she didn't blame him for that. She didn't hate him for the rage she knew boiled in those iron-clad eyes.

It was never supposed to be like this. This wasn't a part of the plan.

She hated what tonight had brought. She hated that he had distracted her from her original plan. Because as the ship pulled away and the three figures in the Red Sea shrank into the distance, Kallie knew it would never be the same. These weeks would be a distant memory and nothing more.

These stolen moments together were never supposed to happen.

Soon, the scent of smoke and whiskey surrounded her, and a heavy hand pressed against her shoulder. Her heart skipped. The familiar scent coated her senses, cocooned her. She would know it anywhere, but she hadn't expected it to be here on this ship. She hadn't expected to be in its presence so soon. Not until she had returned at least.

"You did well, Kalisandre."

Shivers ran down her back. Those words, despite everything she had just seen, despite everything she had to work through in her mind, brought a small smile onto her face. Those words were filled with honey and soothed her aching heart.

Those words were what she had waited for her entire life.

And as she turned away from the shore and looked into those deep brown eyes, she saw the pride that swam in them.

"Thank you, Father," Kallie said.

CHAPTER 36

KALLIE DIPPED HER HEAD, LETTING THE KING LEAD HER AWAY FROM THE railing, away from the blood that stained the deck. While they walked, she fought the urge to look over her shoulder, to see those figures one last time. But she knew what she would see. And she had made her choice long ago. She kept her gaze forward.

"We have much to discuss, Kalisandre," King Domitius said as he reached the door of a cabin. He pushed open the door, and Kallie followed him into the room.

The latch of the door clicked into place behind her, and Kallie took a deep breath, clearing her mind of the battle happening inside of it.

Face emotionless, she stated, "You're early."

He shrugged. "The Frenzians were getting . . . " King Domitius waved his hand in the air, "restless. When they had gotten word that I had ended my search for you, they wanted answers."

She huffed. "Why bother sending a search party for me anyway? I thought we had agreed I could handle this."

"Unfortunately, not everything can go as planned. Someone else had discovered your carriage before I did. Then word spread quickly of your disappearance, so I had no other choice, lest they think me an unfit father. And what would that do to my reputation as king?"

She refrained from rolling her eyes. He was always looking out for his reputation. But a small part of her was thankful he had not thought she was incapable of accomplishing her task.

Blood or not, he was her father.

"Enough about that." He headed toward a small liquor cabinet and spoke over his shoulder, "Were you successful or not in learning how to strengthen your gift?"

Still, there it was. The doubt.

She put her hands behind her back, clasping them together, steadying them. "I did. Though I must say. . ." Kallie hesitated.

He grabbed two glasses from the small cabinet and sighed. "Out with it, Kalisandre."

She had thought she would have plenty of time to form the questions roaming in her mind. She didn't think she would have to confess what she knew so soon. Staring at the king's back, she forced her voice to remain neutral, "You did not tell me my mother was alive."

She noticed the slightest pause in his movement, but then Domitius continued to pour the liquor into two glasses. "And what of it?"

Kallie pursed her lips but wiped the expression from her face as quickly as it came. "And what about the men who kidnapped me? You told me their leader was able to hear people's thoughts, but you left out the fact that he, along with his twin, were my brothers."

"Was he now? Hm. My spies must have left that detail out." He turned, glasses in hand, brow quirked, gaze questioning. "Does that change anything, Kalisandre?"

Her gaze fell to the red plush carpet. She would not answer that question. Not without lying. And the king would see right through the lie.

He stepped forward and the floorboards beneath the carpet creaked from his weight. He offered her one of the glasses. And when she grabbed it, he clinked his glass against hers. The piercing sound echoed in her ears. "Who has cared for you all this time, Kalisandre?"

"You," she answered.

He took a sip, but Kallie had yet to raise her glass. "And who has trained you all of these years?"

"You," she repeated.

"And who has promised you power, the power you otherwise would not have access to?"

Her gaze flicked up to his. "You."

"That's right." He stood in front of her, staring down at her. "Has your time here softened you?"

Kallie scoffed in disbelief. "Of course not."

"Then what is the problem? Do not tell me you have grown to care for our enemy?"

Her mouth fell open, but she could not string together any words. On the one hand, he was right. Over the past few weeks, she had grown to care for the family she didn't know existed. And her shaking hands behind her back were a clear indication of that truth. But on the other hand. . .

She needed to sort out her thoughts. And fast.

Fractures in her mind formed, blurring the lines between the truth and the act. In the beginning, the line between the two was clear, distinguished. But now it was all shades of gray, blending into one another.

When he had given her this assignment after they had announced the request for suitors, Kallie had known that this would be her hardest assignment yet. But she had not expected to discover these truths about her past. Her identity.

After sending out the invitations to her suitors' homes, her father had discovered the Pontians' plans to kidnap Kallie in an attempt to thwart the king. While this had not been shocking since the two kingdoms had long since been enemies, his plan caused her jaw to drop.

Kallie would let the enemy capture her.

According to King Domitius, Kallie needed to go to Pontia to strengthen her gift. Since he was not like her, he could only help so much. He confessed he had heard rumors that there were others on the island who were blessed by the gods with gifts similar to hers. That they knew how to strengthen them. Therefore, she had two tasks to complete on this mission. First, she would improve the strength of her gift. Second, she would learn about their enemies. She would discover their weaknesses and their strengths, their abilities and their limitations, their hopes and fears. She would gain their trust and infiltrate their kingdom.

And Kallie had been successful in both tasks.

From the moment she had stepped onto the dance floor with Fynn, she had guarded her thoughts. She had thrown up the walls the king had instructed her to build inside her mind. With the aid of her gift and the prior knowledge of his ability to read minds, she was able to hide her plans from him.

When they had captured her and she had spent those first few days tied, she had tested their ability to keep her, to track her down. She wanted to know how far they would go. The roles each enemy played. And when they thought she was asleep, she had listened for tidbits of information.

She did what she was good at. She acted, she manipulated, she seduced.

She followed the king's orders.

And she trusted the king's plan. She wanted his approval and would give everything to gain it, so she believed him without question.

However, King Domitius had not been completely honest with her. He did not tell her he had kidnapped her when she was a child. Or that her family would be the ones to abduct her after the ceremony. Those details had been left out.

And those details were the cause of her current dilemma. It was, in plain terms, a mess.

Not bothering to wait for her to respond, King Domitius lifted one shoulder in indifference. "While it is unfortunate what happened to that young man, that was Sebastian's doing not mine. As the commander of their military, he is a little too eager, if you ask me."

Kallie could only nod, having been rendered speechless. Her brother's death was not a minor inconvenience. Nor was it a misguided judgment. It was murder.

"Have you begun to doubt me, doubt our plans, Kalisandre?"

Her mouth fell open, but a knock at the door interrupted her before she could answer.

"Come in," the king stated, his gaze remaining on her.

"My king, I hope I am not interrupting, but one of the soldiers said you require my assistance?"

At the voice, Kallie froze. Slowly, she turned to confirm her assumption.

"Myra? But what are you—" Kallie snapped her mouth shut as Domitius interrupted.

"Yes, come in. Kalisandre and I were just catching up."

Myra shut the door behind her and stood beside Kallie. Myra gripped her hand, the tension in Kallie's shoulders subsiding instantly at her friend's touch.

But why was Myra here? *How* was she here?

Kallie's gaze bounced between Myra and the king, yet Myra avoided Kallie's gaze. And Kallie realized she was the only one who was confused. But the question remained: why? But now was not the time. Not when the king was questioning her loyalty.

Domitius returned his attention to Kallie. "Have you forgotten why we are doing all of this?"

Myra gave Kallie's hand a quick squeeze. A calmness seeped into her skin through that comforting touch allowing Kallie to remember why she had agreed to this and what she would gain. Myra released her hand, and Kallie tugged on the edge of her cloak and shoved her feelings down.

Kallie had betrayed the Pontians, her family. Brought the enemy to their lands. And caused the death of her brother. And more would die soon enough when war broke out. Forgiveness would never knock on her door.

At the end of all of this, no matter what, she knew what she would choose in the end. So she let those walls around her heart return, then fortified it with stone and steel. Locked away the thoughts of the silver-eyed man—eyes that pierced her soul and had, for a moment, made her want to stay and forget about everything else. He would never forgive her for choosing power. For choosing herself. But this wasn't about him.

She took a large gulp of the bitter whiskey. Let it coat her stomach, her mind as she shed the last remaining layer of the facade she had worn for these past few weeks. She put her shoulders back, tilted her chin up. "Of course not, my king," Kallie said.

Graeson had thought that she was a damsel in distress, and Kallie had played right into his fantasy. Those jewel-encrusted heels, the diamond gown were a perfect fit. And she had worn the crown well. She was the epitome of a princess who needed to be saved.

But she was not a damsel.

Nor was she a little mouse.

He had fallen for her trap. And so easily, so carelessly, too. He had thought that she was a mouse he could easily catch. That she had wanted to run away. That she was *his* to catch. But because of his own arrogance and confidence, he hadn't noticed the python slithering behind him. Watching him, waiting for the moment to strike.

Kallie smirked.

The next time she saw Graeson he would do well to remember who she truly was: the sharpest weapon in the king's arsenal, forged to strike with the aim of a queen.

EPILOGUE
GRAESON

GRAESON DIDN'T KNOW WHAT WAS MORE SHOCKING: HIS BEST FRIEND'S body floating in the water, the life drained from him. Or the girl standing at the edge of the ship, staring down at them, watching, unmoving as his world fell apart. As Dani's heart was torn into shreds.

While Graeson had been fighting off the attackers and Dani and her units were fighting the fire that tore through the village, Fynn had managed to run off unnoticed. Before they realized what he had done, Fynn had already crept onto the enemy ship.

There had been only a handful of enemies where Graeson was stationed. And something had felt off. There should have been more soldiers. But the few he fought hadn't tried to escape his wrath. They had come prepared for a battle with foreign weapons.

And when they charged at him with their weapons drawn, he shut everything else down. As though he had flipped a switch in his mind, and he knew nothing but the rage that ran through his bloodstream.

After he had flipped that switch, the rage released from his body. Untethered, unrestrained, unrestricted.

For years he had trained himself to keep the monster that lay asleep inside of him locked up. Where his friends worked to strengthen their gifts and pull them out, Graeson did the opposite. But tonight he had released the beast within him.

He had only done so a few times in the past month and still with a firm leash wrapped around it. Once when they had attacked the carriage, then again when they had been attacked by the soldiers in Borgania. He had almost released it earlier tonight when he had discovered that it was Kalisandre who had brought these soldiers onto his shores—accident or not.

However, once he had cut that leash tonight, the only thing on his mind had been tearing apart the soldiers. Those who had come to take Kalisandre away from him. Fighting against those soldiers, the monster was out in full force.

And his lack of control had cost him.

He had gotten too caught up in what was happening in front of him to realize what it truly was: a distraction.

Graeson should have never let *her* out of his sight. He should have stayed with her. Protected her. He should have done what he couldn't do all those years ago when they were children. But he didn't.

The sight of her standing at the entrance of the palace made his heart shatter. He knew he shouldn't have been mad. He knew she was not at fault. But when she looked at him, she had transformed before his eyes. Reverted to the woman he had seen sitting on that small throne, the woman who stayed at the heels of the king.

In her stare, in the way she held her head, her body rigid and cold, Graeson saw *him* in her. And his blood froze over.

He did not want to be mad at her, he did not want to blame her. She had not known the truth. Despite his wishes, they had not told her everything. And maybe that was their first mistake. Maybe they should have been honest with her from the beginning.

They had spent the weeks leading up to that day discussing—all right, *arguing*—with each other about what was their best plan of attack. What would ensure that they would be successful in not only saving Kallie but also—and more importantly—convincing her that what they said was true?

And even though Esmeray's gift was the key to it all, she could not leave Pontia for the kingdom needed its queen to remain.

Still, maybe they shouldn't have kept Kallie restrained. Maybe they should have trusted her so that *she* would trust *them*. But they didn't.

How could they when she had been under the care of the man who had taken everything from them? Their princess and their king, their sense of security and peace.

On the one hand, King Markos was lucky. Death was a far better fate than what had happened to *her*.

They knew she was too young when she was taken to have any real recollection of her life here—her life with them. And they had spent the years in between preparing for the moment when they would take her back. But they could not barge into Ardentol. Not with the treaty. They had to be smart, level-headed. And as a teenager, Graeson wasn't. None of them were.

Armen had informed them early on in one of his letters that Domitius had the palace well fortified and rarely let her out of his sight.

So they had to make the king think that he was safe. They had to let him open up his kingdom to them.

But maybe they had waited too long. Maybe they should have tried sooner.

Graeson had wanted to. He had begged to break through Ardentol's borders for the past six years. But his trainers had told him he was not ready. He was too eager, too high-tempered. Too uncontrolled.

And they were right. He knew that.

Graeson had been ready this time though.

Yet he still had failed. He had made the same mistake he did that night: he had let her go. Let her slide through his grip.

However, this time it wasn't because he was a mere child going up against a grown man. No, this time Graeson had let his emotions, his anger, and his feelings for her get the better of him.

And he was *still* angry.

Because when he had looked into her eyes, there was something there that felt off, that felt wrong. Guilt and remorse clouded those deep ocean-blue eyes. Still, there was something else that had floated in them, swirling around her irises. Both he and Fynn had seen it when they had first seen Kallie. But neither of them could figure out what it meant. Fynn had been trying to read her, but something blocked him. He had spent countless hours trying to break through her walls, but the walls in her mind were strong. She shouldn't have been able to shield her mind so well, especially without knowing he could read minds.

And now they knew why, but it was too late.

Her mind was gone.

Ironic, really. She had thought she was the manipulator. The one who could control the minds of others. Yet Domitius had found a way to wrap his fingers around her mind, to manipulate her. And his hold was firm, unbreakable.

Fynn had told Graeson one night that he had seen the fractures in her mind starting to form, but they weren't deep enough. He still couldn't break through. He needed time. Time to figure out *how* Domitius had managed to do it. *Who* he had in his arsenal who could shift the loyalties of a person, who could put up impenetrable walls in a person's mind. Who could change its chemistry.

For someone had manipulated her. Influenced her mind. Used her ability against her. It was the only explanation.

And they were making progress. At least Graeson and Fynn thought they were making progress. Kalisandre was warming up to them. They were breaking through the barriers of her mind. When her mind was focused on her training, Fynn had tried to infiltrate her thoughts. And brick-by-brick, Fynn was breaking down that wall.

Graeson *saw* it. The way she leaned into the pull between the two of them, instead of fighting against it.

Then the fire started.

And he had walked away from her. He had left her with Terin, someone he knew would protect her. But he should have remembered that Terin couldn't protect himself from *her*.

From across the water, Kallie's eyes met his, and Graeson's heart burned. The woman before him, the woman whom he had grown to care for and love over the past few weeks no longer stood in front of him. He didn't recognize this woman.

A stranger with death written in her eyes stood staring back at him as if everything they had been through together never happened. As if *he* meant nothing to her.

As if he had *never* meant anything to her.

Dani tugged at his arm. "Gray, help me carry him," she said through tears as she struggled beneath Fynn's weight.

However, Graeson couldn't take his eyes away from Kalisandre despite all of it.

Because when he looked at her and saw those deep blue eyes that pulled at his soul, he knew that this person wasn't who she truly was. This was the Princess of Ardentol, not his childhood friend, not Kalisandre Helene Nadarean.

The true Kalisandre was there though, buried deep inside. He had seen the real Kalisandre when her stubbornness shone through. When she fought with a loyalty made of steel, when she was quiet as she fidgeted with her jewelry.

"I can't leave her. Not again," Graeson said. He had promised he would protect her, fight for her. And he needed to fulfill that promise.

"Graeson! Look around you! Because of her, our homes have been destroyed. Because of her, I have lost my soulmate, our future king."

Graeson knew Dani was right and he hated himself for hesitating, but his heart was being ripped apart from within. Pieces crashed against the floor of his stomach and turned into dust. "She. . .she doesn't know."

"I don't fucking care! Fynn's gone," Dani spoke between sobs as she began to drag Fynn's body through the water. "He's gone."

And it was the way Dani's voice broke that made him finally turn away, forcing him to regain his senses. Graeson squeezed Dani's shoulder, and her head fell forward onto Fynn's chest as she released the anger, the pain. Her tears fell into the sea, indistinguishable in the water.

He helped lift Fynn out of the water. But before they left, he looked at the woman he loved and memorized every inch of her. How her dark chestnut hair flowed around her face. How her skin glowed in the light of the fire behind them. How her blue eyes turned golden, reflecting the flickering flames. How the cloak, a different one than he had seen that first night at the tavern, billowed in the wind revealing her athletic frame. And how she twisted the ring that still encircled her finger.

And it was that small piece of gold that was the last knot that secured his plan in place.

Kalisandre had told him it was her mother's ring. The only item she owned that belonged to her, the only piece of the woman who she believed to be dead. But that wasn't the truth.

His mother, Lysanthia Osiros was the most powerful seer Pontia had seen in the past century. Before his mother had died during childbirth, a tragedy she had known was coming, Lysanthia had left

Esmeray with one last vision. She had told Esmeray that their children yet to be born were destined for each other, their lives entwined.

Therefore, when Lysanthia discovered she would not survive childbirth, she wanted to ensure that Graeson was able to possess the traditional Pontian rings. It was one of his kingdom's many traditions for the partners' families to forge rings out of a unique gold metal found on the small island off of Pontia's west coast. The family members, traditionally parents, chose the piece of metal and partook in the process to forge the two rings. The metal, having been embedded with Pontanius' will and power, was meant to forge a bond between two lovers so strong that once worn and vowed upon was unbreakable. And due to the power within the ring, only the owner could remove the jewelry once on. Which must have been why Kalisandre still possessed it.

Since Graeson would be left in this world without his parents alongside him, Lysanthia and Esmeray preemptively created the rings for their children. Both mothers wanted to provide their future children with this gift that could only be granted once.

As children, he and Kallie wore them as necklaces. They were too young to understand what the rings meant besides that they were important gifts from their mothers. And to this day, Graeson wore his Pontian ring alongside his other rings. And so did Kalisandre.

Although a seer's visions were not definite and could change, the majority of Lysanthia's visions placed Graeson next to Kallie's side. And Graeson believed in his mother's words. He knew she was the best seer who had lived. And he knew that, according to her visions, every path led Kallie and him to each other.

Every path except for one.

And he was determined to not let this moment be the one that put them on the path that would divide them.

So, as Graeson turned and walked away from the woman who was his, the woman who owned him completely, he vowed to rescue her once and for all. To avenge his kingdom, his friend, his family for the havoc that the bull-headed king had brought to his shores.

For nothing else mattered.

No one else mattered. No one but her.

AUTHOR'S NOTE

Thank you for reading *The King's Weapon*, the first book in the Of Fire and Lies series! Pieces of this story have lived within the confinements of my mind for a long time, so finally seeing them come to life on the page has been such a wonderful experience.

I have been a writer my entire life, but this book officially made me an author. I will be forever thankful for that and for you for giving it a chance.

If you enjoyed *The King's Weapon*, please consider leaving a review on Amazon or Goodreads. Reviews are so important to authors and help readers find books that are a good fit for them!

The King's Weapon was inspired by the story of Helen of Troy. According to the Greek legend, Helen was the indirect cause of the Trojan War. There are a few different versions of the story. Some paint her as a victim; some depict her as a traitor. Women in literature often fall on one side or the other. They are either a victim or a traitor. They are either good or bad.

And so Kallie came to life.

Many readers will not like Kallie. Some will even hate her and question her morality. But I hope that some of you will see the layers beneath—the hidden truth that often gets overshadowed by the bad. And Kallie's full story has yet to unfold.

Want to stay updated about upcoming releases, ARC opportunities, and more? Be sure to subscribe to Neena's Newsletter.

ACKNOWLEDGMENTS

At its core, writing is an individual activity. And after the number of hours I have spent hunched over my laptop with only my characters and writing playlists on repeat, it is easy to believe it is just that—me and my work. But in truth, writing flourishes in a community. And I have many people to thank for the creation and publication of *The King's Weapon*.

First, I want to thank my husband, Nathan, who has supported me endlessly throughout the writing and publication process. When I was stuck on the plot or the magic system, you listened. When I told you I wanted to publish TKW and told you how much it would cost, you didn't even blink an eye. I am forever grateful for you and your continuous love and support.

To my family who has always supported my dreams. To my sister Kayla who was my first reader, not only for TKW but for all the stories and snippets that came before—the ones that will stay buried deep, deep within a box and never see the light of day (P.S. sorry that you had to read those pre-teen rambles). To Jessica, Kita, and George, thank you for showing me what it means to be a sibling. To my step-dad George who has shown me what a father can be. And to my mom. Since I was in elementary school, you displayed my artwork and stories with pride. Not just because you were my mother and that was something you were expected to do, but because you always believed others should see my work.

To Mac who forced me to pick a New Year's resolution in 2022, who helped me brainstorm and talk through plot holes without complaint (though I'm sure Anna got that side of the conversation). I am very thankful for you nagging me about actually sticking to my goals.

To Gabby who has been one of my biggest supporters. You have been a friend, beta reader, critique partner, editor, supporter, marketer, and cheerleader all rolled into one. Forever thankful for you.

To my beta reader and friend, Jess. It was beyond terrifying to ask you to read this in its rough form. But I am so glad I did.

To Heather who has been a source of inspiration (Kallie is a Sagittarius by the way). Thank you for being my fiery friend.

And to all my friends who have supported me in both big and small ways. From the interest you all have shown to spreading the word about TKW to following me on social media (even though I know many of you groaned about BookTok slipping onto your FYP). I am thankful for you all.

To my editor, Emma Jane. Thank you for being kind but critical. To my cover designer, Bianca. Thank you for taking the wheel when I didn't know which direction I wanted to go in. To my writing community, thank you for encouraging me, cheering me on, and inspiring me.

To my teachers who helped nurture a love of reading and writing since I was young: Mrs. Fyke, Mrs. Mattner, Mrs. McDonnough, Mrs. Kaminski, Mrs. Rea, and Mrs. Sellman (to name only a few). I hope you know that you have left a lasting impression on me (and I hope you don't find a grammar mistake somewhere, though I am sure you will).

And lastly, and most importantly, to you, the reader. Thank you for taking a chance on me, my writing, and my story.

With love and gratitude, Neena

ABOUT THE AUTHOR

Neena Laskowski lives in Michigan with her husband and their two pets. She earned her Master's in Secondary Education and Bachelor's in English and Classical Studies from the University of Michigan. When she is not reading or writing about morally grey characters, you can find her camping, wine tasting, painting, or spending time with her family and friends.

For upcoming ARC opportunities and to be among the first to see cover reveals, character art, and more, be sure to join Neena Laskowski's newsletter, found on neenalaskowski.com, or follow Neena on social media.

Made in the USA
Columbia, SC
17 December 2024